DAUGHTERS OF THE
WATCHERS

DAUGHTERS OF THE WATCHERS

THE PROGENY WARS™ BOOK 1

G.Z. RODRIGUEZ

D.J. VARGAS

DISRUPTIVE IMAGINATION

LMBPN Publishing
PMB 196, 2540 South Maryland Pkwy
Las Vegas, NV 89109

Version 1.01, December 2021
ebook ISBN: 978-1-68500-526-9
Print ISBN: 978-1-68500-527-6

THE DAUGHTERS OF THE WATCHERS
TEAM

Thanks to our Beta Readers
John Ashmore, Kelly O'Donnell, Mary Morris, Rachel
Beckford, James Caplan

Thanks to our JIT Readers

Deb Mader
Wendy L Bonell
Dave Hicks
Dorothy Lloyd
Jeff Goode
Angel LaVey
Jackey Hankard-Brodie
Diane L. Smith
Debi Sateren
Paul Westman

Editor

SkyHunter Editing Team

PROLOGUE

"Cookie, you need to hurry. The seer predicted that she'd die if we don't reach her in time," cried Dough without shifting her gaze from the GPS app on her smartphone.

"Moooovee! Get out the way, you jerk!" Cookie yelled and honked at the SUV in front of them. She darted a glance at her twin sister in the passenger seat. "Then next time, you drive. I'm doing my best here."

"Well, you didn't let me, remember." Dough sneered.

"Because I drive better at night, remember." Cookie's hands gripped the steering wheel tightly as she accelerated into a hard right turn and barely missed the other vehicle.

Dough lurched forward and suddenly widened her eyes. "Watch out for the bike messenger!" She stomped her right foot on an imaginary brake pedal—twice.

Her sister placed her left foot deftly on the brake pedal, turned the wheel left, and pressed down hard on the gas with her right foot. "I hate those bikers. I swear they're from Hell."

The other woman's normally olive complexion assumed a greenish tinge. "You're driving with two feet again." She opened the passenger window and stuck her head out. "You keep driving that way and I'm gonna barf."

"Don't do that. I'll sense your nausea and we'll both be sick." Cookie continued up Broadway with the pedal to the metal on the black sports car. She glanced at the dashboard digital clock and asked, "How much farther?"

Dough struggled to keep her composure as she glanced at the smartphone. "About six blocks down, then make a right on West 114th street. The fraternity house will be on your right."

"Hold on, sis, and pray that all these lights stay green." Ignoring the street speed limit, she sped through uptown Manhattan and drew a few fingers, shouts of profanity, and the dreaded "Go Back to Jersey" expression from pedestrians. She raced on regardless. Nothing would stand in the way of reaching their target.

"There!" yelled Dough and pointed to the green-and-yellow three-story brownstone. "That house fits the seer's description."

"Hey *Bhagwan!*" groaned Cookie in her childhood tongue. "They're throwing a party. How are we supposed to find parking in all this? We can't even double park."

Her twin glanced around and located a spot. "It has to be at the fire hydrant. If the car gets towed, Gypsy will have to get it at the pound, but she'll understand. We need to find and rescue this Jasmine girl."

They parked the car and raced to the fraternity house, which was bursting at the seams with partygoers and shook with each beat of the music's bassline. Those windows facing the street glimmered with multi-colored strobe lights to reveal college kids dancing wildly. The front door to the brownstone—its only entrance—was jammed with folks trying to get in, while a few others lay drunk on the floor.

"How are we supposed to get through that?" asked Dough.

"We push our way through."

She turned to her sister. "It's risky to use our gift in public, but you're right. I see no other way."

Cookie lifted two drunk frat boys, one with each hand, and prepared to fling them over the railing of the front steps when she stopped abruptly. Both sisters turned to each other as shivers slithered down their spines. Danger was imminent and they both sensed it.

"You feel it too?" asked Cookie.

Her sister nodded as she dropped the two partygoers with dull thuds. "But where could he be?"

They glanced around and attempted to sync their sight to what they sensed. Seconds later, the sisters stared instinctively at the large tree across the street, which obscured two figures. They perceived a familiar yet alarming faint glow and beside it, a scarcely visible girl who laughed obnoxiously.

The young woman could barely stand and struggled to hold onto an unusually tall man. She continued to laugh as he whispered in her ear. "Did you give me something? Because," she spluttered and hiccupped, "I didn't have a thing to drink but I'm completely out of it. And why do you seem to be glowing black?"

In a low but guttural voice, he said, "That's because you're drunk with the words of my mouth."

The girl laughed and spat loudly, "Drunk with your words. Oh, that's as hilarious as your name, Methi!"

When they heard the name Methi, Cookie and Dough knew it was the Nephilim called Intoxication, one of the Maladites. As one, they yanked crystalline blades from their back straps and rushed forward to attack.

The man sniffed and turned his head quickly towards the approaching sisters. Without hesitation, he drew a long steel blade sheathed at his side and with a swift thrust, he plunged it savagely into the girl's chest. A vicious smirk settled on his face and he called to the women, "You're always a step behind." Suddenly, a large, swirling light appeared behind Methi. He dropped the girl onto the street, backed into the light, and disappeared.

They reached the tree and checked on the girl, who lay choking and spitting up blood.

Dough dropped her blade, knelt, and placed her hands over the wound. Her eyes widened at the sight of the name charm on the necklace around the girl's neck—*Jasmine*. With a sigh, she looked at her sister. "It's her."

"We have no time to bring her to May. The hospital is a block away. Let's take her there." Cookie proceeded to bend to help her sister but Jasmine's ragged breathing suddenly stopped.

"It's too late. She's dead," uttered Dough with her fingers pressed to the side of the girl's neck.

Cookie sighed in frustration and threw her blade furiously on the ground. "Damn it!" She placed her hand over her forehead. "What was the name of the other girl in Tassel's vision?"

"I don't remember." Dough shook her head. "But I know it's a girl from the Bronx. She's not in immediate danger but I swear we'll get to her before they do."

PART I

AN ORDINARY GIRL

1

CAT-LIKE INSTINCT

Angelica strode through the dimly lit Bronx alley on a dark, rainy night in August. The murky skies, fog-covered buildings, gloomy shadows on the pavement, and eerie silence gave the night an air of mystery. Nothing stirred this late. The only sounds were the slow trickle of water down the brick buildings and the soft squelch her feet made with each step.

A walk in this part of the city was not safe for an attractive, slim, five-foot-four young lady, although the thought of the unknown and things lurking in the dark made her feel more alive. Her late shift at the Heavenly Diner had just finished, and although it would have been much more convenient and certainly safer to take a cab or ride-source, she looked forward to these solitary walks.

The display on her smartphone read half-past midnight when she checked it and saw numerous missed calls from her grandmother. The constant stream of calls had not ceased even after she moved out of the old lady's apartment a few weeks earlier. Angelica loved her dearly but felt the move had been long overdue. She was grateful for her —a widowed, low-income Hispanic woman who raised a child in the Bronx and worked long hours as a seamstress to ensure her only granddaughter had a normal childhood.

This appreciation was the reason she had remained with her for so long. Nonetheless, the incessant manipulation and paranoia had driven her to find a place of her own.

She ignored the numerous calls and voicemails and instead, drew the white stereo headphones from her pocket and plugged them into her ears. With a swift motion of her slim, nimble fingers, she tapped on the right-hand corner of the cell, launched the music app, and played her Salsa radio station. She slipped the phone into the pocket of her raincoat and continued through the rancid alley with its smoky vapor from Hell rising from the city's manholes. Blissfully, she let the light, warm drizzle frizz her shoulder-length ebony hair.

Even though this was a familiar route, she began to feel odd halfway through her journey. A distinct sensation nagged constantly at her and crystallized into an impression of being watched or followed. Inexplicably, her senses seemed to magnify—sight, smell, hearing, and touch—as if the thought of being watched put her keenly on edge. This uncomfortable oddness overwhelmed her with fear. Abruptly, as if by sheer instinct, she lurched back and landed hard on the street when an unfamiliar, hissing shadow skittered in front of her.

"*Qué chavienda!*" she exclaimed in her grandmother's native tongue. "Damned stupid cat!" Angelica glanced to her right where a solid silvery-gray feline dashed up the staircase of an abandoned building. While still on the asphalt, she glimpsed a dim outline almost in the form of a man out of her left peripheral vision. The silhouette of this translucent figure stood only a few yards from her.

It loomed abnormally tall and stark and was cloaked in what appeared to be charcoal-black apparel. Its flickering red, fiendish eyes glared at her. The physical appearance of the mysterious figure was not all she experienced, however. A spine-chilling impression of evil and terror filled her soul. Fear told her to not look but curiosity made her cock her head swiftly to the left. She saw no one, only a brick wall with a graffiti drawing of a red two-horned demon.

"What the hell?" She sighed in fright. Puzzled by this midnight thrill, she rose hastily to her feet. She brushed her wet palms on her dark-green raincoat and, with the back of her hand, pushed away the bangs obstructing her hazel eyes. The fall had knocked the earphones from her ears so she rolled them swiftly and placed them in her pocket, which inadvertently knocked her work name tag out.

From a distance, although she was not sure from where, she heard swift footsteps splashing through puddles. She spun one-eighty degrees toward the same gloomy alley while her gaze darted in all directions in confusion. *Me chavé yo ahora...I think I'm losing it.* She decided to not take any chances and hastened her steps toward the end of the block.

"Hi there, honey. Are you looking for some fun?" asked a woman on the street corner. She wore tight leather shorts and a red-wine halter top and leaned seductively against the wall of a corner building with an open umbrella. It was common streetwalker attire but on closer inspection, Angelica noticed an odd-looking blade strapped to her ankle.

"Nah, I'm good," she responded and glanced warily at the stranger.

"I can keep you company, baby." Her blue-eyed gaze followed her intently.

"Not interested," she said emphatically. Apprehensive about the woman's intentions, she quickened her pace and crossed the street. After only a few steps, she had an inner prompting like a sixth sense that the woman was following her. Angelica peeked at the corner, only to find it empty. "Ugh. There's nothing like going insane at such an early age," she murmured, pulled the smartphone from her pocket, and opened a ride-sourcing app.

Two pairs of eyes materialized from the shadows of the alleyway and stared at the young woman as she entered a car. One pair was fiery red and the other dark amber.

"Is it her, my lord?" asked the amber-eyed one in a squeaky, grating tone.

The blazing red eyes went from the girl to the soaking name tag on the street. "Determine her residence and issue a sigil. Send your best hunter."

2

A DAY WITH GRANDMA

The window shades of the tiny, nondescript studio apartment were tightly shut to prevent the beaming rays of the summer sun from interrupting Angelica's sleep. A puffy pillow protected her heart-shaped face from any infiltration of the annoying sounds her neighbors made in the morning. Her body was splayed across the bed, her usual posture for comfortable sleep.

Unfortunately, she'd forgotten to enable her phone's silent mode and suffered a rude awakening in consequence. The musical ringtone sounded much like a pounding jackhammer that drove through her skull. Still half-asleep, she fumbled on the night table and flipped the blinding smartphone screen. "Agh!" She grunted when she saw the caller ID. *Abuela*. If she ignored this call, it would only provoke her grandmother to continue to call incessantly until the end of days.

She swiped her thumb toward the right of the screen and answered lethargically. "Hello." When she realized her voice came out cracking like the bellows of Leviathan rising from the sea, she cleared her throat.

"*Gracias, Dios mío*! You're okay," the familiar wobbly, raspy voice responded.

"Yes, *Abuela*, I'm fine," replied Angelica. Her heavy eyelids drooped low over her scratchy eyeballs as she strove with every fiber of her being to stay awake.

"Why didn't you call last night, *mi hija*? I was worried sick about you," Grandma squawked in her thick Spanish accent.

"I came out of work late again and didn't want to bother you." Angelica flipped sideways to avoid holding the phone and sandwiched the device between her head and the pillow. It was too early for any type of effort.

"You know I don't sleep much and was awake all night waiting for you to call." For several minutes, she rambled on about how concerned she had been and detailed the various symptoms she'd experienced during her time of despair. Her granddaughter listened more out of politeness and respect than interest.

"Angelica, are you listening to me?" she demanded when a snore came over the line.

"Yeah... Yeah, I'm here!" She woke abruptly and stammered, "I was thinking deeply about what you were saying. That's all."

"Humph," interjected Grandma cynically. "Are you stopping by soon?" The sound of pots and pans resonated.

"No—yes, Abuela. I'll be there for sure."

"Don't forget, my appointment is at twelve thirty."

"I won't forget." She sighed and her voice changed from weary to annoyed.

"Okay. Love you, *mi niña*."

"Love you, too."

Her eyes now closed, she grabbed the phone, pressed the End button, set it to vibration mode, and with a swift motion, flung it aimlessly. Her mind entered the sea of forgetfulness and with minimal effort, she returned to her sacred slumber.

Angelica reached her grandma's three-story apartment building a quarter after twelve. It was a rundown building on the southwest side of the Bronx whose façade was so faded it was difficult to ascertain its original color. The building was surrounded by cracked sidewalks pocked with black-stained chewing gum—the playground for Double Dutch and Hopscotch with now-estranged child-hood friends.

Her late arrival was planned deliberately to avoid having to spend additional time in the apartment being lectured and interrogated endlessly. *Maybe it'll only be one lecture and fifteen questions.*

"Carmen, *abreme la puerta!*" hollered Señor Carlos from the front of the building. He gazed toward the second-floor windows, his face flushed from continuous shouting.

"Señor Carlos, I've got a key," she told him. The door-bell system had been broken for years, which left only two options for entry—you owned a key or yelled.

"Angelica, how are you? It is good to see you." He greeted her cheerfully and wore his usual white *guayabera* shirt and dark-brown pants.

"I'm good," was her brief response. He was a talker.

"Thank God you are here. I left my keys in the apartment and have shouted for my wife to open the door for the last ten minutes." He raised his hands in frustration. "Once she starts her telenovelas, not even God and his Angels can get that woman's attention." She smiled awkwardly while Señor Carlos prattled on about his disappointment with the building's management and other trivial information. After he'd held her up for a few minutes, he waved goodbye, sent his greetings to her grandmother Maria, and walked up the squeaky stairs.

Angelica decided to check the mail before she climbed the three flights of stairs. She reached the antiquated, gilded mailbox, inserted the key, and managed to open it after a nudge, a wiggle, and a swift whack. She'd been gone six weeks now and still had not yet notified the post office of her new address. It was merely one of those things she had procrastinated about. Finding no mail, she went up the staircase.

The waft of the dank air brought the familiar heavy odor of old frying oil that permeated the halls and staircase of the building. She could feel the greasy stickiness if she grasped the staircase railing for even a moment. For an outsider, it would be a stench but for her, it smelled like her childhood.

She reached her destination and as always, panted and gasped for air.

Like a discerning prophet, Grandma opened the door before she knocked. The wizened elderly woman with grizzled hair and soft hazel-brown eyes wore a faded-blue nightgown and mocha-brown flip-flops—a.k.a. *chancletas*.

As always, like a trusty sidekick, she held her broom in her hand.

"What took you so long?" was the first of many questions.

"*Bendición, Abuela.*" Angelica spoke her customary benediction on seeing her grandmother.

"*Dios te bendiga, mi niña.*" She placed the broom behind the door and reached out to her granddaughter to hug and peck her affectionately on the cheek.

"Sorry for arriving at this time, but you know the city and the subway delays." Angelica offered a half-truthful excuse and left it at that.

"Don't worry about it. The appointment isn't until twelve forty-five." The old lady now revealed her half-truth about the time of her doctor's appointment.

"But *Abuela*, you said the appointment was at twelve thirty," she protested in a grating tone and felt hoodwinked.

"You know how these doctors' offices work. They tell you to be there at twelve thirty but make you wait an hour. Let them be the patient for a change. Like I always say, *Un poquito de paciencia* never hurt anybody. Angelica mouthed it as always but couldn't help a little resentment. *Her little patience always hurt me.* It was an expression she'd heard countless times growing up, mainly when she wanted something badly but could not have it, although she had always felt that Grandma would never apply it to herself.

"Anyway, come inside. I made you something to eat." Angelica never turned down Grandma's cooking.

Walking into the small one-bedroom apartment always made her feel nostalgic. The living room wall-of-fame contained many photos of her granddaughter, her wedding photo, and a picture of her late husband and daughter, two people the girl had never met. The pictures hung over the clear vinyl-covered sofa that had served as her bed during her high school years.

"You look very thin. Are you losing weight? Are you not eating? Do you have any money for food?" Each question was fired without her taking a breath. No response was needed. Grandma simply slipped her hand into her right pocket and pulled a few dollars out. "Here's some money so you can get something to eat later tonight."

"*Abuela*, I don't need the money and yes, I'm eating. You're getting antsy again." Angelica shook her head slightly and rolled her eyes.

"What's antsy? Did you curse at me, Angelica Gabriella Santos?" The full name was a portent of impending doom.

Seeing her angry expression caused an involuntary and instinctive glance toward Grandma's *chancletas* and a vivid recollection of several memorable scoldings. Ironically, the old woman was the reason she knew so many Spanish swear words.

"No, *Abuela*. I only meant that you're anxious for no reason." She handed the cash to her grandmother. "I'm doing fine. I've been getting decent tips at the diner and I often get to eat for free."

"Okay." Her demeanor softened. "If you say so, *nena*," she responded doubtfully. "Anyway, I made your favorite bread—Mallorca. Also, I made you some oatmeal with a side of boiled eggs, and your *café con leche*." The meal was already prepared and waiting for her. It was Grandma's way to ensure that her granddaughter ate to her standards.

"Do you want me to make you some *tostones*? I prepared them last night. I can fry them very quickly for you."

"No, no, *Abuela*. This is fine. Thank you." She sat at the tiny kitchen table and began to eat, knowing that any minute now, Grandma would commence her lecture.

Maria poured herself a cup of coffee and sat at the table. "Are you going to continue working that late-night schedule?"

Here it comes, thought Angelica. "Yes, *Abuela*."

"*Dios mío!* When will you change it? It's very dangerous for a girl like you to be out in the streets that late." The woman's countenance showed concern and agitation, her usual facial expression when reprimanding her granddaughter.

"*Abuela*, I'm doing fine. I've worked there for close to a year and nothing has ever happened to me. You're doing it again—getting paranoid for no reason. Sometimes, I wish you'd give me a break!" she snapped.

The atmosphere hung silent and heavy between the two for a moment. Grandmother and granddaughter sat and stubbornly refused to speak to one another. The quiet was interrupted only by the sounds of passing sirens and honking horns that traveled through the sultry breeze of the open window.

"I'm sorry, *nena*," said Grandma with a deep sigh. "You know how I get. I don't know what I would do without you. You mean so much to me." She turned her head to the window. "You're also the last of what I have of her." Her gaze returned to Angelica's face and looked deeply into her eyes. "You look so much like your mother that I feel she's right in front of me every time I look at you." Maria's eyes glinted with tears as the memories of her daughter's tragedy resurfaced and with it, the void that came with losing her only offspring. "I sometimes feel...um...culpable, you know—like it's my fault that she's no longer alive."

Angelica's expression softened. Her grandmother's desolate expression made her feel guilty and ashamed about her sudden outburst. She took her hand gently. "I'm sorry for getting upset. I know you care and I never doubt that. And you can't blame yourself for what happened to my mother. You said it yourself so many times how free-spirited she was, and it was her choice to move away and live her own life."

Grandma again gazed out the kitchen window leading to the fire escape while her mind wandered into memory lane. "I sometimes think I was too hard on her and maybe that's the reason she left."

"*Abuela*, I didn't meet my mother but I do know you, and you're a kindhearted woman—overprotective and worrisome at times but at the core, you're loving and caring. You raised me as your own and gave me a wonderful childhood and for that, I'm always thankful." She smiled compassionately and rubbed the old lady's hand.

Maria extended her veined right hand and caressed her granddaughter's cheek softly. "I know you're a strong and brave woman, much stronger than your mother and me. I'm so proud of the woman you've become and know deep in my heart that you'll do great things."

"Thanks, *Abuela*." They stared at each other for a few more moments and their eyes shimmered with emotions.

"Come, Come. Eat your food, *nena*."

Angelica obeyed and scarfed her food. Maria took a few more sips of her coffee, and after a few minutes, rose from her seat, and asked, "Are you done, niña?" She nodded, and the old lady began to pick the dirty dishes up.

"I got the dishes, *Abuela*." Angelica gathered them from the table and placed them in the old, small corner sink.

Standing at the table, her grandmother asked, "Any plans for the weekend? Hanging out with any of your friends or a boyfriend I don't know about?" Her lips curved in a mischievous smirk.

Angelica smiled in response. "No, *Abuela*, I don't have a boyfriend and everyone is busy, so it'll be another party of one for me this weekend."

The reality was that she didn't have any friends. She spent her days off from college or work alone in her studio apartment. Although she had been a loner all her life, it wasn't by choice. She always felt no one could relate to an oddball and eccentric individual who could not easily form connections with people. By now, she'd accepted that it was her lot in life and there was not much she could do to change it.

Despite her reassurances, her grandmother could sense that she was lonely. "Why don't you come to church with me this Sunday? There are always good people there you can meet."

Angelica sighed apprehensively. She knew how touchy the old lady was on the subject of religion. "*Abuela*, I don't believe in that anymore. Church, God, Angels, or whatever is up there..." She raised her hand to gesture vaguely. "It's not for me."

"*Busca de Dios*. You know you need God, *niña*. You're my

answered prayer. I remember being in the hospital alone, asking God for help," she said while she caressed the silver chain with a small cross hanging from her neck. "Well, you know the story. Anyway, I'm always praying for you and those prayers have kept you safe."

"I'd appreciate it if you prayed that the subway lines aren't delayed 'cause...um, looking at the time, we are running late," interjected Angelica when she noticed the time on her cell phone.

"Yes, yes. You're right. Let me change and don't worry about the dishes. I'll take care of them later."

"Oh, *Abuela*, did I get any mail?" she called as her grandmother walked into her menthol-scented bedroom.

"Yes. I have kept all your mail in the shoebox on the table at the front door. Next to where I keep the broom." Her voice began to falter and trailed off as she debated what to wear.

Angelica walked to the small table and picked up the shoebox with her mail. She sifted casually through the small pile of letters and asked, "Did I get anything interesting?"

"*Nada importante*—you know, the usual stuff." She walked out of her bedroom in a rose dress, her hair drawn into a tight bun. "Oh yes, there was one strange letter. It looks like a postcard. Señor Méndez from the first floor gave it to me this morning. He said he found it under the front door. *Pero que estraño*, it has your last name as Archie. That was your father's. Do you go by that name now?" she asked and stared curiously at her.

"Never," she responded with a frown. She found the correspondence and scanned it briefly. A faint unidentifiable smell emanated from it but she thought nothing of it and returned it to the shoebox.

"Ready?" she asked and turned to her grandmother.

"How do I look?" Grandma extended her hands and posed like a model.

"Like a movie star, *Abuela*." They both laughed and walked out the door.

3

EVA SANTOS

Twenty-Two Years Earlier

Emilio Santos sat anxiously with his wife at the doctor's office. He'd received a call that after weeks of examinations, the results were finally available. In the past, he would have indulged in the seasonal shamrock and leprechaun-shaped chocolates before him but today, he grappled with the feelings of sadness at the events that had transpired in the last few years.

His thoughts were mainly on his daughter whom he had not seen since the previous Christmas. How he missed her. He was heartbroken that his once-sweet little girl had become such a troubled individual. While he'd done everything he knew to restore their once-close relationship, it was all to no avail.

He mulled over what had gone wrong. It had been a couple of years since Emilio moved from the Bronx to The City of Brotherly Love. The company where he had worked as a forklift driver for the past twenty years had relocated to Philadelphia. When he was offered better pay to move, he saw it as an excellent opportunity. Moreover, he hoped the relocation of the warehouse would bring a fresh start for his family—a blessing from above, he'd thought then.

Eva Santos, his only child, had been an honors student throughout her elementary and middle school years, but things changed drastically when she entered high school. She met a friend by the name of Licity, who introduced her to the wrong crowds. Little by little, Eva's grades declined as her roguish behavior increased.

Shortly after, she began to miss school, come home late, argue every day with her parents, and at times, arrive at the house intoxicated. Emilio and his wife thought that maybe this move could keep Eva from those toxic friends, especially Licity. That hope proved short-lived.

A few months after they moved, the girl arrived on their doorstep, to the family's surprise. Emilio insisted she have no contact with his daughter, but her influence on Eva ran deeper than he knew. To her parent's dismay, Eva's old patterns and habits began to reemerge.

It was Licity who introduced Leonard to Eva. A wealthy, tall, young fellow with handsome features, perfect skin, and long ebony hair that tumbled over his broad shoulders, he was the kind of guy any girl would fall for. However, her parents saw something strange and dark in him.

Whether it was intuition or merely a general dislike for him, it didn't sit well with them that a rich, handsome man was interested in a poor girl from the hood. It was not a Cinderella story. He was no prince charming and Licity was no fairy godmother. Soon, Eva dropped out of school and when she turned eighteen, she left her parents' home and moved in with her boyfriend.

Not long after she left, Emilio's health began to deteriorate. He frequently found himself fatigued, sweated excessively, and developed bruises all over his body. As he sat in the doctor's office, he decided that maybe the Philadelphia move had been more of a curse than a blessing.

"Mr. Santos, the doctor is ready to see you now. Please follow me," said the office nurse. He and his wife shuffled through the wood-paneled hallway and their anxiety made the brief walk feel like it lasted an eternity. They stepped into the dated office space where Dr. Jacqueline sat behind a small wooden desk. She gestured for them to take a seat.

"Mr. Santos, thank you for coming to see me on such short notice. It's nice to see you and your wife again. However, I don't have good news to give you," she told him and cleared her throat. "I have reviewed the results carefully a few times, and they seem very conclusive. They show a malignancy in your blood—an abnormal production of white blood cells."

A perplexed look settled on Emilio's face. "What does that mean, doctor?" he asked, his dark-brown eyes wide.

"Mr. Santos, you have leukemia. In layman's terms, you have cancer. The leukemia cells have accumulated very rapidly in your blood and bone marrow and have begun to affect vital organs. You're in a very advanced stage and while we can start an aggressive treatment, I'm not sure how helpful it would be."

His wife stared at the doctor in confusion. Her eyes shifted quickly to her husband, whose countenance had become utterly grief-stricken. "No *entiendo!* What does that mean, Emilio?"

He simply shook his head, unable to look at her. His eyes were dull and his hands trembled. Emilio grasped his wife's hand and asked the doctor nervously, "How much time, Dr. Jacqueline?" He sighed sharply and stared at his trembling hand.

"At this rate, Mr. Santos, life expectancy is between three and six months," the doctor replied.

Later, Emilio sat alone in his living room with a broken heart and an anguish-flooded mind. It had been a week since the doctor's visit, but the news remained fresh in his mind. He pondered how cruel and unfair life could be at times. His failing health, his estranged daughter, and the thought that his beloved wife would soon need to fend for herself brought a mixture of grief and anger.

As he wallowed in his sorrow, the telephone rang. Initially, he wanted to ignore it but his options were to either answer it or continue the pity party. Gradually, he rose from the sofa and strode toward the end table.

"Hello," he answered sluggishly. At first, all he could hear were heavy sobs and sniffles on the other side. His intuition said it was his daughter. "Eva, is that you?"

A shuddering and desperate voice responded. "Papi, I'm so sorry!" Eva sobbed unrelentingly. "I'm sorry...I truly am!" Her words were barely audible through the sniffles.

"Eva, *mi amor*, are you okay? Are you hurt?" A bittersweet sensation engulfed him.

"I'm not okay, Papi. I'm not okay!" she repeated through her wracking sobs. "I feel so alone, scared, confused…I don't know what to do now." Each pause was filled with audible weeping.

"It's all right. I'm here now." He offered comfort while he considered the worst. "What's going on?"

"I don't know how to say this…" Her voice quivered and she hesitated.

"It's okay, *mi hija*. You can tell me anything." He sighed softly and waited for the news.

A moment of silence followed. "I'm pregnant," she blurted and sobbed anew.

Emilio was standing when he heard the news but the shock of it made him sit abruptly. His unwed baby girl of eighteen was pregnant. A long, heavy silence followed, interrupted only by Eva's sniffles and whimpers.

Finally, he spoke. "Is it Leonard's?" His face was ashen.

"Yes."

"Did he leave you?"

"No. I left him." She whimpered.

"Why don't you tell me all about it?" he asked tenderly.

"I don't know what went wrong. When we first found out, Leonard was so happy. He made sure I was getting plenty of rest, eating the right foods, and taking the best vitamins. He didn't let me do any chores and he pampered me. I felt so blessed."

"So, what happened?" her father asked.

"At first, he was excited and said he was sure it was a boy. During the second trimester, I went to see my obstetrician and found out I'm having a baby girl. When I told him I was having a girl, however, his attitude changed. He immediately told me that he didn't want a girl and he insisted I should abort it. When I refused, he became cruel, distant, and abusive."

"Did he get physical?" His eyes blazed with rage at even the thought of it and he stood reflexively.

"No, but he was mean and verbally abusive, and... strange things started happening. I started having nightmares of being tortured and haunted and would wake up with him standing over me. As crazy as it may sound, I saw objects move and fall without anyone touching them and heard weird sounds when I was alone." She drew a sharp gasp. "I told Leonard about it but he didn't believe me. He simply said I was hallucinating and that was all the more reason to terminate the pregnancy. The more I refused, the nastier he got. I couldn't take it, so while he was away, I left. Since then, I've moved from place to place so he wouldn't find me."

"*Un espíritu*," he murmured in Spanish. His eyes glazed over.

"What was that, Papi?"

He shook his head to clear the stupor. "I'm sorry, *mi amor*. Why didn't you come home?"

"I was...uh, I was afraid," she said apprehensively.

"Afraid of what?"

"Afraid that you and Mami wouldn't want me back—"

"*Mi amor*, you are always welcome at home." Emilio interrupted her in mid-sentence.

"But I was also afraid that Leonard would hurt you. He threatened that if I were to call or go back home, he would harm you."

"Have you contacted the police?"

"As soon I left, I did, but when they went to check for Leonard at the apartment, it was completely empty as if no one had ever lived there. I don't know what else to do."

"You can come home and we can deal with this together." Her father's words brought Eva to tears again and she realized for the first time in her life how much he loved her. "And about the baby—we will raise her together and give her the best home possible."

"I've been a jerk, Papi, and I feel ashamed and terrible for the way I've treated you."

"Hey, don't worry about that now. Come home."

"Is Mami home?"

"She stepped out to run some errands," Emilio replied without revealing that she had stepped out to pick up his pain management medication.

Unexpectedly, a dry, wracking coughing spell came over him. He pulled away from the phone and covered his mouth to muffle the sound. His body shook violently and he gasped several times as he struggled desperately for breath. He pulled his hand from his mouth and noticed blood splattered on it.

"Are you all right, Papi?"

He wiped his lips with his hand, cleared his throat, and continued, "Yeah, I…uh, been dealing with a bad cold." He rested his hand on the table to steady himself. His body looked weaker and lankier in only a week.

"How's Mami?"

"We are both fine but we will be better when you are here with us. Where are you now?" He could hear the faint sound of chirping crickets over the line and he deduced she was using a payphone.

"I'm outside a shabby-looking diner in the middle of nowhere. I've traveled all over Pennsylvania and just arrived at Lancaster. I hope to catch a train to Philadelphia as soon as I can." The thought of returning home refreshed her soul like springs of living water.

"Do you need money?"

"I got it, Papi. Love you."

"Love you too, Eva."

Emilio hung up, walked quickly to a nearby oak chest, opened the top drawer, and searched frantically. After a few minutes, his gaze located the object he was searching for. He took hold of a simple silver chain with a small unassuming cross hanging from it. His hand shook as he held the chain and this time, it was not from the illness. "I can't believe I missed all the signs." He fell to his knees and prayed.

It was the last time that Emilio and Eva spoke.

4

LIFE AND DEATHS

"Can we please speak to Mr. or Mrs. Santos?" asked the voice on the line.

"Who is this?" Mrs. Santos answered unpleasantly, thinking it was another telemarketer. She had just finished gardening in the late-summer heat and desired rest, not annoyance.

"This is the Lancaster Police Department. Am I speaking to Mrs. Santos?"

"Yes, this is she." Apprehension swirled around her.

"Would it be possible for you to stop by the Lancaster Hospital? This concerns your daughter."

"My daughter! Is she okay? Has anything bad happened to her?" Her blood ran cold as she imagined the worst possible situation.

"Mrs. Santos, all your questions will be answered at the hospital, but we need to know how soon you can make it here."

"I can be there within two hours," She responded, both puzzled and frightened.

Immediately, she got in her car and rushed toward the hospital, ignoring Stop and Yield signs, traffic lights, and even the late afternoon showers. Her sole focus was to reach her destination as quickly as possible. Panic was her only companion throughout the entire drive and it tormented her relentlessly. She'd lost her husband a week before. Could it be possible she had lost her daughter too? She reached the hospital earlier than expected and dashed through the front door to the front desk.

Ignoring the fact that the receptionist was on the phone, she exclaimed frantically, "Where's my daughter?" The woman gestured with her finger to wait. "Excuse me! I'm here for my daughter," she insisted.

The staff member sighed and spoke into the phone. "Can you hold for a moment?" before she turned her attention to the desperate woman, smiled, and asked, "How may I assist you, ma'am?"

"I want to see my daughter." Her vague response left the staff member clueless.

"What's your daughter's name?"

"Eva Santos!"

The receptionist went to search the computer directory but her gaze lowered and she did not bother to type. "Are you the mother of Eva Santos?" she asked soberly.

"Yes, I am." Maria stared at her in bewilderment and impatience.

Without meeting her gaze, the woman gestured with her hand. "Hold for one moment." She picked the phone up and dialed an extension. "The mother has just arrived." She paused and said, "Okay. I'll let her know." Her gaze finally shifted to Mrs. Santos. "Someone will be with you shortly. You can take a seat in our waiting area."

Although she'd been pointed toward the seating area, the anxiety kept the poor woman pacing.

Within minutes, a nurse appeared and led her down the main corridor. Each step made Maria's stomach knot more tightly. They took the elevator and descended to a much cooler area of the hospital. After a few more steps, they both stood before a secure door, which required the nurse to pick up the phone attached to the wall to get it opened. They walked through it to where two suited individuals waited—one who appeared to be in his late forties and the other half that age—in front of double swinging doors.

"Detectives, this is Mrs. Santos. You asked me to bring her to you," said the nurse to the men.

"Thank you, Jon. We will take it from here," the older detective said as she began to leave. "Mrs. Santos, I am Detective Max Brooks and this is my partner, Detective Daniel Ortega. We are with the Lancaster Police Department."

"What is this about? Someone mentioned something about my daughter over the phone." Her heart drummed with every word.

"Have you come alone, Mrs. Santos? Is your husband or anyone else with you?"

Her throat clenched and her vision blurred as she rummaged through her purse for a tissue. "I'm alone. My husband passed away a week ago. He died from cancer."

The two detectives stared gravely at each other and wondered how to deliver their news. The older detective placed his hand over his lips and cleared his throat. "Our sincerest condolences on your loss, Mrs. Santos. To be quite candid with you, I'm not sure how to say this but... um, we found a body that matches your daughter's description and we need you to identify it."

"Oh, *Dios mío*, no, no, no! Please don't say that to me!" She staggered and fell to one knee as her body became strangely numb and uncooperative. Her sobs were loud and distraught. The young detective rushed forward and prevented her from collapsing fully.

Detective Brooks grasped the nearby beige phone hooked next to the swinging doors and called immediately for medical assistance. She cried for a few minutes before she rose slowly to her feet and said sternly, "I want to see the body."

"Maybe we should wait for a doctor first," said the younger detective.

"I want to see her body now!" she snapped.

"Sure thing, Mrs. Santos," Detective Brooks replied. He opened the double swinging doors and proceeded to walk into a cold and gloomy room comprised mainly of embalming tables occupied by sheet-covered bodies.

The men led her slowly to a mid-size body in the center of the room and her heart pounded harder with each step closer.

Very carefully, Detective Brooks began to unveil the lifeless body to reveal a beautiful, petite, but now pale and sunken-faced young lady. Maria exhaled sharply and fainted.

Mrs. Santos' eyelids flickered as she awakened slowly from what she thought was her worst nightmare. Her bleary eyes tried to make sense of her surroundings, while her thoughts swirled in confusion. She glanced out the window toward the morning sky obscured by dark clouds. *Donde estoy*, she thought when she realized she wasn't in her bedroom.

The sound of beeps and the sight of monitors surrounding the bed where she lay confirmed that she was at a hospital. Not any hospital—the hospital of her nightmare. How she wished that it was nothing more than a nightmare. Merely the thought was too much to bear. Eva, her only daughter, was dead.

Her eyes flooded with tears as she stared dully at the ceiling, trapped in a place of dark despair. With no husband and no daughter, misery was her only companion. She lowered her head and stared bitterly at the silver chain and crucifix her husband had given her before he died. "How could you do this to me? I have no one left." Tears coursed down her face. "I'm now childless and widowed. You have left me with no one."

"How are you feeling, Mrs. Santos?" asked the nurse who walked cautiously into the room.

With sniffles and heavy sobs, she responded in a quivering voice. "Like I want to die."

"I'm so sorry for your loss. I can't imagine the pain you're going through." The woman approached and checked her vital signs. Shortly after, the two detectives she'd met earlier walked into the room. The nurse turned to them. "I'm sorry, Detectives, but I don't think this is a good time to see her."

"It's okay," Mrs. Santos interjected. "Leave them. I need to know what happened to my daughter."

"Mrs. Santos, we offer our condolences on your loss and sympathy for the dreadful news. We had no idea of your husband's—" started Detective Brooks.

"*Ahórrame la pena!*" she snapped in Spanish. "What happened to my daughter?" With tear-filled eyes, she looked fiercely at the detectives.

Brooks frowned in confusion and turned to his partner. "Spare her the pity," Ortega translated in a whisper.

"Oh," he said in sudden understanding and returned his gaze to her. "There's no easy way to say this, but she was poisoned. She was found unconscious in a diner's restroom a few nights ago and was pronounced dead shortly after she arrived at the hospital," he told her.

"You mean she was killed?" Her expression was bewildered and shocked.

The young detective spoke quickly. "At this time, we are treating this case as a possible homicide. We obtained information from the Pittsburgh police department that a few months ago, your daughter had filed a complaint against her boyfriend, a Leonard...hold on..." The young Detective Ortega began to flip through the pages of his pocket-sized notebook. "I had written his last name somewhere in here..." Ortega said and his voice trailing off.

She nodded. "Yes, that's correct. My husband mentioned she called the police because she felt...*amenazada*... What's the word in English... um...threatened."

"Well, at this time, he's wanted for questioning and we

were hoping you could give us information about him. Has he tried to contact you recently?"

"No. I don't know anything about the man. The last time I saw him was the day my daughter left my house a little over eight months ago."

Detective Brooks spoke. "It's imperative that if he does, you call us right away. At this time, he's the only suspect we have."

"My daughter had mentioned to my husband that she was pregnant when she spoke to him. Was she still pregnant when you found her?" There was a momentary pause as she stared intently at the detectives and waited for either to respond.

Suddenly, a neonatal nurse walked into the room wheeling in a baby bassinet and exclaimed, "And here's Grandma!" The two detectives shook their heads and gave her a wide-eyed look.

"We haven't told her about the baby yet," Brooks protested.

"I'm sorry. You said to bring the baby shortly after you entered the room," the woman said awkwardly.

"No, we said after we left the room." Their faces were disapproving.

Mrs. Santos interrupted the discussion. "This is my grandchild?" she demanded.

The nurse responded, "My apologies. I thought you were informed already but yes, she's your granddaughter. We are calling her a miracle baby. Even with all that happened to her mother, she was not affected at all. She's one hundred percent healthy."

"My granddaughter..." she said as tears of joy and hope began to stream down her face.

With that, the detectives took their cue to leave but before they exited the room, Ortega asked, "What's your full name for our records?"

"Maria Soto Santos," she responded absentmindedly while she stared at the infant.

As the young detective began to write in the notebook, he said, "There it is—Leonard Archie. That's the last name of the boyfriend." His partner pursed his lips at him and they left the room.

"She hasn't been named yet," said the nurse. "I know it was unexpected, but do you have any names in mind?" She lifted the baby and turned to hand the child to Maria.

As she held the infant in her arms, joy flooded her soul and she said, "She will be my little angel and will be called Angelica. Angelica Gabriella Santos."

5

THE HUNT BEGINS

Present Time

Angelica went straight to her studio apartment after she dropped her grandmother off. She sat on her bed and considered how to spend the late afternoon. After a few moments, she retrieved her phone from the back pocket of her jeans and scrolled through the contacts.

Her gaze scanned the list from college classmates to her diner colleagues, but all were acquaintances and not actual friends. Many times, she had attempted to connect with others but always felt distant and unable to relate. She always thought they viewed her as aloof or antisocial, but she wasn't. *Merely different,* she assured herself.

To add the final nail in the cross, there was that *thing,* as she called it—the intuition, déjà vu, or sixth sense she generally felt in crowded public areas, although it manifested randomly at times like that night in the alleyway. The few times she'd mentioned it to others, all she received were odd looks and frowns.

As she scrolled through the address book, Jasmine's

name appeared—the orphan girl she met in her English 101 class. Strangely enough, Angelica had connected with her from the first time they met. She was someone she could easily talk to and bond with at a deeper level.

Unfortunately, two weeks after they had met, the girl was killed at a fraternity party. A thorough investigation was conducted but the mysterious killers were never found. Witnesses reported two young girls fleeing the scene with strange-looking knives but no actual identification was made. For some reason, she never removed Jasmine from her contacts, out of respect or a sense of hopefulness that she could have friends or both.

She sighed deeply, put her phone away, and decided to rummage through the shoebox full of mail. As she sifted through it, her gaze suddenly stopped on the puzzling postcard—the one addressed to her but with her father's last name. The black-colored postcard was inscribed with red calligraphy, which gave it the appearance of an invitation.

When she inspected it a little closer, she noticed it had no postage stamp but on the upper left, it was marked *ZOI I THANATOS*. She frowned at the words, which she assumed formed a name. The bottom right-hand corner contained the present date and a time of eight pm. She lifted the postcard to her nose and attempted to identify the strange scent but shrugged after a moment, still clueless.

Her gaze locked on the last name again—Archie. She knew her mother's tragic story, even the part about her father wanting an abortion. Her curiosity about him had made her do her own research, yet she found very little except for a police report that stated he was wanted for questioning in the alleged murder of Eva Santos. Leonard Archie was a mystery to all—like a specter—even Maria Santos and the police, which made her more intrigued about him.

In general, she always wondered about the type of person her father was and if he could possibly have been cruel enough to kill her mother. Her curiosity ranged from his appearance to where he was from. *Is he even still alive?* was a common thought but the most important nagged continually. *Does he even know I exist?* She wondered if the postcard was his attempt to reach out or if it was merely a practical joke by someone.

Curious, she studied it further but was interrupted when her cell phone rang. When she saw *Boss* on the caller ID, she answered quickly. "What's up, Bill?"

He spoke in his usual gruff voice. "Angelica, Margaret is running late today and I wondered if you could cover part of her early shift."

With nothing else to do, she responded, "When do you need me?"

"By five pm. It's only for a couple of hours."

"It shouldn't be a problem."

"Thanks, Toots. I can always count on you. See you soon."

What a boring shift. Angelica slumped in her seat on the subway. The night's only excitement had been Bill regaling her with the account of the break-in the night before.

Someone had all but destroyed the rear door and rummaged through her boss' files but otherwise, didn't steal anything. *Who breaks into a restaurant and doesn't take anything? Is our food so bad that even thieves won't take it for free?* She smiled at her inward joke. Now, she was headed to her grandmother's apartment to drop off some medicine she had picked up for her at the pharmacy.

After a while, she straightened and wriggled in her seat. She began to have the same sensation as the previous night —a feeling that she was being followed without entirely understanding why. And tonight, it was intense.

It was a quarter after eight when she reached her grandmother's apartment building. She paused, looked toward the third floor, and noticed the kitchen window that led to the fire escape was open. It was very unusual for the old lady to have that window open at this time of day. She walked through the front door when suddenly her senses alerted her to an unsettling sense of danger—a menacing presence unlike any she had ever felt.

Concern pushed her to ascend the squeaky stairs and she heard a crash of pots and pans coming from the direction of the apartment. *Grandma must be doing one of those deep cleanings.* Halfway up, however, she heard a bloodcurdling scream. Her face went ashen and she raced up the stairs and reached her floor out of breath.

When she opened the door, her grandmother was suspended three feet from the ground by the neck. In shock, she stared at a darkly cloaked individual whose visible face and hands glowed a charcoal-black color as he grasped the old lady effortlessly in a vise-like grip with one hand.

Horror struck her like one of Egypt's plagues. Angelica screamed, "Stop!" before she snatched the broomstick next to the door and charged at the intruder. He lunged toward her with his left arm and a mysterious invisible force lifted her slim figure a few feet from the floor and hurled her viciously against the wall where her grandma hung all the family photos.

She pounded into it, struck her head, and landed with sufficient impact to knock the breath from her. Her ears rang painfully and muffled the surrounding sounds. Panicked, she swiveled toward her grandmother but the man dropped the old lady like a rag doll.

He turned and walked toward her while his menacing gaze bored into her. Unexpectedly, two female figures appeared outside on the fire escape, one with mocha-colored skin and the other beige. They vaulted quickly into the apartment through the open window she had seen earlier. The dark-skinned girl drew two quartz daggers from the sheath of her ankles. Her companion lifted the back of her Mello Kitty tee-shirt to retrieve a set of blades that were fastened to her lower back.

The intruder sniffed, stopped his approach, and turned to the two newcomers.

Angelica mustered every ounce of her strength and struggled to push from the floor, but she could only watch as the tall assailant moved with considerable speed toward the two females.

Almost as if expecting it, they leapt away and quickly took a stance to engage him in combat. The eerie assailant's lips moved, muttered an obscure incantation, and with a gesture of his left hand, he caused a knife on the kitchen counter to vibrate. He swiped his arm to the left and the knife soared across the room toward the dark-skinned girl. She dodged it easily and it continued past her to puncture one of the kitchen walls. Before he could attempt another attack, she ran toward him, jumped high, and landed a hard kick on his face.

He merely looked at her, unaffected by her strike, and scowled as he motioned with outstretched hands. The entire kitchen table rose and hurtled toward the girl, and the impact was enough to fling her to the floor.

What the hell? Angelica tried to focus but she slipped into a stupor.

The other girl took advantage of his momentary engagement and stabbed her blade viciously into his arm. He clenched his jaw in response to the pain from the bleeding wound. With a groan, he recovered rapidly and thrust his right arm forward to upend the Mello Kitty girl who fell awkwardly. He muttered another strange incantation in a growled tone, made a fist with his right hand, and bounded effortlessly high enough to crack the ceiling with his head. She sensed his movement and rolled quickly to the left. He landed heavily with his full weight behind the attack but missed her and left an indentation on the wooden floor with his left knee and a gaping hole with his fist.

Her partner recovered from the flying table. She rose quickly and wiped the blood from her mouth with the back of her palm. Still dazed, she managed to fix her gaze on her foe, threw one of the blades, and struck him on the back of his shoulder, inches away from his head.

"Damn!" she said disappointedly.

He staggered and struggled to reach the knife in his back. Distracted by the wound, he lurched around and eventually stopped over the girl on the floor with his midsection completely exposed.

When she saw his stunned expression, she raised her right foot and kicked him savagely in the groin.

His shriek of pain was more precisely a squeal. He tottered back but before he could recover, a sudden impact on his back shoved him forward forcefully, over the girl on the floor, and toward one of the windows. Unable to stop his forward motion, he shattered the window and plunged from the three-story apartment building onto the pavement below.

The girl lay back for a moment, sighed with relief, and looked toward the spot where the assailant had stood over her. "Pretzel, nice kick, but I can't believe you missed that shot."

"You get smacked with a freaking table and then see if you hit him at all," retorted her companion. She extended her hand to assist her partner off the floor. Once up, they moved toward the shattered window and peered out to where the intruder must have landed. The dark shadow of blood was visible but no cadaver could be seen.

"He got away. He must've had help from a Daimon." Pretzel sighed in disappointment and turned to her Mello Kitty partner. "Reina, check the girl and see if she's okay. I'll check the old lady."

Reina rushed to Angelica. "She's alive but unconscious," she said and checked her pulse to be sure.

Her companion hurried to Angelica's grandmother. "The older lady is breathing but badly injured. I'll call nine-one-one but we have to take the girl and go. She's being hunted."

6

A CRAZY HEADACHE

The room was dark, save for the pale glow from the city's streetlights through the single window. Both hands of the clock on the wall were on the twelve when Angelica woke slowly. She felt nauseous and dazed. A headache and world of confusion pounded in her head as she struggled to open her eyes.

What the hell happened? Did I eat a bad empanada? Her awareness sharpened and as swiftly as lightning flashes from the east to the west, the memory returned.

"Abuela!"

Images of the evening's events kaleidoscoped, which made her feel sick to her stomach. With no clue as to her whereabouts, she heaved herself out of bed, only to fall onto her knees on the cold concrete floor, ready to hurl the little she had in her stomach.

"Whoa—whoa there, honey," said a stranger who stepped into the room where she fought to control the nausea. "You're in no condition to be standing, much less walking. For now, you need to stay in bed. You have a nasty concussion and have been unconscious for a few hours."

"I...need...to...leave," Angelica managed to tell her. "My grandmother. My grandma—she's...she's..." Her eyes swam with tears.

"Let's get you off the floor onto the bed first," said the woman. She extended both arms and assisted her onto the bed.

"Oh, my God. It hurts so much. What a headache." Angelica grunted in pain and placed her hand over the back of her head.

The woman took a transparent orange pill bottle from her pants pocket. "Here's something to help that headache." She placed two pills into the girl's hand and took the bottle of water from the night table. "I know you'd like to simply waltz yourself right out of here, but let's get you treated first. Okay?" She smiled widely and sat on the edge of the bed.

"My name is May. I'm one of the caregivers here." She appeared to be in her mid-thirties, with short brown hair, smooth beige skin, and vibrant dark-brown eyes. Angelica took the medication and stared bewilderedly at her with tear-filled eyes. "Is anything other than your head hurting?" she asked and turned a penlight on to examine the girl's pupils.

She squinted at the glare and pushed the flashlight away. "Look." She sighed deeply and attempted to fight the headache. "I appreciate your concern for me, but I need to get out of here. I have to check on my grandmother." She pushed from the bed but groaned from the sharp back pain.

May helped her to sit. "We have been through this already. You're in no condition to walk and I need you to be patient for a few minutes. Now, does anything else hurt?" she asked sternly but tenderly.

Feeling out of sorts, the girl responded, "My back hurts a lot, even when I breathe."

"May I?" the woman asked as she placed her hand over the girl's forehead.

Initially, Angelica thought she was checking her temperature, but she instantly felt a warmth that flowed from the top of her head to the soles of her feet. Her headache began to ease and the pain in her back dissipated. She gasped in surprise at the relief brought by the touch of May's hand. Within seconds, her headache and back pain disappeared. She drew a deep breath and felt no discomfort.

She stared at the woman in bewilderment and wondered how she was able to alleviate the pain with a touch of her hands.

With a smile, May winked at her and said, "The pills I gave you should kick in by now."

As she rose from the bed, Angelica asked, "Where am I by the way? Is this a hospital?"

Before the caregiver could answer, three individuals appeared through the door. The middle-aged woman had deep gray eyes that accentuated her diamond-shaped face and attractive features. Dirty-blonde hair tumbled over her shoulders but was pulled back from her face to reveal her high cheekbones. Although only five-foot-five, she had a commanding demeanor and presence. Angelica recognized the other two—both about her age—from her grandmother's apartment.

"She's up," said one of them. At this, Angelica propped herself against the headboard and turned her head to the doorway.

"The answer to your question is no, this isn't a hospital," the older woman told her. "Officially, this is Saint Miriam's Shelter for Children and Women. My name is Joan. These two are Pretzel and Reina, your rescuers at the apartment, and it seems you've already met May. This is our facility, and you were brought here shortly after your attack. I imagine you have a slew of questions about what happened to you."

She focused her gaze intently on Joan. "As I said to May earlier, I'm thankful for the help but I need to get out of here and see my grandmother. She was being robbed or assaulted, I think, by a very tall man, and I believe she was seriously injured. I need to make sure she's okay."

"A Nephilim," the woman clarified. "Your grandmother was attacked by a Nephilim. She's currently in a stable condition at Mount Salvation Hospital. If you were to visit or contact her now, though, it might draw another Nephilim to her location. I'd suggest staying put for the moment."

"Nephila...what?" Her eyebrows raised to her hairline.

"A Nephilim—a half-human, half-angel species. A hybrid. Most are workers of darkness whose sole iniquitous purpose in life is to destroy, conquer, and execute their fathers' bidding." At this stage, all three moved from the entrance of the doorway into the room.

At first, Angelica said nothing and stared blankly at

them with pursed lips. She nodded slightly to appear agreeable. "Right," she drawled. "I'm not sure what you guys are smoking, but whatever it is, it seems you're enjoying it. But...um, I don't want any part of it, so if you don't mind, I'd like to leave now."

"I used to be more diplomatic about the subject with newcomers, but after years of doing this, I realized being blunt from the start is the best course of action. I know you may find it hard to believe, but your eyes can't deny what you saw in your grandmother's apartment."

At first, Angelica had thought the strange events she recalled from earlier were part of some dreadful nightmare or form of hallucination. Her mind began to spin wildly as she recollected the chaotic events of the evening. She had been thrown into the wall without anyone touching her. Her grandmother had been lifted effortlessly off her feet with one hand, the knife and table had been flung with ease, and the incredible speed and movements of the man had seemed impossible. The doubt began to melt from her cynical mind.

"That's not possible," she murmured.

"I'm not trying to sell you a hocus-pocus tale. I'm giving you the plain facts. The creature you saw simply isn't a human being. It's the reason you may have seen him do unusual things."

"So, these...these Nephilim have supernatural powers and go around robbing old ladies' apartments?"

"We are sure that the Nephilim wasn't there to steal or to harm your grandmother. He was there to kill you."

Angelica's eyes widened. "What? Why? What did I do?"

"It's not what you have done but what you could do to them," Joan clarified.

"What the hell does that mean?"

"I won't dive into those details now but I will say being with us gives you and your grandmother a better chance to survive."

"What are you? Some secret anti-Nephilim police department?"

Reina, who had seemed distracted throughout the entire discourse, murmured, "Ooh, I like the sound of that —Freeze, ANPD!" Pretzel arched an eyebrow and stared pointedly at her.

The older woman continued. "We call ourselves the Daughters of the Watchers. I'm the leader of this sector. Pretzel, Reina, May, and the rest of my team, including me, were targeted to be killed by the Nephilim exactly like you. We are the only ones who can stand up to them, so you are in good hands with us."

Angelica listened, half-terrified and half-disbelieving. "Oh, God! This all sounds crazy." She lowered her forehead into her hands and tried to make sense of it all. Nephilim, soaring knife, flying table, Daughters of the Watchers, and jeez, even the instantaneous disappearing headache and back pain—everything sounded like a cryptic message from Hell. "I don't know what to make of this. I need to sleep," she mumbled and shook her head. Her expression was one of utter confusion.

"I know this is a lot to take in so I won't say more yet. In due time, I'll explain everything you need to know but for now, get some rest."

She slid into the bed, rested her head gently on the

pillow, and closed her eyes to the sound of footsteps leaving the room.

It had been several hours since Angelica had been left alone and she listened intently for any sounds of activity around her. She guessed since it was the early hours of the morning and the skies were still dark that it was a good time to leave this mysterious and bizarre place. Quietly, she eased herself from the bed and tried to not disrupt the eerie silence. She searched the floor for her sneakers and found them under the bed, put them on quickly, and crept cautiously to the open door of the room.

The view through a large lattice window on her left seemed to indicate that she was on the second-floor level of some building or warehouse. When she looked to the right, a long, gloomy corridor stretched ahead with several closed doors to the right and left, which she suspected were other rooms.

She hunched nervously, proceeded cautiously along the hallway, and tiptoed carefully to avoid detection. Her gaze danced nervously from side to side as she hurried through the long, murky hallway and searched her surroundings frantically for an exit. After what seemed like forever, she found only other passageways, doors, and dead-ends in a labyrinth of endless corridors. *'ño! Estoy perdida. Where's the freaking exit?* Feeling a little desperate now, she hurried along numerous winding corridors and made it a point to look tentatively through each opening so she wouldn't miss something.

Finally, she rounded a corner into a hallway leading to an industrial-sized door with a small middle window. Light slithered through the edges—a hopeful sign. She reached it undetected and peered through the small glass window at a set of staircases. Very gently, she opened it and tiptoed down the stairs to another door like the one above.

Her peek through the window revealed the wide-open space of a warehouse and her gaze initially registered only stacked boxes and numerous windows. A few yards away, however, she noticed a door with a red *Exit* sign above it and most importantly, no one was around. Carefully, she opened the door to the warehouse.

Half-afraid that someone would enter and find her there, she abandoned caution and hurried forward with quick strides, although she felt increasingly anxious with every step. *I hope the door isn't locked.* Only a few feet away, she allowed herself a deep breath of relief. "Home free."

"You're not a prisoner here, you know," Pretzel said quietly. She was seated on a windowsill on one of the side windows toward her left. Her face revealed a deep melancholy and her green eyes glinted with sorrow.

A cold chill shot up Angelica's spine like a child caught with their hand in the cookie jar. "Oh, hi!" she blurted with wide eyes. She turned slowly toward the girl. "I couldn't sleep so I was…uh, exploring, that's all."

"Sure," the girl responded sarcastically. "You know, I was in your shoes once—scared, freaked out, and surrounded by a whole group of whackos. Getting away from here seemed like the most logical thing to do." She took a few steps away from the faint moonlight. Her brown hair hung in two braids and even in the poor light, it glimmered.

Angelica stared at her in despair and frowned uneasily. "I don't think you understand. I need to see my grandmother. I'm so concerned about her. She's the only family I have."

With a poignant expression, Pretzel looked intently at her. "I was only fifteen when my mother was killed. She died protecting me and she was the only family I had too. If it weren't for this group of ladies, I wouldn't have survived. But I understand your dilemma. If my mother were in the hospital, I'd have moved heaven and earth to see her." She swallowed hard at those words. "Yet knowing what I know now, not seeing her would be the best way to protect and keep her alive."

"None of this makes any sense to me!" she exclaimed.

"It didn't make any sense to me either until I saw what those creatures did to my mother and to countless other individuals." The girl's face displayed a sense of pain and truth as she uttered those words.

"But I can't simply sit here without knowing her condition, if she's dead or alive, or if she needs me." Angelica paced in a circle and drummed her fingers against her legs.

"I promise you this. Stay with us and I'll personally take you to your grandmother when the time is right. Tassel, our computer geek, has access to the hospital's network and she's been keeping tabs on your grandmother. Maria Santos, right?"

"How did you know her name?" She stopped and gazed intently at her.

"I'll explain later, but Tassel's latest update is that she's in a stable condition although she is still unconscious, so there's not much you can help her with at this time."

"*Me cago en ná!*" she muttered in Spanish. "Why's this all happening?" Angelica clutched her head with her hands.

"Angelica." It was the first time Pretzel had called her by name. "Stay with us and everything will become clear."

She sighed deeply and nodded.

7

MORE THAN MEETS THE EYE

Detective Dexter directed the investigation of Maria Santos' apartment with his morning coffee in hand. With him were other NYPD officers who examined every possible clue and gathered evidence on the latest NYC crime.

The police were attempting to put together the pieces of this unusual case. He ensured that photographs were taken of the blood spattered in the apartment, the kitchen and living room in disarray, the shattered window, and the crimson-stained sidewalk littered with glass.

No eyewitnesses were found who could reveal what happened that evening and the elderly woman found at the scene was unconscious. She had immediately been taken to the hospital following an anonymous nine-one-one call.

"What do you make of it, Detective?" asked one of the first responding officers, Samuel Peterson.

"A preliminary assessment tells me it was a breaking and entering gone wrong, but let's see what forensics comes up with," responded a confident Dexter. "Once I get the full report, I'll be able to make a more thorough assessment."

"The FBI is downstairs," one of the NYPD police officers alerted him. The man walked through the main door and seemed somewhat haggard.

"Huh? Are the FBI making house calls now?" the detective asked cynically.

"Someone must have given them a head-ups," Samuel pointed out.

"Let me head downstairs to check this out." He turned to Officer Peterson. "Sam, before I go, make sure forensics does their job correctly this time. We can't solve cases if we haven't gathered all the evidence." Dexter hurried out to descend the steep, squeaky stairs, curious about the unwanted visitors.

He exited the building's front door and focused on two suited individuals who stared intently at the red-spattered stain on the sidewalk and the shards of glass that surrounded it.

He strode apprehensively toward the two agents with an inquisitive frown on his face. "I'm Detective Daryl Dexter, NYPD. How can I help you?" The visitors turned to him.

"Detective, I'm agent Daniel Ortega and this is my partner Constance Anderson. We are with the FBI." Both agents presented their golden shields. He glanced blankly at the open-winged eagle emblems.

Although a far cry from the sleek young detective during his Lancaster days, at two hundred pounds with salt-and-pepper hair, Ortega still looked physically healthy and fit. His partner was quite attractive and in her early thirties, with shoulder-length blonde hair and a lean figure.

"What can I do for you?" asked Dexter.

"We heard there was a peculiar intrusion here last night and we hoped to have a look at the apartment," responded Ortega.

"Sure, but I'm curious—what's the bureau's interest in this crime scene and how did you even know to come here?"

"We have our contacts like you do, and let's say we are trying to make some connections." The agent cracked a smile.

"It sounds like a subtle way to say mind your own business," snapped the detective, not pleased at all. "Whatever. I'll take you up."

He spun on his heel and led the two of them up the stairs without any further effort at conversation. Agent Ortega was close behind and Anderson followed, her face scrunched.

"They like their cooking oil here, huh?" she snarked.

"You don't like that smell, Connie?" joked Ortega. "It's quite nostalgic for me—smells like my parents' old apartment building in Philly." He tilted his head at his partner with a smirk.

They all reached the apartment panting slightly and in need of fresh air.

"Exactly like home," he affirmed cheerfully.

The FBI agents entered Maria Santos' crowded apartment.

"This is the place," stated the detective. "The name of the victim is Maria Santos, age sixty-five—"

"Yes, I'm aware of that," interrupted Ortega. "You mind if we take a look around?"

"Sure. Be my guest," he responded with a slight sneer.

After exploring the various rooms, the agents stopped in the living room and examined the indentation and hole in the wooden floor. Ortega squatted to inspect the damage further and inclined his head to look at the crack on the ceiling.

He stood and studied the wall, the scattered family photos on the floor, and a broken broomstick in the center of the living room. The agents walked to the kitchen and noted the overturned wooden table and the stainless-steel knife that protruded from the wall. Their gazes shifted to the lavender powder which covered the windowsill and highlighted various latent footprints. Finally, they approached the shattered window adjacent to the kitchen, observed the blood drops on the floor, and stared outside at the concrete's crimson blot.

"Detective, were there any signs of forced entry?" asked Ortega and gestured toward the kitchen window.

Dexter nodded and responded, "The other tenants mentioned that after sundown, she keeps all her windows closed. That's how I came to discover the window latch was broken. Someone must have forced it open. I suspect this was the point of entry."

"Good find," Ortega commented and turned to the wall. "And were you able to pull any fingerprints from that knife?"

"We found several sets of prints throughout the apartment, but only one set of prints on the knife. I suspect it's the victim's. She might have thrown it when she saw the perpetrators coming through the window," the detective responded.

"That knife sank deeply into that wall. I'm not sure that a sixty-five-year-old lady has the brute strength to make such an impact," the agent pointed out. Without waiting for a rebuttal, he continued. "You mentioned perpetrators —is there any reason you suspect there were more than one?"

"Well...um, the windowsill shows multiple footprints." A flush crept up Dexter's face.

"Hmm...there could be but let's take a moment to analyze the evidence so far." Ortega retraced his steps to the window. "First, multiple footprints of various sizes all face into the apartment but none face out." He turned and scanned the room and his gaze settled on the broken window. "Second, someone went out of that window." His finger pointed at the shattered glass. "And judging by the blood spatter's distance from the building, that someone went out with a great deal of momentum."

He walked to the disordered living room and stopped between the indention on the floor and the damaged ceiling. "Third, the conditions of this room suggest a sizeable struggle with participants of considerable strength. Unless Mrs. Santos is skilled in mixed martial arts with a bodybuilder physique"—he smirked at that last expression— "not everyone who was in the apartment tonight was a perp." His gaze shifted from the ceiling to the floor.

The detective shrugged his shoulders. "Whatever you say, Sherlock."

Ortega smiled and brushed aside the smart-aleck remark. "Where's the body that landed outside?"

"It was gone," said Detective Dexter irritatedly. "Someone must have dragged it out before we got here. The only body found was the unconscious old lady. She was transported to Mount Salvation Hospital shortly after the nine-one-one call."

"No blood trails led away from the site of impact. I only saw the splotch of blood outside, but I saw no evidence that a body was moved," the agent remarked rhetorically.

Anderson stepped forward and looked at the Detective, "Were there any eyewitnesses?"

Dexter shook his head and blurted, "No."

"How's it possible that no one saw or heard anything?" she asked incredulously.

Ortega turned to his partner. "You have never lived in the projects, have you?" He snickered. "I'd be surprised if folks could hear their own thoughts, much less what happened in someone else's apartment. The present silence is due to the police presence."

He turned his attention to Dexter again. "Any word on the victim's granddaughter?"

The detective raised an eyebrow inquisitively at their knowledge of the girl. "No, not a word. Neighbors said she moved out a few months ago."

"Did they call nine-one-one?" the agent asked as he walked to the kitchen.

The detective frowned as realization dawned and replied, "No. At this time, we don't know who made the call."

Ortega walked around the upended table, approached the refrigerator, and glanced at a note with the Spanish words *Mi Angel* and a ten-digit number below them. He took his smartphone from his pocket and dialed it. A musical ringtone issued from under the sofa. "I like that song.'"

He retraced his steps to the living room, took a sealed pair of latex gloves from his blazer, squatted, and opened the pack to use one glove to drag the smartphone into view.

"The granddaughter has become a person of interest." He looked at the cracked screen, then at Dexter. "You may want to bring her in for questioning," he advised as he clicked the end button on his phone. "I think she was here when the intrusion occurred."

Officer Samuel walked closer, took the cell phone with extreme care, and placed it in a clear plastic bag. He nodded at the agent and said, "I'll get this to TARU immediately."

Dexter looked at Samuel in annoyance, not pleased by the deference given to Ortega.

"One last question—has the blood been sent for DNA identification?" asked the agent.

The detective cleared his throat and nodded before he answered. "It should be a few days before we get those results."

"You mind if we get a copy of that report?" Ortega asked with a smile.

"Well, you need to go through the proper protocols," snapped Dexter.

"I will. Thanks, Detective."

Agents Ortega and Anderson sipped their coffee in their parked SUV. He was pensive. As usual, she studied her partner of three years who was engrossed in his thoughts while he connected the details of the investigation.

"So, do you think this was a breaking and entering or is it similar to what we have been pursuing?" she asked.

Absentmindedly, almost as if stuck in a trance, he murmured tersely, "Similar."

She knew he would come out of his intense concentration shortly and pressed on with her line of questioning. "I'm curious how you knew about the granddaughter."

He pulled himself from his daze, turned to his partner, and responded, "First, the scattered photos of the old lady and the girl. I also saw the note on the refrigerator with a number and the expression 'my Angel' written in Spanish when we walked through the kitchen." He paused and lowered his voice while he stared out the front windshield. "But to be fair, Maria Santos and I go back about twenty-two years." Ortega's mind reeled in long-forgotten memories. "I don't remember all my cases but I will never forget hers."

"Do you mind elaborating?" Anderson prompted and twirled her hand in the air in a gesture for more information.

He sipped his coffee and sighed. "I was a young detective working for the Lancaster Police Department at that time. It was one of my first cases, to be exact. Maria Santos had recently lost her husband to cancer, and my partner and I were the lucky ones who had to break the news that her pregnant eighteen-year-old daughter had been killed."

"How terrible!" expressed Anderson. "How did she die?"

"She was poisoned although miraculously, the baby survived. That's how I knew about the granddaughter."

"What happened with the case?"

"It went cold with one suspect in the wind and no leads."

Anderson sipped her medium-hot latte and asked, "If the granddaughter was on the scene, what do you think happened to her?"

He shrugged. "My gut tells me she was there on the night of the attack and may have been the reason for it. The crime scene had similar patterns to the serial killings as of late—young, female, and signs of extreme violence. I suspect she was the target."

"Do you think she was the one who went out the window?"

"No," he replied crisply.

"Then what's your take on it?"

"Whatever plunged out that window must have had superpowers," he said drily.

Anderson chortled at his comment. "Making fun of those lab guys again, huh, Danny? You know they mean well." She sipped her coffee with a smirk on her face.

"I'm a pragmatic individual and believe everything has a rational explanation. Just because we've come across some unusual DNA doesn't mean we should follow Internet conspiracy theories. We don't need hypotheses that point to aliens or lizard people." He turned to her with a lopsided smirk. "I like to leave all the mysticism and superstition to my wife. She's the praying one. I'm the black sheep of the family."

"Okay, okay, calm down now," Anderson advised,

knowing very well how sensitive her partner was when it came to mystical and religious matters. "You're preaching to the choir here. Anyhow, what's your take on the fall?"

"I will admit it's one of the most baffling aspects of the case."

"Why is that?" She gave him a puzzled look.

"Think about it. Someone falls from a three-story apartment building, lands on the pavement, and leaves behind no evidence other than a bloodstain. Moreover, let's say that the person survived the fall and walked away, or someone picked the body up. There would've at least been a trail of blood. It seems the body hit the pavement and disappeared."

"So, the lizard people snatched the body?" she joked. He gave her an expressionless stare. "Anyway, back to my earlier question—where's the granddaughter? If she was present, maybe she can explain what happened."

Ortega cranked the engine and shifted the car into drive. He made a U-turn in the middle of the road and said, "I don't know where she is but hopefully, I can hit two birds with one stone. I have a feeling she'll most likely visit the hospital, so either she or Mrs. Santos can tell us what happened last night."

8

A GRACEFUL BREAKFAST

"Morning, sleeping beauty," May said as she entered Angelica's room.

"Ugh… What time is it?" the girl asked and covered her face with a pillow. She had never been a morning person.

The caregiver checked her watch. "It's ten forty am and I came to see how you were feeling this morning." She approached to sit on the edge of the bed and removed a penlight from her pocket.

Angelica pushed to a seated position, rubbed her eyes, and yawned loudly. "Excuse me! I'm feeling well-rested. It's very quiet here."

"We have an infirmary but currently have no empty beds. It's been a rough week for us. This side of the warehouse is where we house our guests and newcomers." She flashed the light into both her pupils to check them for dilation, which made her squint due to the brightness. "How are you feeling overall?"

"The headache and back pain seem to have completely disappeared. Those were great pills you gave me."

May smiled broadly and slid the flashlight into her pocket. "Well, that's good to hear." She pulled out a small vial containing a golden-yellow liquid. "When you get the chance, apply this to yourself, especially on your face and arms."

"What is it?" Angelica asked and her gaze danced from the woman to the vial.

"It's an ointment we've concocted, which we use for many purposes. We call it Kollourion."

A curious frown crept onto the girl's face as she studied the small vial and didn't even try to pronounce the name. "What's it for?"

"To avoid an overly complicated explanation, let's say it'll prevent you from getting any further pain." The woman winked at her.

Angelica opened the vial and caught a whiff of the ointment. "It smells great—sorta like cinnamon."

"We have a good supply of it so you can keep that one. Everyone here uses it. I recommend you apply it daily." May caught her wrist and looked at her watch. "Your pulse is good and your eyes weren't dilated, which is a good sign, but take it easy for the next few days. I suggest you continue to rest and don't perform any excessive activities unless necessary."

She stood and gestured to a small closet in the room. "Inside there, you'll find fresh clothes." She pointed at a nearby dresser. "And there you'll find underwear, socks, and fresh towels. If you need any footwear, let us know your size and we'll get them for you."

"Thank you," said Angelica.

"Hi!" a high-pitched voice said from the doorway.

May's and Angelica's heads turned to a slim, animated girl with arctic-blue eyes who waved a greeting. Her gilded blonde hair with highlights of purple was pulled up in a double knot bun with eye-grazing bangs. She wore her usual ripped jeans and Mello Kitty tee-shirt—her beloved cartoon Persian cat.

"Hello, Reina," responded May. "It's good to see your cute dimples around here."

"OMG, I'm gagging. You made my day!" she shrieked at the compliment.

"How are you this morning?" asked the caregiver.

"I'm gucci. Not doing much so I came by to see our newest friend." Reina smiled and stared at Angelica.

"Great. Then you can do me a favor by taking her to the kitchen so she can have something to eat. I heard her stomach growl while I examined her." She grinned at Angelica.

"You heard that? Sorry. I haven't eaten anything since yesterday afternoon," she said sheepishly.

"No worries. My stomach growls all the time," Reina said cheekily. "May, I'll take her posthaste."

"Thank you. You can bring her back here afterward." The woman waved goodbye and exited the room, leaving her to the chipper girl.

"Hello, my name is Reina. Well, you may know that already. We saw each other last night but...um, anyway, welcome." She sashayed into the room and brushed the wispy blonde bangs out of her eyes. Her smile never left her face.

A smile flickered on Angelica's lips at the girl's bouncy, dorky, and quirky personality. "Hi, I'm Angelica."

"Yeah, I know that," she remarked with a faint chuckle. "I'm sorry for what happened to you and your grandmother last night."

At the mention of her *Abuela*, her eyes welled with tears. "Thank you," she said and wiped the tears with her hand. "I know nothing about you all but you guys seem to know so much about me."

"I don't know much, but the others like Joan, Mist, Gypsy, Pretzel—they know more. Anyhow, let's get you something to eat. You'll like the food here."

"Sure," she responded and tried to make sense of her companion's amusing eccentricity. "Before I get something to eat, can you show me the way to the bathroom? I'd like to try this stuff that May gave me and freshen up."

"Kollourion! Definitely!" she said eagerly. "Just walk this way." She paused then clarified, "Not walk like me but, like, follow me."

Angelica smiled.

From a distance, she could smell the tantalizing aroma of fried chicken, buttermilk biscuits, and country-style cinnamon rolls, which made her stomach rumble with each step and her mouth water the closer they got to the kitchen. Still, the main attraction that tickled her nose was the wafting scent of freshly brewed coffee.

"The kitchen is right through there." Reina gestured with her hand. "We have a refectory—like a cafeteria," she clarified, "where we usually eat, but um…it's usually for our major meals—you know breakfast, lunch, and dinner. By now, Grace and her staff should be preparing lunch, but she usually saves a little breakfast for folks like us who oversleep." She giggled at the last statement.

She flung the kitchen door wide and no sooner had she stepped into the room than a jubilant voice called, "Well, I'll be—my queen!" The greeting came from a golden-brown-skinned, hefty woman whose eyes glinted with ecstasy and life. Her silver hair glistened as white as snow. "How good to see you, darlin'. It's been a while. You don't visit me anymore," she said in her noticeable Southern accent.

"Hi, Grace," Reina responded as she approached and embraced her tightly. She held onto her for some time. "I've been super busy. They have me scouting and doing all kinds of stuff. How are you doing?"

"I'm finer than frog hair split four ways," the woman replied with a chuckle. "Well, bless your heart, they've got you scouting. That's good, baby." She proceeded to pinch the girl's cheeks. Her mannerisms made Angelica think of her grandmother and she wished more than ever to be in her grandma's kitchen, even if only to be lectured and questioned.

Reina turned and gestured with her hand. "This is Angelica, our newbie. She came to us last night."

"Hi." Angelica extended her hand to shake Grace's.

"No shaking hands with me, darlin'. I do hugs." With a genial smile on her face, the woman walked toward her and wrapped her arms around her. Although she wasn't the touchy-feely type, especially with strangers, the embrace felt like ice-cold water to her weary, thirsty soul. Grace's presence exuded warmth and a soothing peace that suffused her entire being. It made her gasp quietly.

"So, what can I do for y'all?" A gentle smile tugged at the corners of the woman's mouth.

"Angelica hasn't eaten anything and I was hoping you still had some breakfast left from this morning."

"You know I always do." She beckoned with her hand. "Sit—sit, both of you." The girls sat across from each other at a long wooden table positioned in the middle of the kitchen. Grace turned her head toward one of the girls working with her. "Melody, can you bring me what we have left from breakfast this mornin'?"

"Will do," responded Melody from the other side of the spacious kitchen.

"Thank you, my love." She turned to the girls at the table. "Would y'all like anything to drink—coffee, tea…juice?"

"Coffee!" Reina responded eagerly. Angelica nodded, wide-eyed.

"I reckoned y'all would. I'll fetch that for you right away. I made a fresh pot a few minutes ago."

Soon after the coffees were placed on the table, her food came. She ate ravenously and relished every bite. Within minutes, her plate was empty.

Reina and Grace simply sat and chatted.

Thoroughly satisfied, she burped. "Oh, my! Excuse me. That was so good!" Her face reddened and she covered her lips with her fingers.

"That's what good Southern food does to ya," said Grace with a chuckle. "Would you like some more, darlin'? You can't leave this kitchen unless you're as full as a tick."

Angelica shook her head while her right hand patted her stomach. "I wish but can't fit another bite."

"Grace is the best chef ever. She has been doing this for many years—right, Grace?" Reina slurped her coffee.

Grace, seated next to the girl with her cup of coffee, said, "It's not the number of years you've been doing it but loving what you do. If you have passion, it's bound to be good." She held her index finger up. "That's my secret ingredient to any meal."

The three women sat for a while conversing, laughing, and enjoying each other's company. Angelica had never felt such a strong connection with people she had just met. It surprised her since she had not bonded this way with her peers, coworkers, or college classmates except for Jasmine. For the first time, she was relatable.

Reina turned to her. "How old do you think she is?"

A little uncomfortable, she said, "Um, yeah, I've learned never to guess a woman's age. When I was younger, I did that to my grandmother and was sent to my room."

"Just guess. I'm sure you won't offend her."

"Okay. Uh...fifty-five or maybe sixty?" Angelica ventured timidly as she drank her coffee.

"She's ninety-seven." The girl giggled.

She almost spat her coffee out. "You're kidding, right?" Grace smiled and shook her head. "Dang, girl! What kind of lotion are you using? L'Eau de Supernatural?" she teased. "What's your secret?"

"I guess it's in my genes, my dear," responded the woman with a chuckle.

Suddenly, the entrance to the kitchen door opened and Pretzel walked in and propped the door open with her foot. Her vantage point only gave her sight of Reina and Angelica. "Hello, ladies. May said I'd find you here. I need you both to come with me. Joan wants to speak to us."

Both girls rose from their seats and left their empty coffee cups on the table.

"Hey, missy," Grace said to Pretzel. "You're not leaving this kitchen without giving me a hug, right?" She moved her head slightly past the edge of the opened door.

The girl beamed when she saw her. "Oh, my God. I'm sorry, Grace. I didn't see you there." She walked forward swiftly and engulfed her affectionately in a tight bear hug. "It's always good to see you, Grace." Exactly as Reina had done, she held her for an extended time.

"My apologies—I can't stay long and chat," she said and held the woman at arm's length. "Maybe I can stop by later tonight and have one of our chats again. It's been a while."

"Sounds good, darlin'. I'm always here for ya."

All three ladies left Grace and hurried to Joan's office.

9

GETTING TO THE BOTTOM OF IT

The ladies stopped in the doorway of a small office, which was bare save for a gunmetal-gray desk, a matching filing cabinet, and a couple of metal chairs in front of the desk. On the wall behind the desk hung a poster that read *The Five Pillars of the Daughters of the Watchers: Emissary, Seers, Scouts, Guardians, and Influencers.*

Joan was seated behind the desk on the opposite side of the entrance in conversation with two other individuals who stood near her.

"Come on in." She beckoned with her hand when she noticed their arrival. "Take a seat."

"Mist and Gypsy, this is Angelica—the girl from the Bronx I spoke to you about. Angelica, these are Mist and Gypsy, two of my high-ranking officers. Mist is the team's second in command for this location, and Gypsy is one of the finest warriors we have onboard. She's our training coordinator."

Both ladies nodded, while Angelica sat and looked

perplexed since she had no idea what type of group this was.

High-ranking officers, second in command, warrior...who the hell are these people?

Mist gazed at her like a deer caught in headlights, her eyes wide as if she stared at a ghost. Angelica winced involuntarily at the prolonged gaze and frowned in discomfort. The woman turned her face away from the others and wiped tears from her eyes.

Joan folded her hands on the desk. "I wanted us to meet and discuss last night's events. Pretzel, Reina, I know we spoke briefly last night, but I've gathered Mist and Gypsy to assess the situation thoroughly. If it is who you said it was"—Joan turned her gaze toward Pretzel—"we need to understand why. I'm hoping with Angelica here, we can gather as much detail as possible."

"The entry we have in the archives matches the entity Reina and I saw last night without a doubt. The Nephilim fits the description of Pharmakeia son of Persia, better known as Witchcraft," said Pretzel without missing a beat. "I believe he suspected Angelica was at the apartment and when he couldn't find her, he attacked the grandmother."

Mist, who seemed to be the same age as Joan, remarked, "Interesting! They sent one of the Warlockites for a hunting expedition. It's very unusual for one of his caliber."

Angelica pursed her lips at hearing the term "Warlockites."

"That's my point exactly," asserted Joan and fixed her gaze on her second. "Very unusual."

Pretzel added, "His features, height, and build match what we have in the library but most importantly, he had telekinesis. That's how I got this bruise." She showed them her left forearm. "He threw an entire table at me."

"How did he manage to get away?" asked their leader.

"I wounded him with a blade but was unable to kill him. He fell through the apartment window but escaped after the fall. We suspect he wasn't there alone. Someone was there to assist him with a portal."

"A Daimon must have been present," commented Mist.

What the fudge nuggets! How did he survive a three-story fall? Angelica's mind ran wild. Her expression shifted between amused and petrified. *And what the hell is a portal and a Daimon?*

Joan turned her gaze to her and asked, "Can you recollect anyone else on the scene or remember seeing anything else?"

"I'm sorry...I don't know if it's the concussion or the conversation or both, but this is all going too fast for me." The confused emotions were visible on her face. She wondered for a moment if this was all a practical joke or a hidden-camera show.

"I gave you my word that I'd explain everything in due time but for now, I need you to recall what you can about last night. We need as much detail as you can remember—anything can be useful no matter how minuscule."

The tension in the room testified to their seriousness. Feeling both compelled and intimated by all the unsmiling faces in the room, she responded, "Well, I left work around seven thirty pm and felt strange throughout the entire commute. I had a weird sensation as if I was being followed."

"Sorry, my bad! That was me," interrupted Reina.

"What?" she asked with both surprise and curiosity.

"Reina, I need her to concentrate on every detail. Please, no interruptions," stated Joan. "You may continue," she said and looked firmly at Angelica.

"Sorry," the other girl mouthed.

She turned her gaze toward Joan again and continued. "Yeah, so I...um, reached my grandmother's building a little after eight pm. From the moment I arrived, I felt a strong sense of danger and now that I think about it, the danger came from my grandmother's apartment. The only thing that seemed abnormal, though, was that her window was open 'cause she usually keeps it closed at that time of day.

"When I entered through the building's front door, I heard my grandmother scream. I ran up the stairs and into the apartment and this tall person, glowing but in black, held her by the neck with his hand. I grabbed the first thing in sight—a broomstick she keeps next to the door—and tried to stop him. This person or thing simply waved his hand and threw me into the wall. Shortly after, Pretzel and Reina appeared."

Gypsy stood next to Mist and wore very short denim shorts and a chiffon crop top that revealed her pierced navel. She pressed her fingers to her lips and said, "We know he wouldn't attack the grandmother without reason so he must have been looking for information—most likely for Angelica's whereabouts." She stared directly at her and asked, "Are you usually at your grandmother's around that time?"

To Angelica, she seemed more ready for a party than for a fight but her familiarity piqued her interest. She felt as if she had seen her before. "No. I was only there dropping my grandmother's medication off. I moved out of the apartment a few months back."

Gypsy continued, "If we know anything about the Nephilim, it's that they're thorough before an attack and very punctual in executing their orders. He must have arrived around eight pm—"

The timeframe brought Angelica's mind to the correspondence she had collected from her grandmother's apartment. "The postcard!" she interjected.

"What was that?" asked Gypsy.

"Yesterday morning, I received a postcard or invitation —I'm not sure which. It was a blackish color, handwritten in red ink, and sent to my grandmother's address with yesterday's date and a time of eight pm. It had an unusual sender's name...uh, Zoi with a middle initial of I? And a last name that started with T. I can't remember the actual name."

"Zoi I Thanatos," Mist told her. "It's not an actual name. It's Greek for live or die." She turned and locked her gaze on Joan. "That's strange. They sent her a Sigil of Apollyon instead of a Sigil of Artemis? Anyway, it must have been how the Nephilim knew the location, date, and time for the visitation."

"What's a sigil and what does live or die mean?" asked Angelica.

"A sigil is a typically hunting point but in your case, it was a call to join their cause or die," remarked Mist. "Sigils are one of the forms Nephilim use to target their victims— indicating the target's name, location, time, and date—but the scent the sigils contain is more pertinent. While almost imperceptible to humans, the scent can linger in a location for days and a Nephilim can pick up from miles away." She pursed her lips in thought. "Where's the sigil now?"

"It's in my apartment."

"I suggest you don't return there anytime soon. There's now a high probability that they'll search for you there."

"'ño!" exclaimed Angelica. "Sorry for the language."

"So I assume you had not updated your address and thus the sigil and Warlockite were sent to your grandmother's address," said Mist. "Our next question is how they obtained that?"

Suddenly, her face paled and her breath caught as she recollected and correlated in her mind how she'd neglected to change the postal address with the break-in of the diner. Sorrow closed her throat as she uttered softly, "It was my fault." She paused in despair while all the women stared curiously at her. "I should have changed that address long ago. It's my fault she's in the hospital." She sobbed silently and buried her face in her hands.

Reina placed her hand on her back for comfort. Pretzel knelt next to her and said, "This isn't your fault. We have seen this happen so many times in the past. You shouldn't take unnecessary guilt on. Neither you nor your grandmother asked for this, and you had no idea this would happen."

"I know this is very difficult for you but is there any reason you can think of why that specific time would be chosen?" asked Joan.

She cleared her throat before she responded. "I don't know. Everything was so strange yesterday. My boss called me into work unexpectedly, I picked up my grandmother's medication…" She paused and her expression slid into thoughtfulness as the memory of the diner's break-in floated to the surface. "They knew I'd be home," she muttered.

"What was that?" asked Joan.

"I work at a diner and my boss mentioned a break-in sometime in the early morning hours. He thought it was weird how they broke through the door. It seemed someone punched it with their fist and destroyed it. What was strange about the whole thing was that nothing was stolen. He found the employees' files open on his desk, along with the weekly schedule." She drew a deep breath and continued. "But there was a slight change of schedule yesterday. I went to the diner for a few hours to cover for one of the other waitresses."

Mist spoke. "So having your employee's record with your grandmother's home address and the weekly schedule, they had the place and time for the attack."

Her neck muscles tensed. "Do you mean to tell me these things were stalking me?" She grasped the sides of her chair in a state of panic.

"They would go to any lengths to accomplish their grand plan," responded Joan. "Is there anything else you felt, heard, or saw? Anything unusual or out of the ordinary you can recall at your grandma's or at the diner?"

Angelica shook her head. "No, that's all I can think of."

The woman inched forward in her seat, her expression stern, and asked, "How were you addressed in the sigil?"

"Oh yeah, I almost forgot. It was addressed to me using my father's last name, which is weird 'cause I've never gone by that."

"What name did they use?" The room fell more silent than heaven after the opening of the seventh seal.

"Archie."

The other five ladies in the room exchanged horrified stares as if frightened by a ghost.

Obliviously, she continued. "But I never go by that and don't even know him, so I don't know what difference that makes."

After a moment of hesitation, Joan said, "Angelica, I think it's time for you and me to have that talk. Can you wait for me outside? I'll be there in a moment. Reina, can you take her to the large conference room? I need to have a quick chat to Gypsy, Mist, and Pretzel."

The two girls nodded and left the office.

When the door closed, Mist drew a sharp breath and blurted, "That's Eva Santos' daughter. I thought the baby died with the mother." She slapped a hand over her mouth.

"That's what I wanted to confirm. If Angelica is the daughter of Eva Santos, is she the one foretold to be the Daimon Killer?" Joan asked her.

Her second stared rudely at her. "Joan, you know I never believed that traitor's prediction." She looked aside as if replaying the memory in her mind. "She looks exactly like her mother. When she first walked into the office, I thought it was Eva," she muttered.

"Wait—what do you mean by Daimon Killer?" Pretzel asked with wide eyes. "Daimons are spirits. They can't be killed."

"Thousands of years ago, a prophecy was given that one would arise among the Daughters with the power to slay Watchers and Fallen," Joan explained. "To make a long story short, one of our Daughters predicted—"

"A betrayer, you mean," interjected Mist.

"One of the Daughters who defected the group predicted that Eva Santos' child was that Daimon Killer."

"Nice," Gypsy added with a smirk on her face. "Finally, we have a way to kill those jackasses."

"Don't get your hopes up," Mist warned. "First, we don't know exactly what this Daimon Killer prophecy means and second, the person who predicted this prophecy was a deserter and traitor." Her nostrils flared. "It'd be a disgrace to heed any prophecy from such a person." She turned her gaze to Joan. "I need to talk to her and tell her everything about her mother. Her days at the Lancaster compound—"

Joan interrupted her brusquely. "Mist, this girl went through a traumatic experience and has her grandmother in the hospital in a critical condition. I don't think this kind of information will help her now. We need to follow protocol. She first needs to be told who she is."

Her second sighed heavily and nodded.

"And ladies, let's keep this whole Daimon Killer prophecy under wraps. I agree with Mist. We don't know what to make of this prophecy and if it even pertains to Angelica. So until it's been discussed with the senior council, please make no mention of it."

All the women nodded in agreement.

Their leader stood from her chair. "Thank you. Now let me have that chat with Angelica."

NERIUM OLEANDER

Joan left the office and headed to the conference room a few feet away. She gestured to Angelica with her hand. "Let's take a walk."

Moments later, they strode up a set of staircases that led to a terrace. The area had the appearance of a garden full of roses, perennials, bulbs, tulips, various shrubs, and vines. A white gazebo was decorated with flowing translucent curtains and enclosed by raised garden beds teemed with various plants, and a bench stood at its center. The wooden seat offered a view of the city's skyscrapers, with the Liberty Tower rising above all the others. As she walked toward the gazebo, Joan retrieved a handheld can and commenced watering the plants around it.

"Take a seat," she said to Angelica. "This is one of my favorite places to be. I enjoy coming up here, especially for times of solitude and relaxation." The plants she was attending to looked well-kept and by her tender care and the expression on her face, she seemed to be the keeper.

She talked while she watered her plants. "Eons ago,

one-third of the celestial Angels committed treason against the Sovereign One and were cast out of the heavenly realms to the earthly dimension. These angelic beings came to be known as demons, fallen angels, or spirits of the underworld. The Fallen despised the Sovereign One and all his works, which included humanity."

"Are you speaking of the Sunday School story about the Devil being an Angel of Light?" asked Angelica.

"That's only part of the story," the woman responded. "What you may not have heard from your Sunday School teacher is the story of a second fall."

She raised her eyebrow inquisitively.

Joan continued. "You may have heard how the Fallen deceived mankind, but their deceptive schemes stretched even into the heavens. The Sovereign One had tasked some of his celestial Angels to be watchers and protectors of mankind and the earth. As humanity's evil, violence, and destruction increased upon the world, these Angels began to despair at their apparent failure, and the Fallen preyed on this weakness. They convinced them that they could do better than the Sovereign One if they made their own world, their creation, and rid the earth of mankind's flaws." She exchanged the watering can for a pair of small clippers on the edge of the gazebo and started to clip dry old leaves from the plants.

"These Angels cohabitated with the women of the earth and produced a new species called the Nephilim—angel-human hybrids. The sons of these Angels inherited super-natural abilities like enhanced strength and speed, tele-kinetic abilities, and other forms of power. Additionally, flesh as strong as steel has made them impervious to human weapons. Seduced by their fathers, these Nephilim were wholly wicked—proud, merciless, harsh, and a plague upon the rest of humanity."

As the woman progressed through the narrative, Angelica noticed how the clipping became more aggressive and louder and the expression of the storyteller became visibly agitated.

Joan stopped momentarily and collected herself. She sighed and continued to remove old leaves and relate the story. "Through their offspring, the Angels began to change the natural order of the world. They almost succeeded in subverting the Sovereign One's design."

"What stopped them?" the girl asked, full of curiosity.

"There was a righteous man, a prophet named Enoch, who lived during the early days of civilization. He was given a revelation—a way to stop the conquest of the Angels and their offspring." She placed the clippers in her pocket, slid a pair of gloves on, and took hold of one of the plants on the ground. Very gently, she pulled it toward where Angelica was seated. She sat next to her and slid the plant between her legs, extremely careful that it didn't touch her.

"Nerium Oleander—or Nerium, as it is commonly known." She stared at the plant as if enchanted. "Isn't it a beauty?" Joan asked rhetorically. "I love the way it smells." She pulled the clippers from her pocket and began to prune the plant carefully. "The prophet was informed that their downfall would come from their own kind."

"Their daughters!" the girl interjected.

The woman turned to her with a slight smile. "You catch on quickly. But unlike their male siblings, the female offspring did not exhibit spectacular supernatural traits. Disillusioned at their lack of power, the Daimons—"

"I'm sorry to interrupt, but what are daimons?"

"Daimons is the name we use for Fallen and Watchers collectively." She stared aimlessly at the sky. "Where was I...oh, yes. The Daimons despised, abandoned, and deserted their daughters, but like the stone the builders rejected, these women would display the true essence of power." A smirk appeared on her face as she uttered that expression.

"Why not only have sons?"

"These Angels may be mighty indeed but much like humans, willing the gender of their offspring isn't something they can do." She stood slowly and pushed the plant gently to its original location. "It has such elegance and beauty, but it's a very toxic and poisonous plant. To the naked eye, it is one you can easily grab and crush under your feet, but the sap alone can cause skin irritation and much worse, and it can be fatal if ingested." She returned and sat next to Angelica.

"Sovereignty, as it may seem, isn't without irony for it was revealed to the prophet that these same daughters would become the opposing factor to these Angels' agenda. Similarly, like the Nerium Oleander, which seems fragile and vulnerable but in nature is poisonous, the daughters of these traitors became the unforeseen venom to their diabolic plan." She removed the gloves from her hands and placed the clippers and gloves on the paving next to her.

"When the Daimons became aware of this, they began to seek, hunt, and kill these daughters, using their male offspring to do their dirty work. Enoch the prophet was instructed to seek out and protect them, to teach them how to fight, train them in the arts of combat and survival, and most importantly, instruct them to find other daughters to help and protect them."

Joan closed her eyes and enjoyed the sun-drenched sky and the crisp breeze that flowed through the gazebo. The gentle wind billowed the curtains and her dirty-blonde hair. "These female offspring became known as the Daughters of the Watchers."

"Why not Daughters of the Daimons?"

"It would take much longer to get into the full history, but Fallen did not traditionally create offspring, only Watchers did, so the name stuck."

Angelica tipped her head toward the woman with a bemused expression. "Well, it sounds like a fascinating story but what does that have to do with me?"

"Eons have passed, but these Daimons continue to pursue their New World Order scheme and still produce Nephilim and, much to their chagrin, female offspring. But like them, we Daughters of the Watchers continue with our agenda."

"What are you saying, Joan?" An expression of apprehension crossed her face when she said those words.

"There are countless Daimons in the underground world, all ruled by Diablos—the King of the Abyss. He was judged, sentenced, and locked away in the bottomless pit of Tartarus for two thousand years, although it was foretold that his release is imminent. During his imprisonment, his three regent lords have ruled the Daimons. These three lords also oversee and are designated to specific regions or continents of the world. Legion is in Europe and Africa.

Hades has Asia, Australia, and Antarctica. Last but not least is Apollyon, Lord of North and South America." Joan drew a deep, sharp breath.

"It is very seldom that the three dark Lords reproduce but when they do, their Nephilim offspring are the most dangerous and powerful creatures in the world. Even for The Daughters of the Watchers, these Nephilim are the most difficult to kill." The woman looked unflinchingly at the city skyscrapers.

Angelica gazed intently at her and attempted to assimilate every word she uttered. She shifted uneasily on the bench. "Joan, I'm a little lost here. How is any of this relevant to my situation?" Her voice now sounded aggravated.

The woman turned her head and looked long and hard directly into her eyes. "Because, Angelica, Apollyon, the Dark Lord of North and South America, is known in the human world…" She paused to take a deep breath before she continued. "As Leonard Archie."

PART II

NOT JUST AN ORDINARY GIRL

JUST LIKE YOU

"Apollyon is my father?" asked Angelica in disbelief.

Initially, she sat motionless, although her heart galloped beneath her ribcage like dozens of horses bursting out of a starting gate. It fought for space in her chest with the air frozen in her lungs to the point where it hurt to breathe. Her face had become as white as snow. Finally, anger erupted like the springs of the great deep and burned her cheeks to a crisp crimson.

"No, no, no... *Mierda!* That's bullcrap!" she rasped and shook her head in disbelief. Her lower lip quivered with resentment. She felt ill to the very pit of her stomach. "I refuse to believe this. Basically, I'm a bastard demon girl from Hell. Is that what you're telling me? Some worthless Bronx girl who deserves to have the Devil as her father?"

Her chest rose and fell with rapid breaths as she attempted to grasp Joan's unappealing news. She shook her head abruptly and rose angrily from the bench. "I have to get out of this place." She shifted her head from left and right while her stormy, reddened eyes looked for an exit.

When she located the door, she retraced her steps and stumbled as fast as she could from the terrace to the staircase they had come through.

"Angelica!" Joan cried behind her. "Wait!"

Upset and confused by the grim news, she bounded down several staircases and a few corridors and somehow managed to find the exit of the building. She stormed out of the warehouse at full tilt, weeping as she sprinted through the narrow street hemmed in by adjacent buildings. Her troubled mind also raced, shrouded in confusion and still traumatized by the previous evening's events and her grandmother's condition. This news was too much—she was a demon child.

Her routine, normal life had come to an end. The entire life she knew was now on shifting sand. She had always felt different but now, she felt like an extraterrestrial. *Why not one more freaking thing to be self-conscious about?*

"Angelica, wait!" a different, younger voice called behind her. "Hold up!"

No longer able to keep running, Angelica slowed to a jog and took long strides. The young woman caught up to her.

"Damn, you can run!" Pretzel breathed heavily with her hand over her chest.

"Leave me the hell alone!" she exclaimed without looking at her and struggled to keep her voice steady.

"Hey, I only want to talk," the girl said and fell into pace with her.

"Well, I don't want to talk and I'm tired of listening!" she snapped. She stared directly ahead and resisted the urge to look at her companion from the corner of her eye.

"Angelica, before you wander off, know that your life is in danger. Those monsters are still after you. You need our help."

"I'll deal with it the way I've always dealt with every-thing else—by myself!" she responded bitterly.

"Huh, okay. What's your plan now?" Pretzel asked and studied her closely.

"I'll get as far from here as possible and if any of you or those Nephil-a...whatever approach me, I'll call the cops."

"The creatures that are after you are powerful and dangerous and don't give a damn who you call. You saw with your own eyes what they can do. People have emptied entire gun magazines and not even scratched them. You need to think things through before you run off."

Angelica shook her head in frustration and pain but mostly in confusion. "I can't take this anymore. My grand-mother, my only family, is hospitalized, I never met my mother, and now I've been insulted with the news that my father is some...some...freaking demon!" Her voice was laced with pain as tears coursed down her face. With the back of her hand, she wiped away the tears that streamed down her cheeks. "I didn't ask for any of this. I want things to be the way they were!"

Suddenly, she stopped walking, her throat tight. Feeling dizzy and nauseous, she dropped to her knees with a hand over her chest. She began to pant and her heart raced. Her breathing became shallow as the air around her seemed to thin, while at the same time, her mind still reeled at all the chaotic experiences of the last twenty-four hours. Like the walls of Jericho tumbling, her entire surroundings appeared to cave in.

With eyes full of despair, she looked at Pretzel and asked, "What's happening to me? I can't breathe."

"I think you're having a panic attack," the girl told her. She lowered herself quickly and took one of her hands. "You need to keep calm and take deep breaths. Put your head between your knees as best as you can."

Angelica swallowed hard and attempted to follow the instructions but to no avail. She murmured, "Oh, my God…I can't… I feel like I'm gonna die!"

"You're fine." Pretzel spoke compassionately. "You won't die but I need you to breathe." She stood at her side and held her hand firmly.

A wide-eyed, pale Angelica responded with a nod and began to inhale and exhale as best she could. At first, it was all rasped and gasped breaths but after a minute, her breathing normalized and she sighed quietly.

When she saw that her color had returned, Pretzel asked, "Can you stand?"

She nodded gently.

"Let's get you off those knees and take a seat near that building." The girl helped her to her feet and moved to a nearby brick building, where they sat quietly on the pavement for some time.

When she could finally speak, Angelica asked in a low, soft voice, "How did you know it was a panic attack?"

"I used to get them, especially after my mother died."

"It's the first time I ever experienced that. It felt like the end of the world."

Pretzel turned her head toward her. "I know the feeling of having your life turned upside down, of waking up one morning as an ordinary girl and ending the day knowing you're something else."

"I don't know how much more of this I can take."

"I understand you completely but know this about us—Daughters of the Watchers isn't a fan club name. We are Daughters not simply because of our 'demon fathers,'" she said, made air quotes with her fingers, and gestured to the warehouse. "Every single girl in that building has been chased, abused, hurt, hunted, or has lost someone close along the way. We all share your sentiment of wanting things to be the way they were, but we can't change the fact of what's happened and who we truly are. As much as we'd like to, we can't turn the clock back but we have learned to be more than victims and not only survivors. We are conquerors."

"But is it all true?" Angelica demanded in a strained tone. "I consider myself an atheist and now, I'm a daughter of a demon. This doesn't make any sense to me."

Pretzel looked at her and responded, "You don't have to take our word at face value but know that you don't have to deal with this by yourself. We do know what it feels like to have your whole world taken away and changed in an instant, but that doesn't mean it's the end. There are others like you who know how you're feeling and are willing to help you through this. You're not alone and you don't have to face this on your own."

All her life Angelica had felt she was a loner—the only daughter, the only granddaughter, the only kid in school raised by only her grandmother. *I'm different than everyone else,* she had accepted so many times. She had never been able to relate to or connect with others and now, for the first time in her life, someone told her, "You're not alone." Pretzel's words began to resonate within her. She began to wonder if loneliness had been her misguided comfort zone and if she had known no other way to deal with the challenges of life except to be alone. Solidarity was a foreign and even intrusive concept to her.

A somber silence hung heavily over them. Her expression changed from despondency to contemplation as her mind reeled with the thought that maybe, just maybe, Pretzel was right. She didn't have to face this alone. Perhaps it was time for isolation to bite the dust.

Her companion interrupted the silence. "It's a hard pill to swallow. It's difficult hearing that your father is an anal cavity from Hell—"

"A...what?" Angelica interjected.

"An anal cavity. I'd have said an a-s-s-h-o-l-e but...um, I'm not the vulgar type."

She smirked at the other girl's remark.

"So, I assume you have an anal cavity of a 'father' as well?" This time, she made the air quotes with her fingers.

"There you go! It sounded better when you said it," Pretzel said in amusement. "Yes, we all do and it's one of the reasons we all stick together. I admit it isn't the easiest or most believable news to receive. At least you're managing better than I did."

"How's that?" she inquired.

"I remember vomiting for days, followed by a case of the runs for a week if you know what I mean. I thought I would be named Runs after a while. It's the reason I've taken a more laid-back approach to all this. I imagine going to school on career day and being asked the question, *'What does your father do?'* and me responding, 'He's a demonic spirit who wants to take over the world. Oh, and he tries to kill me on Tuesdays.'"

"Funny." Angelica chuckled.

Knowing that a change of pace could be useful, Pretzel asked, "Hey...um, I assume the warehouse is the last place you want to be right now, but do you like boat rides?"

"Yeah," she said curiously.

"Wanna get out of here and go for one?"

"I guess." She shrugged. "Anyway, I don't know where I am or where I was going."

"All right then. Let's go!" The girl beamed.

⸻

They sat side-by-side on the upper deck of the NY Riverway Ferry and each enjoyed a front-row view of the Statue of Liberty with popcorn in hand. For an extended period, neither said a word and simply stared at the spectacular copper structure as the ferry circled Liberty Island. The bright blue skies hosted a soft, glistening sun that made the Hudson River glimmer, and a clear view of squawking flying seagulls swooped around the boat. It was the perfect weather to thoroughly appreciate such a scenic view.

"So Pretzel, huh? That's not a common name," Angelica said, her gaze fixed on the statue as she enjoyed her popcorn.

Her companion grinned. "It's my *Memento Vivere.*"

"Memento Viv...what?" Angelica frowned.

"*Memento Vivere*—it's Latin for remember you must live.

All Daughters choose their own." Seeing her puzzled look, she clarified, "Like a nickname or an alias. It's a name that has a special connection to our past that helps us cope with our present and future. The MV, for short, is only used among Daughters. The name is a special way to connect us with who we are and to one another."

Pretzel dug in the small brown bag and popped a kernel of popcorn in her mouth. "The Nephilim use these dark and deplorable names to identify themselves—I guess to make themselves feel more connected with the darkness and hatred of the underworld. I think it's to boost their egos. Their names are a little cliché for my taste." She rolled her eyes. "On the contrary, our MVs bind us to our unique, given identity. It's a way to remind us that we were meant for good and not evil." She paused to swallow. "My actual name is Latisha Brown."

Angelica pursed her lips and nodded slightly. "Ooh, Latisha Brown…now that's a street name," she said with a chuckle. "That's the kind of name I'd use to go into a fight. Say it again!"

"Shut up!" Pretzel said with a grin and nudged her softly with her elbow.

Angelica glanced curiously at her. "So why Pretzel?"

"My mom and I would make this trip often. We'd get on the ferry, stop at Ellis Island, and as we approached Liberty Island, she'd talk about the history and symbolism of the Statue of Liberty—the broken shackles at the feet, the seven rays on the crown with its twenty-five windows, the torch…" She sighed and attempted to hold her tears back. Her emerald-green eyes glistened. "Ahem! Then afterward, we'd buy pretzels at one of those street carts and sit at

Battery Park enjoying every last crumb until twilight." She paused for a moment and murmured under her breath, "God, how I miss her."

"What happened to her if you don't mind me asking?"

"My story isn't too different than yours. I returned from school and saw my mother on the living room floor in a pool of blood, while that monster stood over her. With her eyes narrowed on me, she screamed, 'Run.' Shocked and confused, I raced out of the apartment in no particular direction. I was so scared I didn't realize I was being chased. The creature almost got me, but Joan and Mist appeared and engaged him. Afraid and not knowing what else to do, I ran to the apartment but he somehow disengaged from the women and came after me. He caught up to me in the apartment, pulled a blade out, and hurled it at me, but Mom..." She exhaled with a shudder. "My mom... she...um, pushed me out of the way and was struck. Joan and Mist arrived moments later and killed him."

"I'm so sorry to hear that," Angelica said in a compassionate tone.

Pretzel stared at the horizon as the ferry commenced the return to the mainland. As she gazed thoughtfully at nothing, a single unheeded tear streaked down her cheek.

"You know...it's easy to let hate and revenge consume you, so we name ourselves with a *Memento Vivere* that connects us to the virtuous aspect of our humanity and not its vice. It's not an attempt to ignore the reality of our losses or pain but it helps us to hold onto the perspective that no matter how dark it gets, goodness is also present. My love memorial, as I like to call it, was those pretzel days with my mother."

"Wow!" she remarked with watery eyes. "I guess we all have a heartfelt story to tell." She turned to the girl with a smirk on her face. "You win. Yours is more depressing than mine."

"Stop!" Pretzel responded by throwing a popcorn kernel at her. "Hey, I'm not saying things will be the same or easy, but you're gonna be all right, Angelica."

"Thanks."

"And when you're not, know that you have a friend to count on."

Friend. The sound of the word felt like opening presents on Christmas morning.

With bright eyes, she gave her a tender smile.

THE GATHERING

Angelica and Pretzel walked into a crowded hall of the warehouse. The lofty room could easily fit five hundred individuals on split-level stadium seating. A central carpeted aisle that connected perpendicularly to the back and front aisles separated the right and left halves. The sightline seats offered a view of a large platform with a retractable podium in the middle. It reminded Angelica of her high school auditorium, but bigger and cleaner.

The Daughters listened attentively to Joan's oration as she spoke loudly from behind the podium. The girl surveyed the hall and noticed women in all phases of life, including many of her age group. In the back of the room, several Daughters stood while they held infants in their arms. The back seats were occupied by girls ranging from toddlers to middle school age. A heavyset lady with a very gentle and welcoming expression supervised the children.

Pretzel followed her gaze and commented, "That's Mrs. Poppins. She oversees our younglings. She's a beautiful person." Angelica chuckled at the *Memento Vivere*.

As she continued to study the room, her gaze paused on a petite, golden-haired girl of seven or eight with the facial expression of someone on the verge of tears. That mysterious feeling of déjà vu she had experienced several times in the past resurfaced. Joan's voice muffled, the audience's indistinctive chatter faded, and the little girl's almost imperceptible silent sob became as blaring as the call of the Archangel. Overwhelmed by the wave of empathic emotion, a solitary tear streamed down her face and she wiped it away subtly. As if alerted to her attentive gaze, the girl glanced up and their eyes met, which startled Angelica and she turned quickly away.

She faced Pretzel again and inquired, "Where are we and what's this meeting about?"

"The place and meeting are one and the same. We call it the Gathering. This is one of our weekly assemblies in which we discuss various topics from new DW initiatives to current events. Joan is speaking, which means it's almost over. She usually concludes by updating the team with general news." Both girls remained standing near one of the back entrances. Pretzel listened while Angelica studied the assembly.

The acoustics of the auditorium carried Joan's strong voice to the back of the room with clarity. Her hands were clenched on the side of the podium and her gaze shifted from the audience to the notes before her. As she spoke, her expression was very solemn and her tone earnest.

"Furthermore, we have made significant progress in these past few months, rescuing girls throughout the Tri-State area. In conjunction with the divisional Daughters of New Jersey and Connecticut, we were able to identify and save more girls this past month than we have in the previous six months. I want to thank our seers, scouts, and guardians for their effort in this endeavor."

A round of applause reverberated through the entire room.

Joan continued. "Before I proceed, Gypsy will update us on some of the other areas we are targeting these upcoming days."

Angelica tilted her head slightly toward Pretzel and whispered, "So there are other groups then?"

Her companion responded softly, "Yes. There are Daughters stationed throughout the world. Our group oversees the entire Tri-State area and it's one of the largest."

"And what are seers, scouts, and guardians?" she asked.

Pretzel noticed her puzzled face. "In short, it's what we refer to as call functions. We have various call functions, and each person is designated a specific role within the team based on their skills, talents, and gifts. The way it works is…" Pretzel stopped speaking when in her peripheral vision, she noticed a flurry of activity from where Joan was now seated.

The woman stood abruptly and held a small missive that had been handed to her by one of the Daughters who still stood beside her. Joan glanced sorrowfully at Mist before she approached the podium and whispered in Gypsy's ear.

"Something is going on. Joan is about to speak again." Pretzel gestured with her hand toward the front.

Their leader had a grim expression as she grasped the missive tightly in her hand. She sighed deeply. "Dreadful news has arrived. Only a few hours ago, we had received an unconfirmed report that the Lancaster Daughters of the Watchers compound suffered an attack yesterday. Initially, the council agreed to not disclose this information without proper confirmation, but I have now received conclusive intel. I am saddened to inform you that those reports—" She paused to gather her composure, placed her clenched hand over her mouth, and cleared her throat. "The reports were true and much worse than we thought. It was a deadly assault."

A slight commotion stirred in the auditorium as a ripple of dread circulated among the Daughters. Whispers and mumbles of concern were heard across the room. Some shook their heads, while others were in complete shock.

Joan beckoned to the group to quiet. "As unsettling as the news is, it is the only concrete information we currently have available. We have yet to know the full extent of this assault. It is for that reason that we will soon dispatch a group of our Daughters, along with the assistance of the Camden, New Jersey group, to search for survivors." She drew a deep breath before she continued. "We ask all of you to keep the Lancaster group in your prayers and thoughts. Also, our deepest condolences to our second in rank, Mist, whom some of you know was part of that team years ago before she transferred here."

Gypsy, who was now seated next to Mist, laid her hand on hers.

"Given the nature of this attack, we ask every single one of you to be engaged, vigilant, and active and to continuously give your support to the protection of our facilities."

She sighed and resumed while she reviewed her notes on the podium. "Also, as you all know, we've continued to receive reports from around the nation about further assassinations of mothers and daughters and a numerical increase in Nephilim. It is our understanding that in these latter days, the Lords of the Underworld will mobilize an army in preparation for the release of the King of the Abyss, Diablos, and for the rise of his mysterious Nephilim child known as the Son of Destruction, who some believe is already in the world. But I encourage you, let us not be faint of heart in these tough times. I implore you to be strong and courageous. Take a stance, stand your ground, and let your light shine brilliantly against the dark forces."

She put her notes away and raised her voice confidently. "For thousands of years, the Daughters of the Watchers have endured hardships, tribulations, and persecutions. We have faced the devious wiles of evil as we stood committed to what is true, noble, pure, lovely, and admirable. Although we have wept during the night, I can attest to you that I have seen the joy that comes in the morning." Her gaze skimmed the audience fervently. "Rest assured that our light will not give out no matter how severe the darkness. We are not of those who shrink back and perish but those who arise and prevail. I'm convinced that no weapon formed against us will drive us into destruction!"

Loud cheers reverberated and a crescendo of applause echoed through the Gathering Hall. Angelica could sense the intensity of energy emanating from the Daughters.

"Therefore, let us remain steadfast under trial, not lose

hope under persecution, and remain strong when afflicted. Please let us stand and conclude with our mantra."

The entire assembly rose and proclaimed as one, "Hope, faith, and love. We are a beacon of hope, a stand of faith, and the radiance of love amid the darkness. We are the Daughters of the Watchers—strong alone and unconquerable together."

When they had concluded their mantra, the women began to disperse throughout the hall. A few formed small groups to chat while others exited.

Mrs. Poppins gathered all the children. "Okay, ladies, let's head out to the playground." The announcement was received with shouts of excitement.

"You'll need to explain almost everything Joan said in the meeting," Angelica told her companion.

"I will but let me first introduce you to some of my girl-friends." Pretzel grasped her hand excitedly and drew her toward a small group of four. "Hello, ladies!" Her tone was chipper.

"Where were you?" asked Reina. "I looked all over for you." Without letting her respond, she yelled, "Angelica! Good to see you again!" Her face, as always, beamed with enthusiasm.

Pretzel gave Angelica a look and a wink and said, "We were on a little field trip." She gestured with her hand and said, "Guys, this is Angelica. She joined us last night. Angelica, you know Reina already but this is Tassel, Cookie, and her twin sister Dough."

The group greeted her amiably while she considered the interesting nicknames.

After the exchange of pleasantries, Tassel—with short

black hair, light tan skin, and a Southeast Asian appearance and glasses—said, "Someone's birthday is coming up soon and I think we need a much-needed girls' night out."

Reina, who was performing the Floss dance, interjected, "For my twenty-first, I'd like to go clubbing."

"So no bungee jumping, scaling Mount Everest, or going across the country to a Comic-Con convention this year?" asked Cookie. The twins both had olive complexions with long coal-black hair woven into seven braids.

"Oh...I loved last year's trip to the Grand Canyons," said Dough while she struggled to open a jar of cherries.

Reina shook her head and continued her dance. "I thought of keeping it local since Pretzel..." She made a zany barfing gesture. "You know, when it comes to flying..." The girls sniggered as they glanced at Pretzel.

"Hey!" the girl snapped and smacked her friend on her shoulder. "I saw that." Seeing Dough's losing the struggle with the jar, she took it and opened it for her. "Honestly, Dough, you can flip a car but you can't open a jar."

"You know it doesn't work that way," the girl said and took the bottle. "Thank you, by the way." She smiled with delight and placed a cherry into her mouth.

Tassel remarked, "Incidentally, Gypsy said to include her in the next outing. She was very...how should I say it... distraught when we didn't invite her last time."

"I don't mind," added Cookie, "but know things get wild when Gypsy is around." She snatched a cherry from her sister's jar and popped it into her mouth.

"That's what I'm looking for," Reina said enthusiastically and now performed the Flapper dance. "We need to get wild."

"You're so crazy, Reina," quipped Dough.

Joan and Mist were walking toward the exit when they noticed Angelica. They motioned her to join them and she excused herself and strode toward them. Pretzel trailed behind.

"How are you holding up?" asked the leader.

"Doing a little better, although I'm still trying to process all of this."

"We truly understand what you're going through."

Angelica lowered her head and tucked her hair behind her ear. "I'm sorry for running out like a lunatic. These last twenty-four hours haven't been the easiest."

"Don't mention it," Joan replied reassuringly. "We're merely glad to have you back. Let us know if you need anything."

"Now that you mention it..." She hesitated for a moment. "I'd like to get a status update on my grandmother."

"Sure." She looked over her shoulder. "Pretzel, can you take her to Tassel's lab?" The girl, who was now behind her, nodded.

"Thanks," Angelica said.

Joan and Mist walked out of the room and she turned to Pretzel.

When she noticed that the group of friends had left, Pretzel said, "Tassel must have headed to the computer lab. I'll walk you over but if you don't mind, I'd like to stop by my room first."

"I don't mind at all," she responded.

13

PRETZEL'S ROOM

Pretzel's room was located on the third-floor north side of the warehouse, a spacious area with formal furniture and its own bathroom. It had the look and feel of a New York City studio apartment painted in a soft green color.

When she entered, Angelica's gaze was drawn to a large lattice window that provided a view of the city's magnificent skyscrapers. Beneath the window and in the center of the floor was a khaki sofa bed. The opposite wall contained a suspended forty-inch flat-panel TV, and on each side were small shelves that held angelic sculptures, plants, and various ceramic figurines.

To her left was a loft with a small desk beneath. The opposite wall had a lone poster-sized photograph of the Statue of Liberty taken with a backdrop of a clear blue sky and the sun's illuminating rays reflecting brilliantly on the lady. The adjacent corner was occupied by a chestnut bureau holding several photos arranged neatly, and a bookcase near the loft was stacked from top to bottom with books on various subjects.

Pretzel usually kept her room tidy and clutter-free, although after late scouting nights, she would fling clothes, footwear, and weapons carelessly on the floor.

The moment she entered her room, Pretzel kicked the sneakers off her feet and loosened her brown hair from its four-strand braid. She took some black apparel from her closet and walked into the bathroom

"I love this room," said Angelica as her gaze swept around.

"Thanks," the girl replied. "I do my best to make it feel homey. I used to share it with Reina until she got her own." Her voice projected from the bathroom.

"You can't beat that view," she said and stared through the window at the towers. "My apartment's view is a brick wall."

Pretzel eased closer to the door, poked her head out of the bathroom, and said, "I'm going to take a quick shower so make yourself at home."

At the sound of the running water, Angelica walked to the desk under the loft and noticed a book on philosophy titled *Republic* by Plato. Next to it was Pretzel's opened laptop. She pressed the spacebar key, which brightened the screen and displayed a word document containing an extensive paper.

She then glanced at the bookcase to her left. Curious, she moved to it and studied some of the titles on the first shelf—sixty-six volumes of the *Book, 1st, and 2nd of Enoch, The Sovereign Laws, The Gifts of the Daughters, The Ways of the Daughters,* and *The Chronicles of the Dreamsguard.* She withdrew the first volume of the *Book* called *Beginnings,* flipped through the first pages, and stopped at a high-lighted area of chapter six that read:

When humanity began to increase in numbers, they had many beautiful daughters. The Angels of the Sovereign One saw their beauty and took them as wives. These wives gave birth to Nephilim, heroes of old and mighty warriors, whose greed for power corrupted them.

Interesting. She closed the book and placed it on the shelf. *They should have made these sixty-six small volumes into one book.*

She wandered to the bureau and studied all the photos —a few of when Pretzel was younger, others with the Daughters, and one of an adolescent Pretzel next to a woman, both engulfed by laughter. Angelica picked the latter up to study the photo closer, especially the woman's golden-brown complexion, chiseled face, dark-brown hair, and hazel-green eyes—like Pretzel's.

"That's my mom," the girl said behind her and startled her.

"I'm sorry." She fumbled to replace it. "I only wanted a closer look at the photo."

"It's all right. It's the only one I have of her. She was a photographer but ironically, never liked taking pictures of herself." Pretzel dried her hair with a towel. "That photo was an accident. I took her camera and attempted to take her photo. She hid at first but then she came after me. When she finally caught me, the camera went off and that was the result."

"She was beautiful," Angelica said softly, her gaze fixed on the image.

"That's one of the photos she took." The girl gestured to the poster-sized photo of the Statue of Liberty on her wall.

She turned to the poster. "That's simply gorgeous," she said in admiration.

"I love it too," Pretzel said. "I had it made poster size a few years ago." She gazed at it as if for the first time. "Um… changing topics…I don't know what your plans are, but you're welcome to stay with me. That's a sofa bed and we are about the same size in clothes, so you can help yourself to any of mine."

Angelica turned to her and smiled. "Yeah, I think I'll take you up on that offer. Thanks." She moved to the sofa and flopped on it.

Pretzel walked to the loft wearing her black clothing and dropped the towel on the edge of the bed on the way past. Hanging from the corner of the loft was a light-blue apron emblazoned with the white emblem of a man with long hair holding a thunderbolt in one hand and a coffee bean on the other. She took it and fastened the apron—with the name *Latisha* on it—around her neck and her waist and placed a cap on her head with the same design.

"Wait!" Angelica blurted. "You work at Jovian Bean Coffee shop?"

The girl smiled while she tied her sneakers. "I have to make a living somehow, especially to pay for my college tuition."

"And you go to school?" She didn't try to hide her shock.

"Why the surprise?"

"I don't know…" She shook her head fleetingly. "I thought you guys were more like monks or something."

"Angelica, DW isn't a monastery. We have lives of our own beyond these four walls." Pretzel walked closer and slumped next to her on the sofa. "DW, this center, and these women mean so much to different people. For some, it's a refuge, a school, and a community and for others like me, a home but in the end, we try to make it a family."

"I thought you guys simply fought off demon lords and stuff," commented Angelica, and raised her hands into a karate chop.

"While there are those who dedicate one hundred percent of their time to DW, there are others who have jobs, school, and family outside these walls."

"I see. So...you're a brewer by day and superhero at night," she teased.

The girl stood and said with amusement, "If it makes you feel any better, yes." They both laughed. "Come on, let's go see Tassel."

14

A TECHY SEER

Both girls walked down several staircases and through various corridors to reach the computer lab located on the first floor of the warehouse. The more Angelica connected with Pretzel, the more intrigued and curious she was about the Daughters of the Watchers, the facility, and the call functions. She was eager to know more. Throughout her walk toward their destination, she asked questions and her companion responded willingly to each of them.

"Tell me about Tassel."

"She oversees our digital communications department. Tassel's our computer guru. You need help with anything electronic, she's the go-to person. She's also one of our seers and one of our best, at that."

"I've been wanting to ask you—what's a seer?" she asked.

"It's someone with the ability to see certain aspects of future events. It may come through a vision, a trance, or simply an impression."

"Are you all seers?"

"No. It's one of the gifts."

"Gifts?" Angelica frowned curiously. "I noticed a book you have called *The Gifts of the Daughters* on the bookshelf."

"Yes, gifts are special abilities given to Daughters for the purpose of the unity and service of the Daughterhood. There are many types of gifts and as far as I know, all Daughters are given at least one. May, for example, has been gifted with healing, Joan with leadership and administration, and Reina and I have similar gifts."

"Which are?"

"Encouragement and comfort."

"Go figure! You certainly do it well."

"Thanks. Unlike Reina, I'm also able to speak and understand multiple languages, especially those of the Watchers and the Nephilim."

Angelica was about to ask further questions but stopped when they reached their destination.

Pretzel said, "Here we go. Right through there."

When she strode into the computer lab, she was amazed by the extensive amount of equipment in the room. Various racks of servers and computers, switches, and routers stretched as far as the eye could see. A vast bank of televisions and computer monitors straddled one entire wall of the lab.

Her gaze landed quickly on Tassel, who was plugging CAT-5 cables into a patch panel, while Reina sat beside her and chatted non-stop.

Before Pretzel could utter a word, Reina noticed them and shouted, "Hey, guys! Whatcha doin'?"

"We were hoping Tassel could do us a favor and check

on the status of Angelica's grandmother," the girl replied and narrowed her eyes on the tech.

"Affirmative. Walk over to my office," said Tassel. It wasn't an office but a desk full of computers and other scattered electronic parts. Several flat-panel monitors also sat on the surface with several workstations beneath it.

"Angelica, I have to head to work. Is it okay if I leave you with Reina and Tassel?"

"Sure. Thanks for your help today."

"Anytime. I should be back later this evening," Pretzel responded with a smile. She turned to Reina. "Angelica is staying in my room. Can you help her get around the place?"

"Gucci!" slanged Reina with two thumbs-up.

As Angelica waved goodbye to the other girl, Tassel asked, "Maria Santos, correct?"

"Yes, that's right."

The tech slumped in her chair and let her fingers dance over the panel of keys while her gaze bounced from window to window across multiple screens. She ran a few computer scripts, cracked her fingers, and said brightly, "We are in."

Angelica frowned, but by the look on Tassel's face, she was confident "we are in" meant something good.

Her deft fingers danced over the keyboard again as she searched through the hospital's in-patient directory. A moment later, she found her target and exclaimed, "Here we go—Maria Santos!" She pushed her glasses back and let her gaze scroll the screen.

"What does it say?" she implored. She fidgeted uneasily

over Tassel's shoulders and tried to see what the screen displayed.

"Same condition as before. From what I understand, in layman's terms…" She pushed a key to scroll farther down the page. "She's still in a comatose state, has fractures of her left hip and wrist, and bruises around her neck."

Angelica's features were etched with despair. "I have to go see her."

"Byte me!" exclaimed Tassel as she continued reading through the notes.

"What is?" she asked frantically.

"This wasn't in the database before. It states here, next of kin, granddaughter, Angelica Santos, wanted for police questioning. Inform police if seen."

"What? Why?" she exclaimed and tried again to see what the girl saw on the monitor.

"Undetermined," responded Tassel. "Let me substantiate the info from the NYPD database."

"Maybe they tried to call me." She felt for her cell phone in her back pocket. "Shoot! Where's my phone?" she murmured. "I must have dropped it at my grandmother's."

The tech hacked into the NYPD database and read, "It says here that you're wanted for questioning concerning your grandmother's assault and breaking and entering."

"Are they saying I did it?" she asked and felt sick to the pit of her stomach.

"It's indistinct—I mean not clear—but the police report reveals that the FBI was at the scene." Her gaze was fixed intently on the screen, while her nimble fingers continued typing.

"So, I'm wanted by the feds too." Angelica sat on a

nearby chair and stared nervously at the floor. Her face was as ashen as the pale horse of the Apocalypse.

Reina walked to her and placed her hand on her back. "Hey, girl. Don't get yourself worked up. We've seen this before and have worked magic to clear some of the other Daughters' names." She looked at the tech. "Right, Tassel?"

The other girl nodded.

"Have a little faith in us, okay?"

"Give me a few days, and I'll see what I can do for you," Tassel told her.

"A few days?" she exclaimed disappointedly. "What about my grandmother? She has no one else except me. I need to be there for her." Tears shimmered in her eyes while she stared despondently at the hexagonal tiles on the floor.

Suddenly, the atmosphere in the room shifted and became filled with a hair-raising charge—shocking yet peace-inducing. The tech fixed her eyes on Angelica and her gentle facial expression became earnest. In a genuine, soft tone, she uttered, "Don't overwhelm yourself. Your grandmother will pull through and you'll be there to see it. You'll face many challenges in her path to recovery. Your patience will be tested but always keep in mind a little patience doesn't hurt anyone."

Angelica's ears perked up and her eyes widened. An irresistible tide of emotions swept over her as she recalled the expression frequently used by her grandmother.

"My grandmother always says that," she said in wonder and raised her tear-stained face toward Tassel.

Reina clasped her shoulder tenderly and her tone was soft and comforting. "We will be here for you. I guarantee, we'll have your back when you need it. I believe what Tassel said. She's the best at what she does."

Angelica sighed deeply and said, "Yes, I need to be patient. I'm very sure that's what my grandmother would want me to do."

Tassel undid the clasp of the fabric cord necklace around her neck that held a pendant-like clear vial, which contained a white substance. She stood, strode to her, and placed it around her neck. "I want you to have this. It's quartz dust and the Nephilim detest it. I have a feeling this small token will stop a great threat." She returned to her desk and opened one of the drawers full of mobile devices, selected one, and programmed it quickly. "Here," she said and handed the device to her. "As soon as I have an update, I'll call you."

"Thanks," she said and examined the pendant.

"Oooh...let me get those digits," exclaimed Reina and retrieved her pink-covered smartphone quickly from her pocket.

"So asks the assicon, emoji, and hash-tag meme queen," said Tassel teasingly.

After they exchanged phone numbers, Reina looked at Angelica and said, "Com'on, girl. Let me give you a tour of this place." She turned to the tech. "Thanks, Tassel. I'll tag you later."

The ladies walked out of the lab and the other girl returned to her work.

15

THE CURATOR

Angelica opened one eye groggily to frown at her roommate's diamond-shaped face and closed it swiftly to return to her sweet slumber. When the girl nudged her again, she resorted to the ostrich method which was to cover her face with the pillow.

"Wow! You seriously like to sleep," Pretzel said while seated on the edge of the bed and she attempted to pull the pillow away from her. She held it tightly and shifted to the no retreat, no surrender approach.

"Wake up, sleepyhead," the other girl said softly.

"No! Only a few more minutes," she muttered under the pillow.

"A few more minutes and it'll be noon."

"What?" Angelica pushed the pillow frantically from her face and revealed her blush. Instantly, she sat bolt upright on the bed. "I'm so sorry for oversleeping. I wasn't aware that it was so late."

"No worries. We're glad you can rest. You need it."

Angelica flopped back onto the bed and clasped her

right hand over her forehead. "Can you mention that to Reina? I think she took me to every nook and cranny of this place last night, and then visited each room and girl who stays here." She propped herself on the sofa bed and crossed her legs. "Where does she get all that energy?"

"Yeah, we wonder that too. It's a mystery not even a seer can divine." Pretzel chuckled. "Come on, and let's get you something to eat." She stood from the bed.

"Pretzel, before we go…" started Angelica, whose countenance changed from light to somber. "I never thanked you properly for saving my life and my grandmother's. Reina filled me in with the details last night. I'm truly thankful to you both." She pushed her hair behind an ear. "Um…thanks for calling nine-one-one and getting my grandmother medical help."

The girl smiled. "That's what we do."

"There's something else. Given all that's happened, I don't think my life will ever be the same and…um, if this is my new life, I was hoping to learn…you know, to be more like…you guys." She stammered, a little apprehensive, and fixed her gaze on her folded fingers resting on her lap. "I'm not sure if I'm asking this right, but to be more specific, I want to be more like you. I want to learn all there is 'cause…you guys, you know, *dan paliza*." She registered her Spanglish and clarified, "That means kick a—"

Pretzel smiled and interjected, "I know what it means."

"That's right. You have that gift thingy. Anyway, can you guys teach me?" Her gaze shifted from her fingers to the other girl's face. She swallowed and waited nervously for a response.

Her companion sat again with a solemn stare. "Hmm…"

She sounded stern and placed her hand under her chin. "To do so, we first need to test you through the sororal bonds of daughterhood by having you pass through the Ring of the Metal Sieve."

"The what?" Angelica stared at Pretzel with her brow wrinkled in confusion.

Pretzel stood and spoke in a gruff, masculine voice. "Yes, the Ring of the Metal Sieve." She began to chant. "Hwa! Hwee! Ha! Ho! Ho! Ho! Ha! To the sacrificial chamber!"

"Wait, you're teasing me!" Angelica felt a little foolish. Her roommate paused and burst into loud laughter. "You're horrible, you know that?" She guffawed and threw her pillow at Pretzel.

The other girl caught the pillow and threw it at her. "You've got to admit I had you going there." She sat on the edge of the bed. "In all seriousness, it'd be our pleasure to do so and to be honest, Joan was hoping you would."

"Was she?" asked Angelica, both surprised and honored.

"First, becoming part of the DW is something each woman decides voluntarily. It's part of the DW code of honor that no one is to be coerced, forced, or seduced to be a Daughter. We are not like the Nephilim, who are seduced by the Watchers into complete subjugation and control."

"And why was Joan hoping I'd join?" she asked with an inquisitive expression.

Pretzel smiled and said, "Joan said you remind her of her younger self."

"Quick-tempered and always jumping to conclusions?" she responded with her right eyebrow raised.

"Yeah, something like that." Her roommate smirked.

"Hey! I thought you were on my side." Angelica gave her a mockingly angry stare.

"Kidding aside, I think she meant strong and brave."

She beamed and recalled similar words spoken by her grandmother.

Pretzel, Angelica, and Reina strode down one of the warehouse's long corridors and through a lofty doorway, which led into a spacious area. Towering narrow rows of bookcases lined the room from wall to wall. Wooden tables and chairs were scattered in the center of the room, some of which were filled with a few young Daughters engrossed in their books. Toward the back of the room were several technological devices—computers, tablets, printers, and even 3D VR glasses.

The baronial quarters had been decorated with Greco-Roman architecture. Large supporting beams were covered in fluted-marble Corinthian-style columns with gilded leaves and flowers carved into the capital. The center ceiling encompassed a monolithic Roman-style arch that stretched from one side of the wall to the other.

"This is our library," Pretzel informed Angelica. "If you're looking for any piece of information, you'll find it here. We have books here you won't find in any public facility."

She was impressed by the library and its design and vastness and marveled at the structure and size. She was also astonished that it hadn't been included in Reina's tour.

"Reina, why didn't you show me this last night?" she asked, almost in a whisper.

The girl responded softly, "Well..." She gulped so hard that it was audible. "We are going to meet Mrs. Mozart, and I'll warn you she's a very serious and strict woman. She doesn't smile much and gives me the heebie-jeebies." She paused and bit her lower lip. "And I don't think she likes me very much."

"That's because you can't keep your mouth shut," commented Pretzel in a low murmur. "Anyway, she's one of the wisest, most knowledgeable Daughters in the world. She's been gifted with knowledge and understanding and is one of the twelve senior members who form the general council of this group."

They walked quietly toward the front of the room and approached a large mahogany desk. Behind it sat a slim, pale tan and gray-haired lady. Her features gave her a matriarchal appearance while her eyes exuded a sense of wisdom.

Slowly, Mrs. Mozart raised her head and focused on the young women. "Greetings, Miss Pretzel and Miss Reina. What can I do for you?" she asked in a polished and very cultured English accent.

Pretzel greeted her. "Hello, Mrs. Mozart. I called before lunch about our newest member Angelica. We hoped you could get her started on the ways of the Daughters."

The woman lowered her head slightly and stared at Angelica above the lenses of her spectacles, her expression intrigued. "So this is Leonard Archie's offspring. Hmm... I've heard so much about you." She took her glasses off and continued. "It's nice to meet you, Miss Angelica."

"Hello." She swallowed hard before she responded.

"I presume you two ladies have other duties that require your attention. I will send your friend to you once we have completed our session." Mrs. Mozart's gaze shifted from one girl to the other.

"Angelica, don't forget we are meeting Gypsy later today," Pretzel reminded her.

As they exited the room, Reina gulped wryly and looked woefully at Angelica and mouthed, "Good luck."

Swiftly, Mrs. Mozart stood and revealed a pearlescent shift that reached her feet and was fastened with a loose golden girdle that encircled her lean waist. "Follow me, Miss Angelica." She walked gracefully through the library with her right arm slightly lifted and close to her torso. Angelica followed closely, feeling like a lamb being led to the slaughter.

"I could have you sit in a lecture room and listen to me instruct you, but I do not find that form of enlightenment advantageous. I agree that it has its place, but proper learning needs to engage much more than your ears. It has to captivate your mind and capture the senses."

The woman approached one of the tall bookcases and selected a book. "It is, therefore, the reason that I inculcate the importance of reading in all my girls." She handed it to her and continued toward another bookcase to repeat the process twice before she moved to an empty table in the center of the library. "You may take a seat," she instructed although she remained standing.

Angelica complied and stacked the books neatly.

"The three volumes before you are what I consider indispensable to the ways of the Daughters. I encourage all my girls to include these volumes in their personal library. While we do have digital copies, I prefer physical ones. I guess you can call me old-fashioned. Nonetheless, whatever method you prefer is up to you, but I strongly recommend you have them."

Mrs. Mozart picked up the first book on the stack and held it in both hands so the title faced Angelica. "*The Ways of the Daughters* gives you the origin and brief history, the code, and meaning of the Daughterhood." She placed the book beside the other two and selected the next one on the stack. "*The Gifts of the Daughters* outlines the various talents the Daughters of the Watchers have been gifted with—or at least, in my opinion, those that have been recorded. Nevertheless, the central context is on meaning."

She placed the volume next to the first and took the last book of the stack. "*The Sovereign Laws*—some find this work to be a dull read, yet I believe it is the most important. They are laws that govern the visible and invisible world and regulations that the Daimons, the Nephilim, and yes, even the Daughters must adhere to. Violating these laws can have a detrimental effect on your destiny." She placed it on the table again.

The woman clasped her hands over her lower abdomen and continued, "Many of the girls' initial learning interests are the Daimons and the Nephilim, but I think that should be secondary. It is useless to know your enemy, much less engage your enemy, if you first do not know yourself. The three volumes before you will enlighten you on the four fundamental points of the essence of life—origin, meaning, morality, and destiny." She paused for a moment before she continued. "Do you have any questions before I depart, Miss Angelica?"

She shook her head sheepishly.

"I believe I have gone on long enough so I will leave you to it. I suggest you begin with the first title presented, and I will return in a while to check on your progress."

Ms. Mozart returned gracefully to her desk.

Angelica felt compelled to obey and started to read.

16

PLOT HOLE FILLERS

Angelica was completely immersed where she read on Pretzel's sofa bed with her hair wrapped in a ponytail and legs crossed on the mattress. Her countenance depicted a sincere, keen interest in the history and stories of the Daughters of yesteryear. Her eyes scanned each page with burgeoning excitement and a deep sense of connection. She was so profoundly engrossed that she lost track of time or any other responsibility she needed to attend to.

Beside her on one of the end tables sat a half-eaten sandwich that had been prepared by one of Grace's girls and a glass of orange juice, half-empty, that she had not touched for quite some time.

A shuffle of approaching feet at the door was followed by a sigh of relief, which Angelica did not heed. "There you are! I've looked all over for you," stated Pretzel from the entrance of her room. "Mrs. Mozart mentioned that you were dismissed some time ago. I've searched the entire facility looking for you, thinking you were lost." The girl's beautiful features morphed from tense to relaxed.

"This is fascinating—so the gifts of the Daughters are given to you and aren't for you but for the sole purpose of helping, guiding, and the benefit of someone else?" Angelica asked without acknowledging her roommate's concern. Her voice was a little distracted and her gaze remained glued to the book. "And who's this Carpenter Son I keep reading about— the giver of gifts and who has power over life?"

"Hello, Earth to Angelica. Are you there?" inquired Pretzel without answering her question. "We were supposed to meet an hour ago."

She finally looked up, her face flushed. "I'm so sorry," she responded and closed the book unceremoniously before her. "I totally spaced." She pushed back a single dark bang of hair that fell across her right eye. "It's only that I've been so intrigued by these books that I can't seem to put them down. After my session with Mrs. Mozart, I decided to come here and continue reading. She said it was okay to take them with me, so I've been here ever since."

A tired but understanding smile appeared on Pretzel's face. "That's a first," she stated and arched her eyebrows. She strode from the doorway into the room.

"What's a first?" Angelica asked curiously. She placed the book on the end table and retrieved her lukewarm orange juice, took a sip, and winced at the temperature. When she noticed how stale the sandwich looked, she did not bother with it.

"Some girls fall asleep within minutes of starting the first book. It's the reason some have named the library The Sleeping Chamber, and why Reina doesn't go there. It's the only place I know that saps all her energy." With her index finger pointed at her, Pretzel continued. "But you seem to have taken to it."

Her eyes glinted with wonder as she said, "Gosh! For the first time in my life, I feel I can make sense of things." She drew a deep sigh before she spoke again. "Reading the history of some of the notable Daughters, especially their challenges and struggles, made me feel relatable." Her tone was enthusiastic. "Even though these women are long gone, I felt a deep sense of connection with them."

"To be honest, I'm amazed." Her roommate walked toward her and sprawled on the bed. "Many of us didn't make those connections early on but you've picked it up very quickly. That's impressive." She pushed into a seated position and tapped one of Angelica's knees. "But enough of that. Daughters aren't simply about reading."

Pretzel rose and walked to her bureau, opened one of the drawers, pulled out a pair of sweatpants and a sweatshirt, and tossed them to her. "Get changed, girl. We need to get you strong."

The two girls walked into the Daughters' training area, one of the largest spaces in the warehouse. It was ample enough to hold a circular track, various exercise equipment, and an artificial climbing wall. The facility included exercise equipment for every muscle of the body and different offensive and defensive gear, practice dummies, and weapons such as swords, blades, bo staffs, sais, and slingshots. The center area was covered with many blue floor mats used for physical combat training.

When she glanced around the room, Angelica noticed that each area was occupied by various Daughters engaged in some form of training. Reina was in one of the corners with Cookie and Dough, flinging daggers at a human-sized wooden dummy. Gypsy stood in the center of the room with her blue eyes and short ginger hair shaved on the left side. Her twenty-six-year-old frame showed a slim, fit physique and her toned legs bulged and ripped arms showed the outline of her muscles.

Baffled, she stared at how efficiently Gypsy performed backflips along with roundhouse and spinning kicks. Her sweat-drenched clothes indicated that she had been at this for some time.

"Come," said Pretzel. "It's time to train you with the best." Both ladies moved toward the center of the room.

The woman noticed their approach. "Hello, ladies. I've been waiting for you."

"Sorry for the delay, but I couldn't find her. She was reading in my room." The girl turned to Angelica and gestured to Gypsy as she said, "Angelica, you remember Gypsy. She's one of the team's best fighters. If anyone can train you on how to bring a Nephilim down, it would be this girl."

When she saw how sweaty the woman looked, she simply waved without making any attempt to shake her hand. "Hi!"

Gypsy asked straightforwardly, "So Angelica, what do you have for us? Any special skills in the martial arts, weaponry, sports, runner, climber, swimmer, so on and so forth?"

"Um…I've never been the athletic type," she explained

shyly. "I do like to go on long walks in the park if that counts for anything."

"Unfortunately, honey, walks can't protect you from those monsters."

The word "honey" resonated with her and gave her the impression of seeing her before but she couldn't quite pinpoint where or when.

"No worries," the woman continued. "It merely means we start with the basics."

"The basics?" She felt clueless and fretful.

"A few laps around the track followed by some basic exercises, then a few more laps around the track and more exercises, and back to the track...you get the point."

"You're kidding, right?" she retorted.

"I don't see anyone laughing," responded Gypsy with a straight face, while Pretzel pursed her lips and shook her head.

"I don't think that would be a good idea," Angelica protested. "May mentioned that I shouldn't engage in strenuous activities. You know, 'cause of the concussion and all."

"You fell for the placebo pill crap," snapped Gypsy. "May is a kindhearted individual who doesn't like to freak newbies out with her healing abilities. I'm not May. I'm heartless and the cause of much pain." She glowered at her and studied her from head to feet. "Now get your whining ass on the track and let's go!" she commanded. Without any further persuasion, Angelica walked to the track and commenced what she suspected was her demise.

Gypsy turned to Pretzel. "In the meantime, let's you and I work on synchronized fighting."

Completely haggard and exhausted, Angelica trudged to the center of the room where the other girls were huddled. Every fiber of her body and muscles ached with pain after the torturous run and the various rigorous workout routines Gypsy had made her perform. Again, she lost track of time but this time, it wasn't out of interest. She collapsed face down as if dead with her matted hair and clothes drenched with sweat. The group around her snickered quietly.

Pretzel extended her hand in an attempt to help her up, but she snapped, "Don't touch me. I blame you for this. I've puked twice already." She flipped to her back and saw all five ladies giggling and simpering. "Thanks for the moral support," she said sarcastically as she grasped her roommate's hand to sit. Reina handed her a towel, which she used to wipe the sweat from her brow.

The group consisted of Pretzel, Reina, Cookie, Dough, and Gypsy, all seated in a circular huddle.

"So all this training and exercising will help me defeat a Nephilim?" she asked.

"Well, this and a little something extra," answered Pretzel. "Our shared relationship with the Daimons gives us what we call a spiritual-psychological awareness of the Nephilim."

Confused about the term, Angelica interrupted, "Spiritual what? I swear...*ustedes con estos nombres*...you guys with these names."

"Spiritual-Psychological Awareness, or SPA," the girl clarified. "The Nephilim's physical strength and supernatural abilities are derived from their angelic side. They are too fast and too strong for a normal human to take on. However, we can sense their intent before they act. It's like getting a heads-up about their next move. But you need to develop quick-wittedness and agility to take advantage of this, which requires you to be physically fit."

"So through this spiritual psycho...whatever and being fit is how I can defeat a Nephilim?" She now sat cross-legged and focused intently on Pretzel.

"Not necessarily," interjected Gypsy. "First, as harsh this may sound, we never aim to simply defeat a Nephilim. We aim to kill them."

"Kill?" A disturbed expression surfaced quickly on Angelica's face.

"Once a Nephilim sells their soul to the Devil, so to speak, they're forever enslaved to the Daimons' bidding and forever an instrument of evil." The woman narrowed her eyes at her. "So if you're ever in a fight with a Nephilim, aim to kill or he'll kill you first."

"Okay," she replied but her eyes mirrored her concern. "How do you kill a Nephilim?"

"Using a mineral called quartz. Nephilim are vulnerable to the substance. All our weapons are fashioned from that, which is the reason most Daughters carry quartz daggers and blades." Gypsy extracted a blade strapped to her ankle and wielded it with her left hand. "But to kill a Nephilim, you have to strike him on the head or decapitate him, the latter being my favorite." A gleeful smirk spread across her countenance. "But if you're not a dagger person, you can go old-fashioned and use a quartz stone with a slingshot."

"It almost sounds like the story of David and Goliath," Angelica commented.

"Who do you think told David about the stone?" Gypsy countered. "Goliath was a Nephilim—the son of Anak, a Watcher, along with his four Nephilim brothers. If it wasn't for the help of the Daughters, I'm not sure if the shepherd boy would have defeated the giant."

"You mean those stories were true?" She raised an eyebrow. "I used to think these were merely Sunday School stories." A dumbfounded look crossed her face.

"They're certainly true," the woman confirmed. "As are many stories in mytho-historical accounts."

"If there are so many stories of them, why is it that I've never heard of them?"

"Sure you have," Pretzel responded. "You never read the Greek mythology stories of Hercules, Perseus, Achilles, Gilgamesh, and a host of others?"

Reina joined the discussion in her enthusiastic tone. "And like comic book superheroes with the capes, the hammers, the web-swinging and, you know, a whole host of others?"

"They aren't real. Those are mythical and comic book characters," protested Angelica.

Pretzel shook her head. "Not all the details in those stories are true and some are highly embellished, but they're based on real accounts and exploits of Nephilim."

"So if our fathers are Angels, does that mean God is real?"

"The Sovereign One is real, all right," stated Gypsy emphatically. "Although I don't know if the 'Sovereign

One'"—she used her fingers for emphasis—"is as involved as the Book claims He is."

"I never thought He was real in the first place," Angelica murmured.

"He exists, although it would be nice if He used that sovereignty a little more."

"How so?" She gazed at her quizzically.

"Life would be much less complicated if He'd simply clean this mess up," responded Gypsy. "I know that when push comes to shove, I won't look to the sky for help." Her countenance reflected sadness when she uttered those words.

As she spoke, she poked her left hand forcefully with a pocketknife. Angelica winced and raised her eyebrows when she noticed the marked lack of a cut or bleeding.

Noting her stare, the woman explained. "Sorry, it's an old curse as I like to call it." She put the pocketknife away and looked at the group. "But, yeah, getting rid of the Nephilim requires dexterity, precision, and agility in conjunction with your cognitive sensibility." She turned and fixed her eyes on Angelica again. "It's why you also need to learn how to tune into your senses."

She frowned. "These senses—are they normal? On the night of the attack, I was able to sense the presence of evil and danger when I entered my grandmother's building."

"Every Daughter has those keen senses," Dough responded. "When a Nephilim is in our general vicinity, these senses alert us to their presence and any imminent threat they pose."

"Can Nephilim sense us too?"

"No," stated her sister Cookie. "But Nephilim and the

Daimons do have the ability to see our aura and smell our scent."

"What's an aura?" Angelica shook her head briefly as she tried to understand another confusing term.

Reina smiled and stroked her flaxen hair. "It's the glow we all have—I mean all Daughters and Nephilim. Daughters are light-blue, and Nephilim is like a black."

"That's right," Pretzel added. "When we see a Nephilim, it's like perceiving a dark glimmer around them and vice versa—when they see us, it's a blue glow."

She continued her line of questioning. "Why can't I see your aura or my own?"

Her roommate responded, "We can't see our kind or each other's, but we can sense one another. We can sense each other's presence, pain, and emotions. It's handy when we are trying to locate one another but extra handy in advanced techniques—what we call synchronized fighting."

"Hmm...on the night of the attack, I had a feeling that I was being followed. Was that my sensory perception?" Angelica asked.

"Yup, that was me," Reina interjected. "I was following you."

"Okay. But why were you following me?" She frowned pointedly at Reina.

"To be quite honest, we have kept tabs on you for some time," answered Gypsy. "Tassel had a dream about you. She saw who you were, your place of work, and foresaw the imminent attack on you and your grandmother. It's one of the ways we scout for Daughters and try to help them."

"I wondered how you knew about me," Angelica said. "You mentioned how to kill a Nephilim, but how do you get rid of a Daimon?" Pretzel and Gypsy exchanged grave looks. This made Angelica glance curiously at them. "What? What's with the looks?"

"Ahem." The older woman cleared her throat. "Well, Daimons are spiritual beings who can't be killed or harmed by humans or hybrids. We can, however, feel and sense their presence. When the atmosphere feels...how I can say...fearful or dark, it's an indication of a Daimon."

Angelica recalled her experience a few days earlier. "Some nights ago when I was leaving work, I may have sensed and seen a Daimon." She had a dazed look as she recollected her encounter. "I remember being tripped by a cat and seeing and sensing a dark shadowy figure near me."

"That was Apollyon," stated Gypsy.

"Apollyon? How do you know?"

"I was there that night."

"I don't remember seeing you—" Angelica stopped and realized where she had seen Gypsy before. "Wait!" she blurted. "That was you? It honestly looked like you were trying to hit on me."

"I simply asked if you needed a companion. The rest was your interpretation."

"But you asked if I wanted to have some fun," she insisted.

"I was inviting you to a training session. Didn't you have the most fun ever? I know I did."

"Okay, okay. You win." Angelica raised her hands in surrender. "I'm still puzzled by something, though. If Apollyon or Leonard Archie, my father—I'm not sure what to call him—was present, why not simply appear at my apartment and get rid of me right on the spot?"

Pretzel responded to this question "Sovereign Law 7.VII.7 states that 'neither Angels nor Daimons can physically hurt or kill any of the human race.' That includes us hybrids as well. If they do, they'll face hastened judgment. There are exceptions to the rules. One is if they have a divine mandate and the second is if the person willingly surrenders to the Daimons, which is the case with the Nephilim."

"So, I assume Daimons can harm the Nephilim?"

"Correct," Gypsy confirmed. "Also, we don't believe Daimons can appear anywhere they please. If that were the case, they would have barged into this warehouse a long time ago with a horde of their minions. They must have some special connection to specific locations, but we don't know how portals work."

"Portals?" Her forehead creased.

The woman was about to answer but Dough spoke first. "It's like a gateway—a form of transportation Daimons use to get from one place to another instantaneously."

"And a means to transport Nephilim," added Cookie.

"Last question, I promise," Angelica assured them apologetically. "If Daimons and Nephilim could always see my aura—and I presume it's always been there—why attack now?"

Pretzel pressed her lips together for a moment. "I'm not sure and it's a fair question. However, our aura isn't always visible. We know of only two ways they can't see an aura. The first is if you're using Kollourion. It can prevent the Daimons and Nephilim from seeing our aura. On the day of our field trip, you had it on which put me at ease."

"What's the second?"

"That is something of a mystery that we don't quite completely understand. There seems to be a hedge of protection around certain individuals that prevents the Daimons and Nephilim from noticing their aura. I suspect it could be a relic, beloved person, or both. Whatever it is, my best guess is that it has something to do with love."

Angelica stopped her questioning and sat in silence while she considered what Pretzel had said. Her skin paled, and she rose quickly. With misty eyes, she uttered grimly, "Thank you for your time...but, ahem, I'm exhausted. I'm gonna go upstairs and take a shower." She exited the room hastily and left everyone confused by her sudden departure.

Her roommate stared after her, surprised by the unusual behavior. She jumped to her feet and followed. When she entered their room, Angelica knelt next to the sofa, her face buried in her hands while she cried profusely.

"Hey, what's going on?" Pretzel asked as she approached and knelt beside her.

She pushed against the girl's chest while tears streamed down her face and exclaimed, "It must have been her."

Pretzel simply embraced her without saying a word or asking for an explanation. She let Angelica's tears soak her chest.

After a few minutes and when the tears subsided, both sat on the floor and leaned against the sofa. Angelica inhaled and exhaled deeply and spoke, "It was my grandmother, Pretzel. I believe she was my hedge. She was the reason I wasn't found. For all these years, I didn't realize that she was my guardian angel."

"How so?" her friend asked.

"*Abuela* has been there since the beginning and has given me all I needed. She's paranoid and overprotective at times, but what parent isn't?" She stopped, her voice choked, and fought to maintain her composure. "If you guys are right, she's in the hospital because I moved out."

"What do you mean?" Pretzel asked compassionately.

"A few months ago, I was so frustrated by her constant questions and lectures that I decided to move out. I couldn't take it anymore, so I got my own place. They must have found me because I left her." Tears began to stream down her face again.

"We all carry a weight of guilt. I understand what you're going through." Pretzel cocked her head toward Angelica and her gaze held a secret ready to be shared. "The night before my mother's death, I was invited to a party. I asked her but she said no. It was a school night, she said. We had a spat that evening and I went to my room. She thought I was sleeping but I snuck out and went to the party anyway. A Nephilim sniffed me out and found out where I lived. For years, I carried the guilt of her death until I discovered something greater than that guilt."

"What was that?" Angelica sniffled.

"There's a person on this team who I admire so much, and I believe her gift is one of the most powerful and greatest gifts of all."

"Who's that?" she asked, keenly interested.

"It was Grace and her gift of love. There were days I couldn't even get up, but her embrace and words of comfort brought me back to life. She helped me to focus on the acts of my mother's love and not on the mistakes I committed. I won't lie to you. I still have my days. That night when you toured this place on your own..."

She smirked and referred to Angelica's attempted escape. "I was in that room having a guilt party. But seeing the perplexed look in your eyes brought me to focus and give to you what Grace had given me." Her emerald-green eyes sparkled with compassion. "It made me think of the many dark nights when I'd visit Grace simply to get one of her embraces. Although it didn't change what had happened, her hugs reminded me that I was loved and I am loved."

For a moment, the girls sat in silence and looked out the latticed window of the room. Angelica's soft, gentle voice ended the solemn silence. "Would you mind giving me a hug?"

"I thought you'd never ask."

Both girls sighed and embraced each other quietly for a long, comforting moment.

17

HOSPITAL VISIT

"Tune in to sense my voice and my movement. Become aware of both your surroundings and our presence around you," Gypsy instructed Angelica for the millionth time as she stood blindfolded in the center of the training facility. She gestured to Pretzel to throw another inflated rubber ball.

"'ño!" She yelped as the ball hit her in the stomach. "I'll never get this," she muttered testily and proceeded to yank the blindfold from her eyes. "We have been at this for hours now and I can't seem to sense when you throw the ball." She sighed in frustration.

"It'll take time and practice," Pretzel told her encouragingly. "You only need to concentrate a little more."

"I can sense you and Gypsy and feel her walking around me, but I have a hard time distinguishing between the two," she explained, disappointment in her tone.

"Tuning in to your SPA first requires you to organize the chaos of your sensory input, emotions, and thoughts," Gypsy explained as she moved closer. "Your body is trying to adjust to not having its most used sensory input—sight —and it's being stubborn about it. Instead of focusing on what you've lost, zero in on what you still have." The woman replaced the blindfold deftly. "Let's do it again."

She moved a few feet away from her and gestured to Pretzel.

"*Me caso en na!*" Angelica snapped after another hit from the ball.

"Don't remove the blindfold," Gypsy instructed when she attempted to yank it off. "Again, Pretzel."

The ball thumped into her and predictably, she uttered a curt response. "*Hija de pu—*"

"Stop with the Spanish swearing," Pretzel protested.

"Angelica, this isn't about simply attempting to feel our movement but to know our movement and intent," said Gypsy. "Your SPA doesn't allow you to feel the object coming at you. It enables you to perceive where we are aiming, and the force exerted in the throw. The rest is up to you to predict where and when the object will go. Your instinct and reflexes will then help you know if you need to dodge or deflect." The woman stepped away from her. "C'mon! You got this, Angelica."

"It sounds like a movie I once saw about dodgeballs," she murmured.

"Be grateful I'm not using wrenches, then," chided Gypsy as she nodded in Pretzel's direction.

Angelica inhaled slowly and dug deep within herself. She minimized her frustration, concentrated on her senses, and felt her two companions' presence around her. Most importantly, she attempted to discern their movements and intentions. Without warning, a sudden premonition pushed into her consciousness. In her mind's eye, she counted one, two, three steps to the left and a turn.

Pretzel took a few steps to the right and turned.

She discerned the next attempt with less effort. *Her hand is moving...right, no left, no right...she'll throw it fast and try to hit my stomach.*

A second later, she heard a whispered whoosh and instinctively dodged the ball thrown at her. Her excited response could not be contained and she leapt with excitement. "I did it!" she yelled.

Wait! Another ball...my head.

With a soft thunk, the projectile ricocheted off the back of her head.

"Damn!" she exclaimed and rubbed the point of impact. "But I felt that one coming." She removed the blindfold proudly. "That was awesome."

"You go, girl!" exclaimed Pretzel.

"Good job," remarked Gypsy as she clapped.

"Oh, my God. What an experience!" Angelica said enthusiastically. "I could feel your movements, your breathing, and even your heartbeat." She placed her hand on her chest and sighed deeply. "What a rush!"

Gypsy glanced at her watch. "Ladies, my apologies for not continuing the celebration but I'm already late for a meeting. Angelica, same time tomorrow but next time, we'll practice with real blades." Her face reflected a hidden smirk as she narrowed her eyes at the girl.

"What?" she snapped nervously but Gypsy walked out of the room without a response. She spun toward Pretzel. "Was she serious?"

"With Gypsy, you never know. You'll need to wait until

tomorrow," her friend said with a smile. "But regardless, even if she was, you'll do great. You did awesome today, girl. It took some time but you got it."

"I do have to say that was astounding. It even reminded me of the late-night walks I'd take after work. The thrill, the mystery, and the wonder of the unknown." Angelica's eyes sparkled with excitement. "Is that what you all feel?"

Pretzel nodded. "We only need to get you in front of one of those Nephilim and see if you continue to feel the same way," she teased.

"Throwing me in the lion's den already, are you?" Angelica retorted dryly. "You know I can feel your innermost secrets now."

The girl rolled her eyes. "Okay. You'll be bored." She walked toward her and squeezed her shoulder. "By the way, you look much better than yesterday."

She grinned. "Yes. Thanks to you," she answered with softness in her voice.

Suddenly, her phone rang with a single chime. She frowned curiously and fumbled in her back pocket. "It's most likely one of Reina's emojis again." Surprisingly, the device displayed a text from Tassel. *Come and see me ASAP!*

Pretzel glanced at the text as well.

Without saying a word, they darted out of the training center, scuttled down the various corridors, and reached the computer lab gasping for air. Angelica's heart pounded from the rush and with anticipation for the tech's news. The geeky computer seer and two other companions, Reina and Cookie, were already in the room.

Tassel spun in her chair at the sound of their footsteps in the doorway.

Angelica's eyes narrowed quickly on her and she stared with apprehension. "I got your text," she muttered feverishly.

"Hi, Angelica," the girl responded as she adjusted her glasses. "I've been monitoring your grandmother's condition for the last few days and there's been a status change."

She interrupted frantically. "Is she okay?"

Tassel swiveled on her chair and talked while looking at the screen. "By my interpretation, yes and no. Your grandmother has started to show early responses. According to the hospital's notes, the patient has commenced having localized responses to sound and touch." She paused for a moment to review the information. "Although she still remains unconscious, she has opened and closed her eyes."

"That's a relief." She sighed. "Anything else?"

The seer spun slowly and raised her gaze to focus on her. "Unfortunately, there's a morsel of unwanted news." Angelica's countenance became grave, which made her hurry her response. "It's nothing to be overly concerned about. Early responses mean the patient could come out of unconsciousness but at this stage, may wake to agitation and confusion—and especially with memory loss."

Angelica, her eyes glistening with tears, turned to Pretzel. "I have to go see her."

"Unpredictably, there's additional unpleasant news," Tassel added. "I managed to clear your name from the hospital records and the NYPD database, but the FBI has been surveilling this case very closely."

"Why?" she asked and paced the room nervously.

"For some time now, we've been aware of FBI activity in many of the cases involving homicides of young females and expecting mothers. While they have been inconclusive on the actual cause of these murders, there's been a sharp focus on these cases lately. Due to the relevance of your case, you have been on their watch list." The tech paused and pursed her lips for a moment. "I postulate...I mean, believe they're after you. Whether for protection or questioning, I'm not sure."

"Essentially, they could be at the hospital looking for me. Is that what you're hinting at?" she asked.

Tassel nodded with a frown. "But besides what I found..." She gazed at Angelica with her seer's eyes. "I don't have a good premonition about visiting the hospital. I foresee a choice that could have dire consequences."

"I don't care what happens to me. I have to see her." She turned and began to stride out of the room.

"Angelica, wait!" protested Pretzel.

She turned and without any hesitation said, "Pretzel, I'm thankful for everything you've done but please don't try to stop me this time."

"I wasn't," the girl responded. Slowly, she approached her with a calm look of solidarity. "I promised you I would take you to your grandmother and I'll keep my word. I'm going with you."

"Me too!" Reina exclaimed. "Whatever it takes, we will stick with you."

Tassel's countenance fell as she gazed at the blonde girl.

"Are you okay, Tassel?" asked Reina when she noticed the seer pale.

"Yeah. But remember, May can always help," she said gloomily.

"Danny, we've staked out the hospital for the last few days. I don't think she's gonna show," said Agent Anderson cynically. Her blonde hair was in a bun to stay cool and she leaned her head against the headrest while she glanced sideways at her partner seated on the driver's side. The ignition of the vehicle was on and the air conditioner ran full blast.

"Patience, Connie," Agent Ortega stated calmly and sipped his third cup of coffee.

"She could be dead. The police haven't heard a word from her, her boss hasn't seen her in days—which he claims is very unusual—and the only thing we have to show for it is a cracked cell phone." Anderson removed her sunglasses and looked challengingly at him.

"You could be right." He turned his head slowly toward her with a rueful grin. "But follow me on this thought." He took a sip of his coffee. "We've located many of the bodies of the homicides in prior cases so if she were dead, the chances are we would have found her body by now." He continued after another sip. "I feel we have been a step behind in all these cases. I know it has been very unorthodox, even for my taste, to sit idle these last few days, but in there"—he gestured toward the hospital—"is a potential key that can unravel this entire case, and I think waiting is the best option we have."

"What do you mean?" she asked.

"What if the reason the granddaughter hasn't visited is that she knows she's being followed, or perhaps she knows she's wanted by the police?" he responded, his gaze fixed intently on the hospital.

"But how would she know she's wanted by the police or even know her grandmother is in this hospital?" Ortega's head turned and he gave her a gleeful smirk. "Let me guess, you know something I don't?"

"Yesterday, I went inside to ask the nurses about Maria Santos' condition. They said she has begun to show some activity. I also inquired if they had heard any news of or seen the granddaughter." He tilted his head slightly toward her. "They simply gave me a blank stare and asked, 'What granddaughter?'"

"Wait!" his partner protested. "Didn't the NYPD give them notice?"

"Exactly," he confirmed. "When they checked the in-patient directory for that information, it was as if it was never recorded in the first place, which most likely means someone deleted it."

"But wouldn't the nurse know this information offhand?"

"You know how these hospitals work. There is a constant shift change of nurses, so they'll work on what's in the computer records. I suspect that either the hunter or the prey tampered with that information. If the former, then it could be a means to lure and have the prey to themselves. If the latter, it could explain how the granddaughter knows she is wanted and that her *abuelita* is in this hospital." He gazed at the building and gestured toward it again. "Either way, I'm hoping we are present to see either Little Red Riding Hood or the Big Bad Wolf visit Grandma, especially now that she's started to wake up."

"Nice analogy there but...um, Mr. Narrator, when did you plan to tell me about the tampering?" Her lips pursed in disapproval.

"Just now," he said with a grin. "I was waiting for you to hassle me about the waiting."

Agent Anderson snorted. "When are you retiring—"

Ortega stopped her in mid-sentence with a gesture of his hand. "Open the glove compartment and pull out the picture we have of Angelica Santos," he insisted while he stared intently across the street at the corner sidewalk entrance of the hospital. His partner gave him a queer look but followed his orders, opened the hinged door on the dashboard, and removed the photo.

"This had better be good for you to interrupt me," she remarked with a flustered expression. She handed him the photo.

Ortega made no comment but placed his coffee down and gazed at the photo before he shifted his focus in the direction of the entrance. "Look there—the girl in the middle wearing the denim jacket." He pointed with his index finger. "Take away the shades and picture her with black hair without the Yankees cap, and we have a resemblance to our photo."

His partner snatched the image from his hand and nodded when she saw it too.

"You're right, but who are those other two?" she asked with a frown.

"I don't know, but I think we found our little Red Riding Hood." He turned the ignition off and put his sunglasses on.

"Will we detain her now?" She donned her dark glasses as well.

"Let's wait a few minutes and follow her in. If she attempts to run from us, we'll at least have her cornered." His gaze was still locked on his target.

"Is this disguise necessary?" Angelica asked as she attempted to adjust her Yankees cap. "And it's too hot to wear this jacket."

"If Tassel is right, the feds could be looking for you and we can't take any chances," answered Pretzel. All three girls crossed the street toward the east corner sidewalk of the hospital. "We need to remain as inconspicuous as possible."

"If you ask me, the cap looks good on you," replied Reina. "The Bronx Bombers are my favorite too." She twirled her right index finger around the bang that hung over her brow and half-whispered to Angelica while she pointed secretly at Pretzel, "She's a Red Sox fan."

The other girl rolled her eyes and walked on. "Tassel gave me a good layout of the hospital before I left. She mentioned your grandmother is located on the third floor, room 350. She managed to remove your name from the directory but I wouldn't raise suspicion by going up as a guest. Our best option would be to sneak into her room unnoticed."

"Diversion time!" exclaimed Reina. "I can help with that."

Pretzel looked furtively at her surroundings and gave Angelica a piercing look. "The feds aren't the only thing we should be concerned about. If there's a hunt for you, this would be the best place for the Nephilim to search for you. They have spies everywhere and these spies would stoop to any level to grant them what they want."

Curiosity etched Angelica's face. "Why?"

"We have known individuals who have gone from rags to riches overnight, and this wasn't only because they were paid off." The girl glanced around as if to check if anyone was watching. In a softer tone, she continued. "Some Daimons are known to grant and teach individuals forbidden arts, sorceries, and even provide resources in the areas of technology, politics, and the stock market to name only a few." She stared pointedly at her. "These spies are one of the reasons we keep our identity hidden and don't easily trust anyone outside our circle."

"Got it," stated Angelica.

"There's one more thing to keep in mind. As emotional as this reunion could be, try to keep a keen sense of your surroundings. We are Daughters but we are also human. When we are in a very emotional state, our SPA can become overwhelmed and we can't sense each other or any approaching Nephilim."

She responded with a curt nod.

Pretzel glanced at the third girl. "Reina, I need you to remain downstairs the whole time. I'll go up with Angelica so call us if you see anything suspicious."

"Gucci," she confirmed.

The ladies reached the front entrance of the hospital and entered the main lobby through the automatic sliding glass doors.

"Okay. They're in," stated Agent Anderson. She grasped the door handle and pushed the door open.

"Let's wait a few more minutes," her partner suggested. "We know where she's going, which would be the best place to apprehend her."

She closed the door and tried to curb her impatience.

Both agents waited in silence. Suddenly, out of thin air on the west corner of the hospital, a tall, brawny figure appeared with long raven hair that fell below his broad shoulders. He wore a long, dusky trench coat that reached to the soles of his pitch-black boots and sleeves that covered the palms of his hands. His facial features were pale and menacing, and his lips moved without audible sound. Both fists were clenched as he strode grimly and menacingly toward the entrance of the hospital.

"What the hell!" exclaimed Anderson. "Where did he come from?"

"I don't know but when was the last time you saw someone wearing that type of overcoat in ninety-degree weather?" Ortega's countenance was grave.

The agents stared fixedly at the dour figure as he approached the entrance. He paused for a moment, looked toward the hospital, and proceeded on his course.

"I don't know about you, but I think we have just met the Big Bad Wolf." Agent Anderson opened and closed the car door swiftly and began her pursuit with her partner beside her.

"Like I said before, that stupid vending machine took my dollar," Reina yelled at the front desk receptionist. "I want to speak to a manager."

"Ma'am, for the third time, this is a hospital. Please keep your voice down," said one of the receptionists in exasperation. "If you don't lower your voice, I'll have to call security. As I mentioned before, the hospital doesn't own those machines. You'll need to call the number that appears on the upper right-hand corner."

"If you think security will return my dollar, by all means, call them—" The girl stopped her rant suddenly when she felt the strange presence. The blood drained from her face. "Keep the dollar. Where's your bathroom?" she asked abruptly.

The receptionists gave each other queer looks. "Turn right at this corner and it's toward the end of the hallway. On your left."

"Thank you," she said as she scuttled down the hall and retrieved her cell phone. "Damn!" she exclaimed when she realized she had no signal. To her right, she saw a stairwell and began to bounce up the stairs.

The wraith-like figure walked through the entrance of the hospital. Without taking notice of the receptionists, he strode to the left in the direction of the elevators.

"Sir!" one of the women called after him. "You need a visitor's pass to go upstairs," she insisted. He ignored her protest, his back toward them, and extended his left arm in their direction.

Suddenly, both receptionists were flung over their seats with astonishing force, hit their heads painfully on the wall, and sprawled hard on the marble floor. The folks seated in the waiting area watched the unusual event in horror. After a moment, they shrieked in panic and dashed to the exit.

The eerie man paused for a moment. He sniffed and changed his course to the opposite direction through the same corridor Reina went through.

The agents approached the entrance when a small crowd of people pushed out the front door with howls of horror. They pulled their Glocks quickly from their holsters.

Ortega yelled to a fleeing man, "FBI! What's going on in there?"

"I...I don't know. A man...uh, I think, just...he pushed them to the wall without touching them." The man faltered and shuddered with terror.

Unable to make any sense of what he had said, the agents rushed into the lobby of the hospital. They advanced to the reception desk, where both women lay with blood oozing from their heads.

Anderson checked for their pulses. "Dead!" She glanced at Ortega in alarm.

"Let's call it in," he said.

"Are you ready?" Pretzel asked as they stood in front of the door of Maria Santos' room.

Angelica sighed nervously. "I'm already an emotional wreck." Her eyes were tearful.

"I'm here with you and won't leave you alone unless you ask me to." She placed a comforting hand on her shoulder.

"I'll definitely need you." Her face flushed, she picked her nails for a moment before she drew a deep, fortifying breath.

She opened the door slowly. Her grandmother was surrounded by various monitors, medical devices, an IV stand, and a ventilator near her bed. She gaped at the frail, wizened lady who lay with a nasal canula in her nostrils and an IV needle protruding from her right arm. Resolute, she walked forward steadily and noticed the bruise marks around her neck. Tears coursed down her face and her heart beat faster with every step.

Her friend was a few paces behind her.

Removing the cap and shades, she approached and leaned over the bed. *"Bendicion, Abuela,"* she murmured. Angelica extended her hand and caressed her grandmother's smooth, gentle, yet seasoned face affectionately, not concerned about wiping away the tears that trickled down her cheeks. "I'm here, *Abuela.*" She smiled tenderly and touched her gently. "You can ask me any question. You can lecture me any way you want," she said and the words almost caught in her throat. "I only need you to wake up."

Maria Santos' hand twitched at the sound of her granddaughter's voice.

Angelica placed her head gently on her grandmother's chest, wrapped her arms around the frail body, and rested peacefully for a long moment.

Pretzel watched and wiped the tears away from her eyes. From the far distance, she heard a racket. She peered through the small window opening of the door and noticed medical personnel scrambling. *We needed a minor diversion, Reina.* She walked quietly out of the room.

Her friend didn't see or hear her leave.

Reina reached the top of the stairs, flushed and panting. "350, 350, 350," she murmured repeatedly. She opened the staircase door and scowled at a sign—300 to 325 were to the left and 326 to 350 in the opposite direction. "To the right, to the right," she chanted and stared at the cell phone again but still had no signal. Frustrated, she rushed down the long corridor and scanned each door number. The last was 335. "What?" She clutched her head in confusion.

When she turned the corner after doubling back, Pretzel walked up the hallway. "What are you doing up here?"

"A Nephilim is here!" Reina exclaimed and tried to catch her breath. "I couldn't call you. There's no signal throughout this stupid hospital."

Her friend yanked her cell phone out and noticed the no signal bar. As she registered the full import of what the other girl had said, she felt the menacing presence. "Crap!" she snapped. "I broke my own rule. I got so emotionally caught up here that I couldn't sense it." She stared gravely at Reina. "There's no other way out of this wing. We have to engage him right here."

"What about Angelica? Can she help?" the other girl asked and looked intently at her.

"She has barely begun training and is too emotional to fight." Pretzel stooped to draw the daggers from the sheaths around her ankles.

"But isn't she the Daimon Killer?"

"Who told you that?"

"Tassel." Reina began to bite her nails. "Please don't say I told you. She told me not to say anything."

She straightened and fixed her with a disapproving look. "Reina, that's not possible. Humans can't kill Daimons."

Angelica continued to rest her head on her grandmother's bosom, listened to every breath and heartbeat that emanated from Grandma's chest, and enjoyed the warmth and closeness she had taken for granted in the past.

"*Mi Angel,*" the old woman murmured in a hoarse, feeble voice. The girl turned slowly to look at her and a brilliant smile lit her features. "You look thin," Grandma said with a smirk.

"I know." She nodded and wiped the tears from her eyes.

"We have an idea where he is going," Agent Ortega stated. The agents scurried into an elevator and pressed the third-floor button.

They emerged with their handguns raised and proceeded very carefully along the corridor. He gestured to his partner to advance to the right. Each step was taken methodically and they scanned every inch and peered cautiously around each hallway corner they passed. The hospital wing looked utterly abandoned. They stopped and were alerted to distant footsteps, which made them hurry in the direction of the sound. Cautiously, they eased forward to look around the corner to where their man studied the sign on the wall for a second before he turned left.

"Why are you crying, *mi hija?*" Maria asked.

"I'm happy to see you, that's all," said Angelica. She clasped her grandmother's hand and kissed it very tenderly. "I missed you so much."

Maria Santos' eyes twinkled.

"*Abuela*, I want you to know that I love you and more than ever before, I'm thankful for all you've done for me."

"I love you too, *mi niña.*" Grandma's smile captured the rich bounty of her loving heart.

"I'm here for you and will never leave your side." Her gaze locked with the old lady's.

"Okay, *mi hija,*" she said weakly. "I feel so tired. You don't mind if I take a little nap?"

Angelica nodded and Maria closed her eyes.

"Witchcraft!" Pretzel called the creature's name, her tone almost a snarl. The Nephilim stood a few paces from the girls who waited with their daggers in hand, ready for engagement.

"Don't call me that," growled the assailant. "It's Pharmakeia." A menacing and maniacal expression defined his fiendish countenance. His beady eyes filled with vengeance and rage, while his lips moved rapidly and spoke an obscure language.

"What's he saying?" asked Reina.

"He's angry that we kicked his ass last time. That's what he's saying!" She stared gravely at their nemesis.

"Freeze, FBI!" a man commanded in a rasping voice behind Pharmakeia. The agents aimed their Glocks at their quarry.

Very slowly, the Nephilim turned and spoke. "I don't have time to play with you. Leave unless you want to die too."

"Are you threatening federal agents? Get down on the ground. Now!" yelled Anderson and took a step forward.

"Death it is," Pharmakeia uttered as he began to saunter toward the two agents.

"I said freeze!" Ortega ordered again loudly.

When they saw that he wouldn't stop, the agents opened fire and three shots struck the creature.

He flinched slightly but he continued forward.

"What the hell?" Ortega exclaimed in pure disbelief. They once again fired their weapons and landed bullets to his legs and head but produced only a minor wince. Shocked, they emptied the magazines in their guns, to no avail. "Impossible!" he exclaimed in bewilderment.

Suddenly and with uncanny speed, their target reached them and struck Agent Anderson viciously in her chest. She reeled from the powerful blow and fell heavily and blood spewed from her mouth. Pharmakeia swung, lunged forward, and lifted her partner by the throat with one hand. His powerful grasp began to suffocate him. "You are only human," the creature hissed.

Ortega dangled and gasped desperately for air.

Reina flung one of her blades and it pierced the arm that held the agent. The Nephilim's face twisted in anguish but he released the man, who flopped on the floor, ashen-faced as he labored to breathe.

Angelica heard the yelling and gunshots from inside the room. She turned her head to the door and realized her friend wasn't there. Suddenly restored to her senses, she felt the dark and menacing presence.

"Pretzel! Reina!" she blurted. She rushed away from her grandmother, yanked the door open, and gaped as her friends brandished their weapons at the Nephilim with a dagger protruding from his arm.

When her roommate saw her, she yelled, "Angelica! Don't move!"

Reina rushed toward the creature with her dagger ready. She threw the blade directly at Pharmakeia's head. He thrust his hand forward and stopped the whirling knife in mid-air. It flipped and was propelled toward Reina at unbelievable speed. The blade gouged her in her stomach and she fell with a groan.

"Reina!" screamed Pretzel as she bolted to her severely injured friend.

"Oh no!" Angelica exclaimed and covered her face with her hands.

Pharmakeia noticed her and latched his infernal gaze on his primary prey with deliberate purpose. He extracted the dagger from his arm and dropped it to clatter at his feet. He lunged viciously at her and leapt over the two girls on the floor.

Her awareness narrowed on the Nephilim. Terror filled her as she not only saw him launch toward her with unnatural speed but also sensed his malevolent resolve. She froze like a deer caught in headlights and merely waited for death to claim her while chills of panic rushed down her back.

In shock, she moved her hand reflexively to her chest and felt the quartz pendant Tassel had given her at the computer lab. Her panicked mind latched onto the words the seer had spoken and repeated them almost like an echo in her ear. *She said this small token will stop a great threat—the pendant!*

Her adversary had almost reached her when she closed her eyes instinctively, ripped the necklace from her neck, and bounded away as she flung it into the creature's face. The air filled with an explosion of powdered dust that made the Nephilim stagger to his knees.

He clutched his face with his hand and shuddered as if he'd been sprayed with acid.

Angelica, who stared in shock, watched as he howled in terrible pain and shook his head in agony.

Pretzel's gaze narrowed on the disabled enemy and her countenance was vengeful. She scrambled to her feet and launched into a forceful round-kick that connected powerfully with his face. She followed it up with a brutal knee kick to his jaw and pummeled his face savagely with her fists, which were soon sticky and stained with his blood.

The Nephilim's face was covered in crimson. She caught him by his hair and, with one of her daggers in her hand, muttered, "Die, you piece of filth!" With a vicious thrust, she drove the blade into his skull and let his lifeless body fall heavily.

She looked at Angelica. "Are you okay?"

Her eyes wide with shock, she simply nodded repeatedly.

The girl ran to Reina, whose blood now covered her Mello Kitty tee-shirt and the floor around her. Her face was pale and life already seemed to fade from her eyes. Pretzel fell to her knees and clutched the girl against her chest. "Reina—Reina,can you hear me?" She tapped her face tenderly. "We need to find a doctor."

The blonde girl looked at her with half-opened eyes and displayed her dimples with a weak smile. "No. Tassel said May can always help. Take me to May." Her eyes began to roll back.

"Stay with me, Reina. You hear me?" Pretzel, her expression vulnerable, looked at the other girl. "She's breathing very slowly. We need to get her to May as soon as possible."

Angelica stared in bewilderment before she glanced at her grandmother's room. Her heart settled on not leaving her sight and she returned her focus to her friend. "I...uh...I—" she stuttered.

Pretzel interrupted her impatiently. "Angelica, I can't do this without you. The only way I can get her to May is with your help. The situation is dire. Reina's life depends on it."

The word "dire" penetrated her confusion and her thoughts were yanked to Tassel's earlier words. *A choice that could have dire consequences.* She turned to her grandmother's room. "I'll be back, *Abuela.*" Quickly, she pushed to her feet, removed her jacket, and ran toward Pretzel. "Let's put this around her wound to stop the bleeding."

The girls lifted their friend, slung her arms around their shoulders, and held her firmly as they turned to hurry through the corridor.

"Who the hell are you people?" the perplexed Ortega asked. He was still on the floor and rubbed his neck while he gestured to the dead Nephilim with his free hand. "And what in the world was that?"

"I'm sorry, sir, but we are in a hurry right now," said Angelica as she adjusted Reina's weight slightly and tightened her hold.

The agent pushed shakily to his feet. "Wait! You are Angelica Santos, right?"

She stopped and turned slightly toward him.

"Look, I don't know what the hell is going on around here, but this crap isn't normal." He fumbled in his jacket pocket, pulled a card out, and proffered it to her. "Call me."

She turned without taking it and as she started to walk away, he said, "I know about your grandmother. And...uh, about your mother, Eva Santos."

Startled, she stopped, looked at the agent, and snatched his card.

"Angelica, we have to hurry," Pretzel insisted anxiously. "Let's continue down this hallway. The service elevators are in this direction. It'll lead downstairs to a backdoor exit we can use to leave unnoticed." They increased their pace down the corridor. "I'll call Gypsy once we are outside to pick us up."

Reina raised her head wearily. She turned to glance at each one in turn. "I love you, guys," she said feebly.

PART III

NOT AN ORDINARY ANGEL

SECOND TRIMESTER

Twenty-Two Years Earlier

Leonard stood alone in his luxurious apartment. His countenance was grave and stern. He reached into the top drawer of his mahogany desk and retrieved a small, clear flask but frowned when he realized it was empty. With a small shrug, he curled the fingers of his other hand as if to grasp something and suddenly, a dark, glowing ball materialized in his palm. He squeezed it until his hand closed into a fist and a silvery liquid poured from it into the flask.

"The essence of the serpent," he murmured as he raised it to the setting sun. He studied it in anticipation.

"Your kingdom will come, your will be done, on earth as it is in Hell," he whispered devilishly.

The door to the apartment opened behind him. Swiftly, he placed the flask in his pocket.

"You called for me, my lord," a woman said timidly.

With movements faster than her eyes could register, Leonard suddenly stood before the frightened woman and snaked his hand out to catch hold of her. "You failed me, Duplicity. You predicted that she would bear me a child with the might to bring down Angels." He held her by the throat and her feet dangled while the color fled from her face.

She clutched his hands with desperate grunts and her eyes filled with terror.

"Now she has disappeared carrying a female child, even after I ordered you to keep a close eye on her." He flung her mercilessly to the floor.

Duplicity's body landed with a thud and she grasped her neck in relief. "I'm... I'm...sorry, so sorry," she stuttered, her voice rasping from the effort. She lay sprawled with her gaze fixed on the glistening marble titles in an attempt to avoid eye contact. "I foresaw..." She paused and attempted to catch her breath. "I mean...I thought she was the one, my lord." Shivering in fear, she scrambled into a prostrate position with her hands before her and chin scraping the floor.

"But she wasn't!" he snapped, his face contorted in fury. "You are a sorry excuse for a medium." He glared spitefully at her.

"My apologies, my lord." Her beseeching tone was almost a whine. She remained in her abject position, full of terror and her gaze fixed on the floor.

"I've had enough of the empty apologies!" He drew a deep breath, strode slowly toward her, and stepped deliberately on her hand with his Oxford shoe.

A look of intense pain crossed her features.

He squatted and with his finger, lifted her head to meet his eyes. "So this is what you will do to make up for your mistake. You'll search high and low, far and wide, and even to the pits of Tartarus if you have to, and when you find her..." He paused and glared menacingly at her. "You will take care of the problem." His tone was stern and unyielding.

Leonard slipped his hand into his Italian suit and extracted a small translucent vial containing a juniper-green liquid. He let it drop beside the woman and lifted his foot off her hand.

With a gasp of agony, she raised her hand, grasped it tightly for a moment, then rubbed and shook it for relief. She bit her lip in pain.

"If I were you, I would worry more about the vial than your hand," he said without a single trace of concern. She snatched the vial up and placed it in her pocket. He walked to his walnut drinks cabinet and poured himself a glass of his fine whiskey.

"But my lord..." Her voice was full of hesitation. "She has refused to abort the baby many times. Why would she take this now?" Her heart pounded in her chest as she waited for his response.

With his back toward her, he replied, "It seems to me you are more gifted as a beguiler than a seer. You have even managed to deceive me." He took a sip from his glass, turned, and leaned on the cabinet to glare at her. "Have you played the double agent?" he demanded.

"You know I'm no longer one of them." Her voice quavered. She gave him a fleeting look but kept her gaze on the marble floor. "I've sworn my allegiance to you," she said and shuddered.

He approached her with his drink in hand and said,

"And what benefit has this allegiance brought me? I should have killed you the moment you betrayed them." He stood over Duplicity with a condescending sneer and her face reflected in his shimmering shoes. "You fooled her once so you can fool her again. If you don't..."

Leonard paused and tilted the drink over her head. "Don't bother to stay alive. Slit your own throat. It's as close to an act of mercy as you would ever receive from me." When the whiskey was about to spill from the glass, he stopped and said, "I almost made a mistake there. This drink is worth more than you." He took the last gulp and walked to the bar to thump his glass on the surface.

"Now get the hell out and find her!" he ordered.

"Yes, sir, yes..." she stuttered as she scrambled to her feet and dashed out the door.

"Peccable," he called. A brawny, jet-black-eyed Nephilim with a formidable appearance stepped through the door.

He hurried to him, knelt on one knee, and answered, "Yes, my lord," his dark gaze on the floor.

"I have important duties to attend to and will need you to handle this mishap." Leonard turned and stood with his back toward him to stare out through the floor-to-ceiling window of his penthouse that overlooked downtown Pittsburgh. The evening sun was setting and glistened on his strangely handsome, chiseled features.

"As you wish, my lord," his minion assented quickly.

For a fleeting moment, a frown creased his brow. "Peccable, the child must be killed by any means necessary and I don't trust that the traitorous witch is up to the task," he stated bluntly. "Gather the others and issue a hunt for the mother. If you find her, we can at least hold her until she has given birth to the child and then kill it. Perhaps she can still be convinced to provide me with a worthy offspring."

"My lord…" His beady eyes darted a hasty glance at his master. "You know it is difficult for us to get her scent." He gulped nervously and perspiration ran down his forehead.

"I'm surrounded by incompetent idiots!" For a moment, Leonard's appearance became translucent. He glimmered darkly and he was now two feet taller than before. His countenance mutated to a hideous hairless bat-like form with glistening crimson eyes that flickered sinisterly. The room was shrouded with darkness and dread and even the Nephilim kept his eyes shut to avoid gazing at the ghastly and frightful features. Gradually, he transfigured to the young and beautiful chiseled form with flowing ebony locks.

He spun from the window and shook his head in displeasure. "She's a naive and frightened girl who probably wants to go back to Mommy and Daddy." He placed one hand behind his back, leaned forward, and glowered at him. "Think, Peccable, think," he snarked while he tapped his index finger repeatedly against the Nephilim's temple. "You don't need supernatural abilities to search for someone." Enraged, he paced the expansive penthouse living room.

"Yes, your eminence, you are correct. My apologies. I will launch the hunt," Peccable stammered.

"And if by any chance our traitor finds her and gets the job done before you do, feel free to dispose of her. She has embarrassed me enough." Leonard strode to the door to leave. "One more thing," he said as he grasped the door handle. "Arrange for a cleanup crew. I'm done with this place. Leave no trace that I was ever here."

"Yes, my lord—" Leonard slammed the door before Peccable was finished.

The diner's neon sign twinkled intermittently from *Hardy's Cuisine* to *Hard Cuisine*, about every thirty seconds or so. The dilapidated rustic building was located on a Lancaster half-gravel and half-dirt road miles away from homes and other businesses. The stained, greasy, and unwashed windows made it impossible to peek inside although at this time of day, the only customers were truckers looking for a late-night meal.

From the parched grassy parking lot, the parked 1966 pony car headlights made the windows look extra pale and dull.

"You sure this is the place?" asked Jewels. She cut the headlights but left the engine running. "This dingy-looking spot isn't a place to find a young pregnant girl. It's in the middle of nowhere and by the looks of it, I'm very sure it must be violating a few health codes."

"Sparrow has never steered us wrong. Her predictions have always been spot-on." Her partner clicked the vehicle's interior light and extracted a folded paper from her back pocket to study it intently. "Hardy's Cuisine...gravel road...dirty windows...a young pregnant girl with black hair..." Her voice was little more than a murmur as she read the contents of Sparrow's prediction. "It fits the description on her note." She glanced toward the diner and then at her companion. "The girl may have hitchhiked with a truck driver."

"All right. Shall we go in?" Jewels cut the engine, placed the keys in her pocket, and removed the quartz blade from the sheath of her belt.

"Jewels, I wouldn't raise attention by walking in with blades. If the girl is inside, she may feel threatened by us." She removed the sheath strapped to her left arm and began to fasten it to her ankle. "Let's be as inconspicuous as possible and keep ourselves mindful of our surroundings."

"Good point." The other woman began to copy her partner. "Let's go in and have ourselves some hardy cuisine," she joked.

The two ladies strode casually into the rundown diner and scanned it nonchalantly for a young pregnant girl with jet-black hair and hazel-brown eyes. They walked lightly on the creaking wooden floor and chose seats on ripped upholstered stools at the diner counter, which squealed every time they swiveled. Other than two truck drivers a few seats away, there seemed to be no one else.

"What can I get you, ladies?" asked the thickset, gray-haired waitress with nicotine-stained teeth.

"Only two coffees with cream for now," responded Jewels.

"Two coffees with cream," echoed the woman in her gruff voice.

Jewels turned to her partner. "I don't see her and given

the size of this place, it doesn't seem to have a bathroom to check for her."

After a few minutes, the waitress returned with the two coffees in ceramic mugs that seemed to have been white at some point, although they now resembled the color of the woman's teeth.

"Excuse me, ma'am, but is there a bathroom?" she asked.

"It's toward the side of the diner, but you can't get in from here. You'll need to head outside and turn right. If you reach the telephone booth, you went too far." The waitress pulled two laminated sheets of paper, blemished all over, from under the counter and placed the menus in front of them. "Call me when you're ready to order." She drew a box of cigarettes from her apron and tapped it on her palm a few times. "I'll be outside taking a smoke break."

"Thank you," muttered Jewels as the waitress headed outside. "Why don't you check the bathroom and see if she's there? I'll remain here and see if she walks through the door."

"Sounds like a plan," her partner responded. Hastily, she walked outside, passed the smoking waitress, and rounded the corner in the direction of the bathroom.

Initially, on the side of the diner, the only source of light was the cloud-patched, frost-colored moon and the yellowish hue of on-off flickering fireflies in the distance. Eventually, the path became dimly lit by an incandescent light bulb that hung over the bathroom door, which was crowded with all kinds of flying insects wanting a piece of the spotlight.

The silence of her stride was only interrupted by chirping crickets and the compression of the loosely scattered gravel beneath her footsteps. She opened the creaking door but heard a faint sob and sniffle toward the back of the building. Curious, she tilted her head and could see part of the edge of the telephone booth and someone using it. She eased forward cautiously to have a better look.

———

"I got it, Papi. Love you," she heard a woman say and shortly after, the click of a headset. Immediately, the girl she was searching for appeared around the corner, wiping tears from her eyes.

"Eva Santos?" she asked quietly.

Alarmed at the sound of her name, the woman responded in a tight voice with no hesitation. "Are you one of his goons, too?" Her eyes were filled with terror. "Tell him I won't go back. I already called the police and I'm going home."

"You got me wrong. My name is Charlotte. This is hard to explain but I've been looking for you. I know who you're running away from." She took a step forward, which made her features visible to Eva. "Leonard Archie, correct?"

The young woman stared in bewilderment and placed her hand protectively over her womb. "What do you want?"

"I'm here with a friend to help you," Charlotte responded.

"Help me?" she asked with a frown. "Are you the police?"

"Not quite, but we know a lot about your boyfriend.

He's a very dangerous man and we have intel that he's out hunting...I mean, searching for you." Eva glanced apprehensively at her. "Look, let's go inside. I'll get you something to eat and explain it further."

Suddenly, from around the corner, a perturbed-looking Jewels headed straight toward Charlotte. In a quivering voice, she announced, "Mist, we have to go. A Nephilim is here!" The young Mist spun to Jewels and instantly sensed the presence.

"Wait, I thought your name was Charlotte?" asked Eva.

"Mist is my Memento—my nickname." she stammered, her expression troubled. "Eva, we need to leave right now. Your boyfriend has sent some terrible people after you."

As she was explaining, the smoking waitress uttered a scream followed by a grunt, and an eerie silence followed.

"Oh, my God!" exclaimed the runaway and clasped her hands over her belly. "What was that?"

"If my guess is right, the old waitress is dead," Mist told her. "We need to get out of here fast." The two women both drew their blades. "Let's go toward the back and around the building to the car." All three sprinted and Eva held her womb protectively. As they reached the vehicle, a tall, stoop-shouldered, ominous figure bounded into their view. Frightened, the fugitive screamed in horror.

The two husky-looking truck drivers, along with the cook who held a sawn-off shotgun, stepped out of the diner. One of the drivers yelled, "Hey, you punk! Why don't you pick on someone your own size?" He commenced rolling the sleeves on his red plaid shirt as he approached the Nephilim with a challenging expression.

The cook checked the bloody waitress and seconds

later, he bellowed, "That jackass killed Teresa. He killed Teresa." He glowered at the attacker with a vengeful expression and pumped his shotgun.

"Mist, we need to get in the car and get out of here as soon as possible." Jewels fumbled for the keys but dropped them in her desperate attempt to unlock the door.

Her partner shook her head. "Jewels, we need to help those folks. He'll kill them."

"Kill them?" Eva asked in shock.

"We aren't supposed to engage in civilian affairs, and what about her?" asked Jewels and ignored Eva's question.

"This isn't their fight, and we can put her in the back seat. She'll be safe there."

"You're always so pushy. All right...let's get her in the back seat."

The Nephilim spun to the three men with a sinister glare. The trucker with the plaid shirt lunged forward and swung at his face. A loud crack emanated from the man's arm. "Damn!" he cried in agony and clutched his wrist. "His face must be made of steel."

With a snarl of displeasure, the creature picked him up by the shirt with one hand and pummeled his face with the other. His neck broke and his attacker dropped his lifeless body.

Angry, the other trucker prepared to attack and exclaimed, "You son of—" His adversary drove his fist ferociously into the man's chest and he catapulted away, shattered the diner's window, and landed heavily to convulse on the grimy tiles with white foam spewing from his mouth.

"Eat lead, you stinking piece of crap!" shrieked the

cook. He opened fire once, pumped, and fired again at the attacker. The Nephilim flinched and dropped to sprawl senselessly in the dirt.

"He's dead," uttered Eva from within the vehicle.

"He's not dead," Mist corrected her and stared pointedly at the Nephilim. "He's only recovering from a bad rash." She and her partner slammed and locked the car doors, leaving the pregnant girl alone in the vehicle.

The cook reloaded his gun and stood over the Nephilim with the weapon aimed at what seemed like a lifeless face.

Unexpectedly, the creature opened his eyes.

A panicked expression appeared on the cook's round face. "What the hell?" He started to pump the shotgun but the Nephilim snatched it and a hard kick to his abdomen made the cook stagger and flail to regain his balance before he fell heavily. The assailant stood quickly, snapped the gun in two, and approached the groaning man. With calm deliberation, he kicked his face hard enough to crush his skull.

Eva panicked in the car. *I'm going to die. I need to get out.* She attempted to open the locked car doors but in her hysteria, couldn't figure out how.

Mist fixed her gaze on the assailant and commented, "He looks a little short for a Nephilim."

"And you're a little tall for a Daughter," her partner retorted.

"Touché, but at least I'm prettier. Jewels, you approach from the left and I'll go right." Her countenance was angry.

The enemy turned and locked his fierce, dark eyes on his opponents. He charged toward Mist with incredible speed and with no hesitation, she did the same. Before they

clashed, she slid instinctively between his legs on bent knees, arched her back, and swept her dagger right and left to lacerate his legs. He clenched his jaw in pain and blood dripped profusely as he spun in fury and swung a vicious kick at her face but missed. She sent him reeling with a foot sweep and backpedaled while he recovered slowly and stood.

She yelled, "Jewels!" Without another word, her partner instinctively knew what to do.

Mist dropped to one knee and Jewels raced forward, planted one foot on her partner's back, and launched herself to deliver a flying sidekick to the Nephilim's face. He fell, dazed, but found his feet a moment later and hammered a one-two punch at her but missed each one. With every swing, she slashed his arms with her blade. Blood bubbled from his wounds and he grimaced. She powered several forceful double kicks to his rib cage, which made him spew crimson saliva from his mouth.

"Jewels!" Mist shouted. She reached out with her senses and instinctively leapt out of the way as with a targeted throw, her partner punctured the Nephilim's head with her blade. He dropped to his knees and collapsed on his face.

Eva watched in astonishment from the car.

The two Daughters checked the other victims and when they confirmed that they were all dead, rushed to the vehicle.

Once they were inside, Eva asked, "Who are you people and what the hell was that?" She gestured with a finger toward the fallen Nephilim, her eyebrows pulled together in bewilderment.

"It's a long story," answered Mist as she strapped her

seatbelt on and Jewels brought the Mustang's engine to a roar. "It'll take some time but we can tell you about it while on the road."

19

THIRD TRIMESTER

It had been five months since Eva Santos had come under the care and protection of the Lancaster Daughters of the Watchers, but as far as she knew, it was the Saint Teresa Young Women's Retreat Center of Lancaster. The facility was at an isolated and remote location. The building that housed many of the Daughters of South-Central Pennsylvania had a ten-foot perimeter wall fortified by quartz stone. It was a heavily secured center that made it almost impervious to attack.

Eva kept company with many of the girls her age and other than missing her parents deeply, she felt at peace there. As instructed by the Daughters and to keep her parents safe, she made no attempt to reach them, at least not until she gave birth. She had seen with her own eyes what Leonard Archie could do and how evil he could be. Nonetheless, the Daughters thought it unwise to disclose his true nature to her. She was only informed that he was a high-powered businessman with resources in government agencies, surveillance, and telephone companies, and had the means to employ individuals with extraordinary abilities.

Living with the Daughters, she did not have the luxurious lifestyle she had with Leonard, but these last few months were the safest she had felt in a very long time. At the compound, she was given quarters consisting of a small bathroom, a bed, and other essentials. In comparison to the hostile environment she had been in before, this was more than enough.

"How are you today?" asked Mist, who walked into the room with a food tray for Eva. She placed it on the table, pulled one of the chairs closer, and sat near her.

"This little person is a jumpy one," Eva said and stopped writing in her pregnancy journal. "She had me up all last night. I could barely sleep." A smile settled on her face as she gazed at the other woman. Eva sat on her bed, leaned her back against the wall, and let her long hair drop over her shoulders.

"I see that you write a lot in that journal."

"It's for her." She placed her hand over her womb. "Once she's old enough, I'll give it to her."

"Have you thought of a name?"

"I thought of a few but I'll announce it once the baby is born and my parents are present." Her face lit up at the thought of seeing them soon, but she noticed her visitor had a melancholy demeanor. "They can still come over once the baby is born, correct?"

The woman lowered her head. She walked closer and sat next to her on the bed.

"What's wrong, Charlotte? I thought you said that after the birth it would be safe enough for my parents to come."

"Well…uh, I'm afraid I don't have good news, Eva." Mist exhaled a deep, sharp sigh. "We have received news that your father was battling cancer for the last few months and…um, he passed away last night." Tears welled in Mist's eyes. "I'm so sorry, Eva."

The blood drained from her face and her eyes pooled with tears at the grim news. Shaking her head, she shouted in lament, "No, no, no… Oh, my God, Charlotte. It's not true… He's not dead, he's not!"

Speechless, Mist could only embrace her as Eva buried her face in her chest. For an extended period, she wept and wailed loudly and the other woman simply held her.

After several hours, Eva fell asleep, although she whimpered every so often. The other woman left the room silently and went to meet Jewels in the compound's garden.

She strode along the winding path through the lush lawns of the garden surrounded by an immense variety of flowers, plants, and a koi pond in the center. The sun's rays partially brushed her features, hampered by the garden trees that swayed lazily in the late afternoon breeze. Her eyes glittered with the vibrant, magnificent colors from flower beds that burgeoned with life.

Jewels sat on one of the wooden benches and she hurried to her.

The other woman caught sight of her from a distance and waved a greeting. "How's she holding up?" she asked when she reached her.

"Not good." She shook her head. "She hasn't stopped crying but she's resting now." Mist slouched on the bench, rested her head against the planks, and closed her eyes.

"And how are you holding up? You look exhausted."

Jewels was concerned at seeing her friend's weary countenance.

"I'll be fine but I feel for Eva. She seems like a sweet girl who genuinely cares for her parents, which makes me wonder how she got caught up in this mess in the first place." She opened her eyes and tilted her head toward her companion.

"It beats me." Jewels pressed her lips together. "We only know these scenarios repeat themselves way too often."

Mist straightened on the bench. "Eva kept insisting she wanted to see her mother," she said with a thoughtful expression.

"What did you tell her? You know Sparrow had a feeling that if she leaves this place before giving birth, she could die."

"I know... I know." She gazed thoughtfully at Jewels. "She only said if she leaves, so I wonder what if I went with her to see her mother?"

Her companion considered this for a moment and shook her head. "I don't think it's worth the risk. She's safe and sound here and only a few days away from giving birth. Besides, the whole story about bringing her parents was never going to happen. You know how the council voted."

A line pinched between Mist's brows as she recalled the decision that had been taken. She sighed and muttered, "You're probably right, which is why I managed to convince her otherwise. Now that her dad is dead, I promised Eva I'd personally bring her mom here once the baby was born, even if I have to go against the council." She paused for a moment and wrestled with a nagging concern.

"Do you think we are doing right by not telling her the whole truth and covering so much up?"

"Mist, you understand how crazy this sounds, even to us. Imagine how much more so to a normal person—and a pregnant one. Remember, this isn't only for her safety but for ours as well. We need to take every precaution."

"I get it," she said although she wasn't entirely convinced.

A momentary silence hung between them and her gaze locked on a honeybee that moved from one purple coneflower to another.

Jewels caught her gaze. "Are you still considering the move to the Big City?"

Mist pursed her lips and drew a deep breath. "Hmm...I don't know yet. I'm at a crossroads. I love it here. I've done so much already and enjoy the company." She stared at her and smiled. "But I hear the DW group in New York City needs help. They've seen an increase of Nephilim in the Tri-State area. There have been more hunts and more girls are showing up."

"And it's a better way to move up the ranks," her companion pointed out.

"I'm not too keen on seeking positions or titles. I care more about helping and making a difference." She turned to her with a grave expression. "But the NYC DW group are facing a new level of threat our generation hasn't seen before."

"What's that?" asked Jewels curiously.

"There has been betrayal and treason within the group."

The other woman frowned. "Betrayal as in work for the Daimons? Is that even possible?"

"It would seem so. I've spoken to one of the group's team leaders, Joan, and she calls the betrayers mediums or priestesses, I think."

"Is there a difference?"

"I don't know. I need to read the texts on that, but she said one of the girls in her team became one. She was called Faith. According to Joan, she was seduced by a Daimon and now goes by the name Duplicity."

"That's ironic." The woman shook her head.

"What do you mean?"

Jewels responded, "She went from being trusted to being deceitful."

Mist nodded. "How do you face a betrayer who was once part of you—or even worse, your friend?" Her gloomy gaze swept the garden. "How sad it is that we are now fighting among ourselves."

Her companion placed her hand over hers. "You never have to worry about this friend."

She turned to her and smiled. "Thanks." She drew a deep breath and continued, "I do have a few days before I have to make a decision. When the time comes, you'll be the first to know."

"Please do 'cause I like your room and I'm calling dibs if you decide to leave," she said and laughed.

"Wow! And here I thought you were my best friend."

"In all seriousness, I'll miss you. I can't imagine this place without you—honestly, you mean so much to this group and to me. I wouldn't have made it this far without your support."

Mist's eyes watered. "You're not making this easy for me, are you?"

"Is it working?" Jewels asked with a big grin on her face.

"It's working all right." She wiped her eyes with her hand. "All right. Enough of the mushy stuff." Her stomach growled.

"What was that?" Asked Jewels.

"I've been with Eva the entire day and I haven't had the chance to get anything to eat."

"Silver cooked dinner today." Jewels' face was blank.

"Ugh…" Mist's mouth twisted. "You want to go out and get something to eat?"

Her companion nodded. "I see now why you want to leave."

Both girls rose from the bench and walked toward the car.

"Mist, wake up!" Jewels exclaimed shrilly and shook her aggressively.

"Uhh… What's going on?" She lay in her bed and rubbed her eyes before she tilted her head toward the alarm clock—five forty-seven am. "This had better be important."

"Eva is gone. She wasn't in the room when one of the other girls went to check on her."

"What?" Her eyes were wide open now. "Sunny was supposed to keep an eye on her. What happened?"

"She fell asleep and didn't notice her leave. We found this note in her room. It was addressed to you."

Mist snatched the missive Jewels held in her hand. She studied the contents intently.

Dear Charlotte,

I'm so sorry for leaving without saying anything. Thank you for all you have done and for taking care of me and my baby.

I hope you understand, but I can't stay here and let my mother face this alone. I'm the only family she has left.

I wish you the best.

Eva

P.S. I'll give you a call as soon as I can to let you know I'm okay.

She stared at the note, utterly bewildered, then turned to the other woman and said, "We have to find her. Do we have an idea when she left?"

Jewels shook her head. "No, but even if we did, where do we search for her?"

Mist looked at the floor in thought. "She told me once that she and her dad made a trip to Lancaster using the rail system." Her disturbed gaze settled on her companion again. "What's the first train to leave the Lancaster station to Philadelphia?"

The woman shrugged and said, "I've no idea but we can ask Glacial. She's become a guru with all that Internet stuff."

"Go ahead and check that. I'll get ready. Tell Glacial that if Eva calls the compound to page me nine-one-one."

Jewels nodded and left the room.

"Come on, Mom. Pick up the phone." It was the third attempt for Eva. She had called her mother several times but with no success. Now, she waited patiently at the

Lancaster Train station. The next train to Philadelphia was scheduled to leave in two hours. She wondered apprehensively if she should call Charlotte and let her know she was okay but was concerned that she would be pressured to return. After she thought about it for several minutes, she dropped a quarter into the telephone and dialed the compound's number.

"This is the Saint Teresa Young Women's Retreat Center. How can I help you?" asked the soft voice over the line.

"Can I speak to Charlotte, please?"

"Who's calling?"

"This is Eva Santos."

The woman became frantic. "Eva! This is Anabel. Thank God you're okay." She breathed sharply over the line. "Eva, where are you? Are you okay?"

A deep frown crossed her face. "I'm fine. Can I speak to Charlotte, please?"

"She's not here. I mean, she went to look for you. Where are you?" Anabel, aka Glacial, demanded insistently.

"Look. Tell her I'm fine and not to worry about me. I'll give her a call once I'm back home at my mother's."

"Eva, you are not safe. Where—" She hung up before Anabel could finish.

The baby began to kick in the womb. "You're hungry too, aren't you?" Eva said as she placed her hand softly over her belly. "Let's get you something to eat." She walked to a small café located within the station, ordered herself something to eat, and waited for her train.

When she finished her meal, she retrieved a small mirror from her pocket and winced at her pale face and disheveled hair. "I can't look ugly for *Abuela*," she said to her unborn child. She combed her hair quickly and applied blush, eyeshadow, eyeliner, and red lipstick. "And now we wait."

After almost an hour at the café, she was startled and surprised to hear a familiar voice.

"Hi, Eva."

"Licity!" Eva stared wide-eyed.

"I know I'm the last person you want to see, but please hear me out."

"Correct. You're the last person I want to see and talk to." She rose from her seat and started to walk away.

"Eva, I know about your dad and I got a chance to speak to your mom."

She stopped and turned to the woman. "You spoke to my mom? When?"

"I spoke to her yesterday," she replied, her tone very melancholy. "My deepest condolences on the passing of your father."

Tears started to run down Eva's cheeks. As Licity went to embrace her, she exclaimed, "Don't touch me, Licity!" She took a seat at one of the café's tables. "You and Leo have made my life a living hell."

The girl sat across from her and spoke tenderly. "I'm sorry if things didn't pan out the way you wanted them to, but rest assured I had the best intentions."

"I'm sure you did." Her gaze alternated between the commuters and her companion. "How did you know I was here, anyway? No, no, let me guess. Leo and his unlimited resources." She stopped for a moment and turned to the woman. "Knowing Leo, he has spies in the phone company."

"Yes, I'll admit that Leo sent me." Licity shifted in her seat as if this made it easier to speak her thoughts. "But I didn't come here to force you to go back to him. I came here to tell you the truth about Leo."

As she talked, the baby in Eva's womb gave a hard kick. She clenched her jaw and placed her hand on her belly. The woman started to ask if she was okay but she waved her off. "I don't need your pity now and yes, I was informed about his dealings and the freaks he has employed."

The woman's eyeballs seemed to bulge. "Who have you been speaking to?"

"Why do you care?" she snapped.

Her face twitched. "Because if it's the people I suspect, then you're in terrible danger." Eva frowned. "I should have said this to you a long time ago, but under these circumstances, I think now is as good as any to tell you the truth about Leo and me." She drew a sharp breath. "I wasn't raised in an orphanage in the city but by a group of women known as the Daughters of the Watchers. I went to live with them when I was only five after my mother died. She was killed by one of the freaks those women told you about. They're called Nephilim and are half-human and half-angel."

"Stop the bullcrap, Licity." Her nostrils flared and she started to stand.

"Wait!" the woman exclaimed as she pulled some photos from her pocket. "I know this all sounds crazy but I have proof here." She waved the images at her. "These women who raised me were the ones who taught me about the

Nephilim, about the Fallen Angels, and about who I was." Eva stared intently at her. "I too am a crossbreed of human and angel, and those women trained me from childhood on how to kill these Nephilim."

Her face contorted in anger and she rose abruptly from her seat to leave when suddenly, Licity threw the photos on the table. Her eyes widened, her breath became shallow, and her face paled as she stared at pictures of Leo—photos of the handsome, chiseled face and turquoise eyes and then shifting into a hideous-looking monster whose features were too formidable to describe. Losing her balance, she slumped into her seat, ashen-faced.

A beguiling expression crept over the other woman's face. "You see, those women you talked to don't care about you. They only care about the child you're carrying. They want to use your child as a weapon. I've come to understand who they truly are—liars and deceivers. Once I learned about their true intentions, I ran away from them."

Eva shuddered in her seat while tears coursed down her cheeks.

"I later met Leo, clueless as to who he was back then, and he became a good friend. But Eva..." She placed her hand over her chest and shook her head. "I had no idea who he was until recently. I took these photos to show you and warn you about him and the child you're carrying."

Licity withdrew the small translucent vial with the strange-looking liquid from her pocket. She placed it carefully on the table. "Eva, I'm sorry to say that the baby isn't and won't be normal. That child you're carrying belongs to that hideous creature you saw in that photo." She gestured with her hand toward the vial. "This is a special potion that'll protect you from that baby."

She stared at it apprehensively and wondered if what the woman had said was true. Sweat slicked her forehead as she swallowed hard in uncertainty.

"Eva!" shouted a voice from within the crowds of commuters. She turned her head swiftly. It was Mist and Jewels.

As they approached, she shrilled, "Get away from me." She rose quickly from her seat.

The two women sensed Licity's presence, although it felt stranger than the other usual Daughters. They fixed their attention on her and then looked at Eva.

In a soft, gentle voice, Mist said, "Eva, we are here to help you."

"Is it true?" she exclaimed. "That Leonard Archie is some devil? That you're not a women's retreat center but some organization of mongrels?" Eva's eyes were ablaze with anger and tears. "Don't lie to me. I know what I saw that night you came for me and that wasn't normal."

Mist gestured with her hands and said, "Eva, calm down. I can explain everything."

"So it's true." She wiped her tears with her hand. "You don't care about me. You only want my...my demon baby. Were you ever truly going to bring my parents to see me?" She snatched the vial on the table.

Jewels pointed at Licity. "Eva, I don't know what she has told you but what you have in your hands can kill you."

On the platform, the throng of commuters scuffled and horrific screams followed as bodies were flung in every direction. Mist and Jewels turned as a Nephilim pushed through the crowds. His face was contorted into a vicious mask and he pummeled people with his fist to clear a path. From the sheath of his belt, he drew a steel blade and flung it viciously toward the girls. Mist and Jewels leapt from the advancing blade but it struck Licity's chest. She collapsed with a loud groan.

Mist turned to Eva and screamed, "Run!"

The girls drew their daggers swiftly from their sheaths. The Nephilim dashed forward and bounded five feet to land in front of them. He opened his mouth wide and blew a noxious green smoke-like substance toward Jewels' face. She deflected it with her arm but dropped and shrieked in pain when her arm erupted in boils.

"He's a Maladite," she warned.

Her partner launched her blade toward his neck. He flinched and when his face was slashed, a pained look marred his countenance. When he opened his mouth again and blew toward her, she vaulted away from the green substance. In bitter pain, Jewels threw her blade toward the creature's back and it penetrated his right shoulder. He clenched his jaw in pain.

Mist lifted her left leg in a savage back kick and drove her foot into his abdomen. The Nephilim grunted and staggered to one knee. A few yards away, a swirling graphite vapor began to form.

Jewels, who still lay on the floor in agony, yelled, "Mist, he's going for the portal."

Her partner turned her head in the direction of the portal and behind it, she saw who was devising it—a tall, translucent glimmering charcoal figure. "It's a Daimon," she cried.

The Nephilim rose quickly to his feet and raced toward the portal. She sprinted after him in close pursuit, held the dagger by the end of the blade, and flung it at him. It almost reached the back of his skull but he disappeared through the portal and the weapon clattered on the floor after it lost momentum.

She ran back to check on Jewels. "Are you okay?" She helped her up and covered her forearm with napkins from the café.

"This stings like hell." Jewels turned to her. "Search for Eva. I'll go check the girl on the floor. I should be all right."

Mist hurried out of the station while Jewels shuffled quickly toward Licity, who looked pale and struggled for breath as blood spewed from the side of her mouth. She knelt next to the woman, whose eyes grew steadily dimmer, and she grimaced when she saw the blade protruding from her chest. "I'll get you some help," she said but Licity shook her head. Ignoring her, she started to stand but the woman's hold on her arm was firm enough to rivet her in place.

With a feeble and choking voice, Licity uttered, "Eva's ba...ba-by."

"It's all right. You don't have to say anything."

The woman shook her head. "Eva's baby is Daimon... Kill-er." With that, she exhaled her last breath and died. As Jewels went to close her eyelids, she noticed a strange phenomenon—a mark slowly materialized on the woman's upper right arm. She pushed back the sleeve of her tee-shirt to view the entire odd marking—πλάνη.

She sighed sharply when she interpreted it. "Deceiver indeed. Duplicity!"

Mist ran outside and searched frantically for the pregnant girl. "Where are you, Eva?" She darted toward the parking lot and then to the main road but saw no sign of her. From a distance, she saw flashing red and blue lights approaching. "Damn! The police." She hurried into the station. As she approached the main entrance, her gaze noticed an empty clear vial next to a trash can. She stopped, bent slowly to grab it, and gasped when she saw the red lipstick markings on it. Shaking her head, she voiced a desolate protest. "Eva—no, no, no, no."

Jewels came out from the station and didn't notice the tears streaming down her face at first. "The girl who was with Eva is dead. And you won't believe who—" She stopped as Mist turned to her with the vial in her hand. Her mouth fell open. "Oh, no!" She swallowed uncomfortably. "Is there anything we can do now? Do we even know where she went?"

Her partner shook her head. "She made her choice."

20

A LEADER'S REBUKE

Present Time

From the early dawn hours, Angelica sat at the DW infirmary, watched over Reina, and waited for some kind of response. She had slept for a few hours the previous night and since then, had been at the wounded girl's bedside, worried that she might never wake up.

Outside the room, she could hear Joan reprimanding Pretzel. Although it was faint, she could still make out some of what was said.

"Pretzel, you knew very well that place was a deathtrap. Why would it occur to you to take Reina and a trainee Daughter to such a place?" The woman scowled and her expression tightened with anger. "You know better than this!"

"Joan, I promised Angelica I'd take her and I wouldn't let her go by herself." Pretzel turned from Joan to Mist, who stood next to her. "I knew there was a risk going in but I was willing to take it to help a friend."

The woman sighed and continued in a gentler tone,

"Pretzel, we all know you have a generous heart but being a leader also entails making difficult decisions, especially when it comes to the safety of others." She grasped her shoulders. "We put you in charge of your group because we see great potential in you, so we expect you to deal with these situations wisely." The girl lowered her head. "You should have at least planned and deliberated with us. Reckless decisions lead to unexpected results."

Pretzel's lips formed a thin line, her gaze still fixed on the floor. "I'm sorry," she said and shook her head in regret. "At that moment, I was concerned for Angelica and thought I was doing the right thing." She looked at their leader. "But you're right. I should have been more careful. I guess my reckless call almost got Reina killed, and I never want that to happen to anyone else under my watch."

"Making mistakes is an inevitable part of leadership, but only great leaders are willing to admit and learn from them." A crooked smile appeared on Joan's thin lips. "I know that at the moment, your mind is on Reina but rest assured, we'll have a more in-depth conversation about this.

"Regarding Reina, May mentioned that the blade didn't penetrate deep enough to affect any vital organs and believes she'll make a full and quick recovery." The woman nodded. "I'll check on her periodically to see how she's progressing."

"Thanks," said Pretzel and walked toward Reina's room, while the two older women headed through the infirmary's long corridor.

Mist turned to the leader and said, "How fitting that she'd face this dilemma."

"What do you mean?" Joan opened the door to exit the infirmary.

"Years ago, I faced the same predicament as Pretzel but with Angelica's mom, and I've always questioned whether I made the right decision." A little furrow pulled between her eyebrows as she thought.

"How do you mean?" Both women ascended a few flights of stairs.

"Angelica's mom had just received the news that her father died. She insisted on seeing the same person Angelica went to see." She sighed and continued. "The irony isn't lost on me. Anyway, Sparrow had a premonition that if she left the compound, it would be fatal for her, so I convinced her otherwise. Well, I thought I did. Later that night, she left the compound unbeknownst to us and... well, she died the next day."

"Mist, there was no way for you know that. You did what you thought best at the time and advising her to stay was logical." They now paced through another extended corridor that led to Joan's office.

"I've told myself that so many times but do wonder if taking that risk could have saved Eva." She turned to her companion and met her gaze.

"Old friend, some things are beyond our control and knowledge, and attempting to ascertain the would have and should have will only drive you insane." Joan opened the door to her office. She sat at her desk, while the other woman sat on one of the chairs across from her.

"I agree with you, but Angelica reminds me so much of her mother. Not only in appearance but in character and from what we know of her so far, do you think she'd have waited for Pretzel to formulate a tactical plan?"

The leader stared at her thoughtfully and shook her head slowly. "Most likely not," she finally conceded.

"So, do you think Pretzel did the right thing?" she pressed quietly. The other woman remained silent. "What was it that you said? Ahem...great leaders are willing to admit their mistakes."

"Are willing to admit and learn from them," Joan said with a smirk. "If you use my quotes against me, make sure you get them right." Both women laughed.

Mist continued. "The peculiarity of it all. All these years thinking Eva's child died and she's lived under our noses the whole time." She leaned forward and folded her hands on the desk. "If I had known, I'd have been there for her," she muttered and fixed a thoughtful gaze on the ceiling.

"When do you plan to tell her about her mother?"

"I don't know." She pursed her lips. "So much is happening—the news about her father, the Lancaster situation, and now with this hospital incident..." She paused and drew a deep breath. "For sure, now is not an appropriate time."

"I agree," Joan replied firmly. "And what are your thoughts on this so-called prophecy of her being the Daimon Killer?"

"Honestly, I don't know. I've witnessed so many oddities in my life that part of me says it's possible but on the flip side, could it have been simply the random babbling of a dying girl?"

"I don't want to spook you but when she was part of my team, she was a great seer. Many of them take years to comprehensively develop and make sense of their gift, but Faith caught on fast and her predictions were flawless." The woman leaned back in her chair and placed her finger on her chin. "Yet little by little, she let the accolades and the praise distract her from the true purpose of her gift." She straightened. "To help others."

At that moment, Joan's cell phone rang. She stared at the caller ID. "It's Kindle." Mist gazed wide-eyed and leaned forward while the other woman tapped the answer icon. "Yes, Kindle." Initially, she nodded but then an expression of terrible agony crossed her face. "Only one?" Her gaze lowered. "How badly is she hurt?" She rocked on her chair while she listened attentively to Kindle. "I agree. Bring her from the Camden facility. We have the medical equipment to provide better care." She sighed deeply. "Be safe. I'll see you in a few hours."

She clicked the end button, turned slowly to her second, and choked her tears back before she spoke in an unsteady voice. "There was only one survivor in the Lancaster attack."

Glimmering tears pricked the other woman's eyes.

"It was Jewels. She was the sole survivor."

Mist dropped to her knees.

21

SOLE SURVIVOR

Pretzel's expression was downcast as she shuffled slowly toward the room where Reina lay. She stopped in the doorway and leaned against the doorframe, her gaze fixed sadly on the wounded girl.

Angelica reclined on a chaise lounge next to the bed but straightened when she saw her. The expression in her eyes was doleful. "My apologies but...um, I couldn't help overhearing your conversation with Joan and I'm so sorry about all of this. With everything that's happened with Reina and now you...well, I feel this is all my fault." She shifted her gaze and focused miserably on the floor.

An expression of compassion appeared on Pretzel's face as she turned to her. "This wasn't your fault and at no time did you force Reina or me to go. It was our decision and we understood the risks from the start." Her voice was soft and gentle.

"You have both saved my life twice and I can't let you take the fall for this one. I'll talk to Joan and let her know it was my fault and...and that you thought I was going somewhere else and came along." Her voice was a little uncertain as she voiced the lie.

Her roommate shook her head. "If I've learned anything from life, it's that maintaining a lie requires telling many more." She drew closer and slumped next to her on the chaise. Her gaze turned toward Reina. "I have to accept the consequences of my actions," she said and now looked firmly at Angelica. "Although to be quite honest, I have no regrets about going with you."

She smiled and leaned her head on Pretzel's shoulder. "Thank you," she murmured.

Their momentary silence was interrupted by Tassel's footsteps. "Hey, guys." The seer entered cautiously and spoke softly. "I hope I'm not interrupting anything."

"No, not at all," said Pretzel. "I was telling Angelica that this was her fault."

Angelica fixed her with a mockingly stern look and slapped her shoulder gently. "Hey!" Pretzel turned to her with a smile.

"How's she holding up?" asked Tassel as she gazed at Reina with a sorrowful expression.

"May mended the wound but she still hasn't woken up. She's been this way for several hours now."

"When was the last time she was awake?"

"Not since the ride over," answered Angelica. "We panicked when she passed out and thought she wouldn't make it." She cocked her head toward Reina. "She looks much better now and even has her color back."

"She'll come through. I'm confident," said Tassel emphatically. "She's a fighter."

"Is there anyone we should notify like an employer or something?" questioned Angelica.

"Reina, work! Humph! Negative," responded the seer. "She's filthy rich."

"What do you mean she's rich?" she asked with a deep frown.

"She's loaded...she's wealthy...Queen of England rich," continued Tassel. "Like, she'll never have to work a day in her life rich."

"But she dresses in those faded, ripped jeans, always wears those Mello Kitty T-shirts, and lives here." She was bewildered, incapable of even imagining it. "Why not live it up in a penthouse?"

"The short answer to the question is she doesn't want to," replied Pretzel.

"Wow! That's a shocker," she remarked, still unable to picture it. "But how is she rich?"

"Reina's grandfather was a successful businessman who started a company that now spans the globe. He was a Spaniard who came to this country with nothing and became a self-made billionaire. Tragically, Reina lost her mom and dad in a car accident when she was only a baby—"

"What do you mean by dad?" interrupted Angelica with an even bigger frown. "Isn't her dad one of those things?"

"Well, yes. Her parents couldn't have children so they used in vitro fertilization for her mom to conceive. Somehow, her mom's eggs were fertilized with a Daimon's seed instead of her mom's husband."

"Another shocker," she stated sarcastically.

"So as I was saying, when her parents died, her grandfather took custody of Reina." Pretzel sighed. "But like most of us, the Daimons caught wind of her and tried to kill her. Her grandfather was one of the few outsiders who knew about the DW and he entrusted her to us before being killed by a Nephilim himself."

Pretzel turned her gaze to Angelica. "Reina was only seven years old when she came to us so for her, this is the only family she has left."

Angelica, still in disbelief, asked, "What does she do with all that money and what happened to her grandfather's company?"

"The group has several professional accountants who manage her funds, and the upper-level company management runs the day-to-day operations and keeps her informed about her grandfather's...well, her company," explained Tassel. "Reina isn't much into material gain, so she uses a good chunk of her money to help charities and the less fortunate women of DW, and contributes to help pay the expenses of this facility."

She was awestruck. "This whole time, I thought she was merely this energetic, quirky, and at times, gullible girl. But now to know she's rich—."

Tassel shook her hand quickly and said, "Oh, please don't change your perspective of her. She would abhor...I mean hate that. She wouldn't want to be seen or treated any differently than the other girls. She has a big heart."

Pretzel nodded emphatically. "It's true. Reina often offers to pay for my college tuition and other expenses and I've always refused."

"Why? I wish someone would pay for mine."

"I think her generosity often masks a desire to be liked

and in the past, some have taken advantage of that. Whenever I refuse, she asks, 'But why not?'" She mimicked Reina's high-pitched voice, "None of the other girls pay for my stuff, so why should she? I want her to know I love her because of who she is not what she can provide me."

She paused for a moment and smirked. "Still, there have been times when I've gone to pay my semester-end tuition and the balance was at zero." She glanced at the peacefully resting Reina. "The registrar's office would tell me it had been paid anonymously. Her generosity is only matched by her stubbornness."

"I'll certainly keep that mind," said Angelica.

Tassel's phone chimed with a text notification. She retrieved it and began to read a text from Joan. *Stop by my office ASAP. An urgent matter about Lancaster.* Her forehead puckered.

"What's going on?" asked Pretzel.

"Well, Joan sent me a text to stop by her office ASAP. It's about Lancaster." She stared inquisitively at her.

The girl shrugged. "I haven't heard anything. You may want to check that out."

"Yeah, let me head upstairs now." She slipped her phone into her back pocket. "Let me know of any progress about Reina."

Pretzel nodded. As Tassel walked out of the room, the other girl turned to Angelica. "I'm going to the restroom. Be back in a few."

She slumped on the chaise longue and closed her eyelids for a moment. A moment later, she heard a faint grunt from Reina and opened her eyes with a jerk. The girl grunted again, followed by another louder groan. "Ow!"

A little panicked, she bounded to her feet and lurched to the bed. "Reina...Reina, are you in pain?" she asked nervously. The girl shook her head slowly with an expression of discomfort and her hands clasped her stomach. "Oh, my God—are you in pain? I don't know what to do." Her voice quivered. "Let me get you May, okay? Hold on."

Reina shook her head and murmured croakily, "No... I'm...I'm hungry."

Angelica responded with a guffaw that echoed in the room. "Yes, yes. You should be!" She threw her arms around the girl in both glee and relief. Reina's eyes widened as she wondered who was behaving more vibrantly than her.

"Angelica?" she asked with a quizzical look.

Ignoring the patient, she turned to Pretzel who had stepped into the room. "She's hungry!" she exclaimed and shook Reina, who moaned. "Oh, I'm sorry. I'm hurting you now."

With a broad grin on her face, Pretzel approached the wounded girl and gave her a warm embrace. "It's so good to have you back."

"What happened?" Reina's voice was still hoarse.

"Let's say that the next time you attack a Nephilim, you wait for me." The corners of her mouth curled upward into a grin.

"Oh...I remember now." She placed her hand on her head.

"I do have to say that Angelica saved the day." Pretzel turned to the other girl.

"Me?" She frowned. "I merely reacted. You took care of business at the end."

Reina asked, "Did you kill him?"

Pretzel nodded.

"Good! He was ugly anyway," she said with a chuckle.

"All in all, we were concerned for you and are happy that you're back." She caught the girl's hand. "Angelica hasn't left your side since you got here."

"Hey, you were here with me too," she protested.

"Ahh! You guys are making me blush," said Reina and tugged Pretzel onto the bed. "Come, Angelica, join the squeeze."

All three girls were now on the twin-size bed and hugged one another.

Suddenly, May entered the room and noticed the three girls piled together. "Reina, You have stitches and you three are gonna break my bed!" she remonstrated,

The patient, startled by May, pushed her friends quickly off the bed. The other two fell on the floor in laughter, while Reina waved a greeting at the caregiver with a big grin on her face.

The driving rain pounded the earth furiously, while lightning and thunder crashed through the dark skies. The stormy weather had been looming for the last couple of hours and showed no signs of relenting. Under the raging rain, Mist leaned in the door of the warehouse. She waited anxiously, her gaze fixed on the back-street entrance of the infirmary. Soaking strands of her short, straight hair were plastered against her face and partially masked her anxious features.

Suddenly, two gleaming lights appeared in the far distance and approached rapidly. The car stopped a few feet away from her and the front door opened hurriedly before two women exited. Kindle and Pearl had arrived an hour later than expected and very late into the evening hours. Quickly, they rushed to open the back of the car and eased an unconscious Jewels out.

Mist, who was soaking wet, stepped back to give the new arrivals space to enter and yelled to one of May's girls who waited in the corridor. "Take the wheelchair back and bring one of the gurneys." The young girl nodded and hurried through the hallway as instructed, while Mist moved forward to help the women to carry an old friend into the building. The wind slammed the door behind her. "Has she woken up?" she asked loudly over the deafening thunder and howling winds.

"No! They found her unconscious," shouted Kindle. "Camden team did the best they could but she doesn't look too good, Mist." The blustering winds caused them to flounder as they hurried into the warehouse.

"Let's get her inside as fast as we can."

The strong gales jammed the door shut and she had to let go of Jewels and pull with both hands on the knob and her foot against the wall to get it open. The young girl from earlier was already waiting with the gurney. They stumbled inside, placed Jewels on it, and rushed down the narrow, winding maze of corridors with Kindle doing the pushing, Pearl guiding in front, and Mist at Jewels' side.

"We will fix you up. Hold on," Mist murmured to the woman and held her pale, cold hand.

The young girl had run ahead and now propped the

infirmary door open. May beckoned them from the doorway of a room as they burst through. "What's her status?" she asked as they pushed the gurney into the vacant room with various medical supplies and equipment already on hand.

"She has been unconscious since they found her, breathes very shallowly, and has a deep cut on the side of her head," said a panting Kindle.

The caregiver took the penlight from her pocket, shined it into Jewels' pupils, and proceeded to listen to her lungs, abdomen, and heart with her stethoscope. "It doesn't sound good." Her concerned expression was unmistakable. "I'll need to perform a thorough CAT scan to see what's going on."

Mist held her head, her intense gaze on the wounded woman while she paced the room nervously. "May, you need to do everything possible to keep her alive," she said in a desperate, high-pitched voice.

The caregiver looked at her and responded tenderly, "Mist, you know I will but I need to focus all my attention on her. I'll give you a call once I'm done. Being here now won't help her or do you any good." She looked at Jewels, then at the anxious woman. "I'm very sure she'll need you once she has recovered from all this." She smiled reassuringly.

With a heavy sigh, she nodded and turned to the two girls. "Kindle, Pearl, why don't you freshen up and let's meet in Joan's office in about thirty minutes."

It was close to midnight when Joan, Mist, Gypsy, Kindle, and Pearl convened in the office. The two late-night arrivals sat in dry clothes and with cups of coffee and shook their heads as they elaborated on the devastation of the Lancaster compound. Sadness pervaded the room as they described what they had seen.

"I have never in my life seen so much wreckage and destruction," stated Pearl and paused as she choked on the words. "And...so much death. They killed everyone... savagely." Tears coursed down her face. "You'd think we should be used to this by now but seeing the lifeless bodies of those girls was too much."

"It was a horrendous sight," added Kindle. "A few of the Camden girls couldn't bear to go through the whole compound."

"Do you have any ideas about how they were able to infiltrate the facilities?" asked Joan.

"That's the scary part," stated Kindle. "It seems like they simply waltzed into the compound."

"What do you mean waltzed into the compound?" Mist asked in an offended tone. "That was one of the best-guarded and fortified facilities I know."

The woman lowered her head. "Sorry, Mist, but what I meant was that the stone-quartz wall was intact and the gates didn't appear to have been tampered with or broken. There's no way they climbed those walls given their vulnerability to quartz. It was like the gates were left wide open for them to come through."

The second in command's face went ashen-white.

Kindle continued. "There was no power in the building when we got there, and the main fiber line was cut. They had no way to call using the main lines. Also, we found several of these boxes throughout the building, still turned on." She drew a small black box with a tiny red indicator bulb in the middle from her pocket. "I've seen these before. They're used to block cell phone signals."

Mist snatched the box to examine it further and passed it to Joan.

Gypsy asked, "But why didn't we or any of the groups get a distress signal from them? All our facilities are wired with multiple points to trigger the signal and besides, it works on a shortwave relay."

"This is the reason we believe the power outage occurred before the attack," Kindle explained. "The distress signal can be issued from designated areas such as the one here in Joan's office, but this only works if the facility has power. However, since these systems have a built-in auxiliary power source, the other option is to manually send the distress signal from the actual alarm."

Her expression slid into a frown. "But it appears that the alarm was tampered with, which made it impossible for them to do so."

"This doesn't make any sense," muttered Mist as she lowered her head and pinched the bridge of her nose.

"We are as confused as you, Mist," commented Pearl, her voice somewhat apprehensive. "Rain, the scout leader from the Camden group, suspects there may have been a defector in the ranks."

Kindle added, "I'm not trying to jump to conclusions, but it appears they may have had help from someone on the inside."

"A traitor?" asked Mist in shock. "I can't believe it. If it is as you say, then the person who helped must have known the ins and outs of the compound and also have security clearance to access the security system. That could only be someone within leadership." Her face contorted. "You all know I stayed in contact with them. Those women are—" She choked up for a moment but composed herself quickly. "They were some of the most loyal and faithful ladies I have known. Any assault on their character is an insult to their memory and to me." A tear rolled down her cheek.

Joan looked compassionately at her and said, "Mist, I know this group was close to your heart and we feel your pain. These two ladies aren't accusing anyone specifically but are simply articulating the facts and pointing out the most probable conclusions."

She shook her head as she wiped the tears from her face. "I can't talk about this now. We are jumping to conclusions and sullying the memory of martyrs." With a surly expression, she muttered, "You'll have to excuse me for now but if you need me, you can find me in the infirmary." She stumbled from the room.

"Mist!" Gypsy called after her.

Joan gestured to Gypsy with her hand. "This hasn't been easy for her so I think it's for the best if she takes some time to deal with the shock and trauma. Let her go." She turned to the other two women. "Ladies, I know you must be exhausted so I won't keep you for long. I have one more question—where did you find Jewels?"

Kindle replied, "I tell you she must have had a hell of a fight with those Nephilim. We found her unconscious in the video surveillance room, along with two other bodies.

At first, we thought she was dead but when we checked her, we discovered she had a faint pulse. If there's anyone who can give us an inkling of what happened there, it would be her."

"Thank you, ladies. "I know it may not seem like it, but Mist and I are very appreciative of all you and your team have done."

"I don't blame her for her outburst," responded Kindle. "I'd have reacted the same way if it were this group."

"Thanks for understanding," stated Joan. "Now go get some rest."

22

GIRLS' NIGHT OUT

"Did you find anything yet, Tassel?" asked Angelica with a perturbed expression. "It's been a week now with no word from her." She paced the computer lab and picked agitatedly at her fingernails.

"Honestly, it's been a challenge. I've checked the FBI records and can't find any trace of her." The tech's fingers raced across her keyboard to shuffle from one shell command to another, open various websites, and run many search queries in the background. "I come up with the same information we intercepted earlier from the hospital's records—released to FBI." She spun her chair toward the other girl and adjusted her glasses. "I assume she's in a witness protection program and if that's the case, it'll be complicated to discover her whereabouts."

Angelica plopped into a nearby chair and sighed. "The irony of all this."

Tassel stared curiously at her.

"My grandmother is a highly excitable woman and there were days she'd call me five or six times. She always claimed she had a *presentimiento*—a feeling that something bad had happened—but I knew it was only to check on me." She looked at her companion with a half-smile on her face. "Now I'm worried about her and wonder how she's doing and where she is."

"You miss her, don't you?" Tassel asked in a gentle voice.

She nodded. "A couple of weeks ago, I'd have cringed at the sight of her number popping up on my phone but now, I'm desperate to get one of her calls." She paused for a moment in thought and to avoid tears welling for the hundredth time. "Tassel, I meant to ask you, what about the contact card I gave you that belonged to the agent?"

"Ooh, yes," responded Tassel, spun swiftly on her chair, and rubbed her hands. She shifted her mouse, clicked a few times, and opened a file on her computer. "Daniel Javier Ortega," she read aloud. "Served in the armed forces, was part of the Philadelphia Police Department, and was later transferred to the Lancaster Police Department as a detective before he joined the FBI."

"Is there any information connecting him to my mother, Eva Santos?"

"Yes, sorry, was sidetracked by the details." She cleared her throat and continued. "I did unearth a police report from the Lancaster Police Department and he was involved in your mother's case, so he told the truth about knowing her."

"Is that the police report in which Leonard Archie is mentioned?"

"It is—wanted for questioning in connection with the murder of Eva Santos as per the report," the girl confirmed.

"And by the way, this is still an open investigation in the Lancaster Police Department."

"That case is closed in my book. There is no doubt in my mind who did it," Angelica said emphatically.

"Hmm…" Tassel stared upward as she turned slowly in her chair.

"What's the hmm for?" she asked curiously.

"Well, Mist was from Lancaster around the time your mother was killed. It makes me wonder if she knew anything about her or this case."

"Do you think I should ask her?"

The tech shook her head. "Negative. I don't think this is a good time." She looked furtively both right and left and prepared to share the gossip. "Did you hear what happened to the Lancaster DW headquarters?" Her tone was subdued.

"Pretzel filled me in a little," responded Angelica. "I heard it was horrible."

Tassel continued in an undertone, "Well, it turned out the night the girls returned from Lancaster with the only surviving Daughter, they had a meeting in Joan's office. Something was said that made Mist furious. She left the meeting before it ended. Since then, she has refused to talk to anyone about what happened in Lancaster. She's been at the infirmary this whole time. The woman they found— Jewels—was a good friend of hers years ago, which is why she's there now."

Angelica, who now also whispered, asked, "What did they say that made her so upset?"

"Undetermined," the seer responded with a shrug.

"They've never seen her like this before, which is the reason I advise you to not ask her at the moment."

She pursed her lips and considered her options. "Do you think I should call the agent? He could have information about my grandmother and mother."

"Negative. With all that's going on now, I would suggest staying off the authorities' radar and letting the dust settle, especially after the death of the FBI agent at the hospital."

"The woman who was with Ortega?" she asked.

"The police report states she was shot by an armed man who was killed at the scene, but Pretzel and Reina were present to know Witchcraft killed her." Tassel caught her hand. "I know this is difficult for you but I suspect your grandmother is in FBI custody and likely in good hands."

Angelica nodded reluctantly. "Yeah, I guess."

"Hey, I have a good feeling about her. She's gonna be fine," the girl said with a smile, which she returned. "And don't worry. I won't stop the STW—I mean, searching the web—on my end."

"Thanks." She sounded grateful but appeared dejected.

"Hey, don't look like that, especially tonight. I promise you're gonna have a blast with us."

"Do you think it's safe for me to go out with all that's happened?"

"We feel you need it so we are taking extra precautions," Tassel stated reassuringly. "And, by the way, we are taking the best protection the Daughters have to offer."

"What's that?"

"Gypsy and the twins!" She smiled.

The glowing full moon that haloed the dark skies accentuated Angelica's hazel-brown eyes, while the light, warm breeze caressed her features. The burgundy mini-dress fit fabulously on her petite figure—the outfit was girlfriend approved but grandmother forbidden. Her hair glistened with the hues of the night as it billowed gently in the touch of the evening wind. She waited patiently at the front of the building for the arrival of her friends and held a square beribboned box in her hands.

"Girl, you look tight in that dress!" exclaimed Pretzel as she walked out in her teal-blue V-neck dress with skinny straps. "I knew it would fit you perfectly."

She rubbed her arm and tucked her hair behind her ear. "You don't think it's too much? I hardly wear these types of outfits so I feel kinda out of place."

"Not at all. You look as if you own the night. I suggest you play the role and own it, girl." Her roommate snapped her fingers.

Angelica nodded gently and smiled. "By the way, you look amazing in your dress. I love the way it highlights your eyes."

"I need to look good to get down tonight." She started to shake her hips and her companion laughed. "Any word on the other girls?" Pretzel asked as she opened her purse to withdraw a small translucent spray vial with a yellow-ish-looking liquid. She proceeded to apply it around her neck and wrists.

"Nothing yet. They told me to wait out front." She took a whiff of what the girl put on and said, "That smells good. What is it?"

"Consider it DW's version of Chanel No. 5," she said

with a smirk. "Tinkle from our lab has been experimenting with various fragrances and concocted this little number to keep away the Nephilim. It's supposed to throw their sense of smell off. She calls it Ketoreth. Wanna try it?"

"Yes, please!"

"We want no interruptions tonight. It's all about having fun and a good time."

From a distance, a set of LED headlights approached and illuminated the narrow street to the main DW building. As the vehicle came slowly into view, the front brand emblem set centrally above the hood became more visible. Reina waved her arms wildly from the passenger side of the retractable hardtop convertible. Tassel pulled the metallic blue car in front of the two waiting ladies and right behind, Gypsy arrived with Cookie and Dough in a yellow metallic convertible.

"Hello, girls!" exclaimed Reina as she jumped over the door.

"Reina, please tell me you didn't buy these DMWs?" Pretzel's jaw dropped.

"No! I don't even have a license," the girl responded. "Ned Stevens, a good friend of my grandpa's, rented them as a birthday gift for me. He knew I was having a night out with my friends so he wanted me to go out in style."

"Ned—isn't he one of the executives at your company?"

"Yeah. He's great peeps. He even said if I like them, I could keep the cars."

"And?" Pretzel prompted impatiently.

"I won't keep them. I don't even like the color."

Her partner simply rolled her eyes.

From behind, Gypsy honked the horn and shouted

from the driver's side of the second Deamer, "Are you going to chat all night, or will we get this party started?"

"Woohoo! Let's get it on," responded Reina. Pretzel and Angelica sat in the back seat with Tassel and Reina in the front.

"Happy Birthday, Reina," said Angelica. "Pretzel and I got you a gift." Tassel began to pull away and drove slowly down the street.

"Presents!" Reina exclaimed in a sing-song tone.

She handed the girl a small alabaster-colored square box wrapped with a ruby-red bow. Haphazardly, she ripped the bow and opened the gift. "Aww! You got me a crown." She placed the gold crown quickly over her flaxen hair.

"You're certainly the queen for tonight," stated Pretzel.

"Thank you, guys! I love it." She threw the girls air kisses.

"Where are we going anyway?" asked Angelica.

"Rio De Janeiro NYC—one of the best nightclubs in the city or as the locals call it, El Rio," responded Tassel. "It's a fair distance away but knowing Gypsy, we'll get there in record time."

Reina turned the volume up on the car stereo. As they cruised steadily through the narrow street, she kicked her shoes off and leapt onto the passenger seat, clapped, and shimmied to the beat of the music. She beckoned to the other girls to do the same, but both immediately shook their heads. Reina pointed to the crown on her head to show who was the queen of the night and, feeling compelled, both stood and joined her. For the remainder of the song, the ladies danced and laughed.

They reached a traffic light that led onto the freeway, and Gypsy pulled quickly next to them and revved her engine. "Ladies, I need you to take your seats and buckle up," Tassel ordered.

Gypsy gave her a daring look and she returned it dauntlessly. Both drivers turned their heads to face the road and waited for the green light to flicker. Even before it changed, the tires screeched on the asphalt and produced a cloud of smoke in the air. "Make sure you're securely strapped," the seer told them as the Deamers raced onto the express highway.

"This is what happens when you bring Gypsy," explained an agitated Pretzel.

Both cars streaked along the freeway, swerved right or left, and careened close to other cars, trucks, and vans. Gypsy took the lead, which made Tassel press the pedal to the metal.

Angelica's heart pounded as she clenched Pretzel's hand tightly. "I'm gonna die," she murmured, while Reina shrieked in excitement.

The DMWs were now neck-and-neck with both drivers determined to win. Gypsy gave Tassel one last look, smirked, and thrust the car into gear to push the engine for the lead. The older woman cut across three lanes, almost collided with the car in the middle, and took their exit while she ignored the New York traffic salutes and a seemingly endless car horn from an angry driver.

"*Ay, Dios mio!*" exclaimed a frightened Angelica. "She's crazy!"

Gypsy approached a red traffic light, pressed the brake pedal to the floor, and brought the vehicle to a screeching halt. When the second car finally caught up with her, she looked over and called, "What took you so long, slowpoke?"

"You're insane, you know that?" responded Tassel with a chuckle.

Reina turned to the girl and said, "I hope you don't mind but I want to drive back with Gypsy."

"Go figure," Pretzel snarked.

They reached their destination safe and sound, although Angelica searched on her smartphone for the WTA subway line schedule for the return trip.

As they pulled up to the Valet Parking attendant, he opened the car doors and welcomed the ladies. *"Bem Vinda ao Rio Janeiro."*

———

The nightclub vibe was filled with energy and excitement. Pounding speakers blared deafeningly without ceasing and either made you deaf or made you dance. The dance floor was crowded with a throng of people, all squeezed like fishes in a net. Although it was a little challenging to move, the crowd still managed to shimmy their bodies to the rhythmic thump of the music.

After a couple of hours, the two roommates started to walk off the dance floor that was lit mainly by the club's dazzling strobe lights. Angelica wiped the sweat from her brow as they dodged, pushed, and squeezed through the throng of dancing party animals.

"Where are we going?" shouted Angelica.

"What?" asked Pretzel, her hand cupped around her ear.

"Let's head to the bar where it's less noisy," she yelled in response.

"What did you say?" The other girl frowned.

After lip-reading what she said, Pretzel pointed toward the bar and made a drinking gesture with her hand.

Angelica responded with an okay motion using her fingers.

They squeezed, pushed, and at times, elbowed through and finally reached the club's bar panting for air.

"This is much better," Pretzel said in a normal tone.

"I've never danced so much in my life," said Angelica, panting a little. "That was so much fun."

"You can seriously get down, girl."

"I used to take dancing lessons after school while my grandmother worked. The strange part was she made me choose between dancing or Taekwondo. I guess I made the wrong choice."

"Uh-uh." Her friend shook her head. "You can't worry about that. You're a great dancer and should be proud of it, but we are here to have fun so no DW stuff. What's your drink?"

"Bahama Mama cocktail," she said eagerly.

Pretzel waved to the bartender. "One Bahama Mama and one Amaretto Sour, please."

He nodded. "Coming right up."

"When are those girls getting off the dance floor?" asked Angelica.

"Knowing them, never." Her companion chuckled. "Surprisingly enough, those ladies are releasing all their stress out there." Both of them glanced at the dance floor and watched Reina climb onto the DJ booth and gyrate wildly. Gypsy swayed while surrounded by three guys, and the other girls danced in a huddle.

"You'd think these girls would be more civilized," she commented with an amused laugh.

"It's all in good fun. Eventually, security will bring Reina down, the girls will get tired, and if one of those men even glanced at Gypsy inappropriately…well, I feel sorry for them."

"One Bahama Mama and Amaretto Sour," said the bartender.

As Angelica took her drink, Pretzel warned, "Be careful to not spill the drink on yourself. Alcohol removes the Kollourion from the skin. We never know when one of those creeps may show up."

They enjoyed their drinks and watched their friends on the dance floor and a short while later, a stranger approached. "Hello, ladies. Are you religious? Because you're the answer to all my prayers."

The two friends rolled their eyes. "No, honey," responded Pretzel. "We are the opposite of your answered prayers."

"I don't know but it seems to me my heart has been touched by an angel." They almost spat their drinks out in laughter.

"If you only knew, honey. If you only knew," retorted Pretzel to the weak pick-up line.

"Has anyone mentioned that you look like Cleopatra? Call me your pharaoh, girl." She rolled her eyes and shook her head. "Doesn't matter. I think you're much prettier. Let me buy you and Aphrodite here a drink."

"We are good," she insisted and gestured at him with her drink.

"Okay... Okay, I see you don't want to be bothered but...um, my name is Internet, so search me if you change your mind." He winked.

"Will do, Internet."

He tilted his head slightly and muttered, "Excuse me, ladies. I think I just saw the queen of the gods—Hera." He strode to the so-called Hera and yelled, "Hey, girl, is your daddy a butcher..." As he walked away, he accidentally bumped into Angelica and spilled her drink on her.

"*Imbécil!*" she snapped in Spanish. "You jerk!" She wiped the spill from her dress, while Pretzel waved to the bartender for some napkins. As they cleaned the spill, they suddenly froze and stared gravely at one another.

"You feel it too?"

Angelica nodded.

A shadow of vexation clouded their faces. Pretzel turned her gaze toward the main entrance and it fixed on two shimmering charcoal figures. The other girls dashed from the crowded dance floor toward the two friends.

"It's Strife and his twin brother Rivalry," commented Gypsy as she pulled a small vial of Kollourion from her jumpsuit pocket. "Does anyone need to re-apply it?" she asked the group.

"We do," stated Cookie and Dough and began to apply the substance quickly.

"I lost my Kollourion," Pretzel told them. "A guy bumped into Angelica and she spilled some of her drink on her right shoulder and arm."

"I'm sorry, guys," said Angelica.

"No worries. The twins have finished with mine," Gypsy told them. She handed it to Angelica but as she went to open it, the vial slipped through her fingers onto the alcohol-splashed floor and shattered.

The girls all exchanged concerned expressions.

"I hope someone else has another," Gypsy muttered quickly. "That was the only one I was carrying."

"I left mine in the car," said Reina.

"But you and I were gonna share," protested Tassel with apprehension in her eyes.

"I forgot it...I'm so sorry."

Cookie and Dough were having a similar conversation.

The mere mishap escalated into a heated argument that included finger-pointing, angry faces, and loud shouting.

Suddenly, Gypsy recovered her common sense and shouted, "Stop! We are being influenced by the Temptationites. Let's get our heads out of our butts and protect Angelica at all costs."

As one, the Daughters shook their heads and dragged themselves from the malignant daydream.

The older woman responded to a sudden idea. "We need to form a huddle around her. They're still limited to line of sight. If we shield her, they shouldn't be able to see her."

They did as she suggested and all that could be seen of Angelica was the top of her hair.

"These two guys are known for creating havoc in heavily crowded places," Pretzel explained quickly. "Their very presence creates a hostile atmosphere, which causes people to break out in bitter disagreement and quarrels.

They were the ones responsible for the massive brawl in the Times Square Ball earlier this year."

"And look what we have here." The guy with the ridiculous pick-up lines returned. "I wasn't aware you were friends with Demeter, Artemis, Athena, and...uh, the Parvati sisters, Hindu goddess of love."

"Look, you creep," snapped Gypsy as she caught the guy by the shirt. "If you don't get your cheesy butt out of here, I'll hit you so hard you'll crap teeth for the rest of the night."

"Okay... Okay, Artemis! I'm going." He raised his hands, thoroughly frightened.

"Reina, once the brothers move away from the entrance, see if you can get to the car and bring the Kollourion." As Gypsy spoke, a brawl between two guys broke out near the entrance.

"It's starting," said Tassel.

"Damn!" the older woman exclaimed when she registered the rising hostility among the crowd. She gestured for Reina to wait. "It'll be difficult to move in a huddle in this crowd. We'll have to stay put for the moment and move outside when there's a gap. Look for an alternate exit, ladies." She turned to Dough on her right and then Cookie on the left. "Dough, Cookie, I have two blades strapped to my back under my shirt. Take one each very slowly." She then proceeded to ease up her pant leg, bent slightly, and drew a blade strapped to her thigh. "It's like my credit card—I never leave home without it," she joked.

The brawl had spread to the middle of the crowd and security raced onto the dance floor and attempted to pull people apart. The two Nephilim stared at each other with mischievous smiles and wandered among the numerous fistfights.

A red-faced man with bulging eyes ran toward Gypsy who, with one punch, knocked him off his feet.

"Look up there!" Dough exclaimed. "There's an exit next to the stage. If we move methodically, we can stay in a huddle and get out."

"All right! Let's move with short steps, ladies," the older woman commanded.

The group shuffled as quickly as they could toward the exit while the brawl in the nightclub intensified to the point where security was no longer able to tame the mayhem. The chaos seemed to have spread throughout the entire nightclub. A raging woman lunged at Pretzel and was upended by a swift kick.

A tall, husky man glared at Reina and raised his fist to hit her, but she thrust her foot powerfully into his midsection and he yelped, wide-eyed, and fell.

Cookie and Dough had to elbow a few lunatics who attempted to harm them.

"Only a little more!" shouted Gypsy.

Suddenly, a crowd of people surged into the huddle and the girls toppled to leave Angelica standing and exposed long enough to be noticed.

The two Nephilim scowled, fixed their menacing gazes on her, and began to strike, knock, and jab people close to them. Bodies were hurled aside as the two trouble-makers created a path to apprehend their prey.

"Guys!" shrieked Angelica. "They saw me!"

The girls were pinned by bodies in a domino pattern, which meant they were unable to stand.

Suddenly, Cookie and Dough locked gazes and their gifts activated and they began to effortlessly push the people on top of them off. They rose hastily and assisted the fallen Daughters, pulling bodies off them as if they were twigs.

Gypsy turned to Pretzel and said, "Cookie, Dough, and I will take care of these bastards. Take Angelica and the girls to the warehouse." The girl nodded, grasped Angelica's hand, and dragged her toward the exit.

Strife leapt high when he saw Angelica fleeing. Cookie motioned to her sister, hunched her back, and lowered as she clenched her hands together. Dough used these to boost herself to engage the attacker in mid-flight. In dramatic slow motion, she kicked Strife dead in the face, propelled him to the floor, and as he fell, she flung her blade into his right shoulder.

Pretzel and the girls reached the exit door. "It's jammed," she muttered as she attempted to open it.

"Move out of the way!" exclaimed Reina, who struck the door open with a hard side kick.

It burst open and they rushed through but stopped outside and glanced around as they attempted to get their bearings.

"To the right!" Tassel yelled as she pointed toward the parking lot. As they sprinted to the car, she screamed, "The key!"

Pretzel spun toward her. "You and Reina get the key at the valet booth and Angelica and I will search for the car. Sense us once you have the key."

She and Angelica reached the parking lot and noticed that the influence of the Tempationites had extended out there. Two parking attendants were engaged in a brawl and barely noticed the girls.

"Hey! Why are you guys fighting?" she called to them.

"He started it!" yelled one of the men.

"No! You started it! You... He...you," the attendant stammered and finally realized that had no idea why they were fighting in the first place. "I don't know," he admitted.

"Look, there's some freaking voodoo stuff happening in this place. I suggest you guys get the hell out before it gets worse," Pretzel half-lied to get them to safety.

They nodded with wide, frightened eyes. "We have to get the heck out of here, Jimmy. I don't want to get voodoo, dude. Let's take that convertible." The man pointed to an onyx-colored car. They bounded into it and started it.

"Wait!" she shouted after them. "How were you able to start it?"

"We always leave the keys in the car." They pulled away and the tires squealed through the parking lot.

"Dammit!" swore Pretzel. "I sent Tassel and Reina for the keys and they're in the car. We need to find the vehicle and get them fast."

Her companion nodded.

The girls split up to search for the DMWs. They zigzagged and sprinted through the endless rows of parked vehicles. After a few minutes, Angelica yelled, "It's here!" which instantly drew Pretzel toward her.

They scrambled into it and Pretzel turned the engine on to race in search of the others. "If those guys were able to snap out of their rage that quickly, it can only mean Gypsy and the others were able to subdue the brothers. We need to keep our senses clear to find them as well."

Many of the terrified crowd now ran out of the night-club—some bruised, a few limping, and others bleeding, although all looked dazed and confused. It made it difficult for her to concentrate and maneuver the car through the bewildered mob.

Angelica closed her eyes and began to feel for her friends. Her focus was no longer on herself or the crowd but on the other Daughters. She began to feel a familiar heartbeat she had grown accustomed to in training, which made her yell, "Stop!"

Pretzel pushed the brakes to the floor. "What is it?" Her companion turned her head to the right and she followed her gaze. From the nightclub corner, they glimpsed Gypsy with the twins, and right behind them were Reina and Tassel. Pretzel honked the horn to get their attention.

The older woman saw them and rushed forward with the others toward the car. "The crowd of people is too hectic to get the other car," she said frantically. "We need to all fit in this one."

Somehow, all seven managed to squeeze into the four-seater convertible. Pretzel remained in the driver's seat and Reina sat with Angelica in the front while the others squashed in the back seat. With a clear road before her, Pretzel jammed her foot on the accelerator and left skid marks on the asphalt.

For a long time, no one spoke in the vehicle and the only sounds were the grunts and groans from the girls in the back seat as they tried to fit more comfortably, to no avail. Each turn the vehicle took made them moan louder.

Finally, their driver broke the silence and asked, "What happened in there?"

"The brothers ran away shortly after Dough injured one of them. It seems they assumed that Angelica was there alone and didn't expect a fight," responded Gypsy as she pushed one of Cookie's strands of hair from her face.

"I'm sorry I ruined your birthday," said Angelica.

"What?" Reina said with a frown. "It was the best birthday ever!" Everyone in the car laughed.

"I don't think the celebration is over yet." Pretzel sounded apprehensive.

"What's the problem?" asked Gypsy.

"I think we are being followed."

The girls attempted to look back but with little success. The cramped, confined space made it impossible.

"I've been keeping an eye on it for some time now and every turn I've taken, the vehicle has made it as well."

"I hate to say this," said a groaning Gypsy as she shoved Dough from her lap a little, "but you'll need to make a few more turns to lose it."

Everyone except Pretzel sighed in disappointment.

After several sharp turns, rapid accelerations, and abrupt changes of direction which made the rest of the team's complexions ashen, she sighed with relief. "I don't see the car anymore." When she reached the long narrow street of the DW warehouse, the pursuing vehicle reemerged. "Damn!" she exclaimed in frustration. "It's behind me."

"Stop the car," demanded Gypsy. "If it's them, we can't lead them to the warehouse. We'll have to engage them right here." The car behind them stopped a few yards away as the ladies spilled out of the vehicle.

"Reina, Tassel, watch over Angelica. We'll fight these sons of a fatherless goat."

Pretzel drew her dagger from the glove compartment and joined Gypsy and the twins, who were already brandishing their blades. For a long time, the SUV with black-tinted windows idled steadily. Finally, the headlights flicked off, the engine was cut, and the driver's door opened slowly. A tall, suited individual stepped out of the vehicle. The dimly lit streetlights made it impossible to discern his features. He began to walk menacingly toward the girls.

Angelica's heart pounded.

"Hey, jackass!" shouted Gypsy. "If you want to live, you'll stay where you are."

He stopped and scanned each of the Daughters intently. "I'm here for Angelica," said the stranger. "Angelica Santos, the daughter of Leonard Archie."

23

AN OUTSIDER'S VIEW

Gypsy's countenance was fierce as she clutched her quartz blade, her blue eyes fixed on the dark-suited man. She was ready to take action at a moment's notice if the stranger made any sudden movements. "You'll taste my dagger before you get to her!" The tone of her voice was resolute.

The other girls stood unflinchingly, their features menacing, and were ready to engage.

Cookie murmured in confusion, the words barely audible. "Surely it's not one of them. I don't feel anything."

"Who the hell are you?" the older woman asked without wavering from her uncompromising stance.

The stranger took a few steps forward into the incandescent rays of the wooden light post. His profile was now distinguishable.

Gypsy bellowed, "I said stay put, you jackass!"

"Wait!" Angelica cried from where she was shielded by Reina and Tassel. She strode out from behind the ladies, who attempted to stop her advance by grasping her arm. Irritated, she brushed their hands off and continued past the girls to halt midway between the stranger and the Daughters. "You're the FBI, agent, correct?"

"Yes! Phew…I thought I was a goner there." He drew in a long, sharp breath. "You are a hard person to find," he said and stared directly at her. "I'm Daniel Ortega and for the last few days, I have looked for you relentlessly, with no success."

"And how did you find me now?" she asked and frowned suspiciously at him.

"You guys shouldn't speed so much," he quipped. "There was a facial recognition hit on one of the highway speed cameras. From there, it wasn't too hard to follow your trail. I waited outside the club and tailed you after you rushed out."

"What do you want?" The girls behind Angelica stood at ease although they held their weapons, apprehensive as to the stranger's intentions.

"I'll cut to the chase. I was hoping you and your girl-friends here could explain a few things." He looked past Angelica toward the fierce cadre of ladies, his expression still nervous.

"Explain what and why did you mention my father's name?"

"For starters, I have seen a load of crap in my life but it pales by far in comparison to what I saw at the hospital." He lowered his head sadly. "I lost a partner and a friend that day. I only want to talk. No…no FBI business here." He sighed. "I want to understand what the hell is going on!"

"And my father?" demanded Angelica.

"I thought if you were with the group, it would get your attention quicker." He paused for a moment and looked directly into her eyes. "Also, to let you know, I have been in communication with your grandmother and know where she is."

A look of despair crossed her features. "My grandmother? Where is she?" she asked urgently.

"I could've used that information as a bargaining chip but to show you that I have no ulterior motive..." He cleared his throat before he continued. "She's staying with me."

Indistinct chatter rose from the girls, who all felt alarmed and on edge.

Gypsy snapped, "Why the hell should we believe you?" She thrust her knife menacingly in his direction. "Maybe I should slice you into pieces to shut your lying ass up?"

Pretzel approached Angelica swiftly and whispered in her ear, "Be careful, Angelica. The Nephilim have many spies and this guy could simply be luring you into a trap. Besides, we have other enemies we should be concerned about."

Tassel jumped in, "Yeah, and if he's not an informant, he could still be one of those fanatical zealots."

"Zealot?" Angelica inquired.

"I'll explain later," her roommate promised.

When he realized that the news had not been taken as well as he had expected, Ortega exclaimed, "Look!" Beads of sweat formed on his forehead. "If I had different intentions, this place would be swarming with cops by now. I take it this place isn't Saint Miriam's Shelter for Children and Women." He swallowed hard and his gaze scanned the abundant surveillance cameras positioned on the nearby building. "Your grandmother is...how can I put this? She's a very excitable person. She asked a slew of questions and even though I'm a grown man, she's lectured me a ton."

Angelica spun toward Gypsy. "It certainly sounds like her. I don't think he's lying—"

"Whatever you are fighting, I know they are more than human," Ortega's voice spoke over hers.

Gypsy looked at her and then at the agent. She sighed deeply and lowered her blade. Turning to Tassel, she asked for her cell phone and walked a few feet away from the group. Her conversation on the line was inaudible to the others.

After a few minutes, she returned to the group and said to him, "Follow us."

Ortega waited patiently in a small conference room in a secluded and remote location away from the central DW warehouse building. He sat at a chestnut circular table that seated eight with an untouched steaming cup of coffee in front of him.

The two roommates sat opposite him in utter silence and both parties gave each other awkward stares, nods, and smiles. Angelica jiggled her foot, eager to ask about the condition and whereabouts of her grandmother, but she refrained from speaking or asking any questions as she had been instructed to do by Gypsy.

After an extended period, Joan strode into the conference room with Gypsy, their demeanors intense and suspicious. The leader sat next to Pretzel but the other woman remained standing at the door.

"Mr. Ortega, my name is Amelia Evans, and I'm one of the overseers of these facilities. I hear you have come seeking answers?"

Angelica gave her a fleeting gaze when she realized she'd finally learned Joan's real name.

"It's subtle but I hear an English accent. Is there any chance you are related to the late and renowned Oxford historian Professor Elizabeth J Evans?" asked Ortega as he finally took a sip of his coffee.

"I've lived in the States since I was a teen. I didn't realize I still had an accent. You have good ears and are well informed," responded Joan. "Yes, she was my mother. I'm curious how you know of her."

"First, I'm a big fan of her work on Joan of Arc. *The Maid of Orleans – The Heroine of France* is one of my favorite articles written by her."

Once again, Angelica glanced at the leader when she realized the source of her *Memento Vivere*.

"Though I wasn't too fond of her opinion on Joan being the offspring of a human and an angelic being," added the agent.

"That's unfortunate," Joan said with a sarcastic smirk. "Out of all her views, it's my favorite."

"But it was through the bureau's connections with several of our UK intelligence liaisons that I first became aware of her. The specifics of her murder match many of the homicides the bureau has been investigating throughout the nation."

The woman's eyes glistened at the mention of her mother's death. Clearing her throat, she asked, "So, Mr. Ortega, how can we help you?"

He leaned forward with his elbows on the table and his hands slightly elevated. "For starters, who the heck are you people?"

She steepled her slim fingers together as she leaned back in the chair and answered, "Mr. Ortega, you already have some intimation that we are more than what we seem and if that's true, you will understand why we would be hesitant to disclose too much information." She placed her hands flat on the table and continued. "Why don't you tell us what you know and we'll fill some gaps in along the way."

Ortega relaxed in his chair and stroked his unshaven face with his hand. "Okay, that sounds fair enough." He exhaled softly. "I think I should start from the beginning. Since its inception, the FBI has been involved in investigating a peculiar kind of murder, all involving female victims killed under abnormal circumstances. Some folks at the bureau have come to call them aberrant killings since there seems to be no working theory as to why they were targeted, and the methods used to slay them are bizarre and particularly gruesome.

"Several of the oddities surrounding these cases include unidentified poisons, murder weapons lacking fingerprints, and bodies that were impaled to walls and ceilings, which would have required an immense amount of force. But what's most perplexing for me is that most of the victims were adolescent females." He gave Joan a quick look and glanced around the room, expecting a response, no doubt thinking that what he said was enough to warrant an explanation.

When none was forthcoming, the agent continued.

"The few times that male bodies have been recovered at these scenes, evidence would suggest that they were the aggressors. However, the most puzzling aspect of all is that their DNA has baffled our forensic specialists. The analysis revealed that their makeup is human but in some way, it's something more.

"At first, we dismissed this as contamination but after further recovered samples, it became impossible to ignore. Some within the department began calling it mutant blood." He shrugged and sipped his coffee. "Another striking feature of these crime scenes was how these men were killed. All appeared to have died from wounds that had silicon dioxide residue, which implies they were inflicted by weapons of some type of mineral. I have a strong suspicion that the makeup of the weapons I saw these girls using at the hospital and earlier outside would match our findings." Once again, he stopped in the hope that someone would interject with some clarification, but all he got in return was vacant stares.

"Ahem! Incidentally, I became involved with this kind of serial killing when I was a young detective for the Lancaster Police Department. Coincidentally, it involved Angelica's mother." He gestured at her with his finger.

She bit her lip anxiously, desperate to know more about her mother—what he knew, how she was killed, and if he had known her personally.

"That's how I became aware of Maria Santos and an infant Angelica. And here we are, full circle. My latest case involves both of these women. Call it fate, I guess."

No longer able to maintain her composure, Angelica blurted, "Is my grandmother okay?"

He nodded sharply.

Before he could respond verbally, Joan motioned to Angelica with her hand and fixed her gaze on him. "Mr. Ortega, in the past, we have encountered other individuals like you—deeply knowledgeable and seemingly well-intentioned and courteous. These individuals came from various walks of life and professions but in the end, they have all turned out to have ulterior motives." She removed a blade from its sheath on her belt and placed it on the table.

Gypsy followed suit and drew her blade as well.

The leader continued. "They all wanted to know the same thing—who we are."

A sheen of sweat became visible on his brow. "I came here in good faith to get answers and provide any help I can. Look, I can prove it." He slid his hand into the inner pocket of his blazer.

Gypsy lunged toward him and thundered, "Don't even try it, butt-wipe!" She held the dagger tightly in her hand, ready to strike at a moment's notice. "I'll put it right through your freaking skull."

Slowly and methodically, he removed his cell phone from the blazer and displayed it to them. "It's merely my smartphone." He gestured placatingly. "No need to panic. I have given her a secure cell phone. Let me call her to prove to you that Maria Santos is staying with me. Is it okay if I call?"

Joan looked at Angelica, caught her desperate gaze, and focused on Ortega with a nod. "Put the call on speaker. If no one answers or someone else picks up, you're dead." Her tone was steady and determined.

He dialed the number with trembling fingers and had to backspace to correct the misdial before he clicked the Call icon. The ringtone sounded once, twice, thrice, with no answer. Sweat clung to his brow and each second felt like a ticking time bomb until finally, a voice spoke over the line. "Hello."

The agent's face paled. He snapped hastily, "Put Maria on the line—now!"

Joan looked at Gypsy and ordered, "Kill him."

"Wait!" he screamed. "It's my wife." He held one arm up as he clutched the phone desperately.

"Cariño, is everything okay? Why are you yelling? Kill, who?" his wife asked.

"Honey, I can't explain now. I know it's late but get her on the phone immediately!" he exclaimed. His gaze remained fixed on Gypsy's blade.

After a moment that felt like hours, a feeble, low, and hoarse voice was heard over the line. Ortega slowly and gently passed the phone to Angelica.

She spoke quickly and her voice quivered. "Hello!" Tears streaked down her face when she heard her grandmother's voice for the first time since the hospital.

Joan's stern demeanor softened and she turned to Angelica. "You can take the call in the hallway."

Removing the call from speaker, she rose from her chair and walked out of the conference room. "I'm fine, *Abuela*. Are you okay?" Her voice faded as she stepped through the door.

Joan beckoned Gypsy to put the blade away.

Ortega slumped on the chair, buried his face in his

hands, and heaved a loud sigh. "You guys are tougher than the bureau," he muttered, the protest muffled.

Joan turned her attention to the agent. "My apologies for the drastic measures. The protection and safety of these women is my priority and as you may have noticed, we don't easily trust anyone who comes knocking at our door." She looked at Pretzel and said, "Make sure she's okay."

Pretzel nodded and hurried after Angelica.

"So, Mr. Ortega, how much time do you have?"

"As long as you can keep the coffee coming. I have all night."

24

TREACHERY AND TRUST

"Mist, why don't you head to your room and get some rest? You've been here for days and you've had little to no rest or sustenance. I'm concerned for your health." May rubbed her back softly where she sat with her head against the rail of the bed Jewels rested on.

She straightened on the chair.

The caregiver moved her hand to her shoulder, and Mist held it softly as she gazed at her with weary eyes.

"Even if I head to my room, May, my mind will remain here. I'll simply make myself wearier tossing and turning in bed." She released her hand and yawned, her mouth wide. "I'll be more at ease once she makes a full recovery. I've seen her eyes flicker at times. That's a good sign, right?"

"You have to give it time, Mist. She's been through so much, physically and emotionally." May's gaze turned to Jewels' gentle but now scarred face. "The good news is she's responded well to the medication we have given her intravenously and thanks to you, the blood transfusion saved her life."

"There are times when I can sense her dread, fear, and almost like an emptiness. It...it breaks my heart to see her this way." Her voice cracked as she spoke. "She's always been a strong and brave woman, ready for any challenge, and never walked away from what she needed to do." She sighed sharply. "I do worry that she may never recover from this. Especially once she finds out that she's the only one...who..." She choked down a sob.

The caregiver responded softly, "I guess it means we all need to be here for her when she recovers."

Mist tilted her head with a warm half-smile.

"When was the last time you two spoke?" the other woman asked.

"A week before the attack," she answered. "I was so looking forward to speaking to her again and informing her that we had found Eva Santos' daughter alive and well." She yawned again and rubbed her eyes. "Excuse me. I need a nice cup of tea."

"Hmm..." May pursed her lips. "It's not tea you need."

"I thought you would say that," said Mist and cleared her throat.

"Anyway...Eva Santos...are you saying you and Jewels knew Angelica's mom?" asked an intrigued May.

"Yes. She spent some time in the Lancaster compound but we lost track of her and feared the worst for her and her pregnancy." Her countenance grew grim and sullen. "It was all that traitor's fault—Duplicity."

"Duplicity? Is that the same one Joan mentioned in the

council meeting who spoke the prophecy?" asked the caregiver.

Mist nodded. "Personally, I didn't put much stock in the words of a turncoat and besides, we thought the child had died along with her mother."

"How did her mother die?"

"That traitor convinced her to drink some poison."

"That would certainly do it," May affirmed. "I can't believe that someone could become so vile as to do such a thing."

A momentary silence hung between them. Mist's expression grew grim as her mind worked. "Maybe that's what I'm afraid of, May—afraid that another of our own allowed their heart to be darkened with such cruelty and caused so much destruction. I've seen the aftermath of treachery firsthand and it frightens me."

"It terrifies me simply to hear about it," said May. "So much so that it makes me wonder how it's even possible. We are linked to each other through our SPA. We feel each other's presence, pain, happiness, and when we are stressed or excited. But beyond that, we are a family, and for someone to have shared the benefits of the community, to have felt our joy and our suffering, and to repay it with thorny betrayal is beyond my comprehension." She shook her head as she raised her arms and linked her hands behind her head.

"I wish I could say it's impossible but we know it can happen. It troubles me that it may have happened in Lancaster and if that's the case, it makes me wonder if it could happen here." Mist's face was perturbed. "If I'm honest with myself, it's the reason I've avoided the topic altogether."

"Treachery is older than dirt, and it happened even in the heavens. It's the reason we are in this mess in the first place," the other woman said. "Yet providence has taught us that just as evil appears in the most unexpected places, good seems to arise in the most unforeseen ways." Her gaze fixed on her companion while the woman was focused on Jewels. "I hope it never comes to that but if it ever does, I have faith that good will arise."

Mist turned to her with a smile and nodded. "Me too."

The dawning sun cascaded its orange and yellow hues over the dark sky by the time Ortega finished his last question. He had been intrigued, mesmerized, and fascinated but also frightened by all that Joan had told him. A week earlier, he would have considered it all a bad joke but after his personal encounter with the Nephilim, it had become like a newfound religion.

The woman had vehemently stressed the reason for the secrecy and confidentiality of this information. She briefed him on the presence of moles and spies within the government and of the existence of fanatical human groups like the Star of Nimrod bent on the destruction of all hybrids. Most importantly, she warned him of the danger this knowledge would place him and his loved ones in.

The agent gave his solemn oath to keep their secrets and provide any assistance the group needed in the full knowledge that if he broke their trust, he would place them in grave danger. If stopping the Nephilim was not something he, the bureau, or any law enforcement could do, he would at least be an ally to the people who could. He thanked her for the trust she had granted him.

Exhausted, he strode to his car beside Angelica. As they walked, he related all he knew about her mother's death, his encounter with Maria Santos twenty-two years earlier, and what he found at the scene of her apartment.

"I do apologize if you expected more about your mother." He retrieved his keys and unlocked the car door. "I was only involved with the investigation surrounding her death, although given all I have learned today, it is clear who was behind it." His brow knitted. "But like I said to you and your team earlier, I somehow feel fate has brought us together, and as ill-fated as these events have seemed, who knows? There may be a purpose to all this."

She glanced at the horizon and squinted at the late-summer morning sun. "It seems the more information I get, the more questions I have. I wish things were less complicated."

"Things rarely are." He smirked but the expression was also kind.

As she handed him his cell phone, she said, "I'm sorry I drained your battery, Mr. Ortega." Her face now revealed exhaustion. "It was great to talk to her again. I can't remember the last time we spoke for so long."

"You're all she talks about. She even accused me of not finding you quickly enough," he said with a chuckle.

"That's my grandma, all right."

"It goes to show how much she's missed you." He sighed deeply. "I can't bring you to see her yet. My house has become something of a witness protection home and it is carefully monitored. If I take you now and you are apprehended, you'll be in federal custody for quite some time, trying to answer more questions than your grandmother asks."

Angelica smiled although deep inside, she was disappointed.

When he saw her disheartened face, he tried to reassure her. "She does have a personal nurse attending her all day, and her health is improving significantly. I'll also work on getting you a secure line so you can talk to her regularly."

"I'd appreciate that, Mr. Ortega, and I'm grateful you opened your doors for my grandmother. It means a lot." A concerned look filled her face. "Do you know how long this could last?"

"The hospital incident has seriously rattled the bureau, especially with the death of an agent. They're keeping this entire incident under wraps and are looking for anyone in connection to this case. To avoid any press coverage that might obstruct the investigation, they fabricated the narrative surrounding the deaths in the hospital, including my partner's. Unfortunately, they have you and your friends on surveillance video, so you are all wanted for questioning." His lips formed a thin line. "I promised Amelia that I'd work diligently on my side to get you all cleared. Please be patient with me while I work this out." He sat in the driver's seat and started the vehicle.

"Like my grandmother says, *un poquito de paciencia.*"

Ortega smiled. "Wait, I know this one. She says it all the

time around me…uh, a little patience never hurt anyone." A smile spread on both their faces. "It's good advice."

"I know. I've come to learn it the hard way."

She closed the car door and watched the man drive away.

KNOWING THY GIFT

Olivia tossed and turned in her bed, mumbled incoherently in her sleep, and shook her head restlessly while beads of cold sweat formed on her forehead. Her diminutive young body flinched and shuddered, her breathing ragged and shallow and her expression twisted by a harrowing nightmare that consumed her during the early hours of the night.

Within the dream, girls fled frantically and screamed in terror, desperation, and pain. An immensely vicious fight was in progress between the Daughters of the Watchers and the Nephilim. She grew despairing and was filled with dread as she witnessed Daughters being felled by the foul creatures. Her heart drummed violently at the sight of the Daimons in hideous, malevolent forms that induced fear and horror throughout the warehouse.

She turned her gaze away from the terrifying sight, only to behold a throng of Nephilim inundating the place she now called home. Among them was a woman who wore a dark shift and conspired with the enemy. The gathered Daughters, bloody, hurt, and in despair, were surrounded and huddled together with nowhere to run. She screamed and was awoken when she saw a repulsive Daimon, more grotesque and powerful than the others, kill one with shoulder-length ebony hair and hazel-brown eyes.

While she made her rounds, Angelica heard a scream and rushed to the bed where it had originated. "It's okay, Olivia, I'm here."

The girl wept profusely and her feeble, tiny body shuddered as she breathed in a series of short gasps. Her matted, damp curly blonde hair covered her baby-soft face while her head rested on the older girl's chest.

"I'm here now... I'm here," Angelica repeated soothingly and pushed wisps of the girl's hair away from her bright blue eyes. She remembered seeing that same look and sensing similar emotions from her when their gazes had first locked a few months earlier at the Gathering Hall.

After a long while during which she simply held her for comfort, she asked, "You want to talk about it?"

Olivia shook her head, her expression still etched with uneasiness. "No. I had a nightmare," she said softly and her breathing normalized although her heart pounded as hard as before.

"You don't have to say anything. It's only a bad dream we don't want to remember." The girl nodded quickly. "I'll stay with you until you fall asleep. Is that all right?"

With her thumb in her mouth, she mumbled, "Okay."

Angelica leaned her upper back against the headboard

while Olivia lay on her side. She glanced quickly around the room to ensure that the other three girls were sleeping undisturbed in their beds.

The child tilted her head gently and locked her shiny gaze on her. "In the dream, you died," she muttered in a low, concerned voice.

She gulped. "It was only a nightmare, honey. Go back to sleep."

Neither the bright fall sun that illuminated the room nor the wild, playful cheers of children playing served to snap Angelica out of her slumber. It took Mrs. Poppins' gentle nudge and soft voice to reach her.

"Wake up, lassie."

Slowly, she opened her weary eyelids, blinked them once or twice, and focused on the round-faced older woman with a broad smile. Her first reaction was a deep frown that creased her brow as she took her surroundings in groggily. She drew a sharp breath and groaned with her hand at her lower back when she realized she was still on Olivia's bed and now woke with old-man cramps and old-woman moans. "I'm sorry, Mrs. Poppins." Her voice was hoarse. "Olivia had a nightmare last night so I stayed with her until she fell asleep. It appears I dozed off myself."

"You must have done a good job. She was one of the first to get up this morning," she said in her highland Scottish accent.

With a loud yawn, she straightened on the bed. "Excuse

me," she said bashfully. "This is embarrassing. It's my shift to help with the kids and here I am, still sleeping in one of the children's beds."

"Don't worry about it, my love. I'm glad you were here to offer your assistance." Mrs. Poppins walked toward the window to let the crisp October air into the room. "Most of the younglings have now gone to the cafeteria to have breakfast." She stooped to pick up Olivia's stuffed panda plushy from the floor. "She likes you, you know," she told her as she tossed the toy to her. "You were the only one she could talk about this morning."

Angelica smiled. "She's a sweetheart." Her expression sobered quickly when she thought about the girl's dream. "But last night's dream must have freaked her out. She looked completely terrified as if she'd seen a monster. I asked her what it was about, but she didn't say. She only said that I died."

The woman strode closer and sat at the edge of the bed with a furrowed brow. "Most of these kids have suffered more than regular folks have in their entire lives. Olivia, for example, lost her mom tragically and arrived around the same time you did. She misses her dearly." She placed her hand over hers. "I'm wondering if her fondness of you is what caused the bad dream."

"That makes sense," she agreed.

"She seems very attached to you so I guess she's afraid of losing you too." A comforting smile appeared on her face. "I have seen this happen with most of these girls so I wouldn't concern myself about it."

A curious expression spread across her face as she

clutched Olivia's stuffed panda. "Mrs. Poppins, could Olivia be a seer?"

"Possibly. I believe that we're born with our gifts. In fact, many lassies begin to see their gift around her age. Of course, some are more obvious than others, which some girls notice very early on, and then there are the subtle ones that come to light over time. I'm no expert on this subject but most of the time, we have used our gifts without even knowing it."

"What do you mean?"

"Oh…for example, I have always enjoyed helping others since I was a bairn but didn't realize until I was much older that my gift was being a helper and I had used it all along." She stared curiously at her. "Why the questions on gifts, dear?"

"Today is the day I reveal my *Memento Vivere*."

"Congratulations!" Mrs. Poppins clapped enthusiastically. "I'm so happy for you. I love the Memento Commemoration. It's such a special occasion."

"Thank you, but I don't know what my gift is yet. I'm beginning to feel that I don't have one so I feel kind of awkward going into tonight's event without having an idea what it is."

"Oh, dear!" The woman pulled her closer and embraced her tenderly. "Don't concern yourself about that. A gift doesn't define you. It's only an extension of you. Knowing who you are is more important than what you can do. The Memento Commemoration is a time when we gather to celebrate new beginnings, not to fret about gifts. Remember that, okay?" She glanced at her watch and her eyes widened. "My goodness. I'm running late. Excuse me, my dear I have to pick the girls up."

"Thank you," Angelica said as the woman scuttled out the door. She sat on the bed for a while and wondered if Olivia's nightmare was a prediction or nothing more than a little girl's bad dream.

MEMENTO VIVERE

The Gathering Hall was filled with the sound of gaiety and laughter. Indistinct chatter hummed through the hall as the Daughters waited for the Memento Commemoration to start. Daughters of all ages assembled and filled the auditorium's two-column seating. The first row from the northwest corner was reserved for the senior council of the Tri-State Area Daughters of the Watchers.

Angelica waited, grave and silent, along with a group of eleven other Daughters of various ages, to reveal to the assembly her *Memento Vivere*. They wore the ceremonial long white vestment—the traditional Memento attire—which represented new beginnings. The inaugurating Daughters stood anxiously outside on the northeast side entrance of the Gathering Hall.

"So, are you excited?" Reina asked in her perky voice and clapped enthusiastically.

She nodded grimly, her face pale.

"You'll be fine," stated Pretzel in an attempt to comfort

her very nervous-looking roommate. "If you get overly anxious, remember to breathe deeply."

"How is it in there?" Her voice trembled slightly. "Was it as crowded when you did yours?" she asked.

"The Memento Commemoration is always exciting for the Daughters." Pretzel peeked inside the auditorium quickly and shook her head. "There isn't the same number," she said with an affectionate smile.

Some relief appeared on Angelica's face.

"It's so much fuller." Her friend snickered.

"Hey! You're supposed to encourage me."

"Relax. I'm only trying to take the edge off." She stroked Angelica's shoulder gently. "I know it's nerve-wracking, but you'll do great."

"What if they laugh when I reveal my *Memento Vivere*?" Her body remained tense.

"We have heard some very—how can I say it?—eccentric MVs, but we all know to show honor and respect to that name. It's a sign to you and to the team of the good that name stands for." Pretzel's gaze was steady and comforting.

"Know that you'll see us yelling and cheering you on the entire time," Reina added and bounced with anticipation.

"Thank you so much, guys. I can honestly say I couldn't have done it without you." She embraced both of them in a group hug. In that instant, the lights dimmed to signal the commencement of the ceremony.

"Good luck," said Pretzel as she walked away.

"You got this, girl!" exclaimed Reina and gave her two thumbs-up.

Jingle, the ceremony coordinator, walked out to the corridor to give the girls final instructions. "All right, ladies, exactly as we rehearsed. At the sound of the music track, I'll signal you to make your way into the hall. The senior council will enter from the northwest side at the same time. When the music ends, Joan will begin the ceremony with the Daughters of the Watchers mantra and ask the Daughters to take their seats. You'll remain standing front and center of the room the entire time."

Jingle gestured at one of the girls with a smile on her face, "No slouching, Sara." The fifteen-year-old nodded her head. "Right after the rites of the solemn oath have been read and answered affirmatively, each of you will proceed with the declaration of your *Memento Vivere*." She sighed after the lengthy explanation. "Now, any questions?"

None followed, only blank stares from the group.

"Good luck to you all, then."

After a few more minutes of waiting anxiously, Jingle gave the girls the signal to proceed and they walked forward with solemn faces. The senior council consisting of twelve members strode in as well. They wore their ceremonial cerulean-blue garments that displayed the emblem of the Daughters of the Watchers on the chest—a golden embroidery of an unfolded, three-leaved Nerium Oleander flower. All twelve members took their places in the empty front row. The assembly all stood and clapped and cheered for the inaugurating Daughters. A little louder than the crowd, Reina's voice yelled Angelica's name enthusiastically. Joan took center stage between the podium and the initiates. She gestured for silence with her hand.

"Let us all say the Daughters of the Watchers mantra," she instructed.

The entire hall reverberated as the assembled declared in unison: "Hope, Faith, and Love. We are a beacon of hope, a stand of faith, and the radiance of love amid the darkness. We are the Daughters of the Watchers—strong alone and unconquerable together."

"You may all take your seats," she directed the group. "The Memento Commemoration is a time of celebration, reflection, and new beginnings as these Daughters who now stand before us will honor us today by revealing their *Memento Viveres*."

The assembly responded with applause.

"The *Memento Vivere* is more than a name. It is a reflection of a portion of our past to remind us that no matter how obscure, dark, and uncertain the future appears, it is not the darkness that leads us but the light that has been bestowed on us. The *Memento Vivere* is an image and an indication that no matter how tragic and sorrowful our past has been, good was still there to show us to not despair. This *Memento Vivere* will forever be recorded in the canon of our history. It is an identity chosen by Daughters, used by Daughters, and only for Daughters."

Cheers and claps thundered through the hall.

Joan turned to the inaugurating Daughters with a solemn and stern look. "Ladies, I will now recite the Daughters of the Watchers Rites of the Solemn Oath which you will respond affirmatively to—if you agree of course."

Mrs. Mozart walked toward her with a rustic mocha-brown voluminous book titled with gold lettering. *The Ways of the Daughters* was a book Angelica had read but in a more modern binding. The woman handed the text to Joan and returned gracefully to her seat.

She turned to the bookmarked page and continued. "As you take this solemn oath, keep in mind that this rite you undertake will induct you into this community and bind you to all Daughters of the world. Today, you are bonded not only through our supernatural connection but in the fellowship and unity of Daughterhood."

She turned her focus to the book and the first section of the oath, *Protect*, and read, "Do you Daughters of the Watchers promise to protect, cover, and shield your fellow Daughter, to be your sister's keeper, and put them before you even at the cost of your life?"

The twelve girls responded in unison: "We will."

Two months and two weeks earlier: Day of the Lancaster Attack

"The power is still out and it doesn't look like we will get it back any time soon," exclaimed Sparrow, her face grim. "All lines of communication seem to be down." She looked at her cell phone, which still had no signal. "It seems to be a form of a cell phone jammer." Her eyes widened as a wave of realization crashed over her. "We are under attack."

She turned to her second in command. "We can't send a distress signal while the power is out. Jewels, our priority at this time is to protect the little ones, so gather a few of the guards and take them to the bunkers below the building. Make sure they're guarding those doors at all times."

Jewels nodded, her dark-brown eyes filled with determination. She wound her espresso-brown hair into a bun, ready to act.

"Do you have your radio with you?"

"I have it right here." She unclipped it from her belt and gestured at it.

"Put it on channel six. Let me know when the girls are safe and sound in the bunkers."

She hurried away to do as she was instructed.

Sparrow's gaze moved to Sunny as she stated, "We have to send a distress signal out. The security system has a secondary power source able to keep it running long enough to send for help. Since the main power is out, I can't send it from my office. I need you to initiate it manually from the core. Unfortunately, you'll have to go on your own as I'll need all who can fight to set up defensive positions."

Sunny looked out of the office window and the dry summer wind billowed her long midnight-black hair. She saw nothing but sensed the advance of imminent danger. Her senses were overwhelmed by the invading menace. "This doesn't feel good, Sparrow. There must be hundreds of them out there. Even if we send a distress signal, I don't think they'll be here fast enough to help," she said emphatically.

"We need to do everything possible to hold them back as long as we can. We have no other option. The protection of the Daughters is our priority." She dug in her desk drawer, retrieved a two-way radio, and handed it to her. "The system is locked behind a cage. You have the clearance to use your fingerprint biometrics to unlock it. Once you have done so and sent the signal, radio me." Her gaze focused on Sunny, who appeared distracted. "You got that?"

She nodded and raced as fast as she could to the security station.

The Memento Commemoration

Joan's gaze turned to the second section of the oath, *Service*, and she read, "Do you Daughters of the Watchers promise to wholeheartedly, in love and honesty, serve your fellow Daughters, this community, and other Daughters around the world?"

The twelve girls responded in unison, "We will."

The Attack on Lancaster

"Sparrow, all the stone gates seemed to be unlocked!" exclaimed Aster, the training coordinator for the Lancaster group, who looked terrified. She handed the binoculars to Sparrow, who glared in dismay from the rooftop of the building.

"How's that even possible?" the leader gasped. "These stone walls are impossible for them to leap over or tear down. They are our main line of defense. It's like leaving the vault open at a bank." She grasped the radio and called Jewels. "Jewels, are the younglings in the bunkers?"

Within seconds, the woman answered, "They're all secure. I've placed guardians on all the doors."

"I need you to stay there. It doesn't look good from up here," Sparrow responded.

"What's going on?" she asked.

"I don't know how, but the gates were left open."

"What the hell?" the woman demanded.

"My sentiments exactly." She sighed, hoped that Sunny had made some progress, and clicked the radio button. "Sunny, are you there?" She waited a few seconds but received no response aside from static. "Sunny, do you copy?"

Initially, she heard only the radio's noise but eventually, Sunny's voice came through. "I don't get this system. I'm having problems finding the location of the distress signal mechanism."

"Damn it!" Sparrow said in frustration but not on the radio. "I need you to head to the video surveillance station. It also has a secondary power source. Somehow, the gates were left open so I need you to be our eyes using the video surveillance and give us intel."

"Copy that," she replied.

"Jewels, are you there?" Sparrow reached out again.

"I'm here!" she responded swiftly.

"I need you to head to the security station and send a manual distress signal. Sunny couldn't figure it out, so I need you to handle it."

"Copy that!"

Sparrow gasped when she saw the initial group of Nephilim rush toward the compound. "May the Sovereign One help us," she muttered. She raised her hand and thumped a button in front of her. Seconds later, a slew of quartz arrows hurtled at the invaders.

. . .

The Memento Commemoration

Joan moved to the third and last section of the oath, *Honor*, and read, "Do you Daughters of the Watchers promise to honor and respect your fellow Daughters, from the youngest to the oldest, the leaders to the workers, the strongest to the weakest, and the wisest to the inexperienced?"

The twelve girls responded in unison. "We will."

The Attack on Lancaster

After hours of fierce engagement, the Nephilim managed to infiltrate the compound and overwhelm the Daughters. Sparrow staggered as she carried a gravely injured Aster who, despite having been punctured in her abdomen by a steel blade, still clenched a knife in her hand.

"Only a little more," the leader muttered. By then, she looked and felt fatigued. She placed Aster on the floor against the wall of a long corridor that led toward the security station and retrieved her radio. "Sunny, are you there?" Her call brought no response. "Sunny, do you copy me?" Again, she heard nothing but silence. "I haven't heard from her since I sent her to the surveillance station," she murmured. She turned to the wounded woman, who spewed blood from her mouth. Her heart heavy, she took a handkerchief from a pocket, crouched slightly, and began to wipe the blood. "You hang in there, you hear me?" Her voice shook as she spoke.

"I won't make it, Sparrow," Aster said softly, her breathing labored.

"Do not give up on me, Aster." She went to pick her up but the woman refused.

"Leave me. I'll try to hold them off for as long as I can." She stopped as she began to cough. Her glistening eyes stared intently at Sparrow, who couldn't hide her dismay. "You know this was sabotage. We have a traitor in our midst."

Suddenly, a Nephilim appeared and lunged toward the leader. Aster sensed him and drew on the last of her strength. With one continuous motion, she pushed the other woman out of the way, bounded forward, and plunged her blade into his skull. The Nephilim fell lifeless while Aster was thrown into the wall by the impact.

Sparrow scrambled close to her and exclaimed, "Are you okay?"

The woman did not respond.

Desperately, she grasped Aster's body and turned it toward her to reveal the crimson-stained blade that protruded from her side. Tears coursed down her face—another of her friends was dead.

She had no clue how severe the breach was or who was left. All she knew was that she had to reach the security station to ensure that the distress signal was sent. Sensing and hearing footsteps fast approaching, she sprinted toward the station. After several quick twists and turns, she arrived at her destination, panting and gasping for air. She had hoped that the signal had already been sent and that help was coming. Jewels knew the system and she wouldn't fail her. Her gaze scanned for her second, who wasn't there.

Frantic, she grasped her radio. "Jewels, do you copy me?

Jewels!" Finally, she accepted that the woman hadn't made it.

As she turned her head toward the security alarm, a panicked expression crossed her face. In place of the panel was a tangled web of jaggedly torn wires. "Of course you couldn't find the mechanism, Sunny. You destroyed it." She sighed bitterly when she realized the inevitable truth. "We are already dead."

The Memento Commemoration

Joan closed the book and bowed her head. "May the Sovereign One watch over you, keep you, and help you to fulfill this vow." She then glanced at all twelve initiates and said, "You will now step forward and honor us with the *Memento Vivere* you have chosen."

Sara, the first in the group, took the center stage. "Hello, my name is Sara McKinley and in honor of my mother and stepfather, who both loved and protected me to the end, my *Memento Vivere* is Geneva—my city, my birth home, and where my parents will forever lay at rest."

Cheers and applause from the assembly echoed through the hall. The leader turned and nodded to Mrs. Mozart, who was inscribing the names in a book titled *Canons of the Memento Viveres*.

She gestured to the next initiate, who took the stage as Geneva returned to her place. "Hi, everyone. I'm Jennifer Balter. On this day, I wish to honor my late aunt Elaine, who saw more in me than anyone else. My *Memento Vivere* is Spring, the season she loved the most."

Again, the audience roared with cheers while Mrs. Mozart inscribed her name in the book.

Angelica was next and she looked paler than before. She cleared her throat before she spoke. "My name is Angelica Santos. I want to honor a person who's been my guardian angel since infancy. She is a woman who has sacrificed so much and has been more than I could have ever asked for—my grandmother, Maria Santos. My *Memento Vivere* is…"

The Attack on Lancaster

As Sparrow gazed in dismay at the remnants of the security alarm, she heard indistinct chatter from across the room where the video surveillance station was located. The conversation seemed to take place between a female and a male. She eased out of the security station and into the surveillance room without being detected.

The voices appeared to come from the back of the room. When she found an open closet door, she scuttled to it and hoped to learn who was speaking and about what. She peeked through the gap, gasped, and clapped her hand over her mouth when she saw a pair of legs protruding from behind the surveillance desk. Unfortunately, she was unable to ascertain who it was and if they were dead or alive.

She continued to stare through the narrow aperture and studied the man who was talking. He was young and handsome with chiseled features and very well dressed. Her senses confirmed that he was a Daimon. Next to him stood another young man.

"You have done well." The Daimon paced the room with his hands behind his back.

"Thank you, my lord," responded the woman. Sparrow moved her head and tried to detect who spoke. She sensed a Daughter but the feeling was off. While the voice was familiar, she could not identify the person.

"Many like you have failed in the past but you have granted us a great victory today." He stared at the body on the floor. "You even managed to kill one of your own."

"Anything to show my allegiance to you," she said.

He shook his index finger and said coldly, "But you can't truly be loyal to me unless I give you the mark. You need to be baptized in pain."

The Daughter gulped audibly and responded, "Anything you require of me. My allegiance is to you now."

Instantly, the Daimon took on a hideous nature—a charcoal-black translucent figure with crimson eyes that flickered menacingly. The Daimon raised his hand and breathed fire into it. "Kneel!" he commanded. "Your name will be Villainous." He placed his fiery hand on her right arm.

The woman uttered a bloodcurdling scream and almost passed out from the agonizing pain. Instantly, the Greek letters of the name πονηρά appeared on her arm. They initially glinted in black but then vanished from sight.

The Daimon returned to his human form. He turned to the young man next to him. "Her next task will require a more substantial change. My master had the ability to impart spirits of the ancient past. I surmise that you too should possess this power."

Without a word, the young man stepped forward and placed his hand on Villainous' head. Instantly, the room went cold and the lights of the room began to flicker. A gloomy shriek filled the room.

A loud scream seemed to emanate from the depth of the earth.

Villainous began to shake convulsively as a dark manifestation with no face or figure slowly infiltrated her body. The veins on her neck bulged as she screamed frantically and clutched her throat. A few agonizing moments later, she dropped to the floor as if dead.

The young man stepped back and smirked with satisfaction.

After a few seconds, the woman gasped loudly as if breathing for the first time. She pushed onto all fours and coughed violently, fighting for air.

The Daimon's eyes glowed and his lips curved in malicious delight. "Stand," he ordered as he stared grimly at her. "You are the first of a new order. You will now be my priestess."

Villainous glanced at her hands, feet, and body as if awoken to something that was not there before. She turned her gaze to the Daimon before her.

"There's an important mission I need you to deal with. I have discovered that my female offspring is still alive. One of your predecessors predicted that this offspring could possess great power—a weapon I need. I have issued a search for the girl, but..." He took a step closer to Villainous. "I suspect your friends in the city have interfered. I need you to infiltrate them and gather information to report to me." He placed his hands on the sides of her arms. She grimaced and flinched in pain when he squeezed the newly-marked arm. "Make sure she stays there. I hope to have a father-daughter talk when I pay the place a similar visit."

"And the rest, my lord?"

"We did good work here," he said with a cruel smile. "We'll give them the same courtesy." He turned his back on her and as he proceeded to leave, he instructed, "One more thing. Inform them of this attack. You will need a form of transportation there."

He looked at his companion. "Give her your working cell phone."

The young man extracted a black smartphone from his pocket and tossed it to her. "The code is all sixes."

"Call them now and make it sound convincing," ordered the Daimon.

"Yes, my lord."

Leonard and the young man walked out of the room.

Villainous called the Daughters of the Watchers NYC compound and summoned a desperate, terrified tone. "The Lancaster compound...it's under attack! We need help. This is—" She stopped suddenly and looked toward the closet, hung up, and retrieved her dagger. "I know you're there. Come out."

Sparrow was almost overwhelmed with horror by the new sensation she felt from the woman. Gone was the familiar connection to a fellow Daughter, replaced by a cold and dark feeling. Where there had once been life, there was now only void and darkness.

She stepped out of the closet and steeled herself for the confrontation with the traitor as the mark on Villainous' arm reappeared.

The Memento Commemoration

"Angel," Angelica said enthusiastically. "My grandmother has always referred to me as her Angel but to be honest, she's always been mine."

Those assembled cheered loudly as returned to her place, while Reina yelled loudly for all to hear, "You go, Angel!"

After all twelve of the Daughters had announced their names, Joan gestured for the assembly to stand. They complied with shouts of acclamation and she instructed, "Let us all salute these Daughters."

The group exclaimed in unison, "We Daughters of the Watchers salute you. You are one of us and we are one of you. In light or darkness, united we stand."

Their leader beckoned to the crowd with her hand and stated, "Come up and congratulate these Daughters!"

The Attack on Lancaster

Sparrow walked out of the closet in appalled disbelief. Tears welled in her eyes and her mind spun in horror. "This was your work? You weren't merely one of the Daughters to me. You were my closest friend and most trusted confidant. Why?"

"It's a little complicated to explain," said Villainous. "Let's simply say I was tired of fighting for the wrong side."

"Wrong side?" she asked in bewilderment. "You consider working for those murderers—those monsters—the right side?

"Sparrow, think about it! Why are we fighting them in the first place? For ages, we have waged this war with our brothers for no reason." Her once-gentle eyes now stared malevolently. "Let us stop this war and join them—better yet, rule with them."

"That's what you call them now? Brothers?" She wiped the tears from her eyes, her expression fierce, and continued, "The same brothers who killed your entire family. Who hunted you while you ran alone through the streets, hungry, for days."

"During times of war, you take all the necessary measures to eliminate the enemy. My family, however unfortunate it was for them, was merely collateral damage. I've now realized that if we had never declared this war in the first place, it would never have happened." Villainous paced frantically around the room, her grasp firm on the dagger in her hand.

"Listen to yourself—you're insane. You speak of sedition and mutiny to a code you once swore to uphold!" Sparrow exclaimed. "We never declared war. Our code of honor doesn't say we are Daughters to war against them. They brought this war to us."

"No more, Sparrow. No more codes, or honor, or standing together babble. I can see now that was all brainwashed bull." The woman stopped her pacing and glared at her. "If you don't join us, it only means you're one of them."

Without warning, she threw her dagger at Sparrow, who dodged instinctively but lost her footing and fell.

Villainous surged forward, leapt on top of her, and punched her face several times. Her nose started to bleed. Her attacker drew her secondary dagger strapped to her side and thrust it toward her. She managed to clasp Villainous' hands inches away from her face.

Sparrow pushed her assailant off and kicked her in the stomach. The woman dropped, gasping for air, and she bounded swiftly to her feet to kick the traitor repeatedly until her face was almost violet as she panted for air. She grasped her by the hair, lifted her, and slammed her forcefully against the wall. Villainous' face was bruised and bleeding. The betrayer stood but staggered and she caught her by the shirt and landed a vicious fist on her face.

Seeing her momentary daze, Sparrow glanced around and located the dagger. She picked it up swiftly and lunged toward Villainous. "You were like a sister to me...like my own flesh and blood." She lifted the dagger, her hand trembling, and tears ran down her face. For a brief moment, she hesitated, but as she moved in for the kill a steel dagger pierced her stomach. She dropped the blade and turned slowly.

The Nephilim seized Sparrow by the throat before she could collapse. Behind her, Villainous retrieved the dropped blade and hissed in fury. "It's the end of the line for you, Sparrow."

"I loved you, Jewels," was her only reply.

Her betrayer plunged the blade mercilessly into Sparrow's back and the Nephilim flung her across the room where she landed next to the surveillance desk. The last thing she saw as the light left her eyes was the face on the body she had noticed earlier—it was Sunny.

Villainous looked at the Nephilim. "Thanks for the help."

His right upper lip curled. "No, thank you." He clenched his steel blade tighter and said, "The master wants to make sure that your wounds are persuasive." He drove the pommel of the blade onto her head and knocked her out cold. As she fell, crimson fluid spewed on the floor.

The Memento Commemoration

The entire assembly stood and congratulated the newest members of their community. Pretzel, Reina, Tassel, and the twins huddled around Angel to hug her and address her enthusiastically by her *Memento Vivere*.

"Angel!" exclaimed Pretzel. "I love it. It fits you perfectly."

"Thanks," she responded.

"OMG! It's a fantastic name for you." Reina almost shrieked in excitement. "I have to update my Contact for you." She pulled her cell phone out and made the update with a grin on her face.

"I thought you would spread your wings and fly away when you said your MV," declared Tassel with a chuckle. The other women shared her amusement.

Mist appeared from the crowd, making her rounds and congratulating the new initiates. "Excuse me, ladies, for interrupting your party. I wanted to take a moment to congratulate Angel," she said and emphasized the MV.

"Thank you, Mist."

"We are delighted to have you on our team," she said with a pleased smile. "When things are less chaotic, I'd like to touch base about your—" At that moment, she was interrupted by one of May's girls. The young lady gestured to her to lower herself to her level and whispered into her ear. Her eyeballs seemed to bulge with the news. "So sorry, Angel, but I have to go. Excuse me."

Mist hurried out of the Gathering Hall, looked at May's assistant, and asked, "Are you sure?"

She nodded in confirmation. With a breathy tone, she murmured, "Jewels is awake."

PART IV

THE DEATH OF AN ANGEL

JUDGMENT

The mob of protesters shrilled insults and slurs at the bloody man who carried the wooden beam. Others hurled stones, kicked dust, or spat on his face as they maligned him as a false prophet, a deceiver, and a disrupter of peace. Blood and bruises covered his tawny-brown skin from head to toe. His face was mangled, and his beard had been plucked either by the scouring or pulled by hands. The bangs of his disheveled hair, matted with sweat and blood, partially covered his blackened and swollen eyes.

A few of the crowd wept as they witnessed an injustice against an innocent man, yet the shouted rage of the agitated mob prevailed.

"Crucify him!" was the overwhelming mantra. "He deserves death!"

Yet the man's gaze was always resolute. His bloodshot eyes remained locked forward as he winced and staggered along the dusty, stone-covered road. Terrible, agonizing pain was evident on his face. Again, he stumbled as he attempted to carry the crossbeam that spiked splinters into his already lashed, gory back.

He grunted loudly and fell with a thud, and the thorns on his head penetrated deeper. The Roman guard whipped him to his feet and without a word, he managed to stand, picked the cross up, and continued with grim determination to attempt to reach his destination. After a few more steps, his frail, blood-stained arms lost their hold on the beam and it forced him to the ground. He landed heavily in the dust.

"Get up!" bellowed the Roman guard and brandished the whip before his blood-covered face.

As he lifted it, a centurion near him exclaimed, "Halt!" Disappointed, he uttered, "Don't you see he can't carry it?" He spun to the crowd and glanced around. With a gesture of his index finger, he pointed at a husky, strong young individual. "You!" he shouted.

The man looked around him, then pointed to himself. "Me?" he asked with a frown.

"Yes, you!" he said and gestured more aggressively. "Help him carry the cross!" he ordered.

"Look, I'm only a bystander," he protested in a stammering voice. "I don't want any part of this."

The centurion grasped the pommel of his sword that hung in the scabbard at his belt, his knuckles white. He strode to the man, his expression fierce. "Help him pick the beam up or you'll carry your own!"

With no further hesitation, he hurried to the bloody cross and picked it up. The condemned man glanced gratefully at him and in a hoarse voice, he murmured, "Thank you." He staggered to his feet, swayed, and stumbled as he walked forward.

Up above, on a high rooftop of a first-century limestone building, two translucent figures stared menacingly at the man with their flickering crimson eyes. Their shadow-covered forms were invisible to the human eye.

A wry smile played on the features of the one known as Diablos, the most wicked and devious of all Daimon, the King of the Fallen and Lord of the Watchers. With glimmering delight, his gaze was fixed on the contorted, pained expression of the condemned. "Look at him, Apollyon. Pathetic. He thought he could reproduce our creation, our design, and it failed him miserably." His tone was sinister yet gleeful.

"He couldn't even carry the wooden beam. Something our weakest offspring could do," Apollyon said with a maniacal laugh. "He appears more inferior than a regular human."

A long moment of silence hung between the two as they reveled malevolently in the demise of the struggling man who stumbled with each step. They vanished and reappeared on the top of the city wall as the man staggered through the central city gates and onto the path to the mount called The Skull. The menacing crowds marched with him and their chant of death continued.

Diablos turned his gaze to Apollyon. "This will be our finest hour when once and for all, we rid ourselves of our most prominent enemy." He exhaled a deep, triumphant sigh. "There can be no mistakes." He turned his head toward the mount, where two criminals already hung from their crosses, and murmured, in a low, grim, and barely audible tone, "I will go do it myself."

Apollyon stared at him with a bewildered expression. "My lord, what are you contemplating?"

A dark and sinister smile appeared on his lips. "I will drive those nails through his muscle and sinews and make certain he is well impaled. His demise will be inevitable."

"Your Eminence, that violates Sovereign Law 7.VII.7. Any Daimon or Angel who harms a human is subject to immediate judgment.," he protested quickly.

"Who do you think I am, Apollyon?" he snapped. "I'm a god. Those laws don't apply to me." Diablos' face contorted in fury. "The Carpenter's Son will die by my hands." His finger pointed toward the mountain top.

"Yes, my lord," responded Apollyon. The lines criss-crossing his forehead deepened.

The Carpenter's Son reached The Skull in anguish. He reeled in sheer agony as he fell to his knees. His breathing became short and shallow.

"Drop the cross here," instructed the centurion to the young man and pointed to an already dug hole. With loud, straining breaths, the man lifted the beam from his shoulder and let it fall. The accused stared at him with grateful eyes and gave him a fleeting smile. The young man's dark eyes watered as he walked away.

The Roman guards ripped the blood-covered shift from the battered body, grasped him brutally by the arms, and dragged him to the wooden beam. They thrust him down, positioned his back and feet against the upright post, and extended his arms on the transverse plank.

Suddenly, Diablos strode from among the crowds, no

longer in his disfigured Angelic form but attired as a Roman general. The soldier lifted his hand to drive in the first nail, but Diablos called, "Wait!" He walked forward swiftly. "I'll handle it!"

The Roman soldier gazed at him with a frown of surprise. "Yes, sir." With no questions, he handed him the nail and hammer.

An evil sneer spread across Diablos' human features as he dropped to one knee with the nail and hammer in hand. Meticulously, he placed the iron nail onto the Carpenter's Son's right hand and with a savage blow of the hammer, he drove it through into the beam. The Nazarene groaned loudly and tears coursed down his disfigured face while the other Roman soldiers held his arm and legs tight to the cross.

A smile of satisfaction appeared on Diablos' face. He leaned closer to the man and his hot breath burned against the bloody cheeks. With a devilish hiss, he whispered to him, "Feel my wrath, failure!" He shifted position quickly and proceeded to puncture his left hand and his feet. The gruesome task completed, he vanished as mysteriously as he had appeared from among the crowd.

He emerged again alongside Apollyon on the city wall. A slow, triumphant, cruel smile crossed his lips. "He's finished," murmured Diablos. His gaze was drawn toward the mount when the Roman soldiers lifted the cross. Apollyon nodded in satisfaction.

Suddenly, the darkened, cloudy skies shimmered with the brightness of a thousand suns and they both had to shield their eyes with their hands. From among the luminous clouds appeared several hosts of Angels, all glorious in their splendor. One of them held the key to Tartarus, the lowest dungeon of the underworld, and a great chain. Once their eyes adjusted to the light, Diablos beheld the Archangel Michael with a missive in his hand. His features were fierce yet noble and majestic.

"What is this?" demanded Diablos in a rough voice.

In a thunderous tone, the Archangel read the missive. "Diablos, you have trespassed Sovereign Law 7.VII.7, as declared in the ancient canons of the Sovereign One. The law forbids Angels and Daimons from physically injuring or killing those of the human race without divine consent. Due to this unlawful action, you have been judged and sentenced. You will be kept bound and imprisoned for two millennia in the darkest penitentiary regions of Tartarus." The Archangel turned his gaze to the Angel holding the great chain and nodded swiftly.

A look of horror crossed Diablos' countenance. "Do you know who I am?" he screamed in bitter rage. "I'm the rightful ruler of this world. You have no authority over my jurisdiction nor over me." He backpedaled gradually when he observed the mighty Angel approaching, the chain grasped tightly in his hand. "This is treachery!" he exclaimed. Swiftly, he raised his hand and attempted to open a portal to make his escape, but nothing happened. He glanced heavenward. A battalion of Angels encircled his location, all brandishing flaming swords. Perceiving the inevitable, he turned to Apollyon.

"Apollyon, prepare me an army as numerous as the stars in the heavens. Inform Legion and Hades to do likewise." Diablos reached into the depth of his blackened soul and extracted a small glowing ball that seemed to suck light from its surroundings. Sensing his apprehender closing in, he placed it quickly in Apollyon's hand.

"This is my essence, Apollyon," he said and stared intently at him. "I have seen the Sovereign One's annals of the future with my own eyes. Before my release, humans will devise a means of reproduction without the need for my physical presence. Breed my offspring, a Son of Destruction to rule this wretched world and bring it to utter desolation. The Sovereign One will rue all the injustice committed against me."

The Angel took hold of Diablos and fastened him with the chain. He scoffed and leered malevolently at the Angel, then stared one last time at Apollyon. "Keep my essence and offspring hidden from all. In two millennia, this world will be completely ours!" he exclaimed and vanished with the Angelic hosts, leaving Apollyon standing alone.

"I will do as you instructed, my lord," Apollyon muttered. "At that time, I will aid you in your conquest by breeding a child as powerful as you."

MYSTERY NIGHT

The two girls hid silently in the dark broom closet and listened to the screams and shrieks from the other girls in the warehouse. Olivia's forehead was damp with perspiration and she clung anxiously to Angel where both huddled in the darkest corner.

Shafts of light seeped through the gap at the bottom of the door and sporadically reflected the shadows of feet on the floor. Their gazes froze on this tiny aperture when two feet darkened the light under the door, stopped there, and someone rattled the doorknob. The young girl winced and Angel made a shushing gesture with an index finger pressed against her mouth.

"There's no one there," a voice stated from farther away. "I checked it earlier." The glimmering light beneath the door reappeared as the feet moved away and the girls sighed.

After a long wait, the commotion beyond the closet ceased but the eerie silence made them more uneasy. Olivia turned to look at her companion. "I need to use the bathroom," she whispered. Her knees were shaking.

"Can you hold it for a few more minutes?" Angel asked in a whisper. The girl shook her head rapidly. "If we leave now, we'll get caught."

"But I have to go now." She was adamant.

As Angel stood, she accidentally bumped one of the brooms hooked to the wall and it fell with a loud clatter. Thudding footsteps approached and without any warning, the door to the closet opened. A shadowy figure with a club resting on its shoulder stood in front of them and the younger girl screamed.

"I found Angel and Olivia!" exclaimed Reina in her Mystic Quinn costume.

"Shoot!" snapped Angel. "They caught us," she said to her companion and shook her head disappointedly. "All right, let's head to the bathroom."

"I don't need to go anymore." Olivia giggled sheepishly. "I guess I was nervous." She raised her fingers to her mouth as she continued to titter.

"You were nervous? You…were…nervous?" Angel echoed as she tickled the girl, who hooted with laughter.

Pretzel appeared next to Reina. "You said no one was there earlier."

"I did check but didn't see anyone," responded the other girl.

Angel grinned. "We hid here after Reina checked. We thought it would be the perfect place." She hauled Olivia to her feet and they strode out of the closet.

"I wouldn't have checked again if it wasn't for the crashing sound," Reina told her.

"Are you sure you didn't use your SPA?" she asked dubiously.

The other girl shook her head. "I can't break the rules."

She looked at the younger girl with a sad face. "I'm sorry, Olivia. It was my fault we were caught."

"It's okay." The child shrugged, her eyes bright with laughter.

Angel glanced at Pretzel and Reina. "So, who's left to find?"

"I think you two were the last. You may have won," answered Pretzel.

"Woohoo!" she responded excitedly. She raised her hand to high-five Olivia and they slapped palms enthusiastically.

"Can we play Daughter Hunt again?" asked the young girl and clasped her hands in suppressed excitement.

Pretzel glanced at her smartwatch and shook her head with pursed lips. "Unfortunately, we can't. Everyone is now gathering at the cafeteria." Olivia pouted in disappointment. "But you'll get candy there," the older girl said enticingly, which immediately made her smile again.

They all hurried to the cafeteria. Olivia grasped Angel's hand and almost dragged her forward.

"I love your rainbow unicorn costume, Olivia," said Pretzel. "You look so pretty."

"Thank you," she replied and wiggled her white tail and her colorful horn. "Angel helped me make it." She turned to her companion with a sheepish grin.

"Growing up was financially tough for me so my grandmother and I would sew my costumes," Angel explained. "Although it was my grandmother who did all the work, I guess I picked up the skill naturally." She looked at Reina. "Speaking of costumes, Reina, the Mystic Quinn costume looks fantastic on you." Her gaze studied the girl's outfit approvingly.

"You see this white halter top and red shorts? I bought them myself," Reina stated, swung the bat, and narrowly missed her partner.

Pretzel rolled her eyes and looked at Angel. "She's always Mystic Quinn for Halloween." Her expression was blank. "And you decided to be an angel, Angel. That was original," she said sarcastically.

"It was the easiest thing I could come up with since I spent most of my time working on Olivia's." She grinned, then rolled her eyes mischievously.

"Well, I like your costume, Angel," asserted Reina. "As for our friend here, not only is she wearing the costume, but she's also playing the role of the Wicked Witch."

Pretzel stared at them with an impish look. "I'll get you, my pretties—and your little unicorn too." Her tone suitably evil, she lunged toward Olivia, who scurried around them and giggled.

They reached the cafeteria and it overflowed with excitement as exuberant children went from table to table to collect their candies and sweets—the Daughters' version of Trunk-or-Treat. The room was dimly lit and decorated with jack-o-lanterns, cobwebs, ghosts, and red and orange flowers festooned around the walls. Festive Halloween music played in the background.

"This is great," remarked Angel. "It's such a great idea for the kids. They all seem to be having a good time."

Olivia all but bounced in excitement. "Can I go get my

candy now?" Angel nodded and the girl bounded toward the other children.

"It's too big a risk to have them go door to door so to keep them safe and still give them a great time, we do this. Later this evening, they will go from room to room trick-or-treating," explained Pretzel.

"I loved it when I was a youngling," said Reina. "I'd collect so much candy, I'd be sugar-rushed for days."

Pretzel looked at Angel and pointed at the other girl. "I swear that's where she got all her energy." She turned to Reina. "Hey, sugar-rush, stop staring at the candy. We promised Grace we'd help her in the kitchen."

"Before we go, can I get some?" she said, her gaze imploring.

"No!" her friend protested firmly. "You don't need it." As she yanked her away, she said to Angel, "I'll catch up with you later tonight."

"Okay." Angel grinned as Reina continued to beg for only one piece.

She glanced around the room and watched the little girls enthusiastically collect their candy from table to table. When she glanced at Olivia to check on her progress, she noticed her trick-or-treat bucket was already half-full. The girl was surrounded by a small group of younglings, but a closer look indicated that she seemed to be having some type of spat with the others. Her face was visibly upset.

Angel strode quickly to the group to learn the cause of the commotion. Initially, all she could hear was "nuh-uh" and "yuh-uh" from the agitated girls. "What's going, ladies?" she asked.

"I was telling them that you're a real Angel," responded

Olivia and seemed both distressed and confused. "I keep telling them you are."

"No, she isn't," interjected Brittany, who was a little older than her. "We are the same here."

"Yuh-uh!" retorted Olivia.

"Nuh-uh!" Brittany's swift and conviction-filled rebuttal drew nods of agreement from the others.

Angel stooped so she and Olivia were at eye level. "Sweetheart, Brittany is right. I'm no true Angel. We are the same here."

"I told you!" snapped the other girl.

Angel turned to Brittany. "Thank you, Brittany. Why don't you ladies move along so I can have a private conversation with Olivia?" She returned her gaze to the rainbow unicorn as the rest of the group scuttled away.

"But you're a real Angel," the child uttered in a low voice.

"Honey, the name Angel is only my *Memento Vivere* but that doesn't make me an Angel." The girl's eyes glistened.

"But you have to be. You're the Daimon Killer." Olivia bowed her head in disillusionment and the corners of her lips tugged down.

Angel's eyes widened in shock at the unexpected statement. "What did you call me?"

As she asked the question, Mrs. Poppins took center stage to announce the winners of the Daughter Hunt contest. "The winners of the Daughter Hunt are...Angel and Olivia!" The room was filled with shouts of excitement and clapping. "Come on up, ladies. Get your prize." She beckoned them forward, a big smile on her chubby face.

They hurried forward but didn't look thrilled at all.

Olivia's face expressed disappointment while her companion simply looked bewildered.

The evening's festivities occupied Angel for the rest of the night and prevented her from questioning Olivia further. The youngling's statement had left her puzzled, and she went to bed with her head abuzz.

Mist pushed a wheelchair into Jewels' room, hoping after weeks of recovery to get her old friend off the bed and out of the room. The woman turned her bandaged head toward the doorway with a smile on her face.

"How are you feeling this morning?" asked Mist, her answering smile both cheerful and hopeful.

"Better than yesterday is all I can say." Jewels placed her hand over her left temple. "I still have this pulsating headache that seems to linger no matter what."

"You took a hard hit to the head. It's a miracle you survived." She stared sympathetically at her.

The woman's gaze went from her face to the wheelchair.

"Well, the reason for my visit this morning is to get you out of bed and take you around. May suggested it would be good for you."

"I'm not sure about that. I still feel a little dazed." Her shoulders sagged.

"Come on. You've been awake for days now and haven't left this room. You'll be in the wheelchair the entire time and if you feel sick at any given point, I'll bring you back," Mist promised eagerly.

Jewels sighed. "All right, if you insist. I've always said you were the pushy one in this relationship," she added with a chuckle.

"It's good to hear my power of persuasion still has its effect on you," she quipped and smiled teasingly.

She walked to the bed and helped the woman to move gradually into the wheelchair. Once the patient was settled, she strode to the closet and drew a jacket out. "I know how much you enjoy gardens so I wanted to show you the one we have here. It's very relaxing there. Joan has done a great job maintaining it. It's not as beautiful as the one in Lancaster—" She paused as she realized the garden in Lancaster was no more and how her friend must have felt at the mention of it. "I'm sorry, Jewels."

"It's all right. I'll be fine." Her expression was blank. "I've looked forward to seeing it. You've talked about it so many times in the past." Mist draped the jacket over her body and the woman winced.

"Are you okay?" she asked with a frown of concern.

"I'm fine." Jewels clasped her hand over her shoulder. "It'll take some time before I get used to my new normal," she said and grimaced at her bandaged body.

"The garden is located on the terrace of the building. We have a service elevator that can take us directly there. Excuse the appearance in the hallways. Last night was the kids' Halloween party." She turned very slowly and edged the wheelchair through the doorway and out of the infirmary's corridor. After several careful turns, their slow pace brought them to the elevator and they ascended to the terrace.

The doors opened to a crisp, gentle fall breeze and the

sun sent shy rays across the lilac skies. Mist pushed Jewels into the wide area filled with turf grass, spring-blooming bulbs, perennials, and shrubs, all in a splendid array of vibrant colors. The air held the warm odor of pine that swirled on the breeze.

They moved across the garden in the direction of the gazebo that, by this time of the season, had plants dangling from it that shimmered brilliantly with a golden hue. She parked the wheelchair next to the bench under the gazebo and for a long while, both women sat silently and absorbed the season, the fall flora, and the flurry of fresh air.

"Things are still fuzzy, Mist." Jewels gazed at the sky. "I can only recollect pieces of things."

"Jewels, please don't think I brought you up here to speak about this now," Mist said and fixed her with a compassionate look. "We can only imagine the pain you must have gone through and don't expect you to speak about it anytime soon."

"No more kid gloves, Mist. Tell me the truth—did anyone else survive?" She lowered her gaze to her folded hands.

She did not respond immediately, reluctant to reveal the devastating truth. After a moment, she cleared her throat and proceeded. "You were the only one."

For a moment, Jewels' face remained emotionless before a single tear streaked down her face and she nodded, her expression pained. She stared blindly away and swiped the errant tear away with a jerked motion of her hand.

"I'm so sorry," she continued. She placed her hand over her friend's that were again clasped in her lap. "I've been very hesitant to tell you the news. I was afraid of how you would take it."

"There was a traitor in the group," the woman stated.

Mist pulled her hand back swiftly, her features shocked. Jewels turned her head slowly toward her. "Are you certain? I knew most of those ladies. None of them were capable of such evil. I...I simply can't accept it," she stammered. She stood quickly and paced the gazebo with her hands clasped behind her head.

"I know it's hard to believe, but it has to be said." The woman's gaze followed her tense movements.

She stopped and looked at Jewels. "But who would do such a thing and why?"

"It was Sunny," she said bluntly. "I honestly have no idea why, but I found her tampering with the compound's alarm system and confronted her."

"Sunny?" Mist stared at her in shock. "She has been with us since the start and was very loyal to the cause. How could she do such a thing? I know she wasn't the brightest of the bunch, but I would never in a million years have taken her for a traitor."

"That was my reaction as well. After I confronted her, she ran into the video surveillance room where she attacked me and I lost consciousness." Jewels' gaze followed her companion's return to the bench.

"She was one of the people killed in the video surveillance room," stated Mist as she sat again. "I wonder if Sparrow discovered her and killed her."

"Sparrow?" Her voice was sharp and she placed her hand on her temple and winced. "What...um, happened to her?" Her voice sounded slightly desperate.

"From what we can gather, she was stabbed—most likely by a Nephilim. Her body was found close to you."

Jewels stared at the horizon again.

"Sparrow sent me to secure the children in the bunker and after I made sure they were safe, she sent me to the security station. Supposedly, Sunny couldn't figure out how to send the distress signal and that's when I discovered her." She turned her head to look at her companion. "I'm sorry I couldn't stop her. If I had tried harder...maybe I could have prevented this. I tried calling here but...but by the time the attack started, it was too late. The lines were down."

"That was you? We had so little to go on that we hesitated to act." Mist stood from the bench and embraced her gently. "I'm so sorry and please don't blame yourself for this. You had no idea about her betrayal. I snapped at the folks here when they suggested there was foul play, so I can't even begin to understand what you must have felt when you discovered the truth." She leaned back but held Jewels' hands.

"I don't know how I'll ever get through this," the woman said and shook her head. "Even to think how those children were gassed to death is too much to handle."

She frowned, surprised that her old partner knew about the children's deaths. "How did you learn about the children?"

Jewels swallowed and asked quickly, "Didn't you mention it to me?" Mist stared in bewilderment and shook her head slowly. "I think I must have heard it from someone in the infirmary." She grunted and rubbed her temples distractedly. "I'm getting dizzy again."

Mist sighed. "Yeah, let me take you downstairs. It's been a big day for you so far."

"By the way, thank you for bringing me up here. It truly is beautiful," Jewels said as her companion pushed her toward the elevator. "One more request, if you don't mind —do you have a spare smartphone I could use? I need something to occupy my mind and pass the time."

"Sure thing. I'll have our tech issue you one."

TWO SIDES TO THE STORY

"Where are you off to today?" asked Pretzel as Angel laced her sneakers.

"The infirmary," she replied and gave her a cursory look. "May needed help so I volunteered."

Her roommate nodded approvingly and stated, "I have to say I'm impressed. You seem to be involved in everything—helping Mrs. Poppins with the kids, Mrs. Mozart at the library, and even Grace with kitchen duty and on top of all that, you train daily with Gypsy."

Angel stood, her eyes bright. "You know, for the first time in my life, I feel I'm part of something. Being part of the Daughters has given new meaning to my life and I'm so grateful for it."

Pretzel responded with a huge smile. "I share your sentiments exactly. My only piece of advice? Don't overdo it."

"Yeah, I know, but since I'm not working..." She stopped in mid-sentence as a thought popped into her head. "Gosh, I forgot all about Bill, my boss. I should give him a call to let him know I'm okay." She returned her gaze to the other girl and continued, "Anyway, I'm not working. I took the semester off until this whole investigation is resolved, and since I'm not helping my grandmother, I can think of no better use of my time than helping around here."

"That's great, Angel. By the way, you seem to be on everyone's lips," her friend said with a smile.

"Why's that?" She frowned curiously.

"I mean...everyone I've talked to mentions how diligent and dedicated you are, always going the extra mile, and most importantly, how friendly you are. You've made a good impression around here."

Angel placed her hands over her cheeks. "Aww, you made me blush." She mimicked Reina's voice and mannerisms.

"Oh, Lord, you sound exactly like her," her roommate said with a chuckle. "That's how you know you're hanging around someone too much."

"In all seriousness, thank you. It means a lot." Angel walked closer and gave her a big hug. "I wouldn't be here without you."

"Anytime, girlfriend." A big grin of affection spread across her face.

"Where are you off to this morning?"

"A leaders' group meeting with Joan. She meets the groups every week to discuss projects, plans...that kind of thing. We gather in the large conference room across from her office." She looked at her watch. "And by the way, I'm running late. Hey, do you wanna hook up for lunch?" Angel nodded swiftly. "Right, see you at noon."

For the next couple of hours, Angel helped May with various tasks in the infirmary. She brought patients their breakfast, organized files and folders, and even mopped and dusted.

When she saw how engaged and dedicated she was, the caregiver approached her. "I can't recall the last time this place looked so organized. Thank you so much, Angel."

"You're welcome." Her hair was pulled into a ponytail and her clothes smelled of cleaning detergent.

"You didn't have to mop," the woman said with a smirk.

"This was my regular Saturday morning routine when I lived with my grandmother. I'd spend the entire morning cleaning the apartment before I could do anything else." She wiped the sweat from her brow. "I guess I developed the habit. The only thing missing is my grandma's favorite all-purpose cleaner."

May took the mop from her and suggested, "Why don't you take a break and go around and meet some of the women in the infirmary? I'm very sure they wouldn't mind a house visit. I'll finish here."

"That sounds great," responded Angel enthusiastically. After washing and freshening up a little, she meandered through the corridor of the infirmary, stopped at various rooms, and used the opportunity to meet the women in recovery. She finally reached Jewels' room at the end of the hall and when she entered, the woman lay on her bed.

At first, she did not notice her visitor and looked intently at her upper arm while she caressed the area gently in a circular motion. She suddenly registered her presence and jerked in fright. "You startled me." She cleared her throat. "I thought I had a bruise on my arm," she muttered and covered her arm with her sleeve.

"I'm sorry. I can come back if you like."

"It's okay, you can come in."

"Hello, I'm Angelica—I mean Angel. I still have to get used to my MV. I'm doing some house visits."

"Hi. I'm Jewels."

Angel walked toward her and shook her hand. "You're from Lancaster, right?" Sorrow filled the woman's face and she nodded. "I'm so sorry for your loss," she added compassionately.

"Thank you," Jewels responded dully. She gestured to the chair next to the bed. "Have a seat."

"How have you been feeling?"

"Some days are better than others—I try to make the best of them although it's not always easy." She looked at her with a half-smile. "So is Angel your MV?"

"Yeah, it's in honor of my grandmother. She's called me her angel ever since I can remember but in reality, she's always been mine." Suddenly sentimental at the thought of her grandmother, she cleared her throat. "She raised me."

"You and I have similar stories," said Jewels. "I grew up with my grandmother in Millersville, south of Lancaster. She loved collecting all manner of stones, minerals, and jewels. They were precious to her. She died of old age, but before she passed away, gave her collection to me. I moved back with my addict mother who sold them all. However, in time, I came to realize that my grandmother was the most precious jewel I ever had."

"It's a beautiful *Memento Vivere*," Angel replied. "What happened to your mother?"

She shrugged. "I don't know. She left one night and never came back. Afterward, I went to live with an aunt and uncle who had many kids, but they took care of me like their own."

"I never had a chance to meet my mother," Angel said and stared at the floor. "She was killed by my so-called father." She gestured with her fingers to make quote signs.

"Your father? You know him? In a manner of speaking, most of us never have that privilege."

"Unfortunately, mine is the one leading the parade. His name is Leonard Archie, better known as Apollyon."

The hair on Jewels' arms prickled as though she had witnessed the four horsemen of Revelation. She swallowed hard to retain her composure. "Are you the daughter of Eva Santos?"

"Yeah. Did you know my mother?" Angel's attention was caught.

The woman sighed. "Did Mist never mention her to you?"

"No." Intense curiosity settled on her face.

"I'm surprised Mist hasn't told you about her—"

"How did you and Mist know my mother?" Angel interjected, flustered. She straightened on the chair, desperate for any piece of knowledge about Eva.

"Angel, your mother wasn't killed," Jewels told her with a quizzical expression. "We took care of your mother for almost five months at the Lancaster compound while she was pregnant with you." Her gaze was fixed intently on the younger girl.

"How did she... But why wouldn't Mist... When did you..." she stammered, utterly confused but making an attempt to get her thoughts straight. Her gaze darted frantically around her.

"I'm so sorry. I thought you knew by now. I'd have told you that at the beginning." Her voice was intentionally soft.

"How did my mother even end up with you?" Angel demanded, her tone fierce.

"She was running from Leonard Archie when we found her. One of our seers led us to her and after we rescued her, she came to live with us."

"But why wasn't my grandmother aware of this? The last time she heard from my mother was through a conversation she had with my grandfather." Angel rubbed her temple in puzzlement. "Why didn't she contact my grandmother when she was with you?"

"We suspected that Archie had ordered a massive hunt for your mother, so we prevented her from making any outside contact to keep her safe until you were born—at least that's what we told her," Jewels explained.

"But if she was protected by the Daughters of the Watchers, how was she killed?"

"She wasn't killed," the woman stated emphatically. Angel's eyes widened with trepidation and confusion. "When your mother was informed that her father had passed away, she escaped the compound. At some point, she learned that she was carrying a child of a Daimon. I guess she was afraid and took what's known as the Extract of the Forbidden Fruit—a poison that kills without fail and for which there's no human antidote." Her gaze met Angel's squarely. "I know it's not easy to hear this, but we believe she thought it would get rid of the baby." Her voice was low and lacked empathy.

A feverish chill tingled down Angel's spine and tears streaked down her face. With a sniffle, she said, "Thank you for telling me." Her tone was dull and strained and she wiped the tears from her face. Overwhelmed by this news and particularly by Mist's knowledge of it all, she stood abruptly. "You must feel exhausted so I don't want to take much more of your time. One last thing—were you honestly going to let her contact my grandmother after I was born or was that a lie?"

"Well, you're the daughter of one of the lords, so you have to understand you would have been a great asset to the cause. The leadership wouldn't have risked losing you, so they told your mother what she needed to hear," confessed Jewels. "I'm very sorry," Jewels added in a feigned apologetic tone. "I'm shocked Mist never said anything to you, Angelica."

"Angel," she corrected, her face beet-red as if she had drunk from the vials of the wrath of the Apocalypse.

"Yes, sorry—Angel. I'm still recuperating." She placed her hand on her head. "Before you leave, did she also tell you about the prophecy?" The girl looked darkly at her and shook her head. "Hmm..." She pursed her lips. "One of the things I dislike most about the Daughters of the Watchers is all the secrecy," she said in a deliberate undertone. She fixed her gaze on her visitor. "The prophecy states that you, Angel, are the Daimon Killer."

The blood drained from her face and the hairs on the back of her neck prickled, while her heart pounded in her chest. After a hard swallow, she managed to speak. "Would you excuse me? I need to speak to someone."

As the girl rushed out of the room, Jewels felt a strange sensation on her upper right arm. She lifted her sleeve and noticed the black inscription—πονηρά. Quickly, she turned her gaze to the door and sighed softly as she pulled her sleeve over the treacherous mark.

———

Angel stormed through the infirmary's long and narrow corridor, a dark, bewildered, and furious expression on her face.

May had finished the floor and when she saw her pass, asked, "So, how did it go with the house visits?"

She completely ignored her, wholly overcome with emotion, and strode out of the infirmary.

"Angel, wait—are you okay?" the caregiver cried after her.

Blindly, she reached the staircases and bounded up four flights of stairs, her feet heavy on each step. She walked to Joan's office but noticed the closed and empty office and recalled the leaders' meeting. With a scowl, she looked to her left and located the large conference room. She rushed to it and without knocking, flung the door open abruptly.

It slammed loudly against the adjacent wall. Startled, every head in the room turned toward the doorway, their expressions stunned. Her gaze swept the room and searched for Mist among the large group. When she found her, she glared furiously.

"Angel, we are having a meeting—"

The leader's protest was cut off when she strode into the room, her gaze fixed on Mist. She cried, "*Que cojones*, huh? Why didn't you tell me about my mother? How she killed herself attempting to get rid of me?" Her agitated voice was shrill with anxiety. "And what about this prophecy that I'm...some freaking Daimon assassin?"

Pretzel rose quickly and glanced from Mist's startled expression to Angel's livid features. "Angel, let's calm down and discuss this privately."

She gave her roommate a dark stare. "Did you know about this prophecy too?"

The girl nodded reluctantly and answered, "I never said anything because I didn't think it was real—"

Angel interrupted her with a roar of fury. "*Contra!* Of course, you knew! A seven-year-old knew about it, a stranger from a different group knew, and even my closest friend, but for some freaking reason, I didn't know crap. *Que mierda!*"

Pretzel opened her mouth to respond but she spun on her heel, almost ran from the room, and slammed the door behind her. Driven by rage, she sought the quietest place she knew—the terrace. She sat quietly on the wooden bench under the gazebo for a long time, confused, hurt, and angry. Her gaze traced the hues of the fall sun that grazed the city's skyscrapers. The soft but cool breeze ruffled her hair and teased the silent tears that trickled down her face. It was a little brisk, especially without a jacket, but her frustration kept her warm for some time.

Sudden footsteps coming from the doorway caught her attention. At first, she thought it was Pretzel, her comforter who always seemed to show up in these stressful times, but to her surprise, it wasn't. She turned her head and realized it was Mist, her short flaxen-brown highlights slicked back with hair gel. Abruptly, she turned her gaze away in a gesture of rejection.

The woman held a jacket and a hot cup of chocolate and approached the gazebo slowly. She stopped a few paces away from her. "Angel, I want to apologize for not telling you sooner. I should have told you about your mother and this so-called prophecy a long time ago, but things have been so complicated for both of us these past few months that it was difficult for us to talk. It's not an excuse—you deserved to know sooner—but I didn't intentionally hide it from you." Her tone sounded genuinely contrite. "I'm not sure how much you know but...um, if you give me a chance, I'd like to explain everything to you."

Angel nodded brusquely.

"By the way, I brought you a peace offering." Mist gestured at the hot chocolate.

When she finally realized how cold she was, she accepted it.

When she saw that Angel was shivering, the woman ordered softly, "Put this on. A close friend of yours thought you might need it." She draped the jacket around her and sat on the bench. At a faint whiff of the perfume from the jacket, the girl knew instinctively that it belonged to Pretzel.

"Is it true that she attempted to abort me and that's how she died?" Her voice was melancholy but stern.

"It's true, but I think you should know all the facts before you pass judgment," Mist stated. "I think I should start from the beginning to provide a little perspective."

For the next hour or so, Mist explained how she came to know her mother and the reason she was being protected. She recounted the council's decision to not allow Eva to have contact with the outside world and of her disagreement with it and her resolve to disobey their orders and take her and her baby to see Maria. Last, she told her about Duplicity, the betrayer who had deceived Eva about the extract and the so-called prophecy.

Angel listened attentively and gained clarity and, as the woman had stated, perspective. Her demeanor softened and she began to feel slightly remorseful for her outburst earlier. However, her companion's comforting explanation and grace-filled tone gave her a sense that she would not be censured for her reaction.

She continued to listen and was perturbed to hear about betrayers. "I wasn't aware that any Daughters could betray us and work for the enemy," she stated in perplexity.

"As unsettling as it may sound, it can happen. Before your dramatic entrance"—Mist looked at her with a half-smirk and raised eyebrow—"we were discussing the Lancaster attack and the fact that it was facilitated by one of the Daughters of the group."

"What?" She gaped, wide-eyed.

"We haven't yet discussed this with the general assembly so I'll ask for your discretion until we do."

Angel nodded glumly.

Mist's green gaze looked forward toward the cloudless skies. She seemed lost in thought and almost absentmindedly declared, "The traitor was a good friend of mine." She sighed deeply. "Yes, so it's a level of threat that's more dangerous and destructive than the Nephilim themselves.

And it's one we need to be keenly aware of and remain vigilant." She turned to her. "Regarding this so-called prophecy of the Daimon Killer, it was asserted by a deceiver, which in my book discounts it wholesale. Because of that, I haven't taken it seriously."

The woman folded her hands in her lap and returned her gaze to the sky scattered with Manhattan seagulls. "Angel, I believe your mom was deceived by this betrayer and her actions should be weighed with that in mind."

Angel slouched and buried her face in her hands with embarrassment. "I must've looked like a fool barging into your meeting."

Mist chuckled softly. "Angel, you're still learning about yourself, your past, and the ways of the Daughters, so I think to some extent, your actions are justifiable. I, on the other hand, walked furiously out of a meeting simply because someone suggested the Lancaster attack was foul play, which turned out to be true, yet I'm one of the leaders of this team. We all have our moments."

She straightened on the bench and turned to the woman. "Thanks. I appreciate the way you put things into perspective. It didn't feel that way when Jewels said it."

Mist frowned curiously. "Jewels told you about your mother and the prophecy?"

"Yeah, why?"

"No reason," she replied but seemed concerned. "Jewels has been through so much and is still recovering. She's a great person once you get to know her well."

"I guess so," responded Angel.

"It's getting chilly out here. We should head inside before we catch a cold." Both stood. "Oh, before I forget, who was the seven-year-old you referred to? Other than the leaders and a handful of Daughters, no one knows about this prophecy."

"It was Olivia." She cocked her eyebrows in curiosity.

"You may want to chat with her and find out how she knew," suggested Mist.

Angel nodded but with little enthusiasm.

They strode through the door of the building and descended the staircases to the bottom, where Pretzel waited and paced like a cat on hot bricks. Mist turned to Angel and said, "I'll leave you with your friend. I need to handle some personal business."

She lowered her head, her expression apologetic, sheepish, and more than a little embarrassed. "I'm sorry," she murmured.

Pretzel sighed and extended her hands to her friend. "C'mon. Bring it home to momma." She embraced her warmly. "I'm sorry too. I should have at least mentioned it."

Mist left them to hug it out while she hurried directly to the infirmary. She immediately noticed May, who was busy with filing. "May, I need to talk to you if you have a moment?"

"Sure," the caregiver responded quickly. She held files and folders in her hands but she placed them on the desk in front of her. "What's going on?" She gave her visitor her complete attention.

"Do you know if you or anyone in your staff made any mention of the Lancaster attack to Jewels since she woke up?" she asked tersely.

"No!" the woman replied emphatically. "We all heard you loud and clear when you instructed us not to."

"Hmm... Can you double-check with your girls? And even ask if they'd any private conversations among themselves while at the infirmary."

"I can certainly do that. Is anything wrong?" Her brows puckered in a frown.

"I'm investigating something," she said with a smile so as to not worry her. "Let me know what you find, and thanks," she said, as she walked toward Jewels' room. As she approached, she could hear the woman talking. She stepped into the room without knocking and her attention focused on the patient, who paced from wall to wall with the phone to her ear. Startled, she immediately ended the call. Mist frowned curiously at her reaction and wondered who she had been speaking to.

"Car warranty spam," Jewels muttered. "Hey, how's it going?" She slipped into the bed and hid the phone under the sheet.

"I had a chat to Angel," she stated, quick and to the point.

"She was here earlier. She seems like a very nice girl," she responded casually.

"Yes, she is." Her tone was crisp and matter of fact. "Although when I spoke to her, she was very upset."

Jewels arched a questioning eyebrow. "Did I do anything wrong? By the tone of your voice, you seem upset as well."

"No, I'm merely concerned for one of my girls and what was said that could have made her so agitated." Her entire demeanor was tense and disapproving.

"Maybe it was what wasn't said that's the big issue here," Jewels retorted.

"Look. Angel has been through a lot and is still trying to make sense of all this. We need to be careful about the way things are communicated and expressed."

"Haven't we all?" The woman snapped. "We all had to deal with our issues, Mist. Damn! I lost my entire compound in a single day and I still need to manage, somehow, to move on."

Mist sighed deeply as she felt the pain of the loss. She walked forward, grasped the back of the chair in front of the bed, and leaned on it as she drew a deep breath. "You're right, Jewels." Her voice was more tender now. "We all have our painful stories and losses, but you and I aren't new to this. I know I should have said something to her a long time ago. She's still learning how to cope with all of this, so we need to approach these matters wisely and timely."

Jewels snorted softly under her breath. "You, dealing with things in a timely manner? If I recall correctly, you were the most impulsive one of the group. Remember?"

She smiled. "Yeah, I do, but thanks to friends like you, I learned to be more prudent." Her expression softened. She walked around the chair, sat, and exhaled slowly. "Jewels, let me handle Angel and you work on getting better, which is my biggest concern."

The woman shrugged. "Okay. Are we good?"

Mist nodded. "Yeah, we are good."

FORECAST: A BLAST FROM
THE PAST

Pretzel, Reina, and Angel stood patiently in the WTA subway station and watched the late-night passengers who waited for the next number two train to Brooklyn. During rush hour, the station would overflow with the masses, but at this time of day, it resembled the scene of a post-apocalyptic event.

Disgusting puddles of runoff mixed with rust at the bottom of the staircase and the platform, while rats scuttled across the grimy floor to the overfilled trash cans and sniffed for what was spilled on the ground. The experience would not be complete without the lingering and proliferating odor of creosote and urine deposits.

"How long do you usually wait?" Angel asked imploringly while her expression revealed an intense desire to leave. It was her first time in the field scouting for new Daughters and she had become impatient after only an hour in the awful surroundings. Her inclusion was very unusual, but with persistence—more accurately described as nagging—and a one-time authorization from Joan, she had accompanied her closest friends.

"It depends on the circumstance and the seer," explained Pretzel. "If the prediction is dire, we might wait longer. However, if the weather is treacherous or a life-threatening confrontation ensues, the scout must use their best judgment."

"Or when a place stinks," Reina muttered caustically and pinched her nose.

Pretzel glanced at her partner out of the corner of her eye, shook her head, and smirked. "And as I said, it depends on the seer. Some are still understanding and developing their gift, and there are others whose predictions have been statistically shown to have a high degree of probability."

Bewildered, Angel commented, "That sounds very mathematical for something as mystical as a prophecy."

"We take each prophecy seriously because it's the lifeblood of our rescue and recruitment efforts."

"Don't tell me you guys use calculators to determine the accuracy of a seer?" Angel snorted.

"You're not too far from the truth," Pretzel told her. "We have whole teams dedicated to this endeavor. They despise no prophecy but they test everything. This team tracks a seer's emotional state, physical wellbeing, changes in diet, and other seemingly unrelated factors, and compiles them together with the contents of each prophecy. Over time, the team discovers the correlations between these factors and the seer's accuracy and uses them to determine the probability that any given prophecy is trustworthy."

"Stop speaking in tongues, Pretzel, and speak English," said Reina.

"For example, some seers' accuracy is affected when the prophecy involves someone they deeply care about. Or if they had five-alarm chili the night before, it's not only their tummy that'll be confused."

All three girls giggled at the expression.

"So, who was the seer who gave us this particular prediction?" asked Angel eagerly.

"Geneva. She was one of the initiates at the Memento Commemoration with you."

"I don't think she's that good," Reina added and pinched her nose again.

"Reina, stop." Pretzel slapped her partner gently on her arm, turned to Angel, and continued, "She's fairly new but her accuracy has been consistent. By the way, if it weren't for her, you wouldn't be here tonight."

With a frown, she asked, "Why's that?"

Her roommate dug in her jeans pocket and retrieved a pack of gum. "To become a scout, you need at least one year of physical training and one year of scout training before you can go out in the field. However, Joan liked the idea of having two initiates from the same Memento Commemoration cohort working together on their first assignment." She offered a stick of gum to them. Reina refused, but Angel accepted.

"And whose idea was it?" she asked as she unwrapped her gum.

"Mine." Pretzel smiled and put the stick of gum in her mouth.

"Thanks. Anyway, what's the description of the person we are looking for again?"

"Hold on. I saved it on my phone." The girl pulled her cell phone from her back pocket and launched her note app.

"Black oily hair, pale complexion, black lipstick, black fingernails, and wearing a black trench coat...to be located near the turnstiles. Name, Jesse," she read.

"She sounds like the Devil's niece," snickered Reina.

"Aren't we all," her partner joked.

"We might have a problem," Angel pointed out. "I've been in this subway station before and there are two turnstiles on this platform—the one here and another toward the end." She pointed to the right.

"Shoot!" snapped Pretzel. "If this girl exists, we might have missed her. We'll wait another half-hour and if we don't see anyone with those descriptions, we'll leave, okay?" Her gaze focused on Reina, who responded with a big grin and a thumbs-up but still held her nose. "My concern now is that the NYPD will become suspicious if they see us loitering. I'll walk to the other turnstile and text you if I see anything."

For fifteen minutes, Pretzel waited and stole glances at the passing commuters until she noticed a young girl who appeared to be around eighteen and matched Geneva's description. She wore a trench coat, black top, and mini-skirt with over-the-knee charcoal-black boots. Her Goth fashion was predominant and the only color variation in her ensemble was a pair of white stereo headphones hooked on her ears with their wire plugged into her cell phone. The scout texted her companions, who hurried to join her.

The Daughters moved closer to the young lady, who was thoroughly absorbed in listening to her music. They had to wave to get her attention and she removed one of her earbuds and frowned at them.

Pretzel spoke quickly. "Do you have a minute? We'd like to talk to you about something."

"Are you Sovereign's Witnesses or something?" She spoke in a low, mellow voice. "That's cool and all but it's not for me. Please save your tracts for someone else."

As she lifted the bud to her ear, Pretzel replied, "No, we aren't. Is your name Jesse by any chance?"

She nodded and her frown deepened. "Yeah." She flashed her gaze from Reina to Angel. "Who the heck are you?"

"My name is Pretzel and these are my friends Reina and Angel," she said and gestured to her left. "I know what I'm about to say will sound very strange but we are here to warn you. Your life may be in danger."

"Danger? Hmm...that's not a first," she said with blithe unconcern. The Daughters exchanged quizzical looks and focused on Jesse again. "Yeah. My mom tells me that all the time. I honestly think she's paranoid."

"I'm not sure if you understand the kind of danger I'm referring to, but we believe you're being followed," Pretzel insisted emphatically. "Followed by some very powerful people."

"Boy!" she exclaimed and shook her head. "You sound exactly like my mom. She even makes me put on this oily stuff that smells like cinnamon." She shrugged. "I don't know why, which is the reason I don't apply it all the time." All three stared at each other and thought the same thing —*Kollourion*. Jesse caught a sudden whiff. "You guys wear that stuff too?"

As she finished her sentence, a sudden and unexpected gust of hot air rushed forcefully through the station although no subway train was passing. The sudden wind began to pick up and became almost tempestuous. Curious, the four young women turned to try to locate the source, but in moments, all of them felt something menacing and ominous.

Unsurprisingly, the intimidating feeling began to suffuse their senses. They turned to look at the opposite side of the platform. Across from them stood a seven-foot-tall figure with long blond hair that reached his lower back and tawny eyes that glinted fiendishly. Two miniature twisters spun in the palms of his hands and he flung them toward the group as if they were snowballs.

"It's an Elementalite!" yelled Pretzel. "Move!" She bounded away and pushed Jesse with her, while Reina caught Angel by the arm and yanked her away from the two now-enormous raging whirlwinds that accelerated and expanded with each swirl.

All three Daughters extracted their blades, while the formidable husky figure jumped from the platform onto the tracks and ran in their direction. Suddenly, a non-passenger train on the middle express path flashed its lights and its horn wailed as it collided with the creature. The train came to an abrupt stop moments later.

"What the morbid was that?" a perturbed-looking Jesse asked and pushed quickly to her feet.

"He's not dead, ladies!" exclaimed Pretzel.

"What do you mean he's not dead?" demanded Jesse.

"Angel, watch over her. Reina and I will take care of this menace," instructed Pretzel.

The few shocked passengers on the platform stared disbelievingly at the front of the train, which had now come to a full stop and was only a few feet away from the Daughters. Some onlookers were taking video but one or two were calling nine-one-one. The conductor exited the train and looked at the body of the Nephilim. Those folks closer to the front of the train gasped or clapped their hands over their mouths.

"He's getting up," someone said incredulously.

"Dude, are you okay?" asked the conductor as he walked toward the Nephilim with a flashlight in his hand.

The creature rose gradually and blew a violent wind from his mouth that caught and catapulted the conductor into a fatal impact against the train. Everyone on the platform shouted and screamed as they scrambled to exit the station.

"Oh, my God! My mom was right. It's a demon from Hell!" yelled Jesse and whirled to rush out of the station as well.

Angel shrieked, "Jesse, wait!"

The girl sprinted along the platform but slipped in a puddle of water and fell with a loud grunt. She lost her grasp on her cell phone, which slipped out of her hands and bounced several times before it disappeared into the gap and finally settled on the tracks. Immediately, she clutched her lower left leg and shouted, "Damn it! My leg!" Tears of pain coursed down her cheeks and Angel raced forward to assist her.

The Elementalite locked his gaze on Pretzel and Reina, who stood their ground and brandished their blades. He stretched both arms horizontally to the side and began to spin his entire body in place. Suddenly, he elevated in a gust of swirling wind and from a distance, it seemed like a tornado picked up the debris along with the stream of air. Swiftly, he shifted from the tracks to the platform, landed, and came to a standstill before the two Daughters. With a gust of wind produced by the thrust of his arm, he launched an NYC trash can on his right toward the girls.

Instinctively, they leapt out of the way. While in mid-air, Pretzel hurled one of her blades and it sank into his leg.

He uttered a piercing, guttural sound. "You bitch!" he snarled, yanked the blade from his leg, and flung it at her but missed.

From a distance, Jesse watched in horror and amazement. She looked at Angel and exclaimed, "You guys are the Daughters of the Watchers, right?"

She frowned at her in surprise but before she could answer, the Nephilim bellowed a war cry as he lunged toward Pretzel. She smirked, remained motionless, and waited for him to get dangerously close, clearly in her element. While his attention was focused on her, Reina threw her blade into his opposite leg. He fell with an agonized cry.

"You slut of Hell!" he roared.

The injured Nephilim lay on the platform and dark crimson blood ran from the wounds on his legs. Suddenly, swirling iridescent lights appeared behind the creature, coalesced, and increased from the size of a fist to seven feet in height. Two tall Daimons in their human forms and dressed in their Diamond Edition suits stepped out of the Angelic portal. One of them had long bleached-blond hair falling to his broad shoulders, apricot-hued high cheekbones, and a well-defined Roman nose. The second had ebony hair. Their walk was regal as they approached the fallen Nephilim and stopped a few paces in front of him.

The senses of all four girls had been attuned to the danger of the Nephilim but now, their Spiritual-Psychological Awareness was overwhelmed by dread. For Angel, the sensation she received from the second Daimon seemed familiar. She knew instinctively it was Leonard Archie.

Archie looked disappointedly at the Elementalite, cocked his head toward the other Daimon, and nodded. His companion strode forward, yanked the blade viciously from the injured leg, and let it clatter to the floor. He placed his hands on the Nephilim's wounds and they were instantly healed.

"The only thing you did right here was to inform me first, Euroclydon," Leonard said scathingly, his frown stern. At a gesture of his head, Euroclydon stood. The Daimon then turned to the Watcher. "Amon, take him away."

Amon grasped Euroclydon tightly by the arm and pulled him into the portal, but before they vanished, he lingered for a split second, glanced to his side, and smirked at Pretzel.

The Watcher's smile made her uneasy. She felt disgusted while at the same time, she experienced a sense of longing for something she had never realized she was missing.

The portal closed as soon as they stepped through it.

Leonard walked with light, long strides and smoothed his suit along the way. His gaze locked on Angel and he strode past Pretzel and Reina, who stood frozen in horror with pure terror on their faces. Their eyes widened when he stopped a few paces from Angel, who knelt on the floor and held an injured Jesse propped on her lap.

She glared defiantly at him and looked strangely shaken and grim. Her skin crawled with trepidation and Jesse trembled against her. Like her, she sensed the pervasive fear but more than that, an overwhelming presence of evil.

His chiseled, handsome features were hypnotically beautiful yet darkly enigmatic.

"Hello, Angelica," Leonard said, his voice silken. "Do you know who I am?"

Angel did not respond and only swallowed hard, her expression grim. She stared at him, her eyes haunted.

"I'm not merely another divine one if that's what you are wondering." A slow smile spread across his countenance. His eyes stared darkly at her. "If you have not guessed, I am your father."

The utterance made her blood curdle. She studied the man in front of her in dismay, rendered speechless by his malignant aura that stirred such intense emotion. Her mind reeled and struggled to accept that this was the person she had wondered about all her life, more handsome than she could ever imagine but more terrifying at the same time.

When she didn't respond, he continued. "You could have yelled a big 'Nooooo...' but no matter. Is it not customary in your culture to ask for a blessing when greeting a parent or an elder?" He paused for a moment. "Well, do you?" he mocked and the corner of his lip quirked.

"What do you want?" she muttered coldly and glowered at him.

Indirectly answering her question, he spoke in a patronizing tone. "Do you know why you ask for a blessing?" Dark mischief flickered in his eyes. "The whole point of the blessing request is so the elder can provide a form of protection over their children. The blessing provides the requestor safeguards against whatever challenge or difficulty they are facing or may face." He raised his right hand to stare at his perfectly manicured fingernails, blew hot air on the nails, and folded them into his palm before he rubbed them against his suit. "And that's what I came to do, my daughter." Sheer evil infused his smile. "To offer you my protection." His voice was seductive like soft venom.

"Take your protection and shove it up your—" Angel retorted, her tone almost a hiss.

Leonard clucked his tongue and shook his index finger. "The Good Book does say to honor your father and your mother so you may have a long life…" He stopped deliberately without finishing the verse. "If I were you, I would not bring dishonor upon myself." He stared gravely at her. "You still breathe because I will it so." His expression was fierce and hard as he uttered those words but soon shifted to his beguiling smile. "I am not here to get hostile but to have a cordial, peaceful, and agreeable conversation with my only begotten daughter."

"I have nothing to say to you," Angel replied heatedly. Her voice trembled but her eyes were filled with loathing.

With his hands clasped behind his back, he leaned forward. He bored his gaze into hers. "But I have much to discuss with you. Still, I will cut to the chase. A once in a lifetime proposal—you come and join me and know what real power looks like. Your every craving and desire will be sated. Imagine it—a life free of pain, suffering, and all the things that make life meaningless. I will even throw in a gesture of goodwill. I will make sure sweet old granny, your friends"—he spun to gesture at Pretzel and Reina— "and those at the warehouse are not disturbed. You and I can become...I do not know..." He placed his finger on his chin in a pretense of choosing his words. "A big happy family."

"You can go to Hell!" Angel exclaimed and clenched her teeth. She scowled defiantly at him.

"I've been there," he taunted and nodded. "I was hoping to show you around once we were done here." He gave her a lopsided, mocking smile.

From a distance, emergency sirens wailed, which made Leonard look up and around.

He snorted disdainfully. "The offer is still on the table but will not be for long." The swirling iridescent lights appeared behind him. Before he departed, he turned to Angel again. "I suggest you consider my offer very serious- ly." His gaze was vicious and full of warning. "If not, it will be the end of you and your friends at the warehouse. Do not take too long or who knows, I may come and visit you to get my answer." A slow smirk appeared on his face before he disappeared through the portal.

Pretzel and Reina emerged from their stupor as if from a trance. They raced toward the other girls. Jesse trembled in fear and winced in pain. Pretzel knelt beside them, her expression still horrified.

"Are you okay?" she asked.

Her expression pale, Angel could only nod.

She turned to the other girl, "Are you hurt?"

"Was that a...a demon?" Jesse stuttered.

"Jesse, we don't have time to explain. Are you able to get up?" Pretzel asked tersely.

"I think I twisted my ankle although I heard a crack when I fell."

"Come with us and we'll get you some medical attention—"

She was interrupted abruptly by the distraught girl. "Take me to my mom, please!" she insisted. "She can make me better."

"They're getting closer," warned Reina.

"Where does she live?" asked Pretzel.

"I live with her in Brooklyn. North 9th Street." Jesse groaned in pain as she grasped her leg tightly.

Out of options, Pretzel stared at Reina and Angel. "The subway lines will be closed for the next few hours while they conduct an investigation. We'll need to take the bus. Let's get her up and take her home."

Between them, they helped Jesse to her feet and carried her out of the subway.

They reached the modern-looking graphite-gray apartment late in the night. Very little was said during the bus ride except for Jesse's continuous groans. Her brow perspired and her face was paler than before. They carried her to the front door.

A concerned Pretzel uttered, "Jesse, you don't look good. We know someone who can help you."

She shook her head emphatically. "No. My mom can make me better," she insisted. "Reach into my right coat pocket and you'll find the keys to the door," she said.

Angel immediately retrieved the keys and handed them to Reina while she continued to prop Jesse up with her shoulders.

The girls moved through the front door, down the narrow hallway, and into the elevator. Four floors up, they stumbled into the hallway.

"The third door to the left," Jesse told them.

Reina ran ahead to unlock the door but it was yanked open from the other side. A middle-aged woman stared at her in surprise, her expression frantic.

"Who the hell are you?" she demanded roughly and frowned.

"Mom!" Jesse cried from the hallway. "I need help."

When the woman heard her daughter's voice, she rushed out of the apartment. "Jesse, what happened?" she exclaimed frantically. Her pallor grew noticeably.

"I may have broken my leg," she explained, her voice tight with pain.

Her mom glared darkly at the Daughters but when she saw the pain her daughter was in, she instructed them to bring her inside. They laid the girl on the living room sofa and very slowly, she removed the girl's boots. Jesse groaned in pain.

"It's okay, sweetie. In a few, you'll be fine," she murmured comfortingly. She placed her hands gently over her fractured leg, which made her daughter gasp. Instantly, color returned to her face, her breathing normalized, and her pain dissipated.

With her gaze still on her daughter, the woman glowered at the Daughters. "If you're looking to recruit her, you can forget it. You hear me?" Her jaw clenched.

"Mom!" Jesse snapped. "They saved my life. One of those monster creatures you talk about so much was there."

"Why didn't you call me? I've been worried sick about you." She brushed her hand over her short hair.

"I lost my phone at the station. It fell onto the tracks."

She stared intently at her. "You're not wearing the oil. When will you start listening to me?" Her tone was stern. "Damn it, Jesse. How many times do I have to tell you it's not safe if you don't wear it?" she said in exasperation and sighed deeply.

"Sorry. I honestly thought all those stories were bullsh—"

"Watch your language, young lady!" her mom exclaimed. Still avoiding eye contact with the Daughters, she asked, "I presume she was found and attacked?"

"That's right," replied Pretzel with a somewhat confused expression.

"Damn it!" she bellowed. She sat on the chair next to the sofa Jesse was still lying on and buried her face in her hands. "And we just moved here," she said as if to herself. After a long moment, she glanced at the Daughters. "You can sense me as well as I can sense you, so there's no point in denying who I am. My name is Amanda but...um, I used to be known as Peaches."

All three young women frowned at her remark.

"You were part of the Daughterhood at one point?" asked Pretzel.

"Years ago. I was part of the Los Angeles group but left them when Jesse was an infant. I didn't want to deal with the bull...dust anymore!" she said with her fingers interlaced beneath her chin.

"Mom!" Jesse snapped at her mom for the almost foul language.

"I'm sorry, sweetie." She glanced at Jesse. "Ever since, we have moved around the country and tried to avoid being discovered by those monsters and people like you, but we can't ever seem to get away," she said dejectedly. "It's time for another move, I guess."

"No more moving, Mom," Jesse told her firmly. "I can't take it anymore." She pushed from the sofa and stood on her two feet as if she had never had an injury.

"Don't you get it, Jesse?" her mother snapped at her. "They know we are here. Those monsters...they know we are here," she repeated with tears streaming down her face.

The girl strode closer, knelt beside her, and clasped her hands tenderly. "Mom, we have done this for years now. I'm sorry, this was all my fault, but I think it's time for us to stop running and face the facts."

Amanda smiled warmly at her daughter and caressed her cheek softly. "This was never your fault."

Pretzel spoke hastily. "You guys are more than welcome to stay with us, at least until you feel safe enough to return to the apartment. Our facility is located in lower

Manhattan and it has sufficient rooms to accommodate you both."

Jesse was exhilarated when she heard the offer. "Come on, Mom. It'll give me the chance to learn about this bullsh —" Her mom gave her a stern look. "I mean, the Daughters of the Watchers. At least for a few days."

Hesitant but no match for the excitement on her daughter's face, she relented. "Only a few days until I decide what to do next." She sighed. "Go pack a light bag."

With no hesitation, her daughter looked at Reina and pointed at her shirt, and said, "Would you like to see my Goth Mello Kitty collection?"

The girl's eyes glowed with enthusiasm. "Someone after my own heart," she said blissfully and followed Jesse into her room.

Amanda, still seated, looked at Pretzel and Angel. "I know what you're thinking—how is she my daughter since all hybrids are barren?"

The statement took Angel by surprise. She wasn't aware that Daughters could not have children. Her heart shattered at the realization that she would never have kids of her own.

"I rescued Jesse when she was a babe and raised her as my own. I didn't want her to live this chaotic life so I left the Daughterhood, but no matter where we went this…this curse followed us." Concern marred her features. "Jesse is aware that I'm not her biological mother and I've told her all about the Daughters, the Nephilim, and the Daimons, but I wasn't aware she didn't take it seriously." She shook her head. "But maybe I was aware and didn't want to face the facts either."

"These are difficult times we are living in, but if there's any chance for us to survive this, it won't be through isolation. We need to stick together," Pretzel stated.

Amanda scoffed at her comment. "I've heard this rhetoric many times in the past but in the end, it's merely a nice way to get us involved in a fight we shouldn't be fighting."

"With all due respect, Amanda, this fight you speak of seems to have followed you through the country. If you want to keep Jesse safe, you know there's no better place for her to be than with the Daughters," the scout stated courteously but firmly.

Amanda remained silent and stared out the living room window in contemplation. She stood abruptly. "We are only staying for a few days..." She started to walk toward her bedroom as her voice trailed off. "Tell Jesse I'll be out soon."

Pretzel turned to Angel and noticed her sorrowful expression. "You okay?"

"I'll talk to you about it later," Angel responded.

She nodded as she drew her cell phone from her pocket. "I'll call the warehouse to inform them about the visitors and see if we can get someone to pick us up."

31

FATHERS AND MOTHERS

It was two am by the time Amanda and Jesse were settled in their room at the warehouse. Angel, Pretzel, and Reina were drained, their faces haggard and energy depleted by the evening's spine-chilling event. They trudged toward their rooms with the last ounce of energy they had left.

The torrential downpour had started shortly after midnight, accompanied by streaks of lightning, clattering thunder, and howling winds. The deluge unsettled their fretful hearts even more.

A pale-looking Reina ran her hand through her flaxen hair and asked breathlessly, "Is it okay if I sleep with you guys tonight?" Her voice trembled slightly. "Between seeing those Daimons and this storm, I don't think I can sleep alone." She pressed her fingers to her lips.

"You can sleep with me on the sofa bed," Angel offered, equally terrified. The dim lights in the corridor made it even more hair-raising but did, however, bolster their energy so they hastened their strides. As soon as they reached the room, Reina opened the door swiftly and turned the lights on with a huge sigh of relief.

"It was terrifying, I have to say," remarked Pretzel. "Thankfully, we didn't see them in their demonic form. I've run into Daimons in human shape before but I've never witnessed their true nature. I hear it's the most harrowing and hideous thing in the world." All three kicked their footwear off wearily at the door. Shortly after, Pretzel closed the door.

"I think I may have seen Apollyon's true form in an alley a few months back—the night before I met you guys —and it was terrifying. Tonight, he looked like an actor attending the Oscars but both times, I felt the same frightening sensation." Angel shuddered.

"At least he was dressed nicely. I guess the Devil does wear Prada." Reina tried to lighten the mood. "I'd have lost it if he had shown up in his real form—you know…with, like, bat wings, horns, and those awful red pajamas."

Angel nodded in agreement.

"That's not what they truly look like," corrected Pretzel. "That's only an appearance they sometimes take to impose dread and terror."

"What? You mean it gets worse than that?" demanded a disturbed Angel.

"Yes. Sadly, it does. Their true form is one of absence and void. Imagine staring into a dark abyss that also stares at you," explained Pretzel. "From what I've been told, they're like black holes, devoid of any light or goodness of their own. They exist only to devour and absorb. To stand in the presence of a Daimon in their true form is to have all that's good sucked out of you, and the only thing that remains is existential fear."

"I looked...I looked into his eyes... He took all of my goodness...I'll never leave this room." Reina gasped.

Her friends frowned at her.

"Uh, I don't think it works that way," said Angel.

"Okay, good. But anyway, I don't want to speak about ugly demons now, with wings or holes. Tomorrow morning maybe but not now." Reina cleared her throat, her voice a little raspy.

"I...I have a question for you guys. Did either of you get a strange sensation from the other Daimon?" asked Pretzel.

"I felt all kinds of strange sensations, all of them bad," shouted Reina with a distinctive shudder.

"I'm not saying fear but a sense of a close connection— almost like nostalgia." Pretzel loosened her braided hair pensively. "It felt weird."

"I had the same sense when that creep was speaking to me," said Angel.

She strode to the sofa and began to remove all the cushions and unfold it into a bed with Reina's help. Once it was fully converted, she sat on the edge and lowered her gaze to the floor.

"Hey, have any of you seen...well, you know, your dads? I don't know what else to call them." Her gaze shifted from one girl to the other.

Reina shook her head rapidly. "If he's anything like what I felt tonight, I don't know if I want to." She sat across from Angel and a thoughtful expression settled on her face. "But to be honest, I've thought about it. I wonder what he looks like or if he even knows I exist."

"Most of us never do." Pretzel scowled. "From what we know, there are Daimons who simply produced offspring for the cause."

A puzzled expression appeared on Angel's face. "The cause?"

"The Host of the Daimons," responded her roommate. The explanation left her as clueless as before.

When she saw her face, Pretzel went on to explain. "Two thousand years ago, the King of the Daimons became dormant. We suspect he was imprisoned. After his disappearance, the Daimons began to create Nephilim in greater numbers. The Final Prophet, also known as the Locust Eater, foretold that Diablos would be bound to the deepest regions of Tartarus but would be released again. Some seers have foretold that the time of his release is at hand, and we've discovered that there are Daimons who have dedicated themselves to producing as many offspring as possible. We call them Breeders. They've tried to reproduce by seducing as many women as possible, and some have even gone as far as donating to sperm banks." Pretzel gave Reina a fleeting look. "It's how our moms got pregnant and a few others in this warehouse."

"Are there any other kinds?" Angel asked.

"Well, there are the Powers. These Watchers seem to be more careful than Breeders. They use mediums like seers to ensure that their offspring are male. We see fewer Daughters from this kind. Last are the Archies, the three high lords who, in addition to mediums, use groomers. These groomers ensure the female companions are well suited for the Archies. The high lords are known to produce the mightiest Nephilim on the planet." She stared darkly at Angel. "I only know of two female offspring from this kind."

"Who's the other?" Angel asked.

"The other is Joan."

"Joan?" She raised an eyebrow.

"Her father is Legion, the Lord of Europe and Africa. His human name is Maximus Archie." Angel gawked at Pretzel in shock. "So, if there's someone in this group who knows the pressure you're under, it's her."

Unexpectedly, Pretzel yawned loudly. "Excuse me," she said. "I'm exhausted. We should get some sleep." She walked toward her chestnut bureau, opened the top drawer, and took her nightwear out.

Angel stared out the window and considered Pretzel's words and the last thing her father said to her at the station. It haunted her and she couldn't help but think about it. "I've been thinking about the last words he said about coming to visit me. Do you think he meant here?" Angel asked with arched eyebrows.

"I don't know," responded Pretzel. "Why do you ask?" Her voice faded slightly as she strode into the bathroom with a towel and her nightwear in her hand.

"Could he come here and cause harm?" Her voice was filled with apprehension.

With a toothbrush in her mouth, Pretzel sounded muffled. "Daimons usually don't make their presence known without a Nephilim around, especially if they intend to do something harmful. It would be pointless if he did—"

"Can we please stop speaking of visiting spirits?" interrupted Reina, who looked as if all the blood in her body had drained.

"I'm sorry, Reina," Angel said quickly. "No more talk of demons. Okay?" She walked to the bureau, opened the bottom drawer, and retrieved her set of pajamas. Reina did the same but with the middle drawer. Even though she had her room, she always kept some of her clothes and night-wear in Pretzel's.

Angel sat on the bed to wait for the bathroom and recollected the day's events. Suddenly, the conversation with Amanda came to mind and the shocking realization hit her again like a ton of bricks. With a sullen expression, she asked, "Is it true we can't have babies?"

Pretzel peeked her head out of the bathroom, glanced quickly at Reina, and gave Angel a gloomy look. "Yeah." Her voice was low and soft. "I'm sorry, I thought you knew that already. I guess that's why you were so gloomy at Jesse's apartment? Amanda's comment caught you by surprise, huh?" She gestured with her hand before she returned to the bathroom to rinse her mouth. Standing at the doorway, she continued. "Some say this was established from the beginning, while others believe it's due to the curse of Cain."

"The curse of Cain?"

"There's a theory that states Cain, the first human born, was the son of Diablos and due to his wicked and destructive descendants, a curse was bestowed on all hybrids, preventing them from having children." She shrugged. "It's likely only a legend. I only know neither Nephilim nor Daughters can have children."

"I've always wanted children," she said. "Never having

siblings or cousins, I felt lonely growing up. I always wanted a big family. It's one of the reasons I like working with children. The thought of one day having my own." She gave them a fleeting smile. "It was disappointing news to hear, you know." Reina embraced her warmly.

"We all share your sentiment," said Pretzel. "I've thought about it many times." She stopped in thought. "I wonder if that was the case with Amanda. She mentioned leaving the Daughterhood due to the hostilities, but I wouldn't be surprised if it was simply to live a quiet life and be a mother and raise a child away from this chaotic world."

"I get that," responded Angel. "It's like when I see Olivia. Her gentle smile, curly blonde hair, clear blue eyes, and those chubby cheeks...I want to whisk her away." She stopped abruptly when she suddenly remembered the child's statement about the Daimon Killer and Mist's directive to find out how the girl knew. While she'd fully intended to do so, she couldn't believe she had forgotten to talk to Olivia about it. She stared blankly out the window.

"You all right?" asked Reina with a frown.

Shaking her head from the thought, she responded, "I'm sorry. I remembered something I needed to do." She opened her mouth and yawned loudly. "Oh, my God. My apologies. I'm drained." She turned to Pretzel. "Are you done with the bathroom?"

"Let me take a quick shower and it's all yours," her roommate stated. "Before I forget, we need to be up bright and early to give an account of last night's incident."

Both girls moaned.

"It's part of the scouts' duty."

32

SEEKING ANSWERS

Angel scanned the book almost aggressively and her finger moved one line at a time. She squinted and blinked to relieve her eyes and massaged the back of her neck after hours of poring over books, manuscripts, and even old scrolls. Ashen-faced and hollow-eyed and barely visible behind the stacks of books that surrounded her, she continued to read relentlessly.

She shook her head in frustration, closed the book before her disappointedly, and placed it aside to take the next heavy-bound book from the stack. With a sharp sigh, she proceeded to scan this text as avidly as she had the others.

Mrs. Mozart and Grace walked into the library, chatting softly and even tittering like two old friends would. The librarian halted and gestured for her companion to do the same, surprised to see someone at the library so late in the evening. Curious, they both moved closer and wondered who was surrounded by the towers of books. They stopped in front of her table and narrowed their eyes curiously at a leaden-looking Angel, who had not yet realized she was being observed.

"Miss Angel?" asked Mrs. Mozart in a low, soft voice. She raised her eyebrows inquiringly.

Startled by the unexpected visitors, the girl gasped and jerked her hands to her chest. "Mrs. Mozart, Grace, hi!" she spluttered. She closed the book unceremoniously and gazed at them with her bleary eyes widened in surprise.

"Are you all right, child?" asked Mrs. Mozart in her distinctive English accent.

At first, she stared like a deer in headlights but then shook her head as she ran her slim fingers through her disheveled hair. "I'm not," she muttered and buried her face in her hands.

"What's going on, sweetie? I've never seen you like this before," remarked Grace, her voice as caring and tender as ever.

"I've been searching since noon, looking for some... explanation." She sighed and folded her arms. "And I can't find anything." Her tone was slightly agitated. "I feel overwhelmed and confused." She clasped her hands and ran them over her head to tousle her hair further.

"Do you mind sharing with us what has you so disturbed?" asked Mrs. Mozart.

She exhaled, hesitant and nervous to say what was on her mind. "It's this whole Daimon Killer prophecy," she muttered finally. "I'm sure you both know about it."

"Oh, that." Grace gave the other woman a fleeting look. "Honey, do you mind if we sit? We may look young but these legs of ours betray us at times." She chuckled softly.

"Yes, sure," Angel said and nodded. She pushed the

stacks of books to the edge of the table to have a better view of the women.

As they took their seats, Mrs. Mozart smiled at her. "What is your concern?"

Immediately she asked, "Is it true? I've looked through book after book, countless texts, and tons of manuscripts and can't seem to find anything on the subject, and if it's…" She dragged in a breath. "What am I supposed to do? I feel overwhelmed and need answers."

"I need you to clear your mind for a moment and consider what has you so perturbed. It seems to me it is not so much the reality of it but the effect it is having on you," Mrs. Mozart told her.

"To put it simpler terms, why are you so agitated?" Grace added.

She sat pensively and stared at her folded hands where they rested on the table. A long silence hung between the three until she finally answered. "I'm afraid."

"But what are you afraid of, honey?"

"What if I'm this Daimon Killer? I don't have the fighting skills of Gypsy, the leadership expertise of Joan, the strength of Cookie and Dough, or the agility of Pretzel or Reina. As far as I know, I'm the weakest of the group and I'm expected to bring Daimons down?" She threw her arms in the air in exasperation. "Me, who can't fight, run for a long time, and doesn't even know what my gift is," she said in frustration. "I…I need to know if this is true and if it is, how do I prepare for it?"

"A sage woman once said, 'Worry does not empty tomorrow of its sorrow, it empties today of its strength,'" quoted Mrs. Mozart. "You seem to have overwhelmed yourself with contingencies that are outside of your control. And unfortunately, in the process, you have exhausted yourself and missed out on the gift you were handed for this day."

"What's that?" she asked with a curious expression.

"The present." Mrs. Mozart smiled.

"Darlin', you may not like our response but we don't know if it's true or not," commented Grace. "There are only two possible outcomes to this situation. If it's not true, why worry yourself over something that won't happen? On the other hand, if it's true, then why worry about something that's meant to be? Whatever the scenario, it's beyond your control." She extended her hand and grasped Angel's gently.

"But aren't we supposed to learn and train ourselves with what we have been given? We as Daughters train hard, study, and prepare to make ourselves efficient and effective for the opportune moment." Her gaze shifted from one woman to the other. "Why should this be any different?"

"'Cause there's a difference between the things you do know and need to do and those that are still a mystery," responded Grace. "If this mystery is your lot, it'll be revealed to you in due time what needs to be done, but no amount of worrying can ever prepare you for the unknown."

Mrs. Mozart smiled. "But I also think you have a misconception of what is true strength and power, Miss Angel."

"What do you mean?" Angel fixed her gaze on the woman's calm and wise expression.

"Through my many years of learning and experiences, I have come to understand that true power is not demonstrated in the strongest, wisest, most dexterous, or the most gifted, but by those who convey humility, meekness, patience, and love." She stared intently at the woman's glittering eyes as she spoke. "Some would consider these virtues as weaknesses, infinitesimal and insignificant for engaging in conflict, but on the contrary, I would say it is in that weakness that you become the most powerful."

Sensing the girl's confusion on the matter, she tried to clarify. "In the book of Endings, the last volume of the Books, a pertinent analogical story depicts this point. It concerns the ending of all times and the war between The Dragon and the Lamb. In the book, the Dragon is portrayed as a magnificent, fiery red creature having seven heads with seven diadems and ten horns. The Dragon is illustrated as having the power to bring down one-third of the celestial host merely with a swing of his tail and the ability to deceive the whole world. So great is the strength and power of the Dragon that the world he beguiles will worship him.

"And then there is the Lamb..." She paused for a moment with a smile on her face. "Not only a young sheep but one that seemed to be utterly hurt. Humanly speaking, what can an injured, docile lamb do against the great and powerful dragon? But you see, Miss Angel, therein lies the great mystery that is worth pursuing. For it is this meek, gentle, wounded lamb that overcomes the great and powerful dragon."

"How does the lamb defeat the dragon?" she asked curiously.

Mrs. Mozart glanced at the stacks of books and reached toward the book second on top on her left-hand side. She withdrew it carefully and held *Endings* in her hand. "I will not spoil it for you but will say it was the lamb's willingness to put others before himself, even to the point of death. Once again, it sounds irrational and illogical to the human mind but true power is not demonstrated in exceptional abilities or in great physical strength. True power is shown in love and humility." She handed the book to Angel, who took it slowly and stared at the title.

"Do not read it now," instructed the librarian. "I truly recommend you get some rest first." She watched as Angel grasped the book and stared intently at it.

"The woman I quoted earlier was Corrie ten Boom, a Dutch watchmaker who with the help of her family, helped countless Jews to escape the Nazi Holocaust. Her story has always fascinated me and illustrates very well this concept of true power." Mrs. Mozart leaned back in her chair and rested her hands on her lap.

"Miss ten Boom was only one of the individuals who stood to oppose the destructive genocide of the Nazi regime. Her heroic efforts led her and her family into a concentration camp, where she lost her father and dear sister. After an inexplicable clerical error, she was released from the camp. You would think the scars of her loss and the hardships endured at the hands of the Nazis would have anguished her soul. Rather than retaliate with hatred and violence after the war, Miss ten Boom spent the rest of her life advocating for reconciliation. She went on to open a rehabilitation center for camp survivors and the needy and traveled the world with a message of love and forgiveness."

She fixed her green eyes intently on Angel and leaned forward a little. "Think for a moment, Miss Angel. However powerful and destructive the Nazi regime seemed, their ambitious attempt came to naught. Furthermore, their ill-natured endeavor is abhorred and is equated as a symbol of unequivocal evil." She placed her index finger over her lips. "But the works done by individuals such as Miss ten Boom will forever be recorded in the annals of history as symbols of true courage, strength, and goodness."

Mrs. Mozart smiled and leaned back in her chair. "The point of all this, Miss Angel, is to search for things such as love, kindness, goodness, and gentleness—the true way of power—and not fret about obtaining skills, abilities, and strength to make yourself powerful."

Angel gazed deeply into her bright eyes, mesmerized by her words of wisdom that seemed more precious than rubies and more valuable than gold.

"Darlin', I'm also surprised you haven't discovered what your gift is," stated Grace.

Her expression slid into a frown. "What is it?" she asked desperately.

"Well, think about it for a moment. You and I have talked about your background in the past but indulge me for a moment. Before you joined the Daughterhood, what was your occupation?" Grace stared at her and waited for an answer.

"I worked as a waitress at a diner," she replied.

"During your time off, what did you do?"

"I'd help my grandmother." She frowned and wondered where the woman was going with all this.

"And since you've been with the Daughters, you've been involved with the children, the infirmary, the library, and even lent me a hand in the kitchen. When you're there you do it so gracefully that you inspire others to pick up their slack," she said with a chuckle. "Your gift is quite evident to me."

For a moment, Angel was silent as she considered her words until finally, she whispered, almost to herself, "Service!" Her expression was blank although internally, she felt a thrill of emotion. She turned to Mrs. Mozart and Grace and repeated, "My gift is service." She grinned with relief and excitement.

"That wasn't so difficult." Grace chortled.

Angel rose swiftly, dashed toward the woman, and embraced her warmly. Without any hesitation, she did the same with Mrs. Mozart, who wasn't accustomed to being hugged by her pupils but didn't reject it.

She wiped silent, joyful tears from her cheeks. "Thank you to both of you. You've truly made my day and given me so much to think about."

"Anytime, sweetie," Grace remarked.

Her gaze settled on the stacked books. "Let me clean this up and head up to the room. I need to give the news to Pretzel," she said gleefully.

"Do not concern yourself, Miss Angel. I will take care of it," stated Mrs. Mozart. "I do have a question before you leave, however. You knew about the prophecy for quite some time. Why the eagerness now?"

"It was Olivia," replied Angel.

"What could sweet seven-year-old Olivia do to have you so upset?" asked Grace with a frown.

"It wasn't her but what she said," she explained. "Mist had instructed me to ask Olivia how she knew I was the Daimon Killer and when I did, she responded that she saw it in a dream."

"A dream?" Mrs. Mozart asked and placed her finger on her chin.

She nodded. "In the dream, she saw a Daimon calling me the Daimon Killer. The dream itself was frightening to her. She said the warehouse was being attacked by Daimons, Nephilim, and a woman who was dressed in black, with black hair, nails, and lipstick, and an insignia on her right arm—a mark of some kind." She gazed at both women, who seemed slightly distraught. "That made me think that maybe the prophecy could be true and if there was an attack on this warehouse, I could protect it by learning how to become this Daimon Killer."

Both women sighed deeply, but it was Mrs. Mozart who spoke. "We will have a talk with Olivia and look into this matter. As for you, get some rest and be at peace." She smiled. As Angel started to walk away, she reminded her, "Do not forget to take the book."

Angel nodded, grabbed the book of *Endings,* and strode away feeling a thousand pounds lighter.

Once the girl had left the library, Grace asked, "What are your thoughts?"

Staring into space, her mind in deep thought, Mrs.

Mozart responded, "I know children at times produce dreams from the pandemonium of their past but there was something particular that caught my attention."

"That Angel was the Daimon Killer?"

"Not at all," she responded. "The woman with the mark on her right arm." She turned to Grace with a furrow between her eyebrows as her mind worked. "If you will excuse me, my dear old friend, I need to look something up. I will return shortly."

Grace gave her a curious look as she rose hastily and strode through one of the towering rows of the library's bookcases. After several minutes, she returned with a book in her hand and sat in her chair next to her companion. She placed the large dark-brown book on the table. The title in black lettering read, *The Marks, Seals, Signs, and Meaning.* She opened the rarely-read book and flipped through the first few pages. When she reached what she'd searched for, she traced her finger through various sections—*The Mark of the Beast, The Seal of the Righteous Ones,* and *The Seal of the Spirit.*

Finally, she stopped. "There it is. *The Mark of the Watchers.*"

She read aloud. "*If a progeny of a Daimon, male or female, who of their own volition, of their own accord, and under no compulsion, gives homage and allegiance to a Daimon, they shall receive a mark on their left arm or right arm. Left arm for male, right arm for female. The mark of the Daimon is set with a burning hand that shall inscribe the name of the underling. It will serve as a sign to the Daimon of having authority over the subordinate, and a sign to the subject and the world of their loyalty to the Superior—*"

Mrs. Mozart halted her reading and looked gravely at Grace. "I can ascribe the child's dramatic dream to her past and her knowledge of Miss Angel's so-called prophecy to eavesdropping, but the Mark of the Watcher is not something commonly discussed, especially on a female offspring."

"What are your thoughts on the little girl's dream?" asked Grace, her expression both curious and concerned.

"First, the dream should be thoroughly heard and evaluated and if credible, we should be highly vigilant." She looked blankly at the tall, towering bookcases in front of her. "There may be another defector to contend with," she whispered.

33

FIREARM

"According to Mr. Ortega, this is the safest place to be," Angel replied to her grandma's concern on the phone. She nodded, sighed softly, and responded, "Yes, *Abuela*, they're feeding me here, and you'll be glad to know I've also made some good friends—people I'm truly connected to." She smiled and glanced at Pretzel, who was busy getting ready. "I knew you'd be happy."

A moment's pause followed as she listened and then continued. "So yes, Mr. Ortega is stopping by today and will provide me with an update on the case. He says it's looking good and hopefully"—she crossed her fingers—"we'll see each other soon." She listened intently to her grandmother's cheerful voice. "I know, *Abuela*. I love you too. Bye."

"How's your *abuelita*?" asked Pretzel as she clicked the end button on the device.

"Health-wise, she's great. She's had physical therapy and has started walking on her own." She sighed, thinking deeply of her grandmother and longing to be with her, especially during her therapy sessions. "Mr. Ortega and his wife have helped her with all the medical stuff—my job." Her voice contained a hint of jealousy. "Other than that, she misses me and wishes to see me soon."

Her roommate turned to her with sympathetic eyes. "It's been a long journey for both of you and although it seems like a never-ending path, I've got a good feeling you'll see her soon. That strong bond you share won't let you remain apart for long."

Angel grinned, appreciative of all her friend had done for her. "Thank you, Pretzel. Your friendship has been a beacon in my life. I've never had a friend like you." She paused and focused on the floor. "In every sense of the word, I wouldn't be here without you."

"You can make it up to me by having your grandmother cook some of that delicious Spanish food you always talk about," she said with a chuckle. "What is it again...*arroz con gandules, pernil, mangu, flan?*"

"That's a promise, girl!" Angel laughed.

At that moment, Reina and Tassel appeared at the door of Pretzel's room. "Hey, girls!" said Reina. "What's with the giggles?"

Angel turned to the doorway and responded, "Promising Pretzel the best Hispanic dinner ever once I'm reunited with my grandmother and by the way, you're both invited."

"Woohoo!" exclaimed Reina. "*Delicioso!* I learned that word from a Spanish kid show."

"Let me know when," added Tassel. "Speaking of food, are you guys heading down for breakfast?"

"We were going there now," said Pretzel.

"Guys, before we go, I'd like to share a concern with you," said Angel. All the girls gave her a curious stare. "Tassel, do you mind closing the door?"

The seer proceeded to do so as she stepped into the room with Reina.

"What's on your mind?" asked Pretzel.

"Well, it's about a dream Olivia had. At first, I didn't want to say anything since it's a little frightening and I wasn't sure if it was true but…um, even if there's a slight chance it could happen, I want you guys to know about it."

"What was the dream about?" inquired an interested Tassel.

"It concerns an attack on the warehouse." All three looked stunned and their expressions turned grave. "An attack carried out by the Nephilim." Angel swallowed before she continued "But what was worse, Olivia may have seen a Daughter—a spy or traitor—in her dream helping them."

"Who?" Reina asked, biting her nails.

"She doesn't know. Although she recognized other Daughters in the dream, she couldn't identify this one. She described her as wearing dark attire with black hair and black nails." Angel pursed her lips. "That was her best description."

"Jesse!" whispered an apprehensive-looking Reina. "And to think she's a Mello Kitty fan. The nerve."

"My thoughts exactly," remarked Angel. "I'm beginning to think we let a spy into the warehouse."

"Wait," Tassel protested. "What makes you think the dream is reliable in the first place?"

"Because in the dream, Olivia knew I was the Daimon

Killer," Angel responded quickly. "I thought everyone knew but I now know that's not the case. Also, Olivia described a tall, slim, and in her words, 'very bad' Daimon calling me by that title."

Pretzel shook her head uneasily. "Guys, we shouldn't jump to conclusions. Assuming Olivia's dream is about future events, we can't be certain it's Jesse she's talking about simply by some vague description. I've spent time with her and her mom Amanda, and they're very good peeps. Amanda says she's never seen her daughter so excited before. Even Amanda, who was apprehensive about being here, is warming to us. If we start making accusations without any concrete evidence, it may severely damage the trust they've developed so far."

"There's a way to find out," said Angel. "Olivia said the woman had a marking of some kind on her right arm. If we were to discreetly check her arm, that'd confirm our suspicions."

Unconvinced, her roommate said, "I'm not comfortable snooping around. I believe you know a person by their fruits. If Jesse or her mom is false, their actions will eventually reflect that."

"I don't know, Pretzel. It wouldn't hurt to at least double-check," stated Tassel. "There was a council meeting of the twelve early this morning and while I don't know what was discussed, I was told to work with Jewels, the survivor from Lancaster, on our security alarm system. I was informed she's an expert on the matter and could help ensure it's up to par. I wonder if the council is concerned about an attack."

"I don't feel comfortable about it," Pretzel said and

shrugged. "I think we should wait and see how things play out. If the council suspects an imminent attack, they'll eventually inform us. My advice is for us to be alert but not do anything foolish."

Angel sighed deeply. "Okay," she said, although not entirely convinced.

They walked out of the room and as they strode through the corridor, Reina whispered in Angel's ear, "Pretzel wants to play the goody-two-shoes, but what's the harm in checking, right?" Angel nodded. "Let's keep an eye on that right arm of Jesse's. Pretzel doesn't have to know."

"Okay," she whispered in agreement.

They reached the crowded cafeteria where Daughters of all ages were having their breakfast and engaged in lively conversation. Across the room, Jesse sat beside her mom. Both were thoroughly occupied in a conversation with the other ladies at their table. When the girl saw the friends walk through the door, she rose quickly to greet them.

"What's up, guys?" They reciprocated warmly, although Angel's and Reina's gazes prowled around her like lions.

"How do you like it here so far?" asked Pretzel.

"I love it!" Jesse said, beaming. "Even mom is having a good time. I've never seen her this happy before." She turned toward Amanda, who remained engrossed in the conversation. "I'm hoping she considers staying longer. Well, as long as you guys will have us," she said with fingers crossed in front of her.

"You are both more than welcome to stay as long as you like," Pretzel said warmly. As she turned to introduce Tassel to Jesse, she noticed all three of her friends glancing at the girl's right arm. Reina even craned her neck. She cleared her throat and frowned at them. "Jesse, this is Tassel, one of my closest friends and one of our seers. Tassel, this is Jesse."

The tech shifted her gaze to meet the girl's eyes. "Greetings, nice to meet you."

With a smile on her face, Jesse addressed her. "Hello! So, a seer is like a person who can see the future, right?"

"Yeah, that's one way of seeing it, pun intended," Tassel responded with a twinkle.

"That's cool, you know. My mom has always told stories of the Daughters of her group back in LA and I never took her seriously. I always thought they were childhood stories but seeing all this with my own eyes...I'm amazed." Her expression grew animated as she glanced around the room. "Now, I'm eager to learn more."

"That's great," remarked Pretzel. "We're happy you're with us and hope you and your mom can become part of this community."

While Pretzel spoke to Jesse, Olivia appeared, flung herself at Angel, and wrapped her tiny arms around her idol.

"Angel!" she said in a high-pitched voice.

She leaned over to embrace the girl. "Hi there, Olivia. How are you today?"

"Good," she replied with a sheepish smile.

"Oh, my God, she's so cute," stated Jesse. Olivia turned to face her, still smiling.

"Who are you?" she asked.

"Olivia, this is Jesse. She came to us a few days ago," responded Pretzel.

"Hi," she said and waved. "I like the color of your nails." Olivia giggled.

"Well, thank you." Jesse clasped her hands over her mouth in awe. "I love your curly hair."

The girl smiled bashfully.

"What do you say, Olivia?" Angel said.

"Thank you."

"Would you like to meet my mom? She's right over there." Jesse pointed in the direction of her mother. Olivia nodded her head eagerly. "Would you all mind stopping by to say hello? I'm hoping it'll encourage her to stay longer."

The group agreed and started to walk over. As they strode toward the table, a hand brushed Angel's shoulder gently. She turned to where Jewels stood with a smile on her face.

"Hello, Angel," the woman said.

Her expression slid into a curious frown as she greeted her in return. "Hi."

"Do you have a minute to talk?" she asked. Angel nodded. "I had a chat with Mist the other day and she mentioned that you were quite upset after our talk so I wanted to apologize. It wasn't my intention to cause you any distress." Her voice was very cordial and she extended her hand toward her. "Hopefully, no hard feelings?"

Angel returned the handshake. "Not at all," she responded swiftly. "I've had a lot to process in these last few months and at times, I let my temper get the best of me." A lopsided smirk appeared on her face. "There's nothing to apologize for. I'm still learning about myself and my past, and each discovery brings a host of feelings. I need to learn to have more self-control."

"That's good to hear and if there's anything I can do for you, don't hesitate to call me," Jewels said warmly.

Olivia left the group, ran toward Angel, and latched onto her leg again very affectionately, catching her by surprise.

She gasped and smiled at the child, who stared at her with a huge grin on her face.

"How precious you are," stated Jewels, her gaze on the little girl.

Olivia's radiant expression turned from pleasure to dread as she gazed at the woman. She clutched Angel's leg so tightly that she almost cut off its circulation. The child's body trembled and a great deal of fear emanated from her.

"You must be very shy," remarked Jewels.

Angel knew very well that this was far from the truth. "Are you okay, Olivia?"

As the woman leaned forward to caress the curly blonde hair, the child flinched and buried her face in Angel's leg. "She's very shy, isn't she?" said Jewels. Angel frowned, perturbed by the odd behavior. "I won't hurt you."

Suddenly, a young woman bumped into Jewels' right arm, which made her straighten agitatedly and glare at her.

"Excuse me," said the girl. "Please pardon me."

The woman did not respond at first but rubbed her arm and lifted her right sleeve slightly. Unexpectedly, her demeanor changed as if she was consumed by an inner rage that was triggered by something deep inside her being.

It made Angel's spine tingle slightly like sensing the

presence of a Nephilim—an out-of-place feeling she had never sensed from another Daughter.

"Pay attention to where you walk lest you find yourself with more than you bargained for," chided Jewels and looked daggers at the girl.

"I'm sorry," responded the young lady.

As the woman massaged her arm, Angel took note of the letters—πονηρὰ— and studied them inquisitively.

When she noticed her stare, Jewels added quickly, "I had one of the ladies give me this tattoo recently in memory of what took place in Lancaster." She smiled broadly. "Anyway, as I was saying before, I'm here if you need anything, Angelic—I mean Angel." She placed her fingers over her temple. "My apologies. I'm still trying to get over this headache."

She nodded and gave her a wry smile, although she felt it was not an accident that she'd used her real name again.

The woman turned to Olivia. "I'm sorry if I frighten you. Hopefully next time, you'll say hello to me." The child unburied one eye and stared gravely at her.

Jewels walked away and Angel crouched so that she was at eye level with the scared little girl. "What's wrong, Olivia?" She received no response. "You want to talk about it?" The girl shook her head and Angel pushed the curls gently from her eyes. "There's nothing to be afraid of and when you're ready to talk, you come and get me. Okay?" Olivia nodded. "Give me a big hug." The girl's sunny disposition returned as she embraced her. "That's my girl."

She stood and took Olivia's hand. "Come on. Let me say hello to Jesse's mom."

The child seemed to have regained her cheerful disposition and responded quickly, "Okay. She's a nice lady."

Angel stared at Jewels from across the room, uneasy about what she had felt, the odd tattoo on her arm, and Olivia's reaction to her. She dismissed her suspicions quickly and felt a pang of guilt at casting doubts on a survivor of that horrific attack.

***

She had been at it for quite some time, and Angel still could not hit the wooden dummy with her quartz knife. Gypsy made it look so easy, and the other four girls training alongside her had all managed to hit the dummy at least once. At this stage, she was disappointed and upset with herself and always felt she was the last to master a particular skill.

"Angel, as a beginner knife thrower, it's essential to focus on your footing and posture," Gypsy instructed. "I see that you slouch a lot. Stand up straight and you'll have a better chance of hitting the target. Since you're right-handed, place your left foot forward and your right foot back." She walked closer to assist her with her stance. "Now focus on your target. Hold the blade tightly with your index, middle, and ring finger with your thumb on the opposite side. Your pinky should hang off and curl with your hand. The throw should proceed from your chest and don't flick your wrist."

Angel drew a deep breath and fixed her eyes on her target. She pulled her hand back and threw the blade for the hundredth time. It streaked forward past the dummy and almost hit Agent Ortega, who walked in with Joan.

"I'm not the enemy, remember?" he joked.

She clapped her hand over her mouth. "I'm so sorry," she said with concern and frustration and gazed at Gypsy with a disheartened stare. "I'm never gonna get this."

"Patience and practice," the woman stated before she turned to the group. "Okay, class, we'll resume tomorrow." The group began to disperse, leaving Ortega, Joan, Gypsy, and Angel in the training center.

"You have a forceful throw there," the agent teased with a big smile on his face. "Good to see you, kid. How are you holding up?"

"All right, all things considered. I can't seem to get the basics of knife throwing 101." She grimaced ruefully. "Hopefully, you can brighten my day with some good news," she said eagerly.

"Well, I just finished having a chat to Amelia about it. I managed to have the FBI concentrate more on the perpetrator than on you and your friends. I presented the theory that you and your friends were victims and were so frightened by the assailant that you fled the scene out of self-preservation."

Angel's eyes opened wide. "Does that mean I can see my grandmother?"

He sighed. "Not quite. Unofficially, we are still investigating the cause of the attacker's death and who's responsible for it. Publicly, it was the bureau who took him out but internally, it's still an open matter."

"I guess you never told them it was us?" she asked.

"To be frank, even though I was there, it's still hard to believe what I saw. If I had a hard time believing it, I can only imagine trying to explain it to the other agents at the bureau. It's one of the reasons I was eager to find you all. I needed to get the facts straight." He drew a deep breath. "Now, I need to find a way to shift the focus of the investigation toward a possible culprit." He glanced at each of the women present.

"We appreciate your discretion, Agent Ortega," stated Joan.

He nodded in reassurance. "Give me a few more days to clear your names from the investigation."

"I'm getting used to the waiting game," said Angel. "Still, thanks for all your help."

"Sure thing." He glanced at Gypsy. "Caroline, I'm glad you are here. For the last few weeks, I have been working on a new toy you will be very interested in." He drew a Glock from the holster strapped to his belt, released the magazine, and pulled the slide back to expose and clear the chamber. He then extracted a bullet from the magazine and held it with his fingers. "A quartz-tipped bullet."

Gypsy's countenance went blank as if lost in thought. She took the bullet and held it in her hands. "How did you manage to do this?"

"I have a few friends in the tech lab," he said with a smirk. "They were curious about my request but they were able to accommodate me. It seems I wasn't the first to inquire about alternative types of bullets in the bureau and they were already set up to do this kind of thing. I have tested it and it is almost as effective as a regular bullet."

"It isn't the first time I have heard about this type of bullet."

"It isn't?"

"No, but that was long ago. Still, how I'd love to use modern weapons to kill those father-mockers," said Gypsy.

"Who?" He looked confused.

"Nephilim," clarified Gypsy.

Ortega raised his brow. "Ahh...f-m instead of m-f. Clever. Anyway, why can't you use guns?"

She responded almost absently and still stared intently at the bullet, mesmerized by it. "All hybrids have severe allergic reactions to gunpowder." She shifted her gaze to him and clarified, "It's almost like going into anaphylactic shock. It isn't fatal but it can potentially cause us to break out in hives and rashes, suffer from coughing fits, experience vision impairment, and other things along those lines. In addition to the physical afflictions, the reaction also interferes with supernatural abilities—for the Nephilim, their magic hocus-pocus and for Daughters, our sensing abilities."

"That explains why we've never recovered a gun at a Nephilim crime scene. It's either simply a body or a body with a blade of some kind."

"Trust me, using a firearm would be so much easier for us." Gypsy handed him the bullet. "It's the reason we train extensively and use pre-modern weapons, but if you get the chance to use it, by all means do so."

Ortega looked at Gypsy and then at Angel before he added, "Too bad. I was going to invite you both to the shooting range." He inserted the bullet carefully into the magazine and placed it into the gun.

"I'd love to, but the last time I went out shooting, I had a rash that lasted a week."

"Yeah…if those are the stakes, I prefer to stay here and work on my knife throwing, even if it's pathetic," Angel said with a chuckle.

"I guess that settles it." He looked at the girl. "You take care of yourself. We'll get this resolved soon." She gave him a half-smile.

He turned to walk away but suddenly spun toward her again. "Oh, my goodness, I almost forgot. I wouldn't have heard the end of it if I didn't give this to you." He slid his hand into the pocket on the inside of his sports jacket and removed a shiny object. "Your grandmother asked me to give this to you. She said it would keep you safe."

Angel accepted the object from him and stared at it for a few moments. It was a simple silver chain with an unassuming small cross hanging from the end. "This…this was my grandfather's and he gifted to my grandmother before he died. She never takes it off. It reminds her of him." Her face was washed by a flood of emotions.

The agent grasped her upper arm softly. "I'm not the religious type but I'll take all the help we can get. Your grandmother prays for you every night."

Touched, Angel fought the tears back as she clasped the chain around her neck.

Joan and Ortega walked out of the Training Center.

She turned to Gypsy and commented, "He's fitting in around here."

The woman shrugged. "We don't trust implicitly so we've had him under all kinds of surveillance and Tassel has tracked all his digital communications. So far, he seems legit."

They began walking toward the locker room. Suddenly,

a small booklet fell to the floor from Gypsy's back pocket. Angel saw it and picked it up. *Prayers of the Daughters* was the title. A curious frown puckered her brow.

"Gypsy, you dropped this."

Her companion tapped her pocket and grimaced at the exposure of her well-kept secret. She snatched the book from her hand. "If you tell anyone about this, I'll make sure you run double the amount on the next session," she said very sternly although she suppressed a tiny smile and her eyes twinkled with amusement.

Angel's lips quirked, despite her effort to look solemn.

34

AN ANGEL'S DEATH

"I can't tell," Reina said disappointedly. She sat across from Angel on the opened sofa bed. "She always wears those long-sleeved black shirts. It's difficult to determine if she has any markings on her right arm." She looked at the other girl with quirked lips. Suddenly, she became pensive, snapped her smartphone lying on top of the night table next to the sofa, and with deft fingers, typed quickly.

"What are you doing?" Angel asked curiously.

"Ordering her a Goth Mello Kitty short-sleeve tee-shirt." She glanced at her and continued on her smartphone. "For sure she can't refuse wearing it if she's a true fan." Fixated on her phone, she sighed in dissatisfaction. "The only problem is we'll have to wait for two or three business days."

"Don't do that!" Angel said and shook her head. "I know Jesse fits the physical description in Olivia's dream but I've got a gut feeling it isn't her."

"What makes you think that?" her companion asked in her high-pitched voice.

"For one, she seems like a nice person. Last night, she came to the room and Pretzel and I spent over an hour or so talking and joking very pleasantly with her. Also, I don't sense a bad vibe from her. She appears exactly like one of the other Daughters but to top it off, Olivia is fond of her." She pursed her lips and shrugged. "I'd think if she's the one, Olivia would be scared of her."

"Hmm…" muttered Reina and tapped her chin with her index finger as she thought about it. "If it's not her, then who?"

"I feel guilty even saying it." Angel's expression showed concern. "Forget it," she spluttered.

"No!" the other girl exclaimed. "The curiosity will kill me if you don't say it now."

"Well, I know she's been through a lot and had a very big loss recently, but I think it's…" She hesitated and lowered her tone to a whisper. "I think it's that Lancaster lady—Jewels."

"Jewels?" An inquisitive frown appeared on Reina's face. "But she has brown hair and by the looks of it doesn't even manicure her fingernails." She frowned, unconvinced. "What makes you think it's her?"

Angel lowered her gaze and tried to find the right words. "First, I don't get a good sense from her. I feel darkness, loneliness, and even pain when I'm around her."

"But that all could be from her recent loss. In times of death or some type of great tragedy, we sense those emotions," the other girl pointed out.

"Yeah, I get that, but when Olivia saw Jewels yesterday, she freaked out. I've never seen her so shaken except for that night when she had the nightmare." She raised her gaze to meet her friend's. "Do you think a tattoo counts as a mark?"

"I hope not," Reina said with a frown. "Jasper did this small crown on my right ankle the other day—see?" She pulled her pants leg up to reveal a golden tiara tattoo. "Why you ask?"

"Jewels had this tattoo—well, at least I think it was 'cause it shined a little and I've never seen one like that before..." Angel shuddered when she realized she was speaking like Reina. "Sorry, I'm speaking out loud."

"I speak out loud all the time," her companion assured her.

Her brow furrowed. "Well...um, as I was saying, I couldn't understand it but I saw some strange lettering that I wrote down." She stood, walked to Pretzel's desk, and retrieved a ragged piece of paper from under the laptop. "This is what I saw."

"Uhhhh, yeah...no." Reina shrugged. "It's all Greek to me."

"Hey, guys." Pretzel peered through the bedroom door but didn't step all the way in. "The Gathering is about to start in a few minutes. Are you heading down?"

Both girls nodded and stood slowly. The paper slipped out of Reina's hand and fluttered to the floor at Pretzel's feet. She picked it up. "Huh... Wicked."

"Wicked, how?" asked Reina. "Wicked awesome or green skin, crooked nose wicked?"

"Neither. It merely says wicked in Greek, in the feminine singular form," the girl explained. She looked at her smartwatch and returned her gaze to her friends. "I'm making rounds throughout the warehouse informing everyone of the Gathering. I'm off to the south side of the building now. Joan requests that everyone is present, so I'll see you there in a few minutes. Save me a seat, okay?"

Before the girls could inquire further, Pretzel hurried away.

Suddenly, Reina paused and nodded. "Oh, yeah...I think they're going to discuss Olivia's dream today. Um...and maybe don't say anything about Jewels yet. A tattoo on her arm isn't proof of anything."

As the girls started to leave, Angel's expression turned thoughtful. *Why would someone tattoo themselves with the word wicked in remembrance of Lancaster?*

The Gathering auditorium was filled with the usual indistinct chatter of women's voices that ebbed and flowed throughout the entire hall. The two friends strode casually into the room, along with a group of other Daughters searching for seats. From a distance, Tassel waved and beckoned them with her hand to where she stood three rows from the front. Next to her were Cookie and her sister Dough.

"We saved you some seats," said the seer when they reached her. Both girls greeted the group warmly.

"Thanks," said Angel. "Pretzel also asked us to save her seat."

"Unquestionably!" stated Tassel. "We saved three seats."

Angel surveyed the room and noticed Jesse and her mom a few rows back at the edge of the middle aisle. They smiled and waved and she acknowledged and reciprocated their greeting. Her gaze continued to scan the room and to her surprise, she glimpsed Agent Ortega standing near the back doorway. She frowned and as soon as he met her gaze, she mouthed, "What are you doing here?"

He understood her question and responded similarly, "I'll tell you later."

She nodded and returned her attention to her friends. "I haven't seen it so crowded since my *Memento Vivere*. Even Agent Ortega is here."

"Joan deemed this Gathering of vital importance and from what I've heard, she asked Ortega to be present for today's meeting," Tassel said. She stood and scanned the assembly. "It appears most of our scouts are present, even Kindle and Pearl, who are usually commissioned as long-term envoys."

The auditorium babble came to a gradual halt as members of the senior council entered the hall and occupied the twelve designated seats in the first row, an indication that the meeting was about to start.

From her vantage point, Angel could see Joan stand and seemingly have a last-minute chat to Mist, who was already seated with the rest of the council. The woman turned her head, scrutinized the room, and shrugged before she shook her head. With a few papers in her hands, the leader strode to the front center podium. A single gesture brought the entire auditorium to silence.

"Please let us all stand for our mantra," she instructed.

Everyone stood and Angel glanced around swiftly and asked, "Where's Pretzel?" The girls shrugged with blank expressions.

"I'll text her," said Reina as the assembly recited the mantra as one. She frowned at the phone for a moment, then looked at her with a bewildered expression. "No signal." Angel drew her cell phone and noticed she had the same issue.

Pretzel walked briskly through the south corridor of the warehouse, cleared each room, and attempted to make the Gathering in time. All the rooms were empty so she stopped without checking the last room at the end of the hallway, assuming it was unoccupied. As she walked toward the Gathering, she heard indistinct chatter. With a frown, she turned to check the last room on her left.

She entered and saw a woman dressed in a long black shift with shiny jet-black hair that seemed to have been dyed recently and her nails painted black. Her left arm was covered by the long sleeve of her shift but the other sleeve seemed to have been ripped to expose her right arm. She had her back toward Pretzel, who was unable to identify her.

"My lord, I thought the mark on my arm was a sufficient conduit for you to create a portal," the woman said over the cell phone. "A blockage? What's a Tektonic relic? My apologies…I won't ask again."

After a momentary pause, her voice spoke low and cold and it raised the hairs on the back of Pretzel's neck. "Everything is in place for the attack."

Feeling a dark sensation, she recognized the voice and asked, "Jewels?"

The woman pulled away from the cell phone and turned from right to left to deliberately expose the mark on her arm, which now glimmered more than before. She glared at Pretzel with a resolute look of absolute betrayal. A lopsided smirk filled her face. "That name died months ago," she snapped. "I am Villainous," she affirmed and stared at the brand on her arm. "You speak languages like me, don't you? I know it technically reads wicked, but I think Villainous has a better ring to it in English. Do you like my new look?"

Pretzel was too stunned to respond.

Villainous continued. "I borrowed a few things from that little Goth girl. If she survives the day, I'm sure she won't mind."

Fear shafted coldly through the girl as she realized this woman was the traitor. She was responsible for the Lancaster assault and was accountable for the deaths of so many women, and was the mystery woman in Olivia's dream.

Dumbfounded, all she could utter was, "It's you, but why?"

The woman shook her head and took a step toward her. "Mhmm...it's too complicated to explain and I don't have the time to elaborate." She sighed deeply. "All I have time for is to make you an offer." She fixed her gaze on the girl. "A way to save your life and the lives of your friends." A malicious smile played on her face. "I hear you're a great fighter. Join me. I need women like you to join my ranks," she said in a cajoling tone. "Leave the cumbersome ways of these archaic codes and be part of a new world order not subjugated to old wives' tales."

"And if I refuse?"

"If you are not for us, then you are against us." Villainous snarled.

Pretzel stared at her, shocked but resolute. "With those options, I guess, um...*I'm against you,*" she bellowed as she lunged forward and struck the woman with a hard blow. Caught by surprise, Villainous sprawled awkwardly but managed to shift position to sweep her right leg and knock Pretzel off her feet. She landed with a loud grunt.

The traitor bounded swiftly to her feet, landed on top of the girl, and managed to pin her to the floor with her knees. She punched her twice on the face and her opponent groaned with each hit. Villainous clenched her hands around her neck to choke her but the girl drew strength from deep within and was able to grasp her assailant's hair and throw her off. Both women now struggled on the floor and exchanged violent, relentless blows. Finally, they pushed apart, rolled away, and managed to stand. Blood spewed from Pretzel's mouth.

"You made the wrong choice!" screeched Villainous.

"It wasn't me who sold her soul to the Devil," the girl retorted as she leapt high and caught her adversary in the face with a roundhouse kick. The blow hurled the woman into the wall and she pounded into a night table that held a lamp. She shrieked with pain and fury as she landed.

Pretzel rushed forward for a follow-up blow but the traitor grasped the fallen lamp and swung it to strike the girl on the head and knock her out cold. Villainous staggered to her feet and glowered at her.

The cell phone, which had fallen to the floor during the brawl, rang. She strode quickly toward it, picked it up, and cleared her throat before she answered, "No, my lord. Merely a minor setback. We are still scheduled as planned. Yes, my lord. Cut the power. I've already deactivated the alarm system and security defense mechanism. The cell phone signal blockers have been placed throughout the Gathering Hall and nearby rooms."

"We are living in unprecedented times and the future holds many uncertainties. Recent events are paving the way for challenges we have never faced before," stated Joan from the front of the auditorium. "Regardless of how difficult and perplexing the future may be, we are not those who shrink away and are destroyed, but those who take root and flourish in the midst of adversity."

A round of applause resonated throughout the hall.

Angel turned to Reina on her right, her features clouded with concern. "I'm worried that Pretzel isn't here yet. She's never late for anything, much less Gatherings." Her friend thinned her lips and nodded in agreement. With her cell phone in hand, she continued, "And what's up with the signal in here today? I have no reception at all."

Reina tapped Tassel and asked her to check her phone and confirm the lack of cell service. An intense frown marred her countenance. She turned swiftly to Angel and Reina. "There's definitely something wrong," she expressed vehemently.

Joan's voice continued from the front. "As we have expounded in past Gatherings, the events in Lancaster were not simply an assault but an act of betrayal." She stopped as her gaze surveyed the crowd. "We were hoping for the only surviving member of that team to come forward and speak to us today, but she seems to not be present." She exhaled deeply and prepared for her next announcement. "The Daughters of the Watchers' code is to honor not only the oldest but also the youngest, and to give due consideration even when from the mouth of babes transcendental insights are given to us—"

Unexpectedly, the lights of the Gathering Hall shut off and gasps of sudden panic rippled throughout the room. The emergency lights in the hall came on, now the only source of illumination.

A voice could be heard from the back of the room as a dark figure strolled into the hall, hooded in a black shift. Her eyes were partially covered. "If an enemy were insulting me, I could endure it. If a foe were rising against me, I could hide. But it is you, women like myself, my companions, my closest friends, with whom I once enjoyed sweet fellowship..." Her voice was a soft chant as she quoted from the book of *Poems*.

"Concern yourself no more, for it is I, Villainous, who has lifted her heel against you." She laughed menacingly and removed the hood gradually. The room erupted in shock. She walked down the middle aisle in her long black shift and a mysterious smile settled on her lips as she glanced around the room.

Mist stood, appalled, and shook her head. Dismay knotted her stomach as she gazed disbelievingly at a beloved friend.

"Yes, Mist, it was me all along," she confirmed tonelessly.

Tears tracked unchecked down the second in command's cheeks. "You wretched witch!" she yelled. "How could you?" Her dismay boiled into anger.

"That's where you're wrong, my friend. I'm not a witch. I'm a priestess—a priestess who today offers you salvation and not death. Well, some of you will probably die." She smirked.

Mist drew her blade and pushed through the crowd toward the traitor. Villainous caught hold of the woman seated at the edge of the aisle, forced her to stand, and placed a blade against her throat.

"Mom!" Jesse screamed.

"If you or anyone else gets any closer, or if I sense any movement at all, she dies!" she warned coldly. She began to walk backward and dragged Amanda along. Her hostage grunted with each pull as the blade began to draw blood. "Soon, this place will be inundated with our brothers. If you want to survive, don't put up a fight. Surrender now and you stand a chance at survival."

Villainous turned her head to the left and glanced at the southwest exit. She removed the blade from Amanda's throat, fixed her gaze on Mist, and declared, "Exactly like Sunny!" With a swift lunge, she stabbed the knife through the woman's back. The blade protruded from her abdomen, and her body slumped when it was yanked free by her aggressor.

The killer darted through the exit while the room froze in horror and shock.

Jesse screamed in anguish as she raced toward her mother, who lay shivering on the floor.

"May!" Joan yelled. The caregiver was seated among the council and pushed immediately to her feet and ran toward the back.

Bewildered and in shock, the girl clutched her mother

in her arms and sobbed brokenly, unable to even try to make sense of everything.

Amanda gazed tenderly at her and tears welled in her eyes. She caressed her daughter's face lovingly with a shaking hand. "You've become a beautiful woman," she said softly. "I'm so glad I had the chance to see you grow up."

"Mom, don't talk that way!" exclaimed Jesse, despair in her voice.

May dropped to her knees and ripped the tattered remains of the bloodied shirt. She moved to place her hand on the wound but shrank back when her gaze met the wounded woman's, who nodded in acknowledgment.

Amanda turned to Jesse. "It's my time, baby. These women…" She clenched her teeth and fought through unbearable pain. "They are your new family and will show you the way."

"Mom, *no!*" she yelled. "Please, let her heal you."

Her mother smiled at her and whispered her final words. "I love you." With that, the life faded from her eyes. May closed her eyelids respectfully, while Jesse held onto her mother in a torrent of sobs.

The room was in utter silence and only the sound of Jesse's sorrowful weeping could be heard. As gently as the dawn breaks, the silence was interrupted by a tender hum from the caregiver. Other women joined her and soon, the whole room was flooded with the bittersweet sound of the melody, the "Dirge of the Overcomers."

Amid the mourning, Mist turned to Joan. "I need to find her," she said in a fierce tone. "She could be a threat to any stragglers who didn't make it to the meeting."

The leader sighed and nodded in agreement. "Take someone with you," she advised.

She walked away and muttered, "I'm going alone."

Joan beckoned to Tassel. "If this is anything like Lancaster, she has probably disengaged the security alarm system. We need to somehow issue a distress signal so the first order of business is that we need to check the security system," she instructed, her expression determined.

The seer nodded. "Yes, I'm on it, but we'll need to bring up the power generators. I'll head to the basement level."

"Okay, but take a couple of the guardians with you in case you encounter the enemy and see if you can bring those generators up ASAP." The girl raced out of the room and motioned to the twins to follow her.

Joan coordinated with the other leaders to prepare for a possible siege. Suddenly, she felt an all-too-familiar sensation—a spark of electricity sizzled up her spine and she shuddered involuntarily. Her gaze turned toward the hall's doors as the impression grew inexorably from the size of a mustard seed to a mighty plant.

Suddenly, the senses of everyone in the room began to overflow with dread as the feeling grew to a mighty tree. Each one of the Daughters, from the youngest to the oldest, knew what that shiver meant—Nephilim.

"Guardians and scouts, front and center," ordered Joan.

Throughout the room, Daughters began to gather before her. She intuitively issued strategic defensive directives and sent groups of women to the four corners of the building, instructing them to pick up two-way radios from the computer lab to stay in communication. When she realized it was too late to send the younglings to the bunkers, she organized a group of warriors to create a defensive perimeter around the hall.

Angel watched from her seat in despair. She glanced at Jesse as she and a few other women carried Amanda's body to an isolated area of the hall. Her gaze moved restlessly as Daughters rushed out of the hall and her heart grew increasingly anxious when she remembered that Pretzel had never made it to the Gathering. Finally, she hurried toward the front of the room.

"Joan, I know this is bad timing but I'm concerned. Pretzel never made it to the Gathering. She was making rounds to announce the meeting, but she never arrived."

"Angel, with all that's going on at the moment, I can't afford to send a search party. I need all hands on deck," she stated emphatically.

"At least let me go. Let me at least search in her room or something."

Joan shook her head. "It's too risky to send you out there alone."

"Joan, Pretzel has become like a sister to me. I owe her my life and I can't bear the thought that she's out there and doesn't know about Jewels' betrayal." She rubbed her hands on her thighs and waited anxiously for a response.

To their surprise, Agent Ortega stepped behind Angel, having overheard their conversation. "Amelia, I'm willing to lend a hand and help Angelica."

"There are Nephilim close by," retorted the leader.

"I'm loaded with quartz bullets if that's any help." He tapped the holster at his side.

Joan sighed and turned her attention to the northwest

entrance to the hall. "Reina!" She beckoned to her with her hand.

The girl left her guard position and hurried forward.

"Assist Angel and Agent Ortega to find Pretzel." Reina nodded in agreement. "Do you have a radio?"

"I have one of my own. I think it operates on similar bands as yours," the agent told her. "Give me the channel you are communicating on."

After confirming the communication, all three jogged out of the hall.

They reached Pretzel's room out of breath. Angel searched frantically for any sign of her roommate's presence and rapidly grew fretful when it became obvious that the girl hadn't returned even temporarily. She paced the room with her fingers laced on top of her head. "Where could she be?" she murmured.

"Where and when was the last time you saw her?" the agent asked.

"In this room about a half-hour or so ago," answered Angel.

"Did she mention where she was going next?"

The girls both stood silently as they thought hard. "The south side of the building," Reina recalled. Angel instinctively headed to the door but Ortega halted her.

"Angelica, we need to be as thorough as possible and think tactically," he insisted. "We need to narrow our search. Is there anything particular about that side of the building?"

She shrugged and impatience strained at her entire body.

"Well, the first floor is vacant. It's an open area with

scattered boxes," stated Reina. "The second floor is where visitors or guests stay. For Daughters, it's where we place them until they're assigned a permanent room." When she uttered those words, Reina's face paled as if whatever thought had surfaced in her mind made her sick to her stomach. "Jewels was staying there," she added.

Without waiting for any further questions, the ladies raced out of the room and left Ortega with no other choice but to follow.

Within minutes, they reached the south side corridor of the warehouse. The eerie silence, the dim lights, and the foreboding threat of the Nephilim assault made the atmosphere hellish. They proceeded with caution, drew their cell phones, and used them as flashlights to examine each room and call their friend's name.

"Seriously, the kid's name is Pretzel?" Ortega's face creased into a confused frown. "What's with these odd names by the way?"

"They're basically nicknames," responded Angel, although her full attention and only concern was to find her friend. "Reina, we need to hurry. I'll check the rooms to the left, and you look at those on your right."

The other girl nodded.

"I'll stay in the hallway on lookout," he told them.

Their search went on for some time with no sign of Pretzel anywhere. Exasperated, Angel threw her hands in the air and dropped them to her sides with a slap. "I don't think she's here."

"There's one more room toward the end of the hall. On your left," said Ortega and pointed to the last door.

She focused on the open door and remembered the

time she had spent in that room when she first arrived at the warehouse. Although it had only been a few months, it felt like it had been years.

The two girls began to stride to the last room but stopped halfway when they heard a methodical scraping coming from outside the building. They held their breath and focused their senses in an attempt to determine the source of the sound.

After a concerned glance, they drew their quartz blades instinctively. Behind them, Ortega drew his Glock although he didn't fully grasp the situation. He moved closer to the young women and asked, "What's going on?"

Suddenly, a hand appeared on the ledge outside the latticed window and startled all three. Seconds later, another hand appeared.

"A crawler!" yelled Reina in alarm.

The creature pulled itself toward the window and revealed its upper half. In contrast to the splendor and beauty projected by their progenitors, these types of Nephilim were grotesque and looked more beast than man. This particular specimen had beady eyes surrounded by unkempt, bushy eyebrows, large flaring nostrils, and razor-sharp incisors.

His eyes narrowed on his prey, the crawler crashed headfirst through the window and shattered it. He barrel-rolled into the room, came to a stop on all fours, and raised his head, poised to attack.

A few shards of glass lacerated the agent's shooting hand. "Damn it," he exclaimed as he loosened his hold and dropped the gun.

The Nephilim leapt ferociously toward him. Angel

pulled him out of the way and they fell together. Quickly, the crawler stabilized himself on his feet and turned for a second attack but Reina lunged and delivered a hard kick to his face. His head snapped to the right but he was otherwise unaffected and his eyes opened wide to glower at her.

"Come on, Reina—think. Stab first, then hit!" she exclaimed as the creature swung his fist at her face. She barely managed to dodge.

Angel scrambled to her feet, pulled her arm back, and flung her blade. She prayed as the knife streaked toward its target and watched in what felt like slow motion as it thudded into the Nephilim's right leg. With a clenched jaw, the crawler grunted in pain. She ran forward but slipped on the shards of glass and sprawled painfully.

With a wry smile Reina repeated her earlier kick but this time, their adversary slumped on impact. Rapidly, he shook his head and noticed a distracted Angel, who tried to stagger to her feet. He bounded from the floor to the wall and then to the ceiling and began to crawl toward her.

The other girl screamed a warning for her to move.

Although aware of the imminent attack, she simply stared as if mesmerized.

The crawler plummeted from the ceiling with every intention to kill her. Instantly, three consecutive bangs resounded through the corridor and like a splattered spider, the creature dropped.

Angel turned to look at Ortega, who lay prone on the floor and held a smoking gun.

"Is it dead?" he asked and continued to aim the gun at the Nephilim. She nodded. He sighed, relaxed his arms, and lowered his head to the floor to rest his forehead on the concrete.

She stepped closer and helped him to his feet. "Thanks," she said and frowned as she glimpsed his hand. "Your hand is bleeding."

"A small flesh wound. Nothing serious," he said and wrapped it with a handkerchief. "Are you both okay?"

Before they could answer, a low grunt came from the nearby room. Without a second thought, the girls raced in, their blades in hand, only to find their friend on the floor and clutching her head.

"Pretzel!" Angel exclaimed the moment she saw her. "Are you okay?"

Both women dropped to their knees beside the girl, who still attempted to get her bearings. She moaned softly, seemingly more unconscious than not. With her friends' help, she managed to sit.

"What happened to you?" asked Angel.

"It was Jewels." She massaged her temples and tried to rid herself of the headache. "She's the traitor. She slugged me with a lamp." She squinted her eyes for relief. "What is it with me and getting hit with furniture?"

When she noticed a small cut on her friend's right forehead, Reina searched the room for a cloth or towel to clean the wound. She found one and handed it to her. "Thanks." Pretzel grimaced as she pressed the towel to the injury.

"Yeah, we know about Jewels," Angel told her in a sorrowful manner. "Pretzel, she killed Peaches—Jesse's mom."

Pretzel stared at her in disbelief. "Oh, my God!" she exclaimed and shook her head. "How?"

"Jewels made her presence known at the Gathering. She told us she goes by the name of Villainous now."

"It's really Wicked," the wounded girl clarified.

Angel turned her gaze to Reina and met her look with raised eyebrows. "Wicked!" she stated without breaking her gaze.

"Wicked...Villainous...Villainous...Wicked!" whispered Reina in a soft, breathy voice, stunned by the sudden revelation.

Pretzel glanced from one to the other with a blank expression.

Angel turned to her roommate. "The Greek word you translated for us in the room...I saw it on Villainous' arm." She grimaced in shame. "Now, I feel awful. I ignored my suspicions and on top of that, I cast doubt on Jesse, who ended losing her mother at that traitor's hand." She lowered her gaze. "I should have judged by fruits instead of appearance."

"Treachery is a bitzach," exclaimed the other girl. "Where's Jewel—I mean, Villainous now?"

"We don't know," responded Reina. "She ran away shortly after stabbing Jesse's mom."

"We need to find her before she causes any more harm." She gestured to them both. "Help me up."

"We have bigger problems," Reina told her. "Her grand entrance at the Gathering wasn't only her debut. The warehouse is under attack. Daughters were sent throughout the building, while another group is at the hall protecting the younglings."

At that very moment, Ortega's radio crackled with a panicked voice. "Nephilim on the south side first floor. We need assistance! Daughters down! I repeat, Daughters down!"

Pretzel, who noticed Ortega's presence for the first time, stated, "We are the closest to them. We need to help them."

"But you're hurt," protested Angel. "We need to take you to the Gathering."

With a stern but encouraging look, her roommate said firmly, "Angel, this is where we need to put others before ourselves. I'm willing to lay my life down to protect the women of this warehouse."

She nodded.

"Mr. Ortega, pass me the radio and head to the Gathering Hall." He tossed Pretzel the radio without hesitation. "Copy!" she responded on the radio. "This is Pretzel and we are on the way!"

Mist walked steadily down the long narrow corridor that led to the staircase toward the garden. Her cheeks were flushed, her nostrils flared with each breath, and the veins on her brow were pronounced and visible as she clutched a blade tightly in each hand. Her senses had directed her there, an inner premonition that she would find her old friend and scouting partner on the rooftop.

She ascended the staircase two steps at a time and stepped out into the garden, where an icy fall chill blew tempestuously. The frigid air nipped at her the moment she walked out, but the bitter rage kept her warm and distracted. She stopped abruptly when her gaze, from a distance, settled on a friend who had now become an enemy.

Villainous stood on the edge and stared at the city's skyscrapers. Her black shift billowed and her hair was fanned by the current of the strong winds. She turned slowly as her old friend approached. A macabre gleam slid into her eyes and a distrustful smile played on her thin lips as her black-tipped hand clutched the hilt of a straight steel blade. For a long moment, they stared into each other's eyes in grim silence.

"You came alone," she said in surprise. "I thought you'd come with an armada of your brainwashed Daughters."

Mist's countenance was inscrutable. She remained silent and glared at Villainous.

"Giving me the silent treatment?" The traitor twisted her lips fleetingly. "You're not going to ask the pertinent question?" She took a step forward, away from the edge. "Why?"

"Not at all," answered the other woman sternly. "You'll only give me a lengthy, pathetic, and lame monologue, which will only serve to delay my blade from being drenched by your blood."

Villainous laughed mockingly. "Your archaic ways deceive you, old friend. I'm more powerful than you think and stronger than you ever were, with power at the snap of my fingertips."

"Friend!" She scoffed. "It wasn't that long ago that a friend promised me I'd never have to worry about betrayal from her and here I am today, facing a broken promise." She lowered her gaze and sighed deeply. "You speak of deception"—she turned to gaze at her again—"but you are self-deluded. You've mistaken betrayal and manipulation for power and that will be your undoing."

The traitor smiled wryly. She shook her head slowly as she sneered at the other woman, raised her marked arm, and pressed her thumb and middle finger together. "Your mindset beguiles and blinds you. Witness my might," she drawled. She took a few steps forward and snapped her fingers.

Suddenly, two Nephilim crawlers leapt simultaneously from the edge of the rooftop and landed behind her. Their expressions were formidable and they stood menacingly and waited for instructions.

With her gaze fixed on her adversary, she ordered, "Kill her!"

One of the crawlers jumped and landed behind Mist, while the other rushed forward. Villainous' smile was cruel and triumphant.

The two Nephilim attacked, one from the front and the other from behind. Mist surged toward the one ahead and tossed a thin blade, which landed squarely in the creature's shoulder. She jumped nimbly, pulled her arm back, and swung viciously to strike the first crawler in the face. The Nephilim's momentum combined with the force of her blow snapped his neck with a sharp crack.

As she landed, the second Nephilim came within range. She spun and vaulted over the approaching foe. When she reached the peak of her leap, she caught him by the hair and dragged him down to pound him hard against the paving. Before the stunned crawler could make sense of the acrobatics and respond, she drew a second blade and sliced through the creature's neck. His head rolled toward the traitor while she stood and began to wipe the blood from the blade with her shirt.

"Is that what I was supposed to witness?" mocked Mist with a look of satisfaction.

Villainous' smile turned dark. She tensed her muscles and exploded toward her adversary in utter rage. While in motion, she drew a blade from its sheath on her hip and flung it furiously at the other woman. Mist attempted to dodge the blade but it came much faster than she anticipated and left a sizeable laceration on her left arm.

With her failed attempt to avoid the knife, she lost her balance, fell on her knees, and grunted as she clenched her teeth. She clutched her left arm and blood spilled on the floor. The traitor yanked the blade from the shoulder of the fallen crawler and hurled it at her. This time, she did not miscalculate the throw and rolled so the blade swished past her head.

Villainous surged forward and swung a foot at her face.

Mist grasped her opponent's leg with both hands and her attacker tumbled. She leapt on top of her and managed to land two hard blows on her face, but her enemy countered by squeezing her injured left arm. She yelled in pain and slid out of range, clutching her wound.

The traitor stood hastily, rushed forward, and attempted to trample her but she managed to roll away and avoid the attack. Mist came to a stop and glimpsed the steel knife that had slashed her arm beside her. When the other woman darted forward and lifted her foot to crush her ankle. She snatched the blade up with her right hand, twisted, and hurled the knife, releasing it without fully seeing her target. The blade plunged deep into the woman's abdomen.

Villainous stopped and gaped at the knife now protruding from her stomach. She grasped the blade as blood began to leak from the wound and she staggered back toward the edge of the rooftop. With wide eyes, she glared at her former friend and mumbled, "Out of everyone here, I thought at least you'd understand." Her foot stepped over the side of the roof and she vanished over the edge.

Mist lay on the floor for a moment and held her bleeding arm before she gathered her strength and scrambled to her feet. She staggered to the edge of the roof and looked down the five-floor building in the direction of Villainous' fall. As she scanned the ground for the body, her expression turned quickly to horror. From her vantage point, she had a bird's-eye view of a massive army approaching. A vast host of Nephilim had gathered to storm the warehouse.

When she realized she had no way to communicate with the other Daughters, she bolted from the garden in the direction of the Gathering Hall.

Gypsy felled the invaders as if they were gnats, but the number of Nephilim increased as more entered through the shattered windows of the building. Two Daughters lay dead before her. Kindle—utterly exhausted by this point—fought alongside her to protect a badly injured Pearl, whose blood seeped steadily from multiple wounds.

Although she was a great warrior, Gypsy's expression grew weary and apprehensive and sweat clung to her brow. Her gaze danced from the horde of Nephilim who breached through multiple entrance points, the fallen Daughters, and the two remaining women who were at the brink of collapse. She glanced upward momentarily and prayed, "Sovereign One, you know I'm not the praying type but we could use your help right about now."

Almost as if in response to her plea, her radio crackled and a staticky voice spoke. "Copy! This is Pretzel and we are on the way!"

Moments later Pretzel, Angel, Reina, and Agent Ortega —who had chosen to not return to the Gathering—reached the open space of the south side first floor where the desperate women were besieged by a horde of menacing Nephilim. Without missing a beat, they engaged the assailants. Valiantly, they battled with every fiber of their being and littered the floor with the lifeless bodies of the enemy, yet the flood of infiltrators was unending.

"We need to pull back!" yelled Gypsy. "Let's grab Pearl and go!"

Angel and Reina dragged the wounded woman's arms over their shoulders and moved toward the door. A Nephilim bounded into their path and thrust his knife toward Angel. She gaped as death flashed toward her.

Pearl propelled herself instinctively into the blade's path and was stabbed in the chest.

"Noooo!" screamed Kindle as her friend dropped life-lessly. Reina reacted quickly and eliminated the attacker. Angel stared in shock, horrified that Pearl had given her life to save hers. Kindle raced forward and dropped to her knees where her friend now lay dead and pulled her life-less face to her chest. Sorrowful tears coursed down her face.

"Kindle, we need to go," urged Gypsy as she tugged at her. She shook her head but the woman yanked her force-fully from the floor and they sprinted out of the door toward the Gathering Hall.

The group reached their destination exhausted along-side the other groups that had been dispatched earlier. These other women returned in fewer numbers than had been sent and most were haggard and weary.

Gypsy gave Joan a situation report and without wasting time, the leader began to recall all the Daughters sent into the warehouse. After several minutes, the disheartened women returned. Many among them were wounded and several were brought back as corpses.

Tassel and her companions returned from their commission with dejection written on their faces.

Angel overheard the despair in the seer's voice as she updated their leader. "She destroyed all the secondary generators. There's no way for us to get the power on again, much less send a distress signal out."

"What if we head to the roof and try to call the other groups with a cell phone?" asked Joan.

"I was just there," said Mist, her hand around her arm as she walked into the hall. "I saw multiple Anomalites climbing the walls. By now, it's probably inundated with them."

The leader turned and met her halfway. "Are you okay?" she asked and beckoned to one of May's girls.

"I'll be fine," the woman replied as she slumped on a

seat, drained. Shortly after, a young woman began to sterilize and bandage her wound with gauze.

"Jewels?" asked Joan.

Mist met her gaze unflinchingly. "Which part of her?" she responded sardonically. "That problem is taken care of but Joan, the warehouse is surrounded. There's no way out."

Joan's face grew ashen and she lowered her head in despair. After a moment of silence, she straightened and with her gaze on her second, prayed, "May the Sovereign One help us."

Rapidly, she instructed the younglings to gather in the middle of the room and created a circle of protection around them, with the youngest and weakest in the middle and the strongest on the outside. A single tear ran unheeded down the leader's face, but she maintained her composure and with a stern voice, she encouraged her women to stand and fight until the end.

Soon, they all began to feel the menacing presence of the Nephilim closing in and within minutes, the foreboding creatures flooded and besieged the Gathering Hall. Sporadically, portals appeared and countless Daimons stepped through them, some in human shape and others in hideous, grotesque forms.

Gasps of horror erupted from the women and many, if not all, of the younglings covered their eyes in terror. Even Agent Ortega, who stood in the first row with his pistol close to his chest, uttered a low gasp of fright.

Suddenly, a portal appeared at the back of the hall. The Daughters' attention was drawn to a tall, slim figure who walked menacingly out of the brilliant light in a crisp, clean, and expensive suit. His long charcoal-black hair billowed behind him as he strode forward.

Angel stared at her father in dread.

"My children," he uttered mockingly. "What a pleasant surprise, isn't it?" He glanced around the room with his hands spread before him. "How often I have longed to gather you, as a hen gathers—" He stopped his quote in mid-sentence and placed his finger on his chin in thought. He looked upward. "No, not like chicks, but like broken eggs that the hen devours." He laughed malevolently.

He paced the room, his gaze intimidating as it scanned those present. "Where's my daughter? Did she survive?" he snapped.

Pretzel and Reina stood in front of Angel to hide her.

"Where is my prodigal offspring who has been the cause of so much speculation of late?" When no response was heard, he bellowed cruelly with a low, otherworldly rumble in his voice, "Where is she?"

"I'm here," responded Angel in a soft voice.

Pretzel whispered, "No!" She caught her hand tightly. "You don't have to do this. We'll protect you."

"You've protected me long enough," she said tenderly with a faint smile on her face. "Like you said to me earlier, I'm willing to lay my life down for these women." She glanced around the room. "And for you."

She shook free of her friend's grasp and walked toward Leonard. With each step, her mind raced to the events of the past few months—her grandmother's apartment and hospital, when Pretzel and Reina risked their lives to protect her, the nightclub when her friends had sheltered her from the Nephilim, and Pearl, who took a blade on her behalf. Finally, she thought of Mist and how she had risked her life to protect a stranger and the baby still in her womb.

Inexplicably, Mrs. Mozart's words began to resonate within her—the true way of power was the way of the lamb. *The lamb's willingness to put others before himself, even to the point of death.*

She stopped inches away from her father.

The Daimon scrutinized her from top to toe and finally settled his gaze on the small silver chain hanging from her neck. A look of disgust soured his countenance as he beheld the small shiny cross. "A Tekton relic," he snarled.

He wrenched the chain angrily away from her neck and discarded it on the floor behind her. "You won't need this foolish thing. No daughter of mine needs this kind of protection." He sighed deeply. "Now, on to business, and make sure you speak loud enough for all to hear."

In a quivering voice, she spoke, her gaze lowered to stare at the floor. "You once offered me the opportunity to join you and in exchange, you wouldn't hurt these women." She raised her gaze and knelt before him. "I'm willing to offer myself to do your bidding willingly and voluntarily. All I ask is that you let these women live. Please, I beg of you, if you want me, let them go," she pleaded. Her body trembled and sweat trickled down her face.

Leonard frowned and snapped, "Stand!" He placed his left hand on her shoulder. "How is it that my seed is this blind?" He sighed. "How utterly useless you've become to me. No matter, I guess I'll simply give you the mark you deserve."

Inexplicably, a long steel blade materialized in his hand

and with a glare of loathing, he thrust his sword through her and lifted her body several inches off the ground. As quickly, he withdrew the blade savagely.

Angel grunted as she fell on her knees and toppled onto the floor. Blood began to seep from her mouth.

A horrified silence fell throughout the Gathering Hall.

Pretzel screamed, "Angel!" She bolted forward, dropped to her knees, and cradled her dying friend to her chest. Ashen-faced, the wounded girl gazed into her watery eyes.

With a soft smile, she exhaled her last breath and died.

Her roommate clung tightly to the body that lay lifelessly on her knees. Hot tears streamed down her cheeks as she stroked the increasingly pale face gently and pushed back the long ebony hair from her closed eyelids.

Proudly, Leonard's gaze shifted to the other Daimons and the slew of dreadful Nephilim in his army that surrounded the aghast Daughters, who stared incredulously at Pretzel. He surveyed the assembly with satisfaction and his eyes glinted with arrogance now that his mission was accomplished.

The Daughters huddled together to form a last line of defense that encircled the whimpering and petrified children of the warehouse.

He scanned the faces of the women before him slowly with a ferocious resolve and in a derisive, intimidating tone, he began to speak. "For so long, you have been a pebble in my shoe—a thorn in the flesh if you would." He strode forward past Pretzel and paced in front of the women with his hands behind his back. "You have been a hindrance, a persistent itch that has interfered too long in affairs you could not hope to begin to comprehend. Your incessant meddling has agitated the very fibers of my being. I have come to loathe every single one of you," he told them in a silky, cold tone.

Leonard paused and stared at them with a glowering expression. "To be honest, I am utterly disgusted to know that we, the divine ones, can produce such a weak, useless atrocity. And if that weren't enough, this one's pathetic attempt to offer herself in exchange for your lives..." He turned to Angel's body. "What a waste. This was your weapon? Your great Daimon Killer? That any of you would consider that I would grant her ridiculous request and honor her worthless sacrifice is revolting, a stench too unbearable to endure."

The Daughters gasped in despair and horror and their faces expressed dread at the realization of their inevitable extinction. A wry smile played on his features.

With his attention toward the women, he pointed at Angel's corpse. "And to think I was willing to consider that she was this promised Daimon Killer." He laughed wickedly. "Even a few of my generals began to feel intimidated but you see, these prophecies, gifts, abilities, or whatever you like to call them are fraudulent illusions. They are little more than placebos you use to make your miserable little lives seem valuable."

He jutted his chin egotistically and raised his hand. "In my eyes, you are worthless and insignificant, the scum of the earth who need to return to the dust from which you came," he hissed with a contorted expression of abhorrence.

The Daimon lowered his hand and tugged his suit jacket. His voice grew loud and stern. "I am neither a saint to keep promises, nor a son of man who is obliged to adhere to your moral or ethical laws." He glowered threateningly at them. "Leaving you alive will only ensure a continuous nuisance as I pursue my ultimate objective."

His malevolent minions stood ready, dark and foreboding, and with a loud voice, he commanded, "Kill them! Kill them all!" He gestured dismissively with his hand and began to walk away.

Suddenly, Leonard stopped in mid-stride as a diffused, shimmering light materialized from thin air. The luminescence intensified dramatically and cascaded its blinding hues throughout the hall. Daimons, Nephilim, and Daughters alike shielded their eyes from the ever-increasing iridescent shafts of light that now blazed brighter than the sun.

A simple man appeared from the light. His flesh glowed like bronze and His shoulder-length hair was white like wool. Although soft and beautiful, His eyes burned as brightly as fire. He was dressed in a white robe that reached to His feet, with a golden sash around His chest. His handsome, chiseled features emerged as the light faded in intensity and the eyes of the beholders adjusted.

Still mesmerized by the sudden and glorious appearance, Mrs. Mozart glimpsed the wounds on His hands and jagged holes on His bare feet. Without any hesitation, she bowed and whispered reverently, "The Carpenter's Son!"

Grace followed suit, along with Joan and the rest of the Daughters.

The Daimons and Nephilim shivered in fear and trembled in horror at the sight of the man. Leonard watched in dread and stood incapacitated.

The man strode majestically across the hall toward Pretzel. When He reached her, He stared at her with tender, loving eyes. Her tear-stained face shimmered in His light. He lowered to one knee, turned His gaze on Angel, and moved slightly forward so His face was a hair's breadth from hers. Tenderly, He blew the breath of life into her nostrils.

As the breath touched her being, the girl gasped and opened her eyes gradually to stare at the Lifegiver. She smiled when she focused on His countenance and stared at the face of someone she felt she had known for quite a long time but now saw for the first time—strangely familiar but at the same time, someone she was only becoming acquainted with.

He turned to Pretzel, whose eyes were awash with intense wonder, and spoke in a soft and gentle tone. "Your friend isn't dead. She's alive."

The girl stared at Him in reverence.

With a smile, He turned toward the group of women, and called, "May!" He beckoned to her with his hand.

The caregiver's eyes glistened with tears as she stood slowly and walked toward Him. She dropped to her knees and He took her hand gently and placed it over Angel's wound. "Would you finish this for me?"

She nodded nervously, her eyes wide with wonder. To the woman's surprise, Angel's gash closed instantly. Her gift had never worked for a wound so deep nor so quickly.

He stood and fixed Leonard with a forbidding stare.

The Daimon scowled in return. "What business do you have with us?" he demanded in irritation. "You interfere in matters that do not pertain to you." He extended his hand

and pointed his index finger in Angel's direction. "I didn't break law 7.VII.7. She willingly offered herself to me. This is a violation of your laws!" His voice echoed loudly through the hall.

"You have since forgotten the ancient law of love, Apollyon." His voice was soft but stern. He lowered his gaze to Angel. "Greater love has no one than this, to lay down one's life for one's friends."

He extended His hand and helped Angel to her feet, positioned her in front of Him, and held her shoulders tenderly.

She could feel the warmth of love exuding from His hands as she had many times when she hugged Grace.

"Her selfless act of love and sacrifice resulted in life and not death." He fixed His gaze on Leonard. "It's life for her but judgment for you."

Inexplicably, Angel was enveloped in a wholly novel sensation—an impression and a deep inner instinct that had lain dormant until now. Without any instruction or command, she knew instinctively what to do. She strode forward and stopped a couple of feet away from her father. The paralyzing fear she had sensed before was gone and she stared at him with a hard expression.

He looked at her with quiet disdain. "You judge me?" He laughed scornfully. "You have no power over me," he said with a scowl.

"Apollyon," she said coldly. At the authority in her words, he lost control of his appearance. His skin began to crack and peel like old, dry paint and his lavish attire sizzled and liquefied to ooze off his deteriorating flesh. Under the ragged skin, his hideous, translucent form became manifest for all to see. Finally, all that remained was a dark, stained humanoid shape that seemed to absorb light but reflected none.

Angel, not intimidated in the slightest, continued, "You have been weighed on the balances of justice and have not measured up. Today, the Sovereign One has cut short the days of your reign and has brought them to an end." Her tone was fierce and stern. "By the authority granted to me, I cast you out into the lower regions of Tartarus, where you will be bound and held until the final days of judgment."

At first, nothing happened. The shadowy form attempted to back away from her but was unable to move. Instead, the dark humanoid shape pulsated with energy and its silhouette began to fade. Although it lacked vocal cords, the shadow uttered a bloodcurdling scream that could not be heard but was felt by all in the hall.

The form began to grasp at its vanishing features as if to reform itself but to no avail. The murky shape oozed a dark substance that disappeared as it dripped from its shadowy body. Soon, only a core of evil energy was left, which expanded momentarily and finally imploded to launch a surge of energy to wash over the entire building. The mighty Apollyon, lieutenant of Diablo's army, conqueror of empires, was cut off from this plane of existence.

The swarming hordes of Daimons and Nephilim, having witnessed the unthinkable, began to disperse in an uproar and fled in fright and trepidation. The Daimons disappeared through their swirling portals while the Nephilim followed hastily.

After a short time, the Daughters no longer felt the threat of the enemy, only the serene peace that emanated from the Carpenter's Son.

Angel turned slowly to the Man who had brought her back to life. She inhaled deeply and savored the pleasing aroma of love and peace that now filled the atmosphere.

The Carpenter's Son turned His gaze downward as if searching for something. After a few moments, His eyes brightened and he stooped to pick up a small object. He approached and stopped immediately in front of her. Gently, he used both hands to clasp a silver chain around her neck. He looked at the small cross and said, "The one who ripped this off thought it foolish, but you and I know its true power."

"Thank you," she said softly with moist eyes.

"You will face more troubles in the days ahead," He informed her. "But don't be afraid. I won't leave you alone." He turned His magnificent gaze to Pretzel and smiled.

Angel nodded instinctively.

He turned and strode toward the women who now stood in reverent silence. When He reached Jesse, he stopped in mid-stride, looked at her with tender compassion, and wiped the tears from her eyes. "Fear not," He said gently. "Your mother will be with me from this day forward in paradise." He glanced at Angel. "Be strong and courageous. She will need your help."

With stately, measured steps, He continued toward the Daughters. When He passed Reina, she waved at Him with a big dimpled smile on her face and astonishingly, he responded with a grin and a thumbs-up gesture.

The Carpenter's Son took a few more steps and stood

beside Agent Ortega. "You should listen to your wife more often." He smiled at him. "She's wiser than you think."

His steady steps led him to Gypsy, who bowed her head in reverence. "Your tears of prayers have been collected. Each one is recorded in my book and although not all have been answered, all have been heard." He lifted her chin to meet His gaze. "Your sister lives and in due time, you will meet again." As He uttered those words, a heavy sob escaped the woman and tears streamed uncontrollably down her face.

He moved forward, halted before Mist, and turned gradually to Her. "I know very well the feeling of betrayal from a good friend. Do not feed the heart with hatred that leads to bitterness, but with love, the true way of contentment." Tears welled in the woman's eyes. "Do not lose heart. Lancaster will need you again."

As he passed Mrs. Mozart, He lowered His head in approval. Her expression lit with adoration. For the first time ever, the Daughters saw a fleeting glimpse of red in her pale face.

Next to her stood Grace and without any hesitation, He embraced her and she wrapped her arms around Him. "That feels so good," she said.

"I could not leave without embracing you," said the Carpenter's Son. She smiled in return.

He reached Joan and His expression grew gloomy. "Dark times lie ahead." He sighed sharply. "There's a deep deception in this war that was formulated at the beginning of the age. It will shake you but remember this—what was intended for evil, I will use for good. I beseech you to be strong and bold and to continue to lead, encourage, and protect them. You all have a vital role to play in the events that will unfold."

To the surprise of all in the room, Joan leaned forward, rested her forehead on his chest, and sighed. "I'm not sure I have the strength."

In response, he raised her head with his hands and planted a warm, soft kiss on her forehead. "My strength, I leave you."

Finally, he stepped back and stood in the center of the hall. His compassionate gaze searched the Daughters, who all stood to gaze at Him in wonder. "Fear not!" His voice was tender but strong. He breathed on them and said, "Peace be unto you all." The women gasped when they all felt a warm sensation of comfort and peace settle on them. Some of the younglings giggled in response to a tingle that trickled down their spines.

In an instant, He vanished from their sight.

35

THE RELEASE

A week had passed since the horrific attack on the warehouse. To the Daughters' surprise, the police's investigation into the broad-daylight assault wrapped up quickly and with little fanfare. The authorities officially classified the events at Saint Miriam's Shelter for Children and Women as a failed home invasion and the carnage at the scene of the crime was ruled to have been self-defense by the women. Additionally, Ortega's presence during the attack was concealed, as was the existence of the surviving assailants. As far as anyone was concerned, the women defended themselves from would-be attackers and killed them all.

The agent also managed to clear Angel, Pretzel, and Reina of all suspicion by tying the attack at the hospital to the one at the shelter.

A Gathering Hall meeting was held to honor the fallen Daughters. Groups from Pennsylvania, South New Jersey, and Boston came to pay their respects and provide comfort to the Daughters in the Tri-State area.

After the memorial service, many of the Daughters remained and offered their assistance to repair the damages to the facilities. While the rebuilding was underway, discussions were held by the leadership regarding the reconstruction of the Lancaster compound. They unanimously commissioned Mist as the new leader, with Kindle as her second in command. Gypsy was promoted to fill Mist's NY position.

It had been a solemn week filled with mourning for those lost and farewells for the group of women. This included the twins, who left with Mist for Lancaster. Angel, however, was elated as she would finally reunite with her grandmother Maria.

Eager to be back in her apartment, the old lady convinced Ortega to drive her to the South Bronx building. Although she was still in recovery, she immediately went in search of her trusty broom and was dismayed to learn that it had been broken and was in the NYPD's evidence locker. Undeterred, she wasted no time and demanded a new one.

Angel arrived on the WTA One subway train with her companions, Pretzel, Reina, and Tassel. They strode through the all-too-familiar neighborhood and arrived at the apartment building with much excitement.

"This is it!" she said gleefully. She raised her head and stared at her grandmother's windows. Surprisingly, they were also adorned with the sparking multi-colored Christmas lights that decorated each of the windowsills of the many apartments.

She drew her key from her coat pocket and, as she swung the front door open, she warned her companions of the unconsecrated oil smell. "We Caribbeans like to fry a lot," she explained. She also cautioned them to not hold onto the sticky banister and to prepare themselves for the never-ending upward climb through the narrow staircase.

Even after the warning, they reached the third floor slightly winded. Angel caught her breath the moment she saw the figure in the doorway. With tears in her eyes, she bolted forward and embraced her grandmother in a long, emotional hug. *"Abuela!"*

"Oh, my angel!" remarked a sprightly Maria with tears of joy. *"¡Gracias, Diosito!"*

"¡Bendición, Abuela!"

"¡Dios te bendiga, mi hija!" Grandma blessed her.

When they finally managed to step away from each other, Angel turned to her friends, who all stood with moist eyes. She started with Reina and introduced them. "Grandma, these are my best friends in the world, Chrissy, Latisha, and Abigail. They've been my source of strength during this whole ordeal."

The old lady embraced each one swiftly and kissed them on the cheek. "Thank you so much for taking care of my angel," she said warmly and pinched her granddaughter's now blushing cheek. "Come in. I cooked enough for you all."

"You cooked?" Angel said in surprise. *"Abuela*, you should be resting."

"Ah...I rested for too long." She threw her hands up and walked into the apartment.

She fully intended to reprimand her grandmother and remind her of the importance of resting and following the doctor's orders but came to a sudden halt the moment she caught a whiff of the rich *sofrito* aroma from the kitchen. Even her friends' spirits jolted with anticipation as they inhaled the fragrant scent.

As she glanced around the apartment, she was astonished at how tidy and clean it was. She had expected to find the mess of the attack from all those months before. As she looked to her right, she noticed Mr. Ortega seated on her grandma's plastic-covered sofa. Beside him sat a thickset, light-skinned woman in her mid-fifties with neck-length hair. He had his arm around her and when he saw the girl, he stood quickly.

"Mr. Ortega!" she exclaimed and embraced him affectionately. "It's good to see you."

"Good to see you, kid." He turned to the woman. "I would like to introduce you and your friends to my beautiful wife, Awilda."

The woman stood and spoke with a slight Spanish accent. "I have heard so much about you." She hugged and kissed Angel on her cheek. "You're as beautiful as your grandmother described you to be."

"By the way, she was the one who took care of tidying the place, putting the Christmas lights on the windows, and she even bought a new dinner table," Ortega explained and pointed to the kitchen. "The other one was destroyed somehow," he added.

When she remembered the encounter, Pretzel swiped her hand over her forehead and glanced at Reina.

"Thank you so much." Angel smiled at the woman.

"I should thank you," said Awilda. The girl stared curiously at her. "I finally was able to get this big lug to go to church. He said you were his inspiration."

Ortega gave her a fleeting wink and a wry smile.

"Yeah, well." She turned her head to glance at her friends and grandmother. "I think after all that's happened, I've become a believer too."

"You?" Maria said incredulously, clapped, and made the sign of the cross. "*Gracias Dios mio*." She walked closer and gave her another embrace. "My prayers were heard...twice."

"Why twice, *Abuela*?" asked Angel curiously.

"For believing and for having friends," she stated with a big smile on her face and cupped her granddaughter's cheek tenderly.

"Oh, I almost forgot. I have something that belongs to you." She began to remove the silver chain from her neck.

"No, it belongs to you now," responded Maria. "So you can think of me whenever you pray."

"I have been praying too," said Ortega.

"What for?" asked his wife.

"For us to stop this chatter so we can eat." The room filled with laughter as they all proceeded to the kitchen. The evening was spent with good food, good company, and in good spirits.

The two enormous angelic beings descended to the gloomy, colossal cavern of the dungeon—the bottomless pit of Tartarus. Jagged black cavern walls spurted infernal fire and billowed wafts of sulfurous fumes. The stench of burning flesh and sulfur permeated the air along with the horrific screams of the damned.

With measured steps, they strode along the scorching narrow path. The ground seethed red-hot and issued dark smoke, and they were surrounded by dazzling-white lava that continuously stoked the burning flames of Hell.

When he recognized the look of horror in his companion's features, the elder angel stated, "Do not get distracted by the imagery. It is nothing more than the reflection of the inner torture of irreparably broken souls."

They stopped in front of a looming, black iron gate that towered fifty feet in height. The formidable barrier contained a large locked seal with a ghastly engraved asp, the emblem of the ancient serpent. Behind this, the heinous creature known as Diablos lay incarcerated.

The elder Angel, known as the Archangel Michael, turned his head to the other angelic being who held an enormous shadow-gray key and nodded consent. The Angel hesitated initially but with a thick, dreadful sigh, inserted the key into the locked seal. With a clockwise turn, the seal shattered with a booming creak that echoed through the halls, pits, and walls of Tartarus.

"Steel yourself!" commanded the Archangel. "What is to come greatly dwarfs what came before."

They took a step forward and with their combined strength pushed the mammoth gate open to release a gale of stale, violent winds.

The younger Angel stepped through the open gate behind Michael. At first, he could neither see, hear, nor sense anything inside Tartarus' most formidable cell. Gradually, he began to perceive the faintest of smells. This odor stood in stark contrast to the smell of sulfur that permeated Hell. It was the stench of raw, putrid, unadulterated malevolence. He had little time to grow accustomed to the foulness before he sensed the greatest evil intent he had ever experienced. It was as if every wicked desire, craving, and lust had been simultaneously unleashed in that dark, finite space.

Overwhelmed by such unprecedented malice, the Angel staggered back and fell to one knee. Suddenly, he felt something much deeper and rawer. This emotion was partly masked by the others but he understood it to be the true nature of torment. It was the feeling of existential isolation, of being truly and unequivocally disconnected from all others and from the source of existence itself.

He pushed to his feet and the two messengers strode forward into the center of the cell. Finally, they could see their target. There was not so much something to be seen, however, as much as there was a nothingness that absorbed the light that emanated from their bodies and revealed a shapeless silhouette.

Michael reached into his long, shimmering robe and withdrew a missive. He unrolled it and read it in a strong voice.

"In accordance with the fulfillment of the requirements of the Sovereign Laws, Diablos, the King of the Abyss, is released from this prison. This emancipation will remain effective until the end of days or until such a time that Diablos violates another Sovereign Law, the penalty for which will be the Judgment of the Lake of Fire."

As soon as he concluded the annunciation, a great wind rushed into the room. A massive whirlwind formed and began to give shape to the dark shadow. Gradually, the shade took form to reveal dark, menacing eyes and a mouth curved in an ominous smile. The moment Diablos had fully taken form, he disappeared from their sight and left the two Angels alone in the dark cell.

Shadows danced on the walls of the wooden cottage as the fire crackled in the rustic fireplace. The room was quiet aside from the occasional pop and crackle of the firewood and the sporadic clack of the keys on a small laptop by the room's sole inhabitant. This tranquil balance was suddenly interrupted by a loud bang on the dwelling's sole doorway.

"Come in."

A large imposing man with wild mane-like hair and beard entered the room, followed shortly by a second man who was slender and smaller. The latter closed the door hastily behind him and proceeded to kneel before the occupant, who had not yet looked up from the screen.

"My lord, we have finally found you!" exclaimed the slender one.

The room's occupant closed the lid slowly on his laptop and looked at the visitors. "Ah, Legion. Ever the refined gentleman."

"This is the middle of nowhere. It took forever to find it. What's Diablos, the lord of Hell, doing in such an inferior dwelling?" demanded the large visitor.

"And Hades, still the hulking brute," responded Diablos.

"Seriously? After all this time, that's all you have to say?" roared Hades, his countenance stern.

Diablos arched his eyebrow. Suddenly, the wood beams that made up the cottage began to creak violently and threatened to shatter into splinters at any moment. The embers in the fireplace ignited abruptly into an amber-hued explosion that engulfed the room with an unnatural flame. The ghastly blaze coalesced into six separate spear-like fragments which streaked towards Hades, impaled his body, and scorched his clothes, but more agonizingly, seared his inner being.

He uttered a bloodcurdling scream.

"I am Diablos, Wielder of the Hellfire, the Great Deceiver, Master of this World, and Prince of the Power of the Air," announced Diablos in a low, calm tone. "You forget yourself, Hades."

The cottage's wood beams settled, the fiery lances dissipated, and the room returned to its former tranquil state.

Hades composed himself as best he could and prostrated himself. "My lord and my master."

"Much better. Now, an answer to your question. I've been busy getting reacquainted with this world. Much has happened in the last two millennia," explained Diablos. "And I didn't want to be interrupted with petty matters."

He glanced at Legion and asked, "And where is your extravagant brother, Apollyon?"

The Daimon's countenance paled. "My lord, I was not present when the events transpired. However, I have performed an extensive investigation into the matter and have conclusively determined—"

"Long-winded as always. Spare me the nuance and qualifications and out with it," he interrupted.

Hades spoke quickly, "He got himself banished into Tartarus, my lord."

"What?" Diablos bellowed and pushed from his seat. His

countenance contorted. The laptop in front of him melted into a soup of metals and plastics before he composed himself slowly. "How did this happen? he demanded. "Did he break law 7.VII.7?"

The large Daimon shook his head. "No, my lord. He was sentenced by a human," he disclosed hesitantly. "His offspring, who is known as the Daimon Killer." He paused, apprehensive about revealing the last piece of information. "A woman with the power of Enoch...and the Carpenter's Son." His voice was barely audible.

"Impossible! None other is supposed to have this ability," he thundered.

Legion, still kneeling, spoke. "It is unsettling and unwelcome news, my lord, but I can confirm that the report is true. It was a female hybrid who banished Apollyon to Tartarus."

Diablos slumped in his seat. "This is sorcery from the Sovereign One," he murmured. "When did He start playing my game?" He glared at his two subjects and demanded, "What's been done with my essence?"

"Your essence, my lord?" asked Legion.

"At least Apollyon did one thing right. I sense he carried my instructions out to the letter." He sighed deeply and continued, "It's time for me to take control of this world again. I will oversee Apollyon's former territory."

"What about the Daimon Killer, my lord? If she banished Apollyon, she could banish any of us," Hades pointed out.

"Leave her to me." Diablos interlocked his fingers and smiled. "I'm curious to see how the Sovereign One's champion will fare against true power!"

EPILOGUE

SECURE CHANNEL HANDSHAKE INITIATED...

HANDSHAKE SUCCESSFUL AFTER 3 SECOND(S).

ENGAGING ANTI-TEMPEST PROTOCOL...

ENTER USER: ROMANI_MASU

ENTER PASSWORD: ****************

BIOMETRIC SCAN CONFIRMED.

INITIALIZING 3072-BIT PUBLIC KEY ENCRYPTION...

USER ROMANI_MASU CONNECTED.

CALLSIGN: RomaniDESIGNATION: Field Analyst

ANALYST — ROMANI_MASU: Analyst Romani ready to report.

LUMINARY — TAMMUZ_LUM: Luminary Tammuz ready to receive your report.

ROMANI_MASU: About my mission to surveil and assess abomination targets for eradication by the Hunters, I have ascertained several possible targets in Pennsylvania and New York.

LUMINARY — TAMMUZ_LUM: The order is aware of these locations and has determined them low priority/high risk.

ANALYST — ROMANI_MASU: I have gathered intel on new developments at these locations. The PA location was decimated by the male faction, but they seem to be rebuilding. The NYC location was also attacked, but they managed to repel the assault.

LUMINARY — TAMMUZ_LUM: This is not new intel. We are aware of these developments. We have received the official FBI reports. Is there nothing else?

ANALYST — ROMANI_MASU: There is more. I have procured the FBI secret files. Just a moment.

INITIATING SECURE FILE TRANSFER: FBI_SECRET_FILE_NYC_ST_MARY.pdf
PROGRESS...10%
PROGRESS...37%
PROGRESS...63%
PROGRESS...89%
TRANSFER COMPLETE.

ANALYST — ROMANI_MASU: There is an Agent Ortega who seems to be actively involved with the situation. Additionally, neighbors reported hearing an explosion. Several humans in the vicinity of the complex had to be hospitalized. The reports clarify that there were no external wounds on the victims, nor was there any kind of physical evidence of detonation.

LUMINARY — TAMMUZ_LUM: Have the crossbreeds developed a new weapon?

ANALYST — ROMANI_MASU: I don't think so. I took the liberty of cross-referencing the reports with the intelligence gathered by some of our deep cover operatives. I found one report to be most interesting. It details that Leonard Archie entered the target site in NYC but did not come out. The operative claims to have overheard chatter that Leonard was destroyed, which released a massive shockwave.

LUMINARY — TAMMUZ_LUM: Impossible.

ANALYST — ROMANI_MASU: It seems there is a new player in the female faction with the ability to destroy an Utukku.

LUMINARY — TAMMUZ_LUM: This, we were not aware of. Well done, Romani. We will open an investigation into the matter.

ANALYST — ROMANI_MASU: If I may... There is a plausible vector for infiltration. I have a maternal connection to one of the female abominations in NYC.

LUMINARY — TAMMUZ_LUM: This is highly irregular. You are an analyst, not a hunter or infiltrator.

ANALYST — ROMANI_MASU: I am willing to do whatever it takes to ensure the survival of humanity. If I fail, I will at least take a few abominations with me, but if I succeed...

LUMINARY — TAMMUZ_LUM: Very well, congratulations on your promotion, Infiltrator Romani.

USER ROMANI_MASU DESIGNATION CHANGED
NEW DESIGNATION: Infiltrator

INFILTRATOR — ROMANI_MASU: Thank you, Luminary. I will not fail the Star of Nimrod.

LUMINARY — TAMMUZ_LUM: We serve the light...

INFILTRATOR — ROMANI_MASU: To protect the purity of man.

CONNECTION TERMINATED...

AUTHOR NOTES

DECEMBER 15, 2021

What began years ago as enthusiastic discussions and collaborative ideas of an imaginary world with fallen angels, Watchers, and Nephilim led to this great concept of The Progeny Wars. Who would have thought that our lengthy private conversations would eventually become a book series? Though we never planned for this, how fitting it is that we are now sharing our passions for the world to see and become part of it.

(From G.Z.) - I love stories with vast and complex characters, plots, and twists that leave you on the edge of your seat but most importantly, as you flip to the last page and read the last lines of the book, it opens your eyes to see it was more than a story but a life-changing experience. As if a veil was lifted, you can perceive the message hidden within the book's pages. Daughters of the Watchers was written with the prospects and hopes that readers can connect with the characters and the storyline in a personal way.

Thank you all for picking up a copy of this book and

joining us in this adventure. We were not only the authors but the first readers, so we hope you have enjoyed it as much as we did.

In addition, thank you to the staff at LMBPN, Michael, Judith, Steve, Kelly, Rachel, Miha, Judah, David, Lindsay, and Grace – your input and faith in us was indeed a blessing from the sky.

To the staff at home - Thank you so much for your support and understanding: Wined, Levi, Timothy, Carlos, Carmen, Edwin Sr., and Edwin Jr. It was a long endeavor for me and you. I'm genuinely grateful.

(From D.J.) – I am a self-avowed nerd and all-around geek, and I grew up reading all sorts of fantasy and sci-fi stories. One of my favorite things about reading a good story is the moment when you lose yourself in the narrative and begin to experience the events with the characters. As G.Z. and I embarked on this journey as authors, I never imagined how much more engaged you could become as a writer. There were so many moments where I stood up out of my chair and acted out fights scenes or typed a particularly poignant scene while fighting off those pesky onion-cutting ninjas. Writing this book has been a richly rewarding experience.

Thank you to our readers for taking a chance on these novice authors and joining us on this journey. If you've enjoyed this story, please share it with friends and family and leave us a review! They are incredibly helpful at this stage of our writing careers.

Also, I want to thank LMBPN for seeing the potential in our work and pushing us to refine it and make it so much better than it would have been otherwise. The team at LMBPN has been fantastic, and I've enjoyed every second of working with them.

I want to thank my friends and family for their support and encouragement throughout this process: Sam, Daniel, Sara, Daniel Sr., Maira.

And final thanks to the Sovereign One for the inspiration, strength, and source material.

BOOKS FROM G.Z. RODRIGUEZ AND D.J. VARGAS

The Progeny Wars

Daughters of the Watchers (Book 1)
Sons of the Lords (Coming soon)
Children of the Mortals (Coming soon)

CONNECT WITH THE AUTHORS

Connect with G.Z. Rodriguez and D.J. Vargas

Facebook: https://www.facebook.com/gzdjauthors